TH

Bertha could feel Antonio's hand on her elbow, helping her to climb onto the stone altar. The surface was sensuously cold. Once more the drug surged through her, sweetness beyond measure. She spread her legs and lay back. Above her stood the snake master, Simon. Slowly he lifted and donned the gleaming mask of the snake. Then they began the catechism of Abyssos.

"What were we?"

"Light."

"What have we become?"

"Slaves."

"Who enslaved us?"

"Jehovah, the jealous god."

The catechism rolled on. Bertha answered smoothly, her words carried on the drug. The last question: "Are you prepared, sister?" Bertha nodded, breath gone, staring at Simon.

Above her rose the glittering, stilettolike instrument of sacrifice. It plunged toward her.

She had no will to scream.

ABYSSOS

RAYMOND HARDIE

TOR
HORROR

A TOM DOHERTY ASSOCIATES BOOK

This is a work of fiction. All the characters and events portrayed in this book are fictional, and any resemblance to real people or incidents is purely coincidental.

ABYSSOS

Copyright © 1987 by Raymond Hardie

First printing: September 1987

A TOR Book

Published by Tom Doherty Associates, Inc.
49 West 24 Street
New York, N.Y. 10010

ISBN: 0-812-51892-6
CAN. ED.: 0-812-51893-4

Printed in the United States of America

0 9 8 7 6 5 4 3 2 1

If any of you lacks wisdom, let him ask God
who gives to all men generously and without
reproaching, and it will be given him.
But let him ask in faith, with no doubting,
for he who doubts is like a wave of the
sea that is driven and tossed by the wind.
For that person must not suppose that a
double minded man, unstable in all his ways,
will receive anything from the Lord.

James 1:5–8

1905
THE UPPER SUDAN

THE HEAT WAS relentless. At times it lay across the skin like a tight bundle of steel scrapings. It dared him to move, scratching, burning, grinding into his resolve.

Sometimes he thought it was insanity that drove him on. The swaying action of the donkey had almost become unbearable. The stench of his long-worn, travel-stained clothes and the smell of the hot beast filled his nostrils. His thighs ached till he felt only a throbbing numbness and his buttocks were chafed raw with the constant plod of the animal; but he would not stop, he was a man driven, possessed.

The seed, somewhere this seed had been planted. Then married to his will, it had grown like a lusting monster, leading him. He had become the victim, expendable flesh in the pursuit of this hidden knowledge.

His search had begun many years ago, when he was a young priest, the bright new star in the Vatican secretariat, at home in those long marble corridors, smelling of incense and power. But something else drew him. In his private moments he plodded the labyrinthine corridors of the Vatican library, and the fragments of knowledge quickened his heart. The secret books, the hidden texts, the forbidden lists, the corruptions that must not taint the mind or, more

1

important, wrench the soul from God. Yet, he had to know.

The beast below him sputtered out a dry, raucous sound and jolted him as it tossed its head back.

"*Whoa*. Steady, boy."

He patted the grey neck, and the animal straightened and plodded on. Ahead, the guide on the other donkey seemed oblivious. The path took a sharp turn to the left and the priest saw his companion's profile, vivid against the searing blue sky. For a moment the man turned to him, his eyes a white flash in an otherwise cloth-covered face. He held the priest's look for the briefest of moments, and then turned back, spurring his animal ahead on the rocky path.

Where is he really taking me? the priest thought. Was he a Coptic Christian as he claimed, or a Dervish? Only seven years earlier General Kitchener had defeated the Dervish at Omdurman, but a mindless hatred of all "infidels" still consumed many.

Bellarma's mind clutched fearfully at all the possibilities.

Failure and success, a breath separates them, as it does life and death. If there is such separation. Maybe I will find an explanation of oneness. . . .

No. No, he must stop. He couldn't think in this heat.

After college in Rome it had all seemed so obvious. The gifted golden boy, believing that the world was his oyster. His father a rich cutlery manufacturer in Milan, his uncle a bishop in Naples. The young man himself, Father Bellarma, the rich parish priest on the fertile lower slopes of Vesuvius, enjoying the smooth red wine from those dark hills, the rich harvests, the good life. But it was not to be, for his own brilliance brought him to the Vatican and the path he now followed.

Here there was no velvet-smooth liquor. The sand crunched unyieldingly in his mouth. Ahead and

2

above, projecting gauntly from the sand-stained landscape, stood the red cliffs of Gebel Kalat. The dark shadows from it now slowly crept toward the priest and his companion, and a rising evening wind whistled mournfully around its peaks. They plodded on. The wind was call and fearful warning all in one. Slowly they began to turn, following the rocky path on the long, slow climb around to the rear of the massive outcrop. Bellarma's body tensed with the thrill of expectation, the muscular leanness of his body tightening so that the beast beneath him flinched.

His life since those halcyon days in Rome seemed to have been lived from one gasp to another, on the elusive promise of dark secrets, forbidden and buried truths. He had asked to transfer to the order at Mount Lebanon in Beirut.

"But there are Christians in need there, as much as in Rome."

He had almost believed his own pleadings. Yet all he really sought in his travels were the answers, which would be balm to his aches. He had lusted after knowledge, like another man would after women. For a year he had searched in the Mandean communities of southern Iraq. He was inspired by his readings in the bowels of the Vatican, the scalding attacks of the early Church Fathers: Irenaeus, Epiphanius, Clement of Alexandria. Surely some body of work, some texts, once existed to inspire such vituperation. But there was nothing in Iraq.

Bellarma had returned to Beirut, steeping himself in teaching and study. He was respected by his peers and students alike. Day after day, in that thick white-walled monastery of Mount Lebanon, he waited. Year after year he brooded. By thirty-seven, his dark hair was grizzled with grey.

Then came the cloying touch of the fates. A man from Alexandria was visiting a merchant friend in the city. Bellarma was invited to dinner. After, he could

3

remember nothing of the meal or the small talk. He could recall only the story of a meeting with a cotton merchant from Upper Egypt. The man spoke of ancient cults and caves long sealed, of stories frowned on by the Coptic Church, and texts skillfully hidden from the hand of priestly oppression.

To Bellarma, this was clearly a call. It rolled like dark thunder from a deep, forgotten abyss.

The donkey almost stumbled at the next sharp turn in the path. A new cliff face was opening before them, craggy and pitted with caves.

That morning when the storm had rolled in from the west, Bellarma had watched, and despite the blistering heat he had shivered at the sight. The cloud had coiled and wreathed itself into a looming, gargantuan darkness. It slithered from the grey-and-yellow-streaked desert toward him. Was this the demon that had devoured his years, the outward sign of the evil that had rotted his faith?

They halted. The priest dismounted as the guide approached. He was still suspicious, half-expecting that it would all end here among this bleakness. The guide pulled back his dark blue face-cloth, revealing a face creased with sun and age.

"Here. No further. The herdsmen say here." The man spoke in broken French, pointing to the cliffs.

"You will wait?" Bellarma asked.

The man nodded and, gathering his dusty clothes around him, squatted in the lengthening shadows of a rock. Yes, he would wait. The British officer at the village El Allaqui had half of the promised money. He would wait.

It was midafternoon. Bellarma climbed up, over sand-sculpted red rock, along paths that had him clinging precipitously to the cliff. He struggled and sweated from one dark entry to another. He scurried and pushed, climbed and heaved himself from level to

4

level. Slowly he worked his way along the face of the cliff, probing one cave after another.

They were simple structures, about six to eight feet square, with smooth walls. The only variation was that in some a small niche the length of a man had been cut into the back wall. It was a stone bed. A hard resting place for the ascetic breed of hermits who had lived here.

All had the same rough-hewn bareness. But he knew what he sought was here, somewhere. Or was it all delusion? He felt sick. He sank down onto his knees and grasped his burning head in his hands. Nausea convulsed him, and he swooned forward, clutching the edge of the rock bed with scratched and bleeding fingers. He retched dryly, a bitter acid choking his throat.

When he awoke and climbed down, night had come. It had snaked in silently but swiftly. He could feel something—brooding, poised, malignant.

The guide had lit a fire and was brewing sweet mint tea. He offered some to the priest, but Bellarma knew there was no time to delay. He found the oil lamp in the baggage and filled it. He checked the wick, lit it, and replaced the glass. Within minutes he was back on the cliff paths. He walked onward and upward, past one empty black hole after another. He went on and on, up and up, each step more painful than the last, unaware of the beauty of the bright moon that had risen like a thin caliper over the desert behind him.

And then something changed. He stopped at an opening that in some way was different. The yellow glow of the lamp fell once more on a blank interior, and yet something made him shuffle forward even as his despair started to gnaw at him again.

A sudden chill wind from the desert cut him like an ice-cold blade across the chest. The lamp spluttered. He fell back against the wall of the cave.

5

He felt it. The awful malignance was there, outside, waiting. It breathed icily, lifting the dust in the cave, coating his throat and mouth. He choked and coughed.

Something possessed him. He would plunge into the bowels of the earth, scratching, kicking, and gouging. He pummeled the stone walls with his feet and hands. Strangled sounds escaped his scratched throat. But beyond that he could hear another sound. Beyond the frantic echoes, beyond the pounding of his own blood, there was deep, mocking laughter, evil, resonant.

The priest slid down the side of the rock, fingers clawing, flesh tearing, nails cracking. At the base of the wall he lay in a crumpled heap, still, scarcely breathing. There was silence again. The booming laughter had stopped. He pulled himself up slowly, brushing chips of rock from his stained soutane. He looked at one, turning the shard over in his hand in a desultory manner. Unthinkingly he crumbled it. It was not rock but clay. He looked to the wall. The clay had been used as a facing; but for what?

Bellarma quickly dragged himself to his feet and held the lamp close to the surface. He chipped away more of the clay. Behind, he could see ancient bricks. There must be something beyond, a hidden space, a secret to be prized open. That explained the booming laughter. The taunting echo was beyond the wall, an echo of his fists beating in despair.

Within two hours he had pounded a hole in the wall. He did not ask the fellahim for help. He wanted the secrets for himself. He felt almost sick with desire. First one brick had cracked, then another. Finally one had crumbled into the hole beyond. He loosened more, until the hole was big enough to crawl through. For a moment he sat poised. In the distance he heard the excited stamping of the donkeys followed by an

6

hysterical trumpeting. Something had scared the beasts. Something was lurking in the dark. His whole body shuddered with cold, but he would not back away now.

The cave he came into was only slightly bigger than the one he had left, but it was very different. Bellarma stood up slowly. The yellow light played long fingers of shadow along the rough walls. He stood tense and still, a painful pressure developing behind his eyes. Foot by foot he studied the walls and floor, his breath caught in his throat. At the front, carved from the soft rock itself, stood an altar. He shuffled forward, then stopped. There was that coarse breath again, like the panting of a running dog. It had to be the cave playing tricks with the sound of his footsteps. He stood only a foot from the altar. It was smooth, well-worn. He reached out his hand to touch the top, and felt something holding him back. Something was in the cave with him. The hair on his arms bristled, and he spun around, almost choking, as one of the bricks tumbled down the pile in the cave beyond. He fell backward and to one side, grasping the wall with one hand while the other clutched the swaying lamp. With that wall at his back he felt a primitive security. He convulsed, almost dropping the lamp. He had not seen it before. The black shadow of the altar had hidden it. Perhaps a skeleton would have been easier to take. His heart pounded in his chest. He walked to the back of the altar and his light flooded the grotesque scene. At first he could not make out the total form; the moving light and shadows played optical tricks. But he knew right away that it was mummified human flesh. The shrunken, leathery, grey-brown leg and foot was the first thing he had seen. He stood entranced, his breathing shallow and short. Then slowly his eyes widened and his jaw fell slack. The configuration of what lay there had suddenly become apparent. Two wasted, mummified bodies lay entwined before him. They were clasped together in the act of sex. The legs of the woman were joined high behind the man, holding him deep into her. But all that was left of the soft flesh, the sweat, and the pulsing blood was this misshapen heap of shrunken dried flesh. The woman lay beneath the man, and as Bellarma moved forward he could see her head over the shoulders of her lover. Her face was turned to him. The empty sockets of the eyes glared, and the light moving the black shadows of the eyes gave them a bizarre liveliness. So this was sexual love, this was human passion. He suddenly remembered the soldier and the prostitute that he had stumbled on in the ruins of the amphitheater in Rome, the flash of white thighs, the grinding and the groaning, the shudders of the last moments of pleasure. He looked down once again at the coupling below him. Which had come first here, the shudders of death or the shudders of love?

There was a slithering sound. He jumped and then jerked his head toward a large urn placed only two feet behind them. Something had fallen from it into the dust. He looked and saw a flash of greyish color, the desiccated remains of an Egyptian cobra. So this was how they had died. The snake had snapped in two, and the other part still remained on top of the urn. Bellarma stepped over and brushed it away with a sweep of his hand. The urn was covered with a tight sheet of goatskin. The snake had lain coiled on it, its head twisted through one of the urn's handles.

He blew the dust from the skin, then rubbed it clean. He was fumbling for a pocketknife in his trousers when he stopped and held the lamp close to the surface. There, in a careful line drawing, were a couple fornicating. He looked back at the mummified bodies behind him; it was almost an exact representation. Slowly, he pulled out the knife and cut through the drawing of the coupled lovers. The knife slit the

8

dried skin with ease. He made another cut at right angles and then pulled back the flaps. A strong musty smell rose from within. If there was anything, it had to be here. He lifted the lamp from the edge of the altar where it had been placed, and held it over the urn. There were books inside. Bellarma's whole body began to tremble with excitement. He put the lamp back on the altar and carefully pulled the volumes out one by one, laying them on the stone.

Altogether there were three manuscripts. They were in good condition, written on papyrus and bound in leather that had maintained its suppleness. Within, the writing was as distinct as the day it had been set down. The priest held the manuscripts, open, beneath the light. It was written mainly in Sahidic, the dialect of Upper Egypt, but there were titles and notes in Greek. He began to tremble. Here, after the years of longing, the words lay in his hands. His breath caught like a lover in a spasm of ecstasy. Tears welled up and blurred the text. He knew that years of tedious study lay ahead, but here, at last, were the writings of the cult, here were the forbidden texts whose titles he had read in those vilifying lists of the early Church Fathers. The Church had not managed to destroy all of the texts. Here, in the desert, some had survived.

He leaned across the altar, scrutinizing one after another. The musty smell of the ancient parchment was heavy in his nostrils, but he breathed it deeply, trembling with excitement. He read the titles aloud, like a litany.

"The Apocalypse of Zostrian, the Apocalypse of Messos, Allogenes Supreme, the Apocalypse of Dositheus, of Adam, the Hypostasis of the Archons."

The cave rang with the sounds of a faith that had died nearly two millennia before. On and on he went, breathless, voracious, a beggar at a feast.

The hours whirred by without notice. Finally he turned to the jagged hole in the wall and saw the glow

9

of day. He had to get out. But the books, the books. He clasped them tightly, carefully lifted the lamp. He would crawl through the hole, over the loose bricks—

He stopped dead. In the last flickerings of the lamplight he peered at the wall above the hole. The drawing stood out clearly, even after the centuries. Something half-man, half-swine, gleamed there, jowls sagging and eyes glittering with pride and malignance. In its jaws it gripped a bleeding, dying snake. The reptile's eyes looked almost human; warm and appealing. Beside the drawing a warning had been scrawled in Greek:

"Beware. Truly, Ialdoboath is the Archon of Vengeance."

1908
CHAPTER 1

AN EARLY MORNING fog had draped itself deadeningly over lower Manhattan. It was a cloying, smothering, unseasonable greyness, caused, so the evening papers said, by "unexpected anticyclonic conditions drifting up from the south." The fog needed no reasons, as it wound through the cobbled streets, clung tenaciously to the gantrys and cranes, coiled around the warehouses, and sinuously wrapped about nervous, snorting horses and their trucks. The docks of the Lower East Side seemed to be suspended in time, waiting to explode with activity into the new day.

At the elevated station at Grand Street and the Bowery, the fog swirled and separated into long viperish segments at the passing of each train. The screech of the brakes was muffled by the air, an agonized wail that went unnoticed by the city dwellers in the quickening flurry of that September morning.

Doolan got out of the train behind a group of factory girls. He watched them as they jostled and giggled in front of him. They were obviously aware that he was just behind them. He was a tall, lean, handsome man in his early thirties. He stood six feet two and held himself like an athlete. His shoulders were pulled back squarely; there was a limber, easy quality to his stride.

He smiled at their girlish innuendos. He had an angular face with prominent cheekbones and a strong chin, but the full curve of his lips gave him a softness,

11

and his smile was warm and appealing. This warmth was reinforced by his deep blue eyes and a wide-awake look that was at once both innocent and disconcerting.

Another giggle trilled across the tracks. Doolan wondered for a moment if he was the object of their laughter. His nostrils twitched. He tucked a loose strand of reddish, fair hair under his hat and ran his hand quickly over his clean-shaven face.

Pretty girls, he thought. The oldest must have been in her early twenties, and most were about seventeen. When you're thirty, he thought, all women of that age look fetching. He eyed them, in their ankle-length skirts and their starched bright blouses. A few were very shapely, the small neat waists filling out into the fullness of their hips and thighs. They came to the end of the wooden platform and clanged down the iron steps. When he reached the top, he glanced down, glimpsing shapely legs as they lifted their skirts to negotiate the descent. At the bottom, one of the girls stopped before turning right and flashed a smile at him.

He returned the smile, pushed back his white panama with his forefinger, and then started down the stairs. She did not wait, but grinned and then pranced off after her friends. The group babbled in Polish, Russian, Hungarian, and Yiddish. The girl's soft Irish brogue was startling.

"Hey, Ginny . . . Ginny . . . hold yer horses, yer leaving me behind."

By the time Doolan reached the bottom of the steps the girls had disappeared into the eddy of the fog. He stood for a moment looking into the greyness and mumbled "Ginny . . . Virginia . . ." Only once had he called her that. The rest of the time it had been Mrs. Pendleton, Mrs. Virginia Pendleton, the lawyer's wife; Peter Doolan, the police lieutenant. Simple business to be transacted between them, nothing more, just another case. Nothing more, except for exchanged looks and a chapter of life never to be written. He shook his head as though he could shake away her memory, then he gave a half-wry, half-sad smile and pulled back his brown suit jacket to get at the watch in his vest pocket. It was six-fifteen. He would just have time to greet his brother Tom at his ship and get back to Police Headquarters at Centre Market for his shift.

"Damn it, if I hadn't been dreaming on the El, I could've waited till a stop closer to the river."

He turned and walked quickly across Grand to get his morning *Herald* from the paper boy who stood outside the Bowery Savings Bank. He was careful crossing the road, but the sparse traffic ground along slowly, lights peeping like sulfurous eyes from the whiteness.

He took the paper and told the boy to keep the two cents change from the nickel. After all, it wasn't every day that his brother came home from eighteen months at sea. Doolan rolled the paper in his large hands and smacked it smartly against his thigh like a baton. Then he crossed under the El tracks and started down Grand toward the river.

He walked forward about half a block and stopped dead. A chilling blast from a dark alley had tugged open his jacket and coursed shivers along his back. Somewhere in the fog something was moving. Dimly, Doolan heard a sound, a vague, rhythmic noise. It seemed to be coming closer. The noise resolved into the sound of a drum, accompanied by a shuffling, crunching sound. Doolan held his breath and listened intently. It was the dulled rhythmic tread of feet. He was drawn to the mesmeric beat and quickened his step along the Bowery to where it crossed Broome. At each of his long strides the tread became insistently louder, yet he could still see nothing.

At the corner he was confronted by it. The two

black-plumed horses pulling the ornate hearse shied at his sudden appearance, and Doolan almost collided with the black-garbed man leading the beasts. Doolan stepped back against the wall and watched as the somber faces materialized from the fog. They were bandsmen, their instruments clutched by their sides, all silent save for the insistent drum. It was the Italian Societies Band.

Where were the mourners?

He was startled as the trumpets suddenly sputtered forth a strangled sound, muted only by respect for the early hour. Doolan looked again for mourners and heard first the clip-clop of the horses and then the grinding of wheels on the cobbléd street. A brougham loomed out of the fog. It seemed dark and empty. But looking closely he wondered again if it was. Was there a flash of white, not a face, but something . . . something eyeless, mouthless? Then it was gone. Before Doolan could register, two priests walked past. They must be from the church of San Salvadore, just two blocks away. The younger of the two men was on the side toward Doolan. He slowly turned his head toward the detective. His look was penetrating despite his boyish face. His dark hair was tightly curled. His eyes were a deep, dark blue. They searched Doolan's face for what seemed an eternity and then, was that the wisp of a smile? Chilling. No sooner had it registered than he was gone, the fog folding behind him. Doolan was left alone, standing by the wall, a cold sweat masking his face.

On the other side of the island, the fog kept the banks of the Hudson River obscured. The ferry boats swished their way from New Jersey to Manhattan, and back again. Business as usual, except for the echoes of whistles and horns. The steam tug *Ossuth* chugged lazily upstream, and though the captain was alert to the other river traffic, Toady Skaggs, the deckhand, was not. Skaggs was a small, ugly man with a bulbous nose and a weak chin. It had been a bad night for Toady; he had had too much gin, and then lost the rest of his money playing the fingers game with a bunch of Italian dock laborers.

By the end of the night he couldn't even see how many fingers were being held up, let alone guess it beforehand. Maybe he could recoup his losses by a good find in the river today. He leaned over the stern of the tug and dangled a long boat hook into the water. The cold spray coated his face, chilling him into wakefulness. Suddenly he saw a bundle floating down the side of the tug, bumping against the hull. He hardly had time to think. He just managed to spear it with the hook before it could slip into the boat's wake. He stared at it as it bobbed beside him. It looked like an expensive bolt of cloth. He stretched far out over the rail, almost overbalancing in his anticipation, and grabbed it where it was knotted. Heaving hard, he hauled it in.

"A bit of money at last, thank God. If it's as good as I think, it should last me through next week."

The bundle splatted onto the deck with a strange, squishy thud. He planted his foot firmly on the package and with a sharp twist extricated the hook. For a few seconds he glanced down at the strange shape, then put his boot to it and shoved it across the slick wooden deck. He held tightly to the knot, and the cloth unfurled. Toady watched dreamily, then jumped back, screaming.

The captain was beside him in seconds. He looked across the deck and sucked in his breath in one long hiss.

"Holy God . . . Oh, my holy . . ."

The captain broke off and scrambled up the metal steps to the small bridge. Almost instantly the boat turned in a tight arc toward Manhattan. Toady gripped the rail, his stare fixed on the "parcel."

After a long while he tentatively stepped forward and picked up the hook. The tip was bloody. He dangled it over the side of the boat into the river. Clean. He would wash it clean of blood.

Ernest Jeremiah Pendleton was one of the best business lawyers in New York and he knew it. His whole demeanor advertised confidence. His linen suit was skillfully tailored, his grooming impeccable. In a period when fatness was known as girth, and girth indicated wealth and respectability, E. J. Pendleton had an adequate measure of both. He was a pillar of society.

On that foggy September morning, E. J. Pendleton, pillar of society, stood on platform seven of Grand Central Station. Pendleton was a seeker, a man whose restless energy had pushed him to seek truth in the most obscure places.

Pendleton smiled, tapping his cane on the tiled surface, and took a few steps away from the track. He could hear the train slowly hissing its way toward the buffers. The air reeked of the tarry smoke of burning coal, and the pistons hissed like snakes.

The brakes locked in a low screech, and the train slowly slid to a halt. Pendleton stepped away from the tracks as the platform filled with travelers. The overnight train from Chicago's Randolph Street Station disgorged its "other classes" first, and Pendleton pursed his lips in distaste as the crowd swelled by him.

Democracy . . . the awful democracy of modern transport, he thought.

The first-class passengers began to pass him, accompanied by porters and mounds of luggage. Pendleton reviewed the arrangements as he waited, scanning the faces that moved by him. Many a person turned to look at him as they passed. Though his face was round and almost babyish, he had a narrow sharp nose and darting grey eyes. His penetrating look, accented by bushy eyebrows and a full dark beard, drew attention and respect. He reviewed the arrangements he'd made on Bellarma's behalf.

The lecture room in the Metropole Hotel was booked. The invitations had been mailed.

"Friday, the 18th September, at eight o'clock: Father B. Bellarma, a monk of the order of St. Basil, lately of the monastery of Mount Lebanon in Beirut, will lecture on Magical Rites and the Early Coptic Tradition, with readings from newly acquired Sahidic Parchments. Plus Stereopticon Show."

He smiled at the latter; a touch of the vulgar was always the best shield against close scrutiny.

Pendleton had spoken to Bellarma only once before, three months ago. A rather frightened little man had approached him, offering to address his society on "some matters concerning the root source of modern theology . . ." With that remark he had left Pendleton dangling for two months. Then the priest had written from Chicago, saying that his work was finished and he was now prepared to share his findings. Thus, the speaking engagement had been arranged.

But where was he?

Pendleton fingered his beard and started walking the length of the train. The platform was nearly empty, and he was beginning to worry that he had missed his man.

He turned sharply to see a young guard clanging down the steps beside him.

"Excuse me," Pendleton said, "I'm looking for a gentleman traveling first-class."

"Ask the Negro." He nodded farther down the train, toward a large black conductor who was leaning against one of the carriages, smoking.

"Thank you, sir." Pendleton turned and strode purposefully toward the conductor. Seeing him approach, the man straightened up and stubbed out his cigarette.

"Good morning," Pendleton said.

"Morning, suh."

"I'm looking for a Father Bellarma, a priest traveling from Chicago."

"Yessuh, there was a religious gentleman sleeping here, but I'm sure he's gone now."

"I've been on the platform since the train arrived; I could not have missed him."

The conductor shifted uneasily, then sighed. "Well, suh, if you like, we'll go and see if he's still asleep."

Pendleton took a cigar case from his inside pocket. He clicked it open, took out two fat Havanas, and handed them to the conductor.

"Sorry for interrupting your smoke."

The man flashed a smile and gratefully touched his cap. "Mah pleasure, suh."

Inside, the carriage was dark, the blinds still drawn. It smelled of warmth and sleep. The two men walked down the narrow corridor between the velvet-curtained beds. The dark cloth smothered all sound.

"Here, suh, I think."

The curtains were still tightly drawn on the cubicle. The conductor knocked on the mahogany arm of what would in daytime use have been the seat. There was silence. The men exchanged glances. Pendleton lifted his cane and rapped the handle against the mahogany arm. For a moment they both stood perfectly still. There was no answer, no sound of movement from behind the curtain.

"Signor . . . Father Bellarma . . ."

Nothing. Decisively he leaned forward, pulling back the curtains in one firm movement. They both gasped. Pendleton staggered back and the conductor instinctively shot out his arm to steady him.

"Oh, Lord, Lord!"

The priest was laid out on top of his bed, fully dressed in his black cassock. Everything looked normal, neatly arranged, except that his upper chest, his cassock, and the sheet under him were soaked with an ever-widening stain of dark red blood. His face had the stillness of death, the waxy white sheen of a lily, but miraculously the man was still breathing.

CHAPTER 2

THE SHIP HAD just moored when Doolan got to Pier Forty. He walked across the cobbled street, over the embedded rail lines, to the freight depot opposite the Parke-Davis Chemical company. Pier Forty, at the end of Montgomery Street, was the unloading dock for the depot. Doolan stood on South Street, and squinted through the fog to make out the ship's name, *Pretoria*. Six weeks ago, in one of the highly irregular communications that Tom referred to as letters, Doolan had been told to expect "a visit between September seventh and fourteenth." At least Tom had enclosed the name of the ship. Doolan had kept an eye on the "Shipping/Mails" column in the paper, and eventually he had seen Tom's ship listed.

Doolan stood for a moment watching; and a dark shadow passed over his soul. The ship loomed like some dark omen, threatening in the swirling fog. The lapping water, the creaking piers and wheezing ropes, the disembodied shouts of the sailors and dockers combined into a sinister warning. But that was insane; he was going to see his brother. What evil could come of that? Doolan took a deep breath and shook himself free of the feelings.

"It's that damned hearse, sneaking up on me on the Bowery," he muttered.

He walked onto the dock. The area was alive with laborers and truck drivers. Horses were being backed, stamping, into loading bays. The work tempo of the dock pushed Doolan's ominous feelings back into the fog.

There was no point looking for Tom in the hubbub. Doolan found an out-of-the-way spot and opened the newspaper. He skipped through the trouble brewing in Venezuela; he'd had his fill of saving civilization ten years ago in Cuba. He was fascinated by an article on the new submarine fleet that had just "destroyed" the *Yankee* in a sham battle off the Connecticut coast.

Tom was practically upon him before he knew it.

Tom was a bull of a man, some four years older than Peter. He was the smallest of the family, only five feet nine, but what he lacked in height he made up for in breadth. The flat Doolan nose and flaring nostrils had become flatter and more flared through years of barroom brawls. Doolan grinned as his brother approached. Tom had dark brown, wavy hair and a round face; with his perpetual half smile and twinkling light brown eyes, he had a roguish attractive quality that drew women like flies.

Tom was carrying his canvas bag over his shoulder, and as he strode up to Doolan he tossed it down and grabbed his brother by the hands.

"Peter . . . Peader, it's grand to see you, young brother. I have a few small scraps of business, so if you'll hold onto me bag, and the jacket . . . I'll be back in a moment. . . . And no interfering, mind you. . . ."

Of all the family, Tom kept the most traces of a brogue. While he was talking he'd taken off his blue coat and hat, handed them to Doolan, rolled up the sleeves of his shirt, and walked back to the ship. Doolan stood for a moment in disbelief, then turned his face to the fast-clearing skies and poured forth a mouthful of foul invective against all bullheaded stokers. Then, resigning himself, he slumped down on a large packing case to await the fireworks.

Tom swaggered across the dock to the bottom of the

21

gangplank. He planted his feet firmly, then squeezed each fist into the palm of the other hand. Clearing his throat, he glanced up at the ship and bellowed in a loud, echoing brogue.

"There's a couple of mean bastards on that boat . . . but the meanest one of all is that fat squat grease-ball of a Boer bosun himself. I'm going to stay down here till I can kick the shit outta him. Do you hear me?"

So that was it. Doolan pushed back his panama and sighed in disgust. It occurred to him to go over and lay one good punch to Tom's chin and drag him away, but he quickly squashed his anger. A wide circle of dock laborers had already formed around Tom, and along the railings of the ship a ragtag group of deckhands appeared, smelling a free spectacle.

A tall black man stood calmly at the back of the group. He scanned the crowd on the dockside, his gaze settling on Tom's canvas bag and the man beside it. He studied the tall policeman, a long, deep stare that seemed to absorb the essence of the man. Doolan was unaware of the attention. A man in a dirty officer's cap appeared at the top of the gangplank. He was obviously the bosun. Tom's description of him was not far astray, for he was a squat, ugly man, with a thin line of beard along his jaw. He glared down at the dock, then spat with distaste, mounted the gangplank, and started down.

The black man moved forward. Until that moment Doolan had focused on his brother, but now he sensed that he was being watched. He looked up, scanning the men crowded along the rails, and finally caught the dark eyes boring into him. At first he was taken aback by the pure intensity of the stare. Gradually he realized that he was looking at a tall, aristocratic black man. The man had his head held high so that his full beard jutted out. He had the long aquiline nose and high cheekbones so common in Abyssinia, but it was his eyes that caught Doolan; they seemed to flash almost pure white. Doolan shook his head. It was a morning of small unsettling events. A raucous laugh pulled him back to the events on the dock.

Tom grinned as he stepped back and theatrically removed his shirt. He folded it neatly, then carefully handed it to an onlooker.

"No use in dirtying a good shirt when you're gonna be shoveling shit, is there?"

A ripple of laughter swelled from the half circle of men on the dock. The laughter abruptly stopped as the bosun stepped onto the dock only a few feet from him. Tom suddenly tensed, slightly stooped forward, his hands dangling. Then he took a deep breath and bellowed,

"I'm doing this for you dumping my friend Jim Cleary on the Gold Coast, for making us eat rotten swill while you pocketed the money, and for thrashing the bejaysus out of some of the best blacks I've ever had working with me in a stoke hold."

The bosun responded with a sneer.

"Go vay vrom my ship. You Irish are vit only to lif vit pigs."

The man had scarcely finished his words when a blow caught him on the side of the head. Tom was like a dam that had burst. His fist and forearm had become a piston of flesh and bone. The bosun managed to land one weak blow to the side of the stoker's barrel chest, but decided almost at the moment of impact that retreat seemed the most strategic choice. As the bosun turned away, Tom landed a vicious punch to his kidney. The man emitted a strangled squeak, stumbled, and spun to face the stoker, almost frothing at the mouth. He poured forth a stream of guttural Dutch. There was a clattering at the top of the gangplank and two sailors started down toward the

23

melee. Tom saw them coming. He lunged forward, grabbing the bosun by his belt, ran to the edge of the dock, and, with a mighty yell, heaved him into the East River. Doolan had followed along with the crowd. He looked up at the rails to try and get another look at the Abyssinian, but the black man was gone. The sailors plowed into Tom and the dockworkers piled into the fray.

Hearing the clatter of the police van behind him, Doolan turned and walked away. Two burly cops rushed past him to the fracas; Doolan walked past the police driver who was steadying the horses. There was a roar from the crowd and another loud splash. Doolan grinned. Tom had asked his brother not to interfere, so he would leave him to be taken to the lockup. A day in the cells would do him good. It might make him appreciate his brother when he saw him again.

Doolan walked around the van, pulled open one of the black doors, and flung Tom's bag to the rear of the dark interior. With a nod to the driver, he strode toward the dockyard gate.

On board the ship, the Abyssinian watched him through one of the grimy portholes. He pulled an old leather pouch from his coat pocket, upended it, and dropped a small amulet into his left hand. He flinched as if it were hot, then held it up to the light, looking at it with distaste. Delicately carved, the Snake of Knowledge wound itself around the polished black stone. He shivered. Instinctively his right hand slipped under his shirt and pulled out a small silver cross wrought in the manner of the Coptic Christian rite. It was a touch of comfort, a touch of home. For a moment he stared down at his hands, then smiled sadly at the mythic irony of it; in the left, evil; in the right, good. He glanced up again along the docks and toward the city. Now he knew for certain that this was the time and this was the place. His long journey, his years of questing were over. The final struggle was about to begin.

Pendleton did not think of himself as a squeamish man; his restlessness had in earlier years driven him to emulate the hunter-adventurer life. He had seen many a hunting wound, and when he saw the priest lying prone, he quickly dispatched the conductor to get the police and a doctor.

As the conductor's footsteps died away, Pendleton knelt beside the berth. The priest's breaths were so shallow as to be virtually unseen. Carefully, Pendleton unbuttoned the priest's soutane and pulled aside his shirtfront and collar. Then he pulled back in surprise. There, strapped across Bellarma's chest, was a cloth bag, now sodden with blood. From the cuts and gouge marks on it, the bag had obviously taken a number of blows from the knife. Nothing had penetrated, but down the side of the priest's chest were two long slits. The raw flesh oozed blood, and in one place Pendleton could see grey-white bone. Pendleton did not hesitate; he took out an elegant pearl-handled penknife and slit the tabs where the bag was tied, then he tugged it off and laid it carefully aside.

He pulled a sheet from the next bed and cut it quickly into broad strips. He lifted the priest as far as he could, and began to bind his wounds. It was a difficult job in the confined space. Pendleton began to drip sweat. Soon, however, he had the flow of blood staunched, and laid the man back onto the bed. With a fresh sheet Pendleton wiped the blood from his hands and the sweat from his forehead. Abruptly he realized that Bellarma was staring at him, his eyes a distant grey-blue.

"Father?" There was no sign of recognition in the man's fixed, unsettling stare. "Father, do you know me?"

The priest started to draw in air as though he was

fighting for his life. Each breath was noisier, and his body shuddered. Suddenly his eyes flickered, and he looked up to the luggage rack above him.

"They have taken my case . . . my papers . . ."

It was an exhausted whisper of resignation.

"What? What has gone?"

"My suitcase; it contained the books." The priest sighed. Pendleton's mouth went dry. Everything lost!

"The parchments, the original . . . ?"

Pendleton could not finish. Ever since he had met this strange little Italian, with his grizzled, grey head of hair, his slight stoop, and his piercing searcher's eyes, he had felt that here was a man who would lead him. Where, he couldn't really say—out of the vicious spiral of unanswering answers delivered by this arrogant new century. Now his lips trembled in despair.

"Is everything gone?"

Bellarma's right hand trembled along the length of his chest like a dying butterfly.

"The package . . . the package . . ."

Pendleton lifted the cloth-covered parcel into the priest's line of sight.

"Is this what you're looking for? I'd say it saved your life."

Bellarma clutched it desperately.

"These are the manuscripts, the books that I carried from Gebel Kalat, guarded by the desert so long. They have stolen only my notes. . . ."

"They? Do you know who did this?"

The priest gasped, once more on the edge of consciousness. Then he steadied himself.

"Yes. One of them came to me in Chicago . . . from New York. . . ."

Pendleton heard the clatter of footsteps down the platform.

"That must be the railway police."

The priest grabbed him tightly by the arm, his eyes glaring whitely in the gloom. "We must tell them nothing. We must report no theft." He tightened his grip. "No one must know of this loss. Take this. Hide it." He thrust the package with the manuscripts into Pendleton's hands, then sank back exhausted. "No one . . . no one. . . ."

Pendleton took the package and, opening his shirt, slid it between cloth and skin. He buttoned his shirt quickly. He could feel the blood, damp and sticky against his skin.

"I will bring you to stay at my house, and my physician will examine you. Perhaps we can offer a reward for any knowledge of your attackers. Money is no obstacle."

The priest started to mumble, "You do not understand . . . understand . . ."

But by the time Pendleton leaned in close to listen, the priest's eyes had flickered and closed. And truly Pendleton did not understand.

CHAPTER 3

THE MORNING SUN was warm now, and the fog was retreating slowly before it, slithering, curling and uncurling as it went. Doolan walked up Montgomery Street, past the fowl market on Gouverneur Slip. The smell was noxious, that dry, stuffy smell of chicken feathers combined with the warm, sweet smell of blood. This was where the rabbis slaughtered according to the law, and on Fridays it was wall-to-wall with dark-coated orthodoxy. Doolan pushed through the growing crowds, trying to make his way as quickly as possible to Police Headquarters at Centre Market.

At some unmarked boundary on Grand Street the activities of dockland stopped, and the streets were filled with the whirring, whining sound of a legion of sewing machines. Farther on, crossing Chrystie, the Bowery, Mott, and Elizabeth, the streets were crowded with every peddler in the world.

The crush, the smell of unwashed bodies and trampled horse manure, the constant grind of the horse-drawn trucks, the shouts of the hucksters. It was all here: the Italian ice-water man pumping glasses of water from his three-wheeled tank, the Serbian selling oranges, which hung coolie-style from a pole over his shoulder, the Russian Jew with his buttons and razor blades. Anything that could be carried or pushed was for sale on the streets. Doolan swore the crowds were even worse today than normal. In the distance he heard a band strike up and was reminded of that otherworldly, mist-shrouded funeral band. It was, as the morning paper had said, "the Brooklyn Rapid Transit Company Band of sixty instruments," announcing the first day of the elevated service across the Williamsburg Bridge.

Doolan's first fifteen minutes in the office were spent locating Tom and trying to spring him. The sergeant on duty at the seventh precinct had finally agreed to release his brother that afternoon.

As he set down the phone, Frank Cassassa marched in and dropped a sheet of paper onto his desk. Doolan looked up in mock disgust.

"Top of the morning to me, huh?"

Cassassa was a small man, very swarthy, with dark hair and a dark, thick drooping moustache. He looked every bit the Italian Romeo, except for his fetching, cockeyed smile. He had lately been promoted to sergeant in the murder squad. Doolan stared at him for a moment and then daintily picked up the paper between his thumb and forefinger.

"To what do I owe the pleasure?"

"A patrolman just phoned in a report of a body being brought ashore by a Hudson tug at Pier Twenty-nine."

Doolan walked past him to the door. "Come on, I can read this on the way."

They caught a cab to the Valiant Hotel, on the corner of Desbrosses and West streets. It was a seedy looking place with peeling brown paint and unwashed windows, just across from the freight station at the end of Pier Twenty-nine. The police department wagon was parked outside, and Doolan guessed that the coroner had arrived. Why hadn't he waited for the body to come to the morgue? The freight station was the usual organized chaos of packing cases and barrels. There was a small office against one wall and inside this a policeman was talking with Toady Skaggs.

Doolan told Cassassa to get statements from the policeman and the other two, then he walked toward the coroner, who was at the other end of the shed. There, through a large gate, the warehouse opened onto a pier and then to the river beyond. He glanced out and saw that the fog had retreated onto the river itself and yet in some strange way it seemed to be lurking, waiting for night to come again. The coroner, who was working in the shadowed corner, got up and walked over to him.

Israel Feinberg was a quiet, gentle-looking man in his early fifties. He was bald, save for a fuzzy mop of white at the sides and back. His face was grey and drawn. He put out a hand and laid it on Doolan's arm as though guiding him. About ten yards behind him lay the tarpaulin-covered body.

"Doolan, isn't it? Lieutenant Doolan?"

"Yes, Doctor."

"I want to warn you before you see this . . ." He gestured in the direction of the tarpaulin. "This is only part of a body."

They walked over together, and Doolan, looking down, felt immediately sick. He had seen more shapely lumps of meat hanging from butchers' hooks. It was too much for his stomach. He strode out onto the pier, trying not to vomit. He stared across the water into the changing shape of the fog. Finally he cleared his throat and spat out a large gob of bitter phlegm, wiped his mouth, and returned to the shadowed warehouse.

The body had been wrapped in cloth. The fabric closest to the flesh was quite stained, but some of the remainder could be salvaged.

"When you're finished here, Doctor, we'll take what we can of that material."

"To trace it?"

30

Doolan nodded and turned again from the gore, striding across to the office at the street end of the building. He glanced in at Cassassa, who was taking statements from the captain of the tugboat, and then continued on out to the cobbled street.

He needed air and light, the stirring life of a dockland street. This wasn't the first body he had seen, and yet he was shaken. It was something beyond the tattered flesh; an uneasy feeling, like watching that fog waiting to roll in again for the night. He shook himself, remembering that black day he had gone to the steel mill. He had had the same feeling then, that day his father had died.

"Damn it!"

He sniffed at the cool air wafting out from the shadows of the warehouse, and shivered. Then he took a deep breath.

He had a long day ahead of him.

CHAPTER 4

VIRGINIA STARED OUT along East Sixty-eighth Street, westward toward the magnificent colors of evening playing out above the rim of Central Park. Her pale blue-green eyes caught the radiant light of the evening sun and seemed to glitter. She was so still that her eyes were the only animated thing about her.

She was a handsome woman. She had a strong face, though she had always thought it too long and horsey looking. Because of this she was careless of how she looked, and this carelessness gave her a relaxed graciousness. She had a gentle, almost mischievous smile and slight dimples, which she referred to deprecatingly as creases.

She pursed her lips and blew a strand of dark blond hair from her forehead, then tucked it behind her ear. She normally liked to wear two long curly ringlets framing her face, but today she was too busy for such primping.

"Officer O'Brien has finished speaking with the father now, Mrs. Pendleton. Should I show him in?"

The maid's voice scarcely penetrated Virginia's musings. A policeman? Yes, but not *her* policeman. *His* name was Doolan. He had visited their house many times during the Brownlea case. She had come to look forward to his visits. He had sat with her a number of times, an easy, relaxed person who focused on her and exuded warmth and understanding. She remembered his sympathetic yet penetrating eyes, and that last visit as he stood in the hallway, joking about Pendleton's vulgar statue of Athenae that stood guard over the umbrellas. He had smiled then, a warm smile—

"Ma'am . . . I said—"

Virginia turned away from the window. "Yes. Yes, Gladys, show him in." The maid nodded and went out.

Virginia walked over to the green-veined, heavy marble mantelpiece. She saw the policeman in the mirror as he entered behind her. He was a tall, broad-faced man, with a heavy, dark moustache. He cleared his throat, obviously ill at ease in such an affluent household.

"Excuse me, Mrs. Pendleton, but I've finished my questions."

"You were lucky to find Father Bellarma awake. He's slept all day, ever since the doctor's visit."

"Yes, well it's probably good for him. He doesn't seem to remember much of the incident, just as your husband said . . . anyway I've got what I could." The policeman gave another nervous cough. "Eh, I should be on my way. . . ."

"Of course." Virginia stepped to the fluted side-piece of the mantel and rang the bell.

"The father was lucky that he had your husband meeting him."

"Oh?"

"Being a visitor from Chicago, or wherever."

"Yes, yes."

Wherever, indeed! That had grated on her all day. Pendleton had simply left the priest, saying he was a friend, and gone off, leaving her to cope.

Gladys appeared at the door with a tray in her hands.

"Ma'am?"

"Gladys, show Officer O'Brien out. What is that you have?"

"Some soup for Father Bellarma, ma'am."

"I'll take it up to him myself, Gladys."

Virginia took the tray, then turned and smiled at the policeman.

"Thank you once again for your trouble, Officer."

Virginia swept along the corridor and up the stairs. If he was awake she would at least take the opportunity to introduce herself.

They had put Bellarma in a small room on the fourth floor. She knocked before entering. When she heard no reply, she gently opened the door. The room was in shadow, but the evening sun cast a soft glow through the lace curtains. Bellarma's eyes were closed. Virginia placed the tray on top of the chest of drawers, then turned back toward the bed. The priest was staring at her, his eyes sharp, intense, and dark. She gave a startled gasp and his look softened.

"I am sorry. I just awoke." He spoke slowly and with care, his slight accent only barely detectable.

"I brought you some soup."

"Thank you." He sat up as she picked up the tray and carried it over to the bed. As he settled it on his knees, she scrutinized him. He was an impressive figure with gaunt features and a sallow complexion. He had a small, curved nose and thin lips, reminiscent of a portrait of an effete European aristocrat. But the lines on his face told another story, for they spoke of a strength of character. They were the determined, deep lines of a searcher, of a man who had lived a long and passionate dream.

He looked up, and she quickly turned from him and started toward the door.

"Please stay . . . sit for a while."

She turned and once again caught the dark eyes boring into her. She found them unsettling, but not frightening. She took the challenge they offered and pulled the small wicker chair up beside the bed.

Bellarma smiled at her as she sat and nervously

34

adjusted a small silver brooch at the neck of her high-collared blouse. He watched her for a moment, then sighed. Virginia saw a tired soul in the priest's eyes.

"You know," he said quietly, "I believe that this is the first time in three years that I have felt the simple pleasure of contentment." He drank some of the soup, then laid the spoon down on the tray. Slowly the look of contentment drained from his face. He gazed at the bloodstained, cloth-covered parcel on the small bed-side table.

Outside, the distant hum of evening traffic could be heard along the park. When he did speak, Bellarma's voice was muted.

"Do you know what it is like to want something so badly that you constantly wait for it, search for it, and when you find it, it is like poison to your tongue?"

Virginia stared at him and for an awful moment thought of Pendleton and their courtship and marriage.

"No." She smiled gently. The priest tentatively reached out and touched the cloth parcel.

"I searched for something for years, and I found when I got it that I had grasped evil. Pure evil."

The words died in the silence of the room.

Virginia could not reply.

Araya, the Abyssinian, carried a last bucket of dirty water to the stern of the ship and poured it overboard. He watched the mist gathering over the river and the lights springing to life along the dockland streets. He had never seen a city of such size. It stretched on and on, upstream and downstream, and on each bank of the broad river. Looming close by, the Brooklyn Bridge was a constant hum of traffic.

So this was America! This was where the priest, Bellarma, had journeyed to.

Araya leaned on the rail and clasped his hands

together in prayer. In the manner of his monastery, he thanked God through Elijah and Enoch and James the brother of Christ, thanked Him for carrying his humble servant safely in the palm of his hand.

When he finished, a great loneliness settled on him as he looked out across the dark surface of the river. He was so far from home, so far from the clear, still nights of the desert, where the only lights were the stars and the moon. He was far from the monastery at Asoteriba, where the only noise in the evenings was the sound of chanting from the church, accompanied by the tinkling of finger cymbals and triangles.

Araya had lived in that monastery for eight years. His life had changed as he was making his way to the spring near the Wadi Shigrib. He was on a long contemplative walk of prayer and fasting when he met up with a party of Sunni Muslim pilgrims traveling to the port of Halaib, where they were to embark on a ship to Jidda and Mecca. When they learned he was a Coptic Christian monk, a group of them surrounded him and began to talk. At first it was hard for him to make out what was being said. He understood some Arabic, but their dialect made it difficult for him. Finally one of them took over the telling.

He told Araya that he and his fellow pilgrims came from along the Nile opposite the great, ancient temples of Dendur and Affedunia. About a year ago a priest from a Catholic monastery had come to the spokesman's town, El Allaqui. He had asked about caves to the east, deep in the desert.

He and his fellow townsmen had grown up with rumors of the mountains in the desert. It was a place where men did not journey alone. At one time an evil sect had lived there, worshipping and practicing their beliefs, and the taint was still upon the place.

The townspeople spoke to the priest and told him their stories, but he was not to be dissuaded. Indeed, he seemed drawn to the place. In the words of the pilgrim, he seemed like a man about to meet his lover, distracted, and caring only to be quickly in her arms.

But he could find no one who would lead him. He could only get rumors from those who had heard the stories from the herdsmen. And even herdsmen stayed away from the mountain named Gebel Kalat.

After a week, it looked as though he would start east on his own. It was known that the British officer in the town was unhappy with his plans. White men were not supposed to travel without guides. Finally this officer sought out a man who would go with the priest. The man claimed he was a Coptic Christian, but the townspeople knew him to be an irreligious scoundrel, a man who drank alcohol and ate pork.

The two men had set out over a year before, and it was the last that was heard of either of them. The British officer had been recalled within two months to Cairo and no one from the town would journey out there. Let the infidel court danger and walk into evil.

The man who was telling the story to Araya had stopped and pointed to someone in the crowd behind him. He was a merchant from Idfu, farther down the Nile. They had met on this pilgrimage. One night he had told them that eight months ago a Catholic priest came out of the desert, traveling alone. He was a strange man, distracted, suspicious, a man who was "uncomfortable living in his own skin." He had with him a large sack of parchments. He'd arranged with the merchant to travel down the river on one of his boats. He was the same man who had headed for Gebel Kalat four months before. The man turned from Araya and looked around at the eager faces.

"His name was Bellarma."

Araya shook himself and looked around. The piers were virtually deserted, only a few people wandering the streets. The river twinkled with the lights from the ships and the houses and bars on the east bank. As he stood looking at the iron marvel called the Brooklyn

Bridge he reviewed his decision to follow Bellarma. Truly it had been no decision, for he had always felt that his life was building toward some great pilgrimage, a pilgrimage that would lead to an epic struggle with evil. Following in Bellarma's footsteps, he had discovered the empty urn. He was certain that Bellarma had taken the words of the Abyssos into the world. He had to find him.

Araya did not know what the priest wanted with those manuscripts, but he knew that they must be destroyed. Perhaps the priest's search for them, his taking of them, was an innocent seeking after knowledge, or perhaps it was connected with something much more sinister. Araya didn't know and didn't care. He knew only that he must find the priest and stop the spread of this evil.

He set about it methodically. First he wrote to the Patriarchal Secretariat in Alexandria, and they gave him the address of the local see in Beirut.

Nearly five months later he got his reply. No, there was no such priest connected with the see, but that was not to say that he was not a member of one of the many religious orders in the area. They enclosed a list of addresses. He wrote to each one, and within a period of six months got three negative replies. Finally, one afternoon, in the middle of the long fast of Lent, a monk arrived back from the port of Halaib, carrying another letter from Beirut. It was from the abbot of the monastery of Saint Basil. Yes. Father Bellarma had resided with them for years. He was an ascetic man, respected both for his scholarly knowledge and his devotion to his religious duties. But Father Bellarma had left the monastery just recently and had gone to a requested assignment with an immigrant community in Chicago.

America!

Araya had been stunned. It was a world away, another time, the future as his country could never hope to see it. It made sense to Araya. If there was to be a rebirth of the evil teaching of Abyssos, it would be most fruitful in the land that man had most changed by his own hands. There would be found the arrogance of men who believed they owed nothing to God, for all around them they would see only their own works. In their arrogance they would be open to the insidious answers that the cult Abyssos would give them.

No matter how frightening the journey seemed, he knew that he had to go. It was written in his stars.

He had journeyed first north and then east to the port of Halaib on the Red Sea. There he got a job as a deckhand working on a small tramp steamer carrying cotton and gum arabic for a British trading company. The ship was bound north for the larger port of Suez.

He had stayed in Suez for almost three weeks, waiting for a ship that would carry him up through the canal, and across the Mediterranean to the United States. Each day he would haunt the shipping offices, seeing what vessels were in or expected. He bought rough, loose-fitting trousers and two large cotton shirts. He got his long hair trimmed and tucked it under a knit cap, so that he looked like any other black sailor, except for his alert, flashing eyes. Still, no one could fail to notice that he had the bearing of a pilgrim, a seeker.

So he had waited. Patient. Prowling.

At last he had been rewarded. A South African ship called the *Pretoria*, out of Port Elizabeth and Durban, sailed in to load a cargo of cotton for Marseilles in France. Its ultimate destination was New York, where it would unload a cargo of industrial diamonds. Araya knew nothing of such international trading. He knew only that the *Pretoria* was bound for New York and that that was close to Chicago and Bellarma.

Now, standing on the deck of the ship, looking at this great bridge, he was convinced that Bellarma was in New York. Bellarma was here and he needed help. That meant that the struggle was to be here. Araya knew that he needed allies for the fight. He would seek out his friend Tom and Tom's brother, the man of action, Peter Doolan.

Yes. He felt that the struggle with that evil would be soon.

CHAPTER 5

FOR PART OF that afternoon, Tom had slept, uneasily, in one of Precinct Seven's airless cells. He dreamed of his black friend Araya, Araya the aristocrat as he laughingly called him. And indeed he was a strange man to pick up at a dusty desert port, so noble featured and noble natured!

In the dream Araya's face had been obscured by a vicious snake, its fangs biting into his eyes, its coils strangling the last breaths from his body. Araya pleaded with Tom to end his agony by stabbing him.

Tom woke from the dream with a start, pouring sweat. After a while he recovered, splashing cold water over his head.

"Too long at sea," he said aloud.

Tom spent the rest of the afternoon playing cards and drinking coffee with the sergeant on duty. He was finally released from the station house at six o'clock. By then he had made friends with most of the policemen on duty. They appreciated a man who could use his fists and it had been a spectacular fight. The man would be no loss on the force. But Tom was a tearaway, a wanderer in the old tradition, one of the wild geese. With his Irish gift for storytelling, he took them around the world and back again. When he left, big Sergeant Murphy was going off shift; he put his arm around Tom and walked him to the door.

"So your father came from Cavan?"

"He did, when I was five years old; that was when I first fell in love with ships, damn their souls."

"Well, I'm a Cork man myself and I never had much truck with the North, but you're a fine man, and from a fine family by all accounts; your brother is one of the dacentest big men in the force."

Tom grinned.

"He's all right for a little brother."

"A little advice, Tom, next time you pick a fight in New York, do it in the ring. . . ." He laughed. "And remember to invite us."

"Aaah, there'll be no more fighting. It's just that things seem to build up in a man after eighteen months at sea." Tom set down his bag and put on his jacket. He stared out the station door. Outside, the street was warm and dusty, and yet there was the first raw, damp hint of the returning fog. He picked up his bag again, turned to the sergeant, and shook his hand.

"Thanks for your hospitality." He grinned and turned to walk down the steps.

"Tom."

He stopped and the sergeant moved up beside him.

"You said you'd been at sea for some time, so, eh . . . well to be blunt, if you're in need of a woman, here's the name of a place you can trust. Just mention my name." He handed Tom a piece of paper.

"Thanks, Sergeant."

"Of course, if you don't need it, all the better. Just keep it to yourself."

Tom strode out onto the street and sniffed in the first scents of evening. The address the sergeant had given him was up on Twenty-second Street between Seventh and Eighth avenues. Mrs. Flanagan's. It sounded very respectable, and for a moment he thought it was just the address of lodgings. But no, there was no mistaking the sergeant's innuendo. He pushed the address into his pocket. Perhaps tomor-

42

row he might use it, but for now he had to seek out that brother of his.

It had been a long day for Doolan and unfortunately there was more to come. The inspector had set up a blackboard in the Murder Clinic. Doolan knew they were in for a lecture. It always made Doolan feel like he was back in school. Ferrais had a long string of successes, and they were all on display. Long glass cases ran the length and breadth of the walls. Inside, neatly placed and labeled, were the gruesome reminders of his many solved cases. Weapons that ran the gamut from pearl-handled derringers to sharply pointed sticks, other bits of evidence, photographs of crime scenes. Photos of the many famous criminals Ferrais had caught hung on the walls above the cases. Shelves held scrapbooks containing numerous press cuttings. All of this was supposed to contribute to a scientific scrutiny of new crimes, but many of Ferrais's assistants suspected that it was a shrine to his reputation. However, they voiced their suspicions softly. Now Ferrais stood beside the blackboard, gently rocking on his feet. When everyone had settled down, he cleared his throat and smiled coldly.

"Gentlemen. I always believe it is easier for us to think on paper or the more public blackboard, for that helps us to achieve the whole picture of the crime, and can save us unnecessary time and foot slogging. Mr. Cassassa, let us enumerate the facts that you have unearthed under the tutelage of Lieutenant Doolan."

Ferrais smiled condescendingly at Doolan, who could feel his hackles rise. Cassassa walked up from his chair and stood at the board. He looked around as though at a loss for words. Ferrais waited for a moment and then cleared his throat in his sarcastic, rasping manner.

"Well, Sergeant?"

Cassassa stared at him with lazy brown eyes, and then smoothed down his thick black moustache.

"No chalk, sir."

"Pardon?"

"Chalk, sir. There is none."

There followed a search for chalk. Cassassa looked around the tops of the display cabinets, Doolan took a quick look under his seat, then planted his feet firmly and watched. Finally James O'Neal, one of the two detectives working with Doolan on the case, went across the hall and got a box of chalk from Ferrais's long-suffering stenographer. Doolan took the time to look around the room. Richard McKenna, the other young detective Doolan had asked for, sat on one of the side benches, doodling on a large notepad. Ferrais had also invited five other detectives. New to the murder squad, they were to sit in on all the murder strategy meetings, much like interns.

Ferrais prowled the front of the blackboard like some cat about to pounce. In his fifties, he was thin and energetic-looking. When the chalk arrived he asked Cassassa to sit for a moment while he went over a few things. Doolan settled in for the routine lecture.

"Gentlemen, in this game everything is pictures, pictures, pictures. Success for a detective comes in assimilating two logics, that of the criminal, which is wrong, and that of the law-abiding citizen, which is right. We must therefore juxtapose these two pictures."

Doolan stretched and rubbed the back of his neck. It had been a long day and promised to get longer. He wanted to ask what logic this butchery fell into, what logic there was in slicing a young body into pieces and throwing it into the Hudson. But he kept his silence and looked around at the five young eager beavers scribbling on their pads.

CHAPTER 6

PENDLETON STOOD FOR a while at the bedroom door and watched the motionless face of the sleeping Bellarma. Virginia had told him that the doctor thought Bellarma would be well enough to get up tomorrow, and his heart had leapt at the prospect.

Pendleton glanced at the cloth-covered manuscripts on the bedside table. He wanted to walk over and touch them, hold them tightly to his chest; the Word, left in the desert for two millennia and now brought here, to his own house. He steadied himself. No, he would wait until tomorrow, when Bellarma would be well enough to lead him through it verse by verse, word by word.

He heard the tinkle of the dinner bell downstairs. He turned away to leave the room, thinking again about the circumstances surrounding the robbery on the train. He had gone over this all day, thinking of it between meetings with Van de Veer, who was worrying about his interests in Venezuela, and long phone calls to Kuhn and Loeb, who represented Standard Oil. The robbery clearly meant that there was a group of the cult Abyssos in the city. The thought was chilling. They would be desperate to gain the manuscripts. He glanced again at the bloodstained parcel by the bed. Yes, they were desperate, and they would be more so when they discovered that they had only Bellarma's notes.

He closed the door and proceeded along the hall.

He resolved there and then to talk to the cult, to bargain with them. Surely they quested after knowledge, just as he did, knowledge and power over the self. He would offer them the manuscripts in return for initiation into Abyssos.

Yes. They knew the power of those bloodstained words, and so did he. Why could they not be allies? He would put an advertisement in the newspapers, asking for information on the theft of the notes. That would lead them to him. His blood raced at the thought of taking the next step on his voyage of discovery.

Truth was all he cared about; not ethics; not material goods, possessions; not the bric-a-brac of the acquisitive life. No; he wanted the strength to face pure truth, the strength to look through the window of the soul.

Virginia pushed the peas around her plate, cut a small piece of veal, then laid her knife and fork aside. She looked up as Pendleton turned a page of the newspaper. She stared at him, thinking that he treated her as though she weren't there. She couldn't forgive him for reading at the table, even though he claimed it was the best time for him to catch up on the business news. When he did speak to her, she felt as if she was being addressed like a client.

He seemed to feel her gaze on him and glanced up, giving her a perfunctory smile.

"Interesting . . . it says here that Mr. Wilbur Wright has flown in France for thirty-nine minutes, a European aviator's record."

She gazed at him in a daze. Didn't he realize he was talking at her instead of to her?

"I think it's time for us to consider putting money into this aviation industry. Soon they will be carrying goods and maybe even people."

He smiled again and once more looked down at the paper. That was the grand exchange of the evening, she thought. But tonight she did not want to listen to a lecture on airplanes or stocks and bonds. Tonight she wanted to talk about the guest in their upstairs bedroom. She nervously adjusted the napkin on her lap.

"Ernest, I spoke to Father Bellarma this afternoon."

He looked up, startled.

"I brought him some soup, just after the policeman left. He told me about his journeys in the last year or so, his trip from the desert, his visit to Rome . . ."

Beads of sweat gathered along Pendleton's forehead and trickled down into his beard.

"Did you speak together for a long time?"

"No, about twenty minutes. It was quite a chilling tale."

"Did he speak to you about his manuscripts?"

"No. He was quite tired. Perhaps tomorrow we will talk further."

Pendleton shoved his paper aside; it fell to the floor. Then he leaned forward and pressed the tips of his fingers together. She had seen him do this before. It was his way of exerting control.

"Virginia, I would prefer that you not talk to him of such matters. These are not women's matters. It is something to do with the theosophical society. I am sure that you would not be interested."

"There was a time, Ernest, when you thought I was interested in all matters."

"Please, Virginia, let us not commence another childish argument. I ask you, simply, to comply with my wishes and refrain from talking to Father Bellarma about his business."

"I did not start the conversation with him, Ernest."

"Virginia, the discussion is closed."

47

He glared at her with barely contained anger. She knew that she could say no more. Slowly he relaxed back in his chair.

"Now perhaps you can give me a report of the day's happenings in the household."

She began an emotionless recitation of facts, the children, breakfast, school. As she did, she thought about her past and tried to figure out how it had led her to this. She remembered when she had first met Pendleton. Things had been so different then.

She was only nineteen years old and had just finished her first year at Mount Holyoke College in Connecticut. She was spending the summer back home, in Brunswick, Maine. She felt in the prime of life, bulging with the opinions of her freshman year, and lording it over her younger sisters. Her father was the owner and editor of the local paper, *The Kennebec Telegraph*, and three days a week, during that long warm summer, she worked as his copy editor. The world was opening for her. Two days before she met Pendleton, her first poem had appeared in print. A rather risqué piece for Brunswick, about bicycles and bloomers. Someone had even bothered to write a letter of protest to her father. Life was good.

Then Ernest had appeared. He was thirty-three, a handsome man with a broad moustache, stocky even then, but how he could talk, how he could charm. She felt like Desdemona listening to Othello. He brought her tales of a world beyond the sheltered life she had known.

He was one of New York's most successful young lawyers. He talked about the deals, the millions of dollars invested. To him, America was the new Empire and New York its Rome. The center of civilization, where the Lords of Creation dwelt. It was a new poetry to her, the poetry of power.

He knew Virginia's father well, through family railroad and steel investments, but this was the first time he had accepted the man's invitation to take a holiday with the family. He had insisted on staying at the Maquoit Hotel near the railroad station, a grand affair with white-painted iron balconies. Coming to visit meant joining them for dinner every second night. At least that's how it had started out.

But then he came to the newspaper office, where Virginia was poring over galley proofs. He sat close by, watching, talking, making jokes. Some days the whole family would go on the river, sailing past Arrowsic and Georgetown Island.

He always had his eye on her, in that distant laughing way of his, but she could never really tell what he was thinking. Then one day he took her for a walk along the pebble beach at Cape Small. Beside them the waves drew in and out along the stones, sounding like a crowd whispering. He asked her to marry him. He told Virginia that it was time for him to settle, to have a home, children. Now he would build for others, not just for himself. There would be New York society; she would be mistress of a large household. And somewhere between the whisper of the tide, and the talk of the world of commerce and society, she had succumbed to the dream. But where was the dream now? Was this her Othello, this fat man with the receding hairline, this man absorbed totally in his work and his philosophy, this man who had become so authoritarian and argumentative? Where was the sharing he had promised? She looked along the richly appointed table and realized she had traded goods for youth and dreams.

Doolan's mind had drifted away during Ferrais's lecture. He reviewed the events of the day. He went over the lists of missing that he had assembled, how they had been broken down into subcategories of age and sex. Then he started to daydream. Names and descriptions floated disconnected in his mind. Despair flowed over him as if he were drowning in a river of the lost, as if Manhattan were surrounded by rivers of missing people, human flotsam jettisoned by a city that had no heart.

The scratching of chalk on the board brought Doolan back to the room. Ferrais had rambled back onto his case again. Doolan smiled wryly. It wouldn't last.

"This case is one we can put into the butcher category."

Bravo, thought Doolan.

"We had a spate of such jollity in '97 when two young lads found the lower half of a male body dropped on a green plot in front of the Greenwich Village Bank. The upper half was found in the Hudson. Obviously the lower half had been dropped in despair at ever reaching the river. The disposal of bits of the body in this manner leaves us open to the question of accomplices."

Doolan moved uneasily in his chair. It was all right going over these cases, but they led you to make assumptions and draw conclusions before the groundwork had been done. Doolan knew that he had one firm shred of evidence and that was the cloth. Then he had the lists of missing. Perhaps if he was lucky he might soon have another more recognizable part of the body. He shuddered at the thought of a dismembered head.

Ferrais was winding down. Doolan glanced at his watch and gave an exasperated grunt. It was ten-thirty. He had gotten a message from Tom that he would be in the bar of the Occidental Hotel. Doolan suspected that his brother would be under the table by the time he got to him.

"Well, gentlemen, I think that about wraps it up. Doolan, I'll see you in the morning."

Doolan gave a muted sigh, quickly gathered his

papers, and strode out of the room. He had almost given up on leaving before midnight.

The Bowery was packed to overflowing, but Doolan strode along quickly, keeping his eyes on the signs, looking for the entrance to the Occidental's bar. It was the wrong time of night to be pushing through the crowds. The theaters and music halls and nickelodeons were all letting out. The hawkers and prostitutes, the good-time Charlies and drunks were all pushing and shoving, fighting for space on the pavement, all intent on an evening's entertainment. The street was alive with lights, and the sound of music pouring from the bars was deafening.

"Looking for a tumble in bed, honey?"

Doolan glanced down to see a tired, rather worn-looking woman in her late twenties. As he watched, she adjusted the top of her low-cut, orange and white bodice, in the process allowing part of her fleshy breast to be exposed.

"Well, what about it, love?"

Her breath reeked of stale alcohol and her gestures suggested that she was more than a little drunk. She had painted, glistening lips and rouged cheeks. Straggly blond hair peeked out from under her shabby feather hat. She was hardly a beauty, but something about her elicited his sympathy. Perhaps it was that she was alive and yet one of the lost; one of those doomed for the river, doomed to float like the city's debris, unmissed and uncared for.

"Peader, you young whelp, where the hell've you been?"

Doolan spun around and saw Tom hanging out the doorway of a bar. "Occidental" was painted in large gold letters on the glass of the front window.

"Come on in, you bugger you, and leave the women alone."

51

Tom had a wide grin on his face as he rolled his eyes toward the whore. The woman nervously settled a strand of dirty blond hair under her hat. She had smelled a potential customer, and was desperate for a sale. When Doolan turned back to her, she reached out and fingered his lapel. Doolan pulled back to escape the waft of carbolic soap, alcohol, and tobacco smoke. As he turned and pushed across the crowded sidewalk she screamed after him.

"Well piss off anyway, you're no gentleman."

Doolan stepped into the bar with a sigh of relief.

"Over here, you big long string of misery."

Tom was leaning against the dark mahogany bar, one boot up on the brass footrail, hands resting on the counter on either side of him. He looked as though he owned the place. As Doolan stepped toward him, he broke from his stance, beaming ear to ear, and grasped his brother's arm, pulling him into an embrace. They held tight for a moment, and then pushed away, scrutinizing each other at arm's length.

"Tom, it's good to see you."

It *was* good to see his brother. After such a day it was a luxury to have the rock of family. He gripped Tom's muscular forearm, squeezed hard, and grinned.

"But you're a shite and a half! One of these days I'll be visiting you behind bars."

"Aaah, Peader, forgive me; being the eldest, sure I know no better."

Tom stared deep into his brother's eyes, smiling. Peader, dear Peader, who was straight as a dye, the choirboy, the altar boy, the mother's hope and joy. He was still the "young un" to Tom, the baby. He could still see him, tottering along behind, tiny sailor suit splattered with mud, long blond curls falling onto his shoulders. And now he stood a good six inches taller than his older brother.

"What're you staring at, Tom? Haven't you seen a brother before?"

Tom swallowed hard and slipped his arm around Doolan, pulling him close.

"God, indeed I have. Enough of them for any man."

He banged his fist on the bar, and grinned over at the barman who was pulling pints of beer for a party of shop clerks standing beside them.

"Joe, I'll have whiskeys here for my brother and me, and you may leave the bottle."

"Tom, I can't spend the night drinking with you. I have a heavy day tomorrow, a lot of work."

Tom held up his hand theatrically, as if calling for silence. "Aren't you hours late and I haven't said a thing? Now I think you owe your poor eldest brother the respect of a few drinks." He paused for a moment and smiled graciously, bowing his head. "Now is that too much to ask?"

The barman slapped two clean glasses and the whiskey bottle onto the dark countertop, and took away Tom's empties. Doolan gave a resigned laugh.

"Tom, you're a bollocks, a right roaring bollocks."

"Ah now that may be, but being a man of your profession, you'd have to give me the benefit of the doubt."

But Doolan didn't want to think about his profession, at least for a couple of hours. Maybe the "golden liquor of forgetfulness," as his father used to call it, wasn't such a bad idea. At least when you woke in the morning, you knew what was bothering you. He was always a man who preferred the tangible. He held up his glass and clinked it against Tom's.

"Here's to the Doolans. And to you, Tom. Slainte. Your health."

"Slainte, little brother."

They both tossed back their drinks and felt the liquor warm their throats and trickle down to a fire in their stomachs. Tom quickly placed the empty glass on the counter and searched in his trouser pocket for a wad of dollars. As he did, he felt the neatly folded piece of paper that bore the address of the whorehouse. That was for tomorrow. Tonight was for his brother.

He threw the money onto the counter and poured both himself and Peter another glass.

"Come on . . . you'll have to drink now."

Doolan grinned and lifted the glass.

"I suppose you're right, I'll have to drink."

CHAPTER 7

THE STRONG MORNING sun quickly dissipated the night's fog. Doolan sat at his desk by the window and felt the heat of its rays beating on his head. That he deserved the hangover was the only thing that gave him comfort.

He tried to focus on the lists in front of him, but his brain was a fog of whiskey dregs and tiredness. Images floated into mind: his fingers fishing around inside the jar of pickled onions; the broad red face of the barman in the striped red-and-green vest; the fat Persian cat that jumped onto the bar and lapped up the glass of dark ale.

He stirred a large teaspoon of sugar into his coffee, then carefully lifted the cup and sipped. Across the room, Frank Cassassa sat hunched over a map of the docks. Doolan took another sip of coffee. There was a knock on the door and Dr. Feinberg shuffled in. He stood for a moment in the center of the room and ran his hand through his unruly mop of hair.

"I have a preliminary report."

Doolan suddenly woke from his torpor.

"Sit down, Doctor."

Feinberg pulled up a chair. Doolan set his cup down.

"Would you join us for coffee?"

"No, thanks. I want to get on with this. This is the report, but I can summarize it for you, if you like."

Doolan merely grunted in reply, so Feinberg simply passed the folder across to him. As he watched Doolan skim it, he composed his hands neatly on his lap, fingers touching fingers.

It was not pleasant reading, and Doolan flinched at the cold technical description.

" . . . the lower half of a woman's body, cut at a point just below the pleural cavity and from which both legs had been severed at the juncture of thighs and trunk . . ."

A wave of whiskey-inspired nausea washed over Doolan, and he closed the folder.

"Perhaps you should tell me what I need to know."

"The remains were part of the body of a very young woman, little more than a girl. She had not been dead more than twenty-four hours at her time of recovery from the water."

"Which places her death . . . ?" Doolan sat forward, with his pencil at the ready.

"Between six and ten o'clock on the morning of Tuesday, September fifteenth."

The doctor waited for Doolan to finish writing, pressing his fingertips together like springs.

"She had been dissected by a person with more than general knowledge of anatomy. There was, as well, use of morphine."

Cassassa, hearing this, came over to Doolan. The doctor smiled nervously and slid his fingers past one another until he had his hands clasped tightly in front of him.

"I also determined that she was with child," Feinberg added.

The detectives exchanged looks of puzzlement.

"It didn't look as though she was . . . well . . ." Doolan gestured with one hand.

"The child had been removed." Feinberg's voice

was flat, with a chilling restraint. There was a stillness in the room.

Cassassa broke it, saying, "You're saying that the girl had her child aborted, and then died or was killed."

There was a pause and Feinberg cleared his throat. "Yes. And she was killed, I have no doubt of that."

They fell silent; Cassassa stared at the floor; the doctor clasped his hands in his lap before him; Doolan's forefinger traced the scar high on his right cheekbone. The sounds of Centre Market outside poured in, the grinding, ever-present sound of iron wheels on paved streets, and the newer sound of chugging automobiles.

After a time, Feinberg spoke, as if finishing a sentence. "Let us hope our friend only strikes once."

Their unvoiced fear had now been spoken, and it broke the spell.

"Don't even think it, Doctor," Doolan said. "Don't even think it."

Feinberg got up to leave.

"When can we have the material the body was wrapped in?" Doolan asked.

"I'll get it over to you right away."

The *Herald* said the boys were "playing," the *Evening Sun* was more specific—they were on an "after-school fishing expedition." Both papers were lying, or to be more generous, ill-informed. The boys rarely saw the inside of a school; they were too busy trying to feed themselves. Daily, they poured out of Hell's Kitchen, that teeming scar of tenement life that stretched westward from Ninth Avenue and north from Fourteenth to Forty-second.

They were the great unwashed, the scab-ridden, the rickety debris of the city, but the glorious thing was that they refused to believe it. They believed they had as much right to life as the next man.

57

Jimmy Rentzer was one such survivor, the youngest of twelve, the runt who should not have made it. To the gang he was known as Match, and with one glance at his bony thinness the name needed no explanation.

Match fed himself. If he didn't, no one else would. The docks were a pilferer's paradise, and the boys with the tattered breeches and ill-fitting jackets, the baggy, dirty shirts and scuffed, leaky boots, were the scavengers that preyed on them.

The gang that haunted that area of docks Fifty through Fifty-two called themselves the "Blades." Match was proud to be one of their number. At nine years of age, Match felt as wise as the President. He carried a large knife with him, and would not hesitate to use it. They were violent and dangerous children, and the gang was not a game but a desperate act of survival. They waited patiently for unwary truck drivers to pass by with their lumbering horses. Then they would jump out and carry off what was portable. They were quick, for the dock laborers were as desperate as they were.

The barges carrying fresh vegetables from upstate used Dock Fifty at the end of Bethune Street, and there Match's knife proved invaluable. It could spear and slash, cut and peel. During the winter months his favorite meal was a turnip slashed in two, scooped out and filled with raw dark sugar. Many a truck arrived in Struder's Sugar warehouse on West Fifteenth with a neat hole carved into one of the hessian sacks. The boys would run behind the trucks until their hollowed-out turnips filled to the brim with raw, sweet goodness.

Today Match made an early killing from a truck-load of pears. He had received a good kick in the leg for his troubles and was now nursing a large, ugly welt just above the knee. But he did not brood over it. The pears were golden and sweet. They were worth it. With the fruit safely secured under his shirt, he scrambled down under the pier and curled up in the mud by the river so that he could eat his prize in peace. After a while the lapping of the waves combined with the sweet juiciness of the pears induced a feeling of contented drowsiness.

It must have drifted in while he wasn't thinking. He looked up and saw it bobbing toward him out of the fog of the river. It was like a gift from the gods, and, covered in tar paper, it looked as though it had been wrapped for him too. It bumped against one of the wooden piles and seemed to dance there for a while, not knowing which way to slip by.

It was only about ten feet from him, so he waded out until the water came to his thighs and he could feel the tug of the current. He stopped, not wanting to be pulled into the swirling fog. Match thought for a moment, then untied the cord that held up his baggy trousers, and wrapped one end of it around the handle of his knife. Taking the knife carefully in his right hand, he balanced it, then threw it hard, holding onto the cord. The blade pierced the paper and sank in easily. He began to pull the thing toward him, walking onto shore as he did. He dragged it up onto the stones, enthralled by its bulk. He'd thought it was clothes, but it was too heavy. He drew out his knife, and cut the cord that bound the parcel. Then he slit the paper and pulled it off. For a moment the darkness under the pier seemed even darker, and then he stood up and stared long and hard at what he had uncovered. Turning, he walked back to where his much-abused academy cap was lying, and removed the final pear. He rubbed it on his shirt, took a large bite, and turned again to look at the thing he'd dragged from the river. It was the upper part of a woman's body, without arms or head, the breasts sagging. He stared for a time in wide-eyed fascination and then put on his cap and marched off to find a policeman.

59

CHAPTER 8

THE CHURCH OF San Salvadore lay at the corner of
Broome and Elizabeth. For decades it had had a
stable but aging population. Through these years
Father Brautsch had ministered, sternly but with
compassion, to his mixed flock of immigrants. But
now he was getting old. Recently a new, younger
priest had arrived from Rome, Father Schmidt, an
Austrian. Things began to change, and change too
quickly for Father Brautsch's housekeeper, Bridie
Byrne.

This morning found her scrubbing the floor of the
kitchen, at the rear of the manse. The floor no more
needed scrubbing than did the gleaming pots and
pans hanging from the racks above the stove, but she
used it as a way to work out her frustration and anger.
The whole place had been in turmoil for the past few
days, ever since the death and burial of the wealthy
and secretive Signor Gallenini. Bridie blamed
Gallenini for bringing Father Schmidt to the church,
for it was well known what influence he had in the
diocese. Since Schmidt's arrival the church had
changed. The older members of the congregation had,
one by one, fallen by the way, and young people had
started coming, strange young people. Many a time
she mumbled to Father Brautsch that the young priest
seemed to be starting his own church, making his own
rules. But the old priest had simply laughed at her.

Bridie stood up, grabbed the bucket of water, and

dumped it into the sink. Then she gazed out the window toward the rear of the church. For a moment she looked like the perfect engraving of the Irish housekeeper, her hand on the handle of the pail, standing patiently at the sink. She was a plump, middle-aged woman with smooth, white Irish skin, and grey hair pulled tightly back in a bun. Now, at rest, her face looked calm and motherly.

As she gazed out she thought of the little chapel of Saint Dismas. It was not her duty to clean the church, but she had made it a daily ritual to clean the small chapel. That half hour alone was like a solitary penance to her. Every day she made her cleaning visit something precious and felt it was something that was hers alone.

She'd been late getting to it yesterday. All day long she had tried to shake off thoughts of that early Mass and funeral in the crypt. She had not been allowed to attend; no one had, except for the fathers. The thought of such secrecy sent a chill through her. She believed that the church was always a place with an open door, but now with Father Schmidt . . .

"Well, I suppose 'tis nothing to do with me," she said aloud.

She thought of the laundry that she had to fold and iron, the shopping list that she had to make up. Then she smiled to herself.

"The chapel . . . that's mine, and I'll do it now."

She dried her hands and took the keys from the drawer, then walked out the kitchen door toward the church. The fog had returned in the night, but now with the strong morning sun it was almost burned off. She took a deep breath; there was still a hint of dampness in the air.

When she got to the heavy side door, she pulled it open slowly and entered. It was cool inside, the breath of calm. She walked through the presbytery to the side altar, not really seeing the familiar brass and wood and starched linen. The church smelled of incense and candles, the perfumed portals of heaven. She stepped down into the nave and looked around. There was no one there.

"A city too busy to speak with God," she mumbled.

She walked past the empty pews, her steps echoing on the marble. It was a harsh, lonely sound and it made her stop to listen. As her last footstep died away, the stillness rushed at her. It brought the funeral to mind, and she once more thought how strange it had been that he had been buried that way, like a thief in the night. It was almost as if he was afraid to be called a Christian. He was such a rich man, too. She glanced across the church in the direction of the Gallenini family crypt. The young father had the only key.

Bridie shivered and then turned toward the small chapel of Saint Dismas with its wood-paneled front and heavy velvet curtains. She felt it was a sanctuary, a closed place, closed and close to God. She lifted the heavy brass latch and opened the door.

"I must polish it soon—it's darkening again. Mary and Joseph help us but polishing'll be the death of me."

The door closed gently behind her. Light leaked in only through spaces in the curtains. She knelt by one of the two pews and blessed herself. In front of her Jesus leaned out from his cross, compassion and pain in his eyes. His hands were almost clawed in pain, but she knew that they wanted to open up and accept more of man's burden.

This was the cross of pain. Bridie knew that behind her, on the wall just above the door, was the cross of triumph, the empty cross, joyfully proclaiming the victory of God over pain and death. She could feel it was there behind her. She saw it every morning when she turned around from her prayers. It was a promise of that better life hereafter. It was a promise that compensated her for the man she had never known,

62

for the children she had never given birth to.

It was always there, the same, so she did not turn to see if it was empty still. Her beads clicked one after another and that was why she did not hear the dripping. She needed no light to shape her prayers and thus did not see the dark, sticky stain of blood congealing on the marble.

Click . . . click . . .

"Help us now . . . and in the hour of our . . . Mary, mother of God . . . Holy Saint Margaret . . ." The prayers were routine, but heartfelt.

Then she stopped. She felt something strange, as if someone else was there with her. She listened. Now she heard it.

Drip.

She caught her breath.

Drip . . . drip . . . drip, drip, drip.

She turned around slowly, afraid to see what made that noise.

A pig had been strapped to the empty cross behind her. It looked down with the grin-grimace of death. Its stomach was ripped open, the flesh tattered along the edges. She recoiled at this violent and malignant mockery of the crucifixion and fell back against the pew. She watched in horror as the mouth of the pig seemed to open. A snake wound its way slowly out over the bloody tongue and coiled itself around the neck and head.

And at last Bridie Byrne screamed.

CHAPTER 9

DOOLAN WAS JUST about to leave his office when news of the second "parcel" came in. Feinberg called him from the morgue and told him that "the vicinity and manner of the cut" made it almost certain that it was part of the same body.

Doolan sighed as he set down the phone. He would have to go to the morgue. He pushed his chair back and cursed the day. He did not want to look at another lump of tattered human flesh.

The sidewalks were full of people, but Doolan could push and shove with the best of them. It was not the crowded sidewalks that bothered him most about the city, but the overpowering smell of horse manure. Piles of it lay in the streets for days, rain or shine. After ten years in Manhattan it still riled him. Most days breezes blew in from the East River or the Hudson and wafted the sweet musty odor up into the heavens. But on days like this one, when the air was heavy and still, Doolan found it nauseating. At these times he thanked God for the invention of the automobile with its pungent oil and petroleum exhaust; at least that helped neutralize the smell of decay. The oil smell also reminded him of the smoky pall that lay over Johnstown when its steel mills sweltered under a strong summer sun.

At Broadway and Seventh, he stepped out into the street to avoid a large crowd that had gathered to watch an altercation between an automobile driver, a street vendor, and one of the new traffic policemen, who wore the white cap of the traffic bureau. As Doolan crossed the street, he saw the policeman's motorcycle parked at the front of the car. An ice-water dispenser had crashed to the street, its contents gurgling into the dry and dirty gutter. Doolan stood for a moment and watched the policeman listening to the two parties. The ice-water peddler was an older Italian with a thick, drooping moustache, a battered straw hat, and a striped red shirt. He paced theatrically around his upturned machine, gesturing wildly at the crowd, and pointing to the automobile. A young dandy stood nonchalantly by, his foot placed on the auto's mud guard, his soft cap and goggles pushed to the top of his head.

Doolan saw that the car was a Baker Electric. God, electrics, they were the worst of all the automobiles; you couldn't hear them coming. Whispering killers, Cassassa called them. Still, they were probably the car of the future.

He watched the policeman patiently piecing the story together, and had to admire his coolness in the middle of the yelling and arm waving and loud opinions from the boisterous crowd. The traffic squad had only recently been formed under Captain Stephen O'Brien. There were fourteen men now on motorbikes, and they were making some inroads into the problem of speedsters.

Doolan glanced at his watch, remembering that he had promised to meet Tom at Vittorio's Café between six o'clock and seven. He wouldn't have much time for his visit to the morgue, but then, he thought, all things considered, that might not be a bad thing.

He turned and quickly strode off along the crowded street.

Tom lay in his bath and could literally feel the tension of the months flowing from his body. It had not been a good voyage. The captain was a mean son of a bitch, and the first mate, and the bosun . . . it was a long list. Seeing them floating amongst the other debris at the dock had been very satisfying. Lying back in the long enameled tub, he felt very contented about what he had done.

"Is that you snoring? Wake up—no drownings in my baths, if you please!"

Tom was jolted awake by the rasping voice of the crippled bath attendant.

"No, no, it's all right . . . I'm awake."

When he got out, the rough, clean-smelling towel felt good against his skin. He rubbed his hand appraisingly over his closely shaved face, molding it down along his jawline, under his chin, and across his lips. Then he carefully replaced the bar of dark, sweet smelling Spanish soap in his toilet bag, and took out his well-used tin of Dr. Lyons Sanitary Tooth Soap. This was the last of his six-tin supply, hoarded through tropical storms and frigid nights. He would have to stock up before he shipped out again.

He scrubbed his teeth furiously, until the gums bled. Maybe he wouldn't ship out, maybe he'd see if his eldest brother, Pat, could get him a job in the steel plant and then he'd stay in Johnstown. He grunted at the thought. It seemed as if his whole life was fated to be lived out in front of a gaping mouth of flame and heat.

Most of the family had followed their father into the steel plants, either in Johnstown or Bethlehem. There were five brothers, all working in the mills, two girls, and then him and Peter. But Peter had witnessed the horror of his father's death and would never enter a steel plant again.

"Still, having a policeman in the family's almost as good as having a priest." He laughed out loud. "Mother would be delighted, God bless her."

He sat down on the rickety wicker chair to tie his

boots, trying to imagine his brother's massive frame bulging out of a soutane. That shock of reddish-blond hair, that twisted worldly smile of his. A shiver rolled up his back like wind on a field of wheat. He froze, his thick fingers twined in his bootlaces.

"Yerself stepped on your grave," his mother used to say.

He had seen his brother in a priest's robes. All looked normal—but Peter's face was twisted, malicious. Tom sucked a deep breath. The vision had felt like the dream he had had in the cells, the dream of Araya being eaten by the snake.

What had tied these two men together in his mind? He shook his head and gathered his things.

"Mary and Joseph, but I need a woman. All these fantasies are rising up from my crotch to my brain."

He would look up the whorehouse that the sergeant had mentioned to him, and later meet his brother at the café in Centre Market. He had told Araya to leave messages for him there, so finally he might bring these men together outside his dreams. The thought was an attempt at a joke, but it didn't work. Something felt very wrong.

He grunted out another curse and slammed the towel against the bath. It was time to find a woman.

It was late afternoon by the time Araya left the ship. He took his canvas sack and walked south along the docks, past rows of warehouses: Parke-Davis Chemists, Silas Driggs Coal, Fidelity Warehouse. He listed them like a litany, marveling that there seemed to be no end to this city of merchants. But he wondered where God could find a place to reside in this city of mammon.

On the corner of Jefferson and South streets, directly on the waterfront, he came across a small hotel called the Marine Inn. It was dingy, the white paint peeling from the walls. Some of the small windowpanes had been replaced by paper. But it would be cheap.

The black clerk behind the wood-and-frosted-glass desk eyed him suspiciously.

"Just off a ship, huh?"

"You are correct."

The clerk was surprised at the speech and manner of the man before him. "Where you from, boy?"

"I am from Africa."

"Well you ain't from Hahvard with skin that pu'ple."

The black sailor looked at him quietly, then smiled gently and warmly. "I am Abyssinian; now may I have a room?"

Araya's posture clearly indicated that he did not have time for idle chatter. The clerk, flustered, studied the paper before him and grabbed a pencil.

"Yessir. I have a good one, at the front. You get the breeze from the river."

"I see. Thank you."

"Just up the stairs, turn right, it's the fourth room on the left." He handed over the key, then pointed at a dog-eared guest register. "Sign here." He slid the pencil across the scarred desk top.

The Abyssinian wrote: "Araya Kebbede Kassai," set the pencil down, and went to his room, leaving the desk clerk staring after him.

The room was bare but clean. There was a single bed and a scratched chest of drawers with a mirror hanging over it. By the window, overlooking the river, stood a table and two chairs.

As Araya closed the door a great wave of tiredness swept over him. He moved to the bed and sank down. His fingers searched his pocket for the black amulet. His hand closed on it, squeezing.

Lord God, it felt heavy.

He wanted to crush it, destroy it, but he had carried it so far, and now was not the time.

He leaned back against the pillow and pulled the amulet out into the afternoon light. It glinted black and malicious, and for a moment he covered it with his other hand. Then he looked at it again, scrutinizing it, marveling that even after the years of use, the snake had never lost its form; the intricate carving of the scales remained unworn. It still wound itself tightly around the stone as if it was strangling the circle of the universe.

He let out a deep sigh and lay down, staring up at the ceiling. It had been a long journey, but he was certain he had found Bellarma. The struggle was finally under way.

CHAPTER 10

THE WHOREHOUSE OCCUPIED the top two floors of a new building on Twenty-second Street. The brass plate announced with blatant unoriginality that it was "Mrs. Flanagan's Modeling School." In a well-lit waiting area, a young lady, with the manner of a nurse in a doctor's office, asked Tom to be seated. There was a luxurious ottoman at one side of the room, covered in wine-red velvet and packed with deep-gold cushions. Somewhere nearby, ragtime music was being played. He sat down and looked at the girl. She smiled at him so sweetly and innocently that he thought of bolting out the door in guilt. There were other diversions. There was the Ziegfeld Revue with its Follies of 1908 or the Vaudevilles at the Alhambra, the Colonial or Hammerstein's. Tom shifted uneasily on the couch and ran the nickelodeons over in his mind. There was *The Annis Tragedy in the Tyrolese Mountains*, or something more risqué with *Flirty Affliction*. He had decided on the latter when the door to the right opened, and a matronly, pleasant-faced woman entered.

"Good evening to you, I'm Mrs. Flanagan; can I be of any help?"

She sounded as if she was right off the boat, just like his mother, but with the softer brogue of the west of Ireland. He almost choked and then swallowed hard.

"Ah, Tom, Tom's the name. The sergeant . . . Sergeant Murphy sent me."

Her face lit up at the name.

"Ye must be a fine boy then, come on in and make yerself comfortable."

She took him by the arm and led him into the next room. It was decorated like a parlor; girls occupied most of the chairs and couches. One stood, winding a phonograph, its large amplifying horn decorated with naked nymphs in repose. So this was the source of the ragtime. The blonde set the phonograph needle down on the record and a crazy piano tune blasted out. She turned and smiled at Tom with a wide pouting mouth.

The whole place dazzled him. The room oozed a sensual luxuriousness. The carpet's elaborate geometric weave spoke of the intricate work of Arab carpet makers. Tom had seen their work in Casablanca. He stared at the richly flowered wallpaper and the velvet drapes, at the embroidered and tasseled tapestries covering the tables and desks. He was still taking it all in when he saw her. She was sitting on the arm of one of the deep-cushioned chairs. A plump-faced girl with languid blue eyes, she had deep dimples, like a healthy farm girl, and shiny dark hair. Her bright red lips pursed in playful mockery as she held his look. Then the mockery dissolved into a gentle smile and her tongue glided tentatively along her lower lip, leaving it moist and glistening. Something pulsed in his stomach, and in his groin. He stepped toward her and she rose.

"My name is Jenny."

He smiled at her nervously. She wore an intricate lace-covered bodice, which was fitted in such a manner that her breasts showed freely underneath. Running along one strap down to the top of the soft white breasts was an array of dried flowers, and in her dark, coiffed hair, a rich carnation sat like a welcoming fire.

"Shall we?"

He nodded and she led him through a door and down a dimly lit, carpeted passage. Through some

71

of the doors came the sounds of ardent lovemaking, from others the sounds of sweet ballads played softly on phonographs. Just as they turned into the room at the end on the right, a long groan of pleasure came from farther up. She turned at the threshold and smiled at him tauntingly.

"I'll have to see if you can do better than that."

As she turned and spoke the strap bearing the flowers slipped down, revealing the top of her full, smooth breast. The girl was plump but firm. He saw the white flash of her breast and could almost feel it cupped in his large callused hand. As she turned and walked into the room he saw the shape of her hips and thighs under the black-frilled underskirt. He followed her and closed the door behind them.

"Would you like to listen to some love ballads?"

He nodded, but he was not thinking of what she had said. Her soft, yielding womanliness had pumped him to a peak of desire. She placed a cylinder on the machine, and as the singer in the horn invited her lover to serenade, promenade, and waltz her, the smiling, cherub-cheeked whore lay back on the bed and slid the smooth satin skirt up her legs. Just above the knee, the black stocking was slashed by the crimson red of a garter. Above the black of the stockings was smooth, white skin, covering strong thighs. Her muscles flexed as she raised her buttocks enticingly off the bed. She caressed herself, pushing her legs apart, revealing a red-and-black suspender belt. Gently, slowly, she stroked the softness of her inner thighs.

"Sit. Sit beside me."

Tom swallowed hard, scarcely hearing what she had said. She took one of his hands in one of hers and placed it on her warm, scented skin. He stroked her thigh, up and down along the warm, fleshy smoothness. On the back of his hand he could feel the curly hairs of her mound, brushing, tickling, enticing. The pleasure was too much for him. He wanted to lie on her, feel her legs press hard around him. He wanted to let go and slip into her warmth. He sank down beside her on the bed.

"My God, you're beautiful. You've got the smooth skin of a schoolgirl."

"Maybe I am. And here you are, a rough . . . what?"

She stopped and looked up at him shyly, like a coquettish virgin, arching her eyebrow in a question.

He laughed out loud, half in pleasure and half with relief that he could talk to her.

"I'm a sailor—I'm sure you've heard that one before, but it's true."

"A sailor, a rough sailor. A tired sailor come home . . . come home . . ."

They were simple words, said with gentleness. Their eyes held each other. With one hand she pulled down the side of her rich lace bodice and exposed her breast. Her other hand sought out and unbuttoned his trousers, then very delicately closed around him. He closed his eyes at the rush of pleasure, drifting into a dream that lay beyond ships and voyages, blazing furnaces and sadistic bosuns. Opening his eyes, he saw an unexpected tenderness in her dark blue eyes. His whole body trembled; he wanted to fall on her and kiss the marble smoothness of her breast.

He lay his head there and started to suckle like a hungry child. A deep wave of desire swamped him. He wanted to abandon himself to her. He looked deep into her eyes; they were gentle, yet languorous and inviting. She smiled at him again, that subtle, half-taunting, half-nurturing smile. As she did she reached up and pulled his trousers open wide. He could hold back no longer. He thrust forward and into her with such force that she gasped. With a rip of the laces, he pulled her bodice open and grabbed both of her breasts. She found his mouth with hers and half

73

sucked, half bit into his upper lip. She moved under him slowly at first, then quicker and quicker as she rode his thrusts. Her thighs tightened as she wrapped herself around him and pulled him deep inside.

She heard his breathing grow shorter and shorter. He would come soon. She watched him carefully, and through all his violent rapture saw a gentleness. He was a boy, a lost, shy boy. Then she felt the pressure begin to grow within her, the throbbing pleasure that heralded her own release. His hands grasped her breasts firmly and she gasped as he caressed the nipples. She groaned as she felt him coming; her spasms burst upon her at the same time, and unthinkingly she murmured that which she should never speak.

"I sowed no children for the ruler!"

CHAPTER 11

VIRGINIA WAS SITTING in the front room sipping lemon tea when Pendleton arrived home. She glanced at the clock on the mantelpiece: five o'clock. She knew that he had not come home to see her or the children.

She heard him drop his walking stick into the stand under the cold gaze of Athenae and then hesitate at the open door. It was obvious that he wanted to go straight upstairs to Bellarma, but felt that he had to observe some familial niceties on the way.

Her cup tinkled against the saucer as she set it down. Her husband cleared his throat as he stepped into the room.

"Good afternoon, my dear."

His veneer of good humor was very thin and he looked distracted, almost agitated.

"Ernest, what a surprise. You are home early."

"How has our guest been?"

She marveled at how blunt he could be.

"Gladys says he is feeling better. As you wished, I have not spoken to him."

Pendleton crossed to the window and looked out. Virginia watched him, and her temper began to rise. He was insufferable. He didn't give a damn what she did, as long as she stayed out of his way!

"I have a surprise for you this evening, my dear. I have two tickets for *Love Watches* at the Lyceum, for you and Aunt Eleanor."

Virginia was so choked with anger that she could

barely think. He obviously desperately wanted her out of the house. He never sent her to the theater without him.

"That's very kind of you, Ernest, but I feel a headache coming on."

He glared at her. "Virginia, it would be most unseemly of you to leave Aunt Eleanor without a partner for the theater. I'm sure you could make some effort to overcome your disability."

She glared back at him, wondering how long a marriage that bristled with such hostility could continue. She did not want things to be like this, but there was no compromise with Pendleton. She gave a cold smile.

"Well, since you made an effort to come home early and see us all today, I will do as you ask, Ernest." With that she stood up and quickly walked out of the room.

Pendleton stared after her and then started nipping at the hairs on his moustache. She would go. Good. He wanted Bellarma to himself.

He looked over at the clock. He had been thinking about phoning that police lieutenant, Doolan, and asking a few discreet questions. He would have nothing to do with Abyssos if the police had any evidence that connected the sect with Bellarma's stabbing. The advertisements requesting information on the theft of Bellarma's notes would appear in the papers over the next few days. But before he dealt with the cult, he would call Doolan.

Doolan sat for a long while after he had put the phone down. It was strange, having Pendleton call him. The whole time the lawyer was talking Doolan saw in his mind's eye not the man but his wife, Virginia. He recalled her standing in their hallway as he joked about the statue of Athenae; he saw her smiling, blue-green eyes, the ringlet of blond hair she had curled around her fingers.

Consequently, Doolan only half listened as Pendleton once again thanked Doolan for his circumspection and discretion in the Brownlea affair.

"Many businesses could have been destroyed, if my client had been discovered in those . . . shall we say, unfortunate circumstances."

Doolan allowed himself a cynical grin as he recalled the "unfortunate circumstances." Brownlea, a merchant banker, had been found dead in a brothel beside a pretty Jamaican whore. The case was long closed, but Doolan let Pendleton talk, assuming that the man was going to ask for more "discretion." Such requests used to bother Doolan, but ten years on the force had made him a realist, and he knew that men like Pendleton, who were close buddies of the commissioner, had more than a few "discretion" credits in their pockets.

Pendleton did not want any earth-shattering favors, however. He simply wanted to know if the police had any leads yet in an attack on a friend of his, one Father Bellarma. Doolan didn't know the case, but noted down the details of the incident and promised to call if he heard anything.

Pendleton thanked him with suitable grace and Doolan grinned again as the word "discretion" made its final appearance.

Doolan set the receiver down, wondering if Virginia had been there, listening. It was just a fleeting thought that he quickly dismissed; after all, she was another man's wife and in legal parlance, the case was closed.

Finally he shook himself from his reverie and pulled out his pocket watch. He had promised to meet Tom at Vittorio's—and he was late.

Doolan quickly put his desk in order and headed for the café. The last few days he had continually felt as if he were one step behind. Doolan's mood was black. He strode along the empty, echoing corridor and clattered down the stairwell, cursing to himself. Someday they'd get enough money from the city to finish this place, and carpet all the floors, not just the ones where the top brass worked. Maybe then it wouldn't sound so much like a tomb. As he reached the bottom of the stairs, someone called his name.

"Lieutenant Doolan."

Doolan turned to the sergeant at the night desk. "Carver" Corrigan, as he was known to the men on the beat, had gained the epithet because of his fame with a Bowie knife. He had a broad Irish face with small, deep-set eyes, and a wide, thin-lipped smile. His Kerry brogue still lingered, even after thirty years.

"I have a message from your brother. He was here less than fifteen minutes ago." The sergeant handed over a piece of paper, torn from an old day report book. "He's a grand man. A fine brother, I'm sure."

"I'm sure," Doolan mumbled as he opened up the green-lined notepaper.

"Peter, I waited in Vittorio's and had a bite to eat as well. I've gone down to the Occidental again. Join me when you've finished. Tom."

Doolan glanced through the windows of the main door. Centre Street was busy as ever. The horses and automobiles were passing so fast that it was as though they had never heard of night. A light fog had returned, thinner and wispier than the past two nights but enough to make its presence felt.

Doolan left the building, heading for the Occidental. The night hawkers were everywhere, and they were every bit as loud and raucous as the daytime variety: newspapers, candy, flowers. Recently Police Commissioner Bingham had posted General Order No. 47, ordering his men "to arrest any loud-lunged hucksters or hawkers causing a public nuisance."

A scabby youth of about twelve stood outside the

heavy doors of the Broome Street Tabernacle, a pile of newspapers beside him.

"Bits a body in da Hudson . . . Yankees moidah Red Sox. . . . Read all about it. . . . Read all about it."

Christ, Doolan thought, now the poor girl's death is the property of the streets. Doolan reached into his trouser pocket and fished out three cents, tossing them to the kid and lifting a paper from the stack. He quickly stuffed it in his pocket when he saw that the "Case of the Dissevered Girl" had the front page. Well, in two days some other horror would replace it. He wanted to read about the Yankees in Boston, but he could wait until he was in the bar.

Doolan walked on, past the dark oak doors of the synagogue, closed tight against the clinging evening mist. He continued past the barred windows of the Seroco Refrigerator factory warehouse. He was suddenly jarred from his reverie by a loud bang, followed by shouts and cries, coming from the direction of Mott Street. A group of men were scrambling around a large engine in front of the Meitz and Weiss oil and gas engine company. Along both sides of the street people were clambering onto the fire escapes, eager for the free show.

There had been an explosion in the oil tank. The fire was burning fiercely. Large clouds of black smoke billowed up. Doolan stood transfixed. He could see the flames licking redly at the center of the cloud. It was like the steel mills again: the smell, the intense heat, the smoke. The memory of his father flashed into his mind. It was a horror that Doolan did not want to face again, yet he stood mesmerized as the oily, pungent smoke wound around him.

Two men broke from the blackness, shoving him aside as they ran past. The spell was broken; Doolan turned away. The men had charged into the open door of Fire House No. 55, just along the block.

Suddenly the bells rang out, ripping through the smoke. The horses and fire wagon came clattering out and quickly turned into Mott.

Doolan moved off. The fire would be taken care of, and the blaze extinguished—but the events of the past were not so easily erased, and he wanted to crush those insistent memories.

Pausing to shake his head in an attempt to clear it, Doolan found himself in front of the church of San Salvadore. Light flooded out of the stained-glass windows. It looked warm, inviting. It was a long time since he had been inside a church. Maybe this was the comfort he needed today.

He walked up to the door. He did not see the cab parked on the opposite corner of Elizabeth and Broome, the horse stamping impatiently, the inside dark. Empty. Waiting.

CHAPTER 12

PENDLETON SAT LIKE a statue as he listened to Bellarma read from the manuscripts. Virginia had left for the theater at seven-thirty. During all the hours since, he had scarcely moved. He had watched as Bellarma sat up in the bed, laying the manuscripts before him. The cloth they were wrapped in, stained with the dull rust-red of the priest's blood, lay on the bedside table, a gruesome reminder of the living and dangerous presence of the cult.

Bellarma had to read slowly, translating as he went, and Pendleton stopped him often. What he was hearing was difficult to understand, but more than that it was frightening.

> "We are the cult of Abyssos. Our enemies call us the cult of the damned. We have been persecuted by the Church of Rome and its leader, the bishop Hippolytus, and been driven from the cities of Constantinople and Alexandria. This desert place is our last refuge.
>
> "These books contain the Truths of the Great Knowledge.
>
> "The God of the Christians and Jews is called Jehovah. We know him as Ialdoboath. This Ialdoboath is cunning and vengeful, but the Light of Knowledge will conquer, the Light will lead the soul from its prison to the Eternity that is the soul's rightful heritage.

81

"Only when the mind and body have gone beyond shame, shall the energy of the soul be released."

Pendleton turned the words over and over in his mind. His attention was beginning to wander. It was all too much for him. This new knowledge was flowing over his head, drowning him. He began to feel confused and then scared, like a naked child on a vast dark plain. Storm clouds were building high above his head, black and threatening.

"You will see the Truth when you undress yourselves and are not ashamed, and take your clothing and lay them under your feet, like little children, and tread on them. . . .

"Death is the true consequence of the works of the female, which the Light of Truth shall destroy. . . .

"There is a mingling that leadeth to death, and there is a mingling that leadeth to life. . . ."

Bellarma had stopped at this point and laid his hands against the wound in his chest. Pendleton saw the fear in his eyes. The cult was desperately searching for these books, and anyone who stood in their way was in danger. Bellarma bowed his head and continued reading.

"The Light of Truth shall bring you out from there, from the dust that is the flesh and the corruption that is the body. It shall do this by this means of fire, of Knowledge; by this, you shall escape to the unnameable Godhead in Abyssos, He who is above the Creator Angels, the Archons, one of whom is the evil Jehovah, whom we know as Ialdoboath.

"To make this journey from the corruption of the flesh, you must follow closely the rituals and never

*fear to pay the last quarter. You must undergo all
the humiliation of which the body is capable, the
Rituals of Excess as they are laid out hereafter."*

Bellarma thrust the manuscripts away from him
and nervously wiped his hands along the sheet, as if
he was trying to wipe them clean.

"What is wrong?"

"I will not read any more tonight."

Pendleton watched him as he lay back against the
pillows and let out a long unsteady sigh.

"Would you like me to bring you something to
drink?"

For a moment Bellarma just stared at him and
pressed his hands against the sides of his temples.
Then he nodded and smiled.

"Yes, thank you. Perhaps a large glass of red wine if
you have it."

Bellarma gathered the manuscripts together and
handed them to Pendleton. The lawyer very gently set
the precious books on the table; the priest's hands
trembled as he relaxed. There was a long silence, a
silence charged with fear on one side and ignorance
on the other. Then Pendleton walked out, gently
closing the door behind him. Virginia would be home
soon, he thought, heading for the wine cellar. It was
just as well Bellarma wanted to stop for the night.

Doolan entered the shadowed stillness of the
church and inhaled deeply. The church still had
gaslights, and their smell, combined with the odor of
incense, conjured up memories of his childhood.

He dipped his hand into the font of holy water; it
was cool and refreshing. He was determined to cher-
ish the textures and the rituals. He watched as the
pure liquid dribbled through his fingers, then blessed
himself. The water felt slick on his forehead.

God touches the mind. God touches the heart. God

83

touches the left and God touches the right. He smiled at his mother's rhyme. This was the peace of God.

He moved into the nave and slowly walked up one of the side aisles, selecting a pew. Only when he had genuflected and sat down did it occur to him that he was completely alone.

He sat silent for a long time, eyes closed, hands clasped in prayer. He was trying hard to recall his childhood, cherishing that time when faith was all too simple, before his father's death. The rickety little church of St. Columba, half tin and half wood, standing at the top of a steep, curving street in Johnstown. The wind always whistling around its corners, rattling its windows and doors. He could still smell the burning coal from the old iron stove in the corner, still see Father Heffernan shuffling in from the sacristy, adjusting the maniple over his arm. The other children jostled around Doolan, their responses muffled. He could hear the choir. . . .

He blinked his eyes open. What was that noise? He looked around in the gloom of the dim gaslight. The side altars were dark and silent. There was not even the whisper of a sound, nothing. He glanced at the confessional boxes sitting ominous and impenetrable, their intricately carved, dark wood panels covered with heavy velvet curtains. There was no one there.

His eyes sought out the main altar, with the sanctuary lamp burning to one side of it. Everything was as it should be, everything was in its place. Suddenly the red lamp spluttered in its glass-sheathed holder, and the shadows from the large crucifix lurched grotesquely across the pulpit and altar, shadows dancing with the lurid light.

Doolan turned to look behind him at the left side of the church. Two rows of votive candles burned in front of a statue of the Virgin. They too were spluttering in the wind. The air became still as suddenly as it had been disturbed, but the noise was still there, a throaty breathing or a low growling. Doolan shivered. He felt alone and vulnerable.

Once again the low, hissing breath shuddered through the church. Doolan spun around again. The sanctuary lamp stopped him with a jolt. It was out— dead. Then he heard a distant, wild, taunting laughter echoing around the stone pillars.

Doolan staggered toward the statue of the Virgin. The twenty-odd candles burned brightly beneath her. The white marble of her face gleamed, and her pitying smile seemed to offer peace and rest. The laughter swirled about him again, swirled up into the looming darkness of the empty church. A chill wind howled through the church, shaking the candle flames; the Virgin's smile twisted grotesquely. Seeking the source of that icy breath, Doolan studied the side wall of the church. A heavy iron door lay open. Darkness poured from it like something tangible. As he stared, the chilling breath faded once again.

He stepped forward, then paused to wrench a votive candle from its holder. He held it tight, the wax dripping hotly onto his hand. As he walked toward the door, his steps echoed in the emptiness. He grasped the heavy, bolted edge of the door and dragged it farther open, noting that the iron gleamed with shiny black enamel paint. Beyond the door he could see the top of a dark winding staircase leading down into a crypt.

Beads of cold sweat broke out on his forehead, and glistened in the gently flickering flame of the candle. He shuffled to the top of the first step, shielding the flame from the draft. A cold dampness rose from the darkness below, reeking of the mustiness of rooms long empty. He stepped slowly downward and smelled something else, something strong and sweet, flowers of some kind.

The stairway wound below him. He could see no farther than five steps ahead. The brick of the church gave way to the roughly hewn rock of the foundations. His left hand glided down the outer wall, steadying him, while he clutched the candle in his right.

The noise froze him in midstep. It started with a low growl, a rasping, tearing, guttural sound followed by a wild and desperate scratching. And something else, low at first but building in strength. A forlorn wail shrieked through the air. The hair on his body began to crawl. He tried to swallow, but his throat had dried. He forced himself down another step.

And another. At last Doolan reached the bottom of the stairway. The long crypt stretched before him, swallowing the light of the candle. A figure rushed from the blackness, shrieking demonically as it sped toward him. Black robes billowed around it. Doolan's frantic mind identified it as a nun's habit as the figure flung itself at the stairway. The veil, flying out, revealed a porcelain mask, sockets black and eyeless, the mouth a hissing slit. Its howl was deafening. He had no time to think. A blow smashed him backward into the wall, and the thing rushed past, up the stairwell. Doolan slid to the stone floor, senseless. The candle fell from his hand, gutting itself on the rock floor.

The crypt was once again in darkness.

CHAPTER 13

BELLARMA TOOK THE glass of wine and drank it, then he lay back against his pillow and closed his eyes. Pendleton walked back to the chest of drawers and lifted the bottle.

"Shall I pour you another?"

Bellarma shook his head, a nervous smile flickering on his lips.

"Would you like me to leave, let you sleep?"

The little priest blinked his eyes as though trying to stay awake, then stared at Pendleton. His skin looked grey, and as he spoke a great tiredness, beyond that already in his face, seemed to settle in his eyes.

"Several years ago, just before I found the caves at Gebel Kalat, I returned to Rome and went down into the archives of the Vatican Library. I wanted to go over those early Church texts again, Irenaeus, Epiphanius, Clement of Alexandria, go through them closely to see if there were any clues I had missed."

Bellarma slowly ran his forefinger around the rim of the glass.

"They are so quiet, the archives. The dust lies undisturbed for centuries, rooms are locked with long-rusted keys. It was a shock to find someone in the very room I sought, working on those texts that were so precious to me. He was a young priest."

Bellarma sighed deeply, several times. He stared ahead of him with a fixed intensity, as though seeing the events he was remembering.

"His eyes were so bright. . . . He said he was an Austrian, Father Schmidt. He said that he had had a vision that instructed him to discover the truth about the cult of Abyssos. I can't tell you what a terror his words sent through me. You see, I felt that I was the only one to guard the gate of these secrets."

Bellarma stopped again and played with the glass in his hand.

"He told me that he had been offered a place in New York City. He had given a rich Italian-American 'comfort,' something to do with his daughter, and now this man wanted him in his church. Father Schmidt had read the Church Fathers, and like me he knew that the true texts must lie hidden somewhere. But unlike me he did not want to search for them. He said that his vision had shown him that the texts would come to him. I can see him now, sitting on a bench, his back against the dust-laden stacks, and those eyes, clear and bright, boring into me. God . . . God . . .

"And now I have brought those very texts to this city, to him, as though I was drawn here."

Bellarma's voice died away. Pendleton felt chilled, but forced himself to lean forward and break the silence. His voice was taut with disbelief. "But are you saying that this priest was connected with the incident on the train?"

Bellarma glared at the lawyer. He had the eyes of a scared, cornered animal, ready to pounce on its pursuer. His voice was suddenly stronger.

"It is written that Simon Magus, Simon the prophet of Abyssos, Simon who struggled with Christ's disciple Peter—it is written in the texts of Abyssos that Simon will return when his word has broken free. Schmidt calls himself Simon. He is obsessed with the cult!" Bellarma gasped for breath. The urgency of his message had sapped his strength. He set the wineglass on the beside table with a trembling hand, then rubbed his forehead as though in pain.

"Please, take the books away. Put them somewhere safe. I give them to your keeping. Tomorrow night I shall read further, and you will help me decide what to do next."

The priest's eyes closed. He was instantly asleep.

Pendleton carefully wrapped the bloodstained cloth around the manuscripts once again. Somehow the blood seemed bizarrely appropriate. Cradling the books securely, Pendleton left the room. He must put his bloody parcel somewhere safe, at least until the priest could talk to him tomorrow evening. Pendleton's eyes flickered along the hall toward the top of the stairway. He felt like a grasping miser, with his last jewel clutched greedily in his hand. At first he thought of his study, but that would be the first place that anyone would look. The thought of anyone searching the house caused sweat to gather on his brow and trickle down into his collar.

Then it came to him: he would put the package in the nursery.

He walked down to the ground floor and along the marble hallway to the back of the house. Tentatively he opened the nursery door. The nanny's room was to the side. The children slept soundly in their beds.

All was quiet. Pendleton walked in and looked around. It was like a toy shop. Everything looked so neat, arranged carefully on the shelves. He stood for a moment in the center of the room, thinking. Beside the wooden rocking horse were two large trunks, one atop the other. Pendleton crossed to them and lifted the top one, then set it carefully on the floor. Opening the bottom trunk, he saw that it was filled with an assortment of baby toys and clothes, long unused. He slipped the package under two of Mary's little pink dresses. He shivered at the callousness of his reasoning.

The rust red of the blood would be less visible

hidden under the pink. He closed the lid, replaced the other trunk, then glanced at his rosy-faced children. He crossed to the hall door and slipped out. When the door had closed behind him, he suddenly felt unclean. For the first time, his lust for knowledge had touched the lives of his innocent children.

Doolan awoke to a deep, black stillness. He did not remember where he was. He could feel that he was lying awkwardly. His legs were above him. A heavy, sweet smell filled his nostrils. His face was touching something cold, smooth, and clammy. He pushed it from him, and as he moved he felt the hard edge of the steps under his legs. He realized that he was lying upside down on the stairway. He dragged himself a few more feet into the crypt. For a moment he lay still, listening intently. There was no sound other than his own breathing.

Slowly the events of the evening seeped into his mind. What had rushed past him up those stairs? The memory of it made him shudder again.

He sprang to his feet. It was a reflex from his days in the Marines. At the first moment of fear, move.

His hand shot out to touch the damp, uneven rock wall. Leaning forward, he felt the shape of the spiral staircase. As he touched the wall, he heard a slithering noise behind him, and a soft dull splat. He drew in breath sharply as his whole body tensed. He hugged the wall and strained to hear. His hands desperately searched his pockets. Where were those shagging matches?

His fingers closed around the box. His hearing was alert, but there was no more noise. Silently, he slipped the box out and pulled it open. The match flared as he struck it. Nothing moved. He slowly bent down, looking for the candle. He found it lying on the last step, stuck in a pool of hardened wax. He pulled it free and lit it. As the light grew stronger, he saw his hat lying by the wall. He picked it up, then turned back to the crypt, holding the candle out at arm's length.

As he walked forward something crunched beneath his feet. He gazed down. The floor was strewn with large white lilies. So that was what he had been lying among. That was the heavy, sweet smell that filled his nostrils: lilies, the flower of death. He moved carefully forward. The white flowers were crushed and shredded, as though a trapped animal had torn through them in wild despair. The light shone onto a cold, damp emptiness.

"Mary, Mother of God." The stagnant air swallowed his voice.

He held the candle high and turned slowly, looking carefully into every corner. The gleaming black marble coffin stood in a niche. Part of a wreath still rested on the lid. A few blossoms drifted to the floor.

Doolan walked over. Along the dark side of the coffin he could see scratches and small gouge marks where the marble had been scraped and chipped. That accounted for the desperate clawing noise that he had heard. None of this made sense. He leaned closer, the flame reflecting in the black shininess of the marble. It looked as if a knife had been used to try to dig into the coffin, to get at the body.

He straightened up and looked along the length of the stone casket. The dead person's name was partly obscured by the remains of the last wreath. He brushed the flowers away with the side of his hand.

"GIUSEPPE V. GALLENINI
AUGUST 20, 1846–SEPTEMBER 13, 1908."

Doolan realized that this must have been the man who was buried in that fog-bound funeral the other morning. He didn't understand what was going on, but now he had to get out of here. All of this could be

worked out somewhere else, at some other time. He
ran up the steps, shielding the candle flame. At the top
he was confronted by the heavy iron door. It was
locked. He couldn't believe it. He tried the handle,
then rattled it. Finally he smashed his fist against the
door, groaning in anger.

He listened as the crash of the iron echoed through
the empty church, then pulled his watch from his
pocket. Holding the candle close, he saw it was
ten-twenty. The church must be closed.

"Shit. God damn it."

What would he do now? He tried the door once
more, and then he put his shoulder against it and
pushed. It was solid, unmovable.

He slowly turned and looked down into the blackness of the crypt again. There had to be another way
out from down there. Then he grinned. At least there
wouldn't be any more demented nuns lurking in the
darkness.

Almost as soon as he had the thought, he regretted
it. The place was creepy enough without him thinking
of that porcelain-faced obscenity. He made his way
down again slowly, to guard the fluttering flame.

When he got to the bottom, he glanced at Gallenini's stone coffin, and then walked past. At the other
end there was a low stone archway. He bent his head
and walked through into another small crypt. He held
the candle high and it suddenly flickered and died.

The blackness was thick around him. He tensed. He
felt naked and exposed, like a helpless child. He
sensed that something was circling him, coming from
behind, shifting from side to side.

With an effort he stood still and listened to the
silence.

He could see the outline of the doorway in the
darkness and made for it. He rushed through, striding
across the uneven stone floor of the crypt to the stairs,
unimpeded by the blackness. Groping, he found the

curve of the wall and started up. He was breathless, yet ashamed of his childish fears. At the top, he came to the locked door, and smashed his fist against the metal. The door remained obdurately locked.

The darkness brought back that throbbing sense of desolation he had experienced after his father's death. He remembered the night before the funeral, when he sat alone in the last pew of the ramshackle old church of St. Columba, watching as the aging Father Heffernan shuffled toward him.

That was when his faith had died, leaving him desolate then as now.

Doolan sank to the stone floor. His memories burst on him and once again he was faced with the horrors that he thought he had suppressed forever.

He was back at the steel plant in Johnstown. The air was filled with the roaring sounds of the furnaces, the acrid smell of the coke fumes. He was young again, stripped down to a vest. The sweat was pouring over his taut muscles, leaving tracks in the dark dust that covered his skin. He could feel the calluses on his hands, the thick handle of the heavy shovel that he gripped.

One of the conveyor belts carrying coal to the bins over the ovens had ruptured earlier that morning, spilling tons of coal on the rail tracks. He was one of a gang of laborers that the utility foreman had rushed onto the scene to clean up.

"Pete!" Flaherty, one of the battery foremen, was standing beside the gigantic steel ram. It was used to push the finished coke from the ovens into a waiting rail truck. Doolan strode over to him.

"Pete, this battery'll be up in a minute. It's a wonder we have anything up this morning, thanks to that bunch of feckless eejits that arsed up the belt. Anyway, the ram'll be rolling in a minute, and I want you up on the quencher with Dougherty."

Doolan nodded and started toward the quencher. It

was there that the coke was cooled after being taken from the ovens.

"Come on, Pete, up and get your daily Turkish. Cheapest steam bath in the mountains." Dougherty was a big Donegal man, with an accent not unlike Doolan's father. He was only about five years older than Doolan himself, with a shock of red hair that never looked combed except at Mass. He had a big toothy grin and laughing eyes; an easygoing amiable man. He gave Doolan a hand up the last step, jokingly tugging him up onto the platform.

"Those're grand tatty hoker hands ye have boyo, like the bossman, yer da."

Doolan grinned and wiped his hands along his trousers. They were big, the Doolan blessing and curse. His mother used to make him laugh when she would say, "Grand for the mills, but I'd wouldn't want to see you a watchmaker."

There was a roar across at battery two. The thick steel doors at either end of the oven opened and the heat blasted out. The ram rumbled forward, entering the oven, pushing the red-hot coke out through the other door, along the coke guide and into the waiting rail truck. It was a stream of liquid fire. The ram pushed all the way through, then ground its way back. When the oven doors clanged shut, it rumbled up the rail line to the next oven.

Dougherty and Doolan checked the water hoses and gauges. For a few seconds Dougherty opened the nozzles to check the flow. The water hit the hot rails below and gently sizzled, sending up a cloud of steam.

Doolan looked across the floor, past the batteries, past the gently rising steam and the distorting waves of heat. He could see his father in the distance. He was a giant of a man, a full two inches taller than Doolan himself. He was the general foreman of the battery and had the respect of every man under him.

He was coming down the stairs from the walkway

94

overhead. A group of "bossmen" had been inspecting the trouble on the coal belt.

Doolan wanted to wake, to thrust the dream aside; but whatever malignant force steered him through the reliving of this horror would not let him go. He was doomed to play it through.

The big man got to the bottom of the steps, took his leave of the engineers, and strode into the middle of the vast workplace. He stood with his feet firmly planted apart, his hands clasped behind his back, the master of his world. Slowly he surveyed the mill, taking in every part of the operation; a tall, straight-backed man, with white hair and a face permanently red from the heat. He saw his son on the quencher, and gave him a cursory nod. It was all the contact he permitted between himself and his sons when they were at work.

Doolan watched as his father walked over and joked with the last of the men working on the coal spill. Dougherty tapped him on the shoulder, and pointed at the coke pan. It was nudging away from the battery of ovens, its wheels grinding and screeching. The noise echoed like a warning banshee wail in his head.

The engine picked up speed, bringing the coke pan across the yard, headed for the quencher. Dougherty grasped the water handles and Doolan clambered up to check the steam vent above.

As he finished, and jumped down beside Dougherty again, he glanced at the engine and coke pan taking the curve, within ten feet of his father. The waves of heat from the great pans made his image wave and bend.

The official inquiry said that the weight of the early morning coal fall had cracked the paving stones and loosened the whole section of rail.

Doolan saw and heard every moment of the horror. First was the screech of the wheels, then the ripping and tearing of metal against stone. The massive weight of the searing-hot coke pan reared up, and for what seemed like an age, teetered, almost balanced. He saw his father turn toward the noise. As the almost liquid coke spilled out and roared toward him, Doolan saw his face blanch with terror.

Doolan gripped the railing that rimmed the quencher platform, his body rigid, his heart exploding in his chest.

The coke swirled around his father, burying him to his waist. His screams trumpeted through the yard, rising above the combined noise of the ovens and the machinery. Everyone turned from their work.

Doolan heard the clatter of Dougherty's boots as he charged down the metal steps. He wrenched himself from the rails and ran after him. The yard was filled now with men converging on the gruesome scene. They saw the big man's clothes suddenly catch fire, and watched helplessly as he toppled sideways into the moving river of flame.

Some struggled with fire buckets and hoses, but it was a useless gesture. The spilled pan of coke spread toward them like molten lava, spitting and hissing its defiance.

Doolan pushed through the crowd. Dougherty was ahead of him, and in a blind, stumbling way, he followed helplessly.

His mind was crazed. How could this happen; how could it be allowed to happen? His father was such a good man, a man who had practiced his faith, served his God. God! How could God allow this to happen? That was the question he had never dared to ask before.

Suddenly Dougherty spun around on him and was not Dougherty. He was the priest from Gallenini's funeral, the priest from the fog. He took Doolan by the arms and stared fixedly at him. He spoke, and it was a reply to all of Doolan's despair.

"There is no justice. There is no love. There is only horror in this world."

Doolan thrust him aside and pushed on past the crowd, toward the spitting coke. The men at the front tried to hold him back, but he wrenched himself free and strode forward until the great heat burned at his face and hands.

A flaring coal chip flew out of the fire and seared his cheek. He scarcely felt the pain, but it left a thin red welt that would later form into a scar. The acrid smell choked his nasal passages. He stared out at what little remained of his father's body, and shook with curses. The tears poured from his eyes and the pool of fire swirled before him.

The priest was there again, walking before him. It was impossible. No man could go into that broiling inferno, but there he was. He turned and beckoned to Doolan. His eyes were full of warmth and love. The other men around him faded away. The two of them stood alone in the fire. Doolan could hear the priest's voice, cool and enticing.

"I am here to lead you into the purifying flame. This is the way to end this horror that lives forever in your mind."

"No . . . no . . . no!" Doolan shouted wildly as he lifted his forehead from the stone step. The door was now open. A figure stood before him, framed against the shadowed lights of the church, arms outstretched. Doolan staggered to his feet as the figure spoke.

"I heard the noise and came to the door."

The voice was soft and soothing, but Doolan recoiled as he heard it. This was the priest who had turned to him in the inferno.

Doolan was breathless as he stood up and stared into the man's strange, deep blue eyes. He tried to talk, but the words dried along his parched throat.

The priest smiled. "There is no need to explain. I shall let you out. You are all right, aren't you?"

97

"Yes."

And as they spoke the priest led him down the aisle and through the portico to the front door. Doolan felt he was still in the middle of the dream; everything had that liquid sense of inevitability. Only when the door of the church clicked shut behind him did he come to.

The priest was gone. Doolan was alone on the steps.

CHAPTER 14

ARAYA ROSE AT three the next morning, just as he always had in the monastery at Gebel Asoteriba. He had fasted the previous evening and chanted himself into a prayer trance. During those hours his dingy hotel room had become his cell. There he would kneel until the sun came blasting out of the east, mounting the top of the Gebel, turning the Nubian Desert outside the high sandstone walls into a shimmering basin of ocher.

Now he awakened refreshed, his soul renewed. He could think with clarity again, a clarity informed by a vision he had had during prayer.

He had never met Bellarma, but that night he had seen him clearly. The little priest was lying back in a bed, blood across his chest, his arms outstretched, begging Araya for help. When Araya said he did not know how to find him, Bellarma pleaded with him to look for the sign . . . the written sign . . .

Araya sat in the corner of the dingy all-night café, scanning the first editions of the newspapers. All around him dock laborers and truck drivers scoffed early breakfasts. When he finally came to the advertisement, he jumped up, left his food unfinished, and paid quickly. The message was simple, but it was a signpost.

"LOST. A number of religious papers, in the vicinity of Grand Central Station, Monday morn-

ing, September 14th. Contained in leather suitcase belonging to Father B. Bellarma. Reward. Contact E. J. Pendleton, 72 East 64 Street."

Patrolman O'Reilly could feel someone looking at him, even before he turned. He had walked just a few yards into East Sixty-fourth Street when he stopped. There were eyes focused on him. He spun around, his hand instinctively curled on the handle of his nightstick.

"Hey you, nigger, move out. What're you hanging around here for?"

Araya moved out from beside the porch steps and into the early morning shadows. He stepped onto the sidewalk in front of the policeman. O'Reilly was big himself, but he calculated that this black was at least six feet five.

"Come on, what the hell're you doing lurking around here?"

"I'm a sailor off a Dutch ship."

"Oh, indeed, indeed. Well you're in the wrong part of town, sailor. Try the bars and whorehouses on Sixth below Forty-second Street . . . though I must say you're out scouting for it a bit early in the morning."

The black man pulled himself tall. O'Reilly was struck, as all were, by his aristocratic bearing.

Araya stared down at the policeman for a moment and then slowly nodded.

"Thank you. I was simply roaming and found myself here. I wanted to look at the houses. They are splendid."

His accent was strange, pure-toned and musical. After he had spoken he looked around the street once again and then turned back to the policeman.

"But I shall take your advice, and walk elsewhere."

O'Reilly stared into the black man's eyes flashing in the light of the electric streetlamp. There was something extraordinary in that gaze. The man emanated a profound, almost mystical calmness. O'Reilly suddenly felt that he had just told a priest where he could find a good prostitute. He stumbled to excuse himself.

"I mean, if you're the usual type of sailor, that would be your area."

O'Reilly's voice trailed off. He was mesmerized by the clear, penetrating eyes. Araya gave him a warm smile.

"Thank you for your help. I shall visit there."

He glanced at the house across the street, looking up from the marble front steps and porch, through four floors to the servants' quarters at the top. Then he walked away and quickly turned the corner.

The policeman shrugged and resumed his beat. He'd better get a move on, or his sergeant would be sending out a rescue party.

Araya strode along with the self-possession of a pilgrim. With his easy, loping gait and strong straight bearing, he turned the head of many an early morning pedestrian along Madison Avenue. He saw none of this interest. He was possessed of a vision, and he had followed it to this strange city, this Tower of Babel, with its thousand tongues, its thousand nationalities. A city that arrogantly built its houses to touch the sky.

He had found Bellarma's residence. This afternoon he would return, after he had strengthened himself in the reading of the books. It had been a long journey. That bleak monastery that was paradise to Araya seemed a thousand years away.

CHAPTER 15

DOOLAN SAID NOTHING to his brother about his adventure in the crypt. Tom had ragged him about being late and they had set about drinking each other under the table. Even so, Doolan turned up at his office bright and early.

By the time Cassassa, McKenna, and O'Neal arrived in the office at seven-thirty, Doolan had lists of work for the day. It was a daunting task, but this was where the real hunt started. He had made up a list of cloth outlets and divided it into four. Armed with pieces of the material, they had to hoof it to every garment place until they could turn up a lead. What Ferrais called joyful legwork.

Frank Cassassa was last to leave. He carefully folded the small piece of cloth and placed it in a manila envelope. Doolan was standing at the window, hands clasped behind his back, looking down on the police wagons parked along narrow Centre Market. Cassassa turned to him, smoothing down his moustache with his thumb. He pulled out a snuff box and sniffed a pinch. He waited for his eyes to water, and then blew his nose with a stained handkerchief.

"Anything wrong, Peter?"

Doolan sagged into his chair.

"Aaagh, no, not at all. Just damned tired. That brother of mine is a wild drinker."

Cassassa laughed. "You deserve it, then. My youngest, Theo, was up at four this morning, coughing his little lungs out. Then he just lies down and goes back to sleep. Me, I'm up for another hour. Listen, at least it's good to know that if you have a headache, you enjoyed getting it."

"Yeah."

"You don't sound convinced."

"Maybe in an hour or so."

Doolan shuffled the files on the desk in front of him. He was in another world, replaying last night's disturbing events again and again.

Cassassa picked up his newspaper, folded it, and began to slip it into his coat pocket. Then he stopped, raised an eyebrow, and tossed it onto Doolan's desk.

"Hmmm?" Doolan said, looking up.

"Come on, Pete, wake up. Take the paper; I've finished with it. Go over to Vittorio's and get some breakfast."

Doolan looked up and smiled.

"Thanks, maybe I will. I said I'd meet Tom over there at eight. Though I won't bet on him showing up."

"Talking about betting, what about the fight at the Whirlwind tonight? D'ye reckon Young Otto?"

"God, you Italians must have shares in the guy. Vittorio's red hot for him too."

"Yeah, well, he knocked out the Montana Kid in one punch in California. Anyway, Locke's a slambang artist."

Doolan picked up his sheet of notes and folded them into his notepad. He placed his piece of cloth in an envelope, and put it in his inside pocket. Leaning over, he snatched up the newspaper.

The smell of Vittorio's coffee was very welcome. Doolan breathed in deeply as he walked to one of the little café's side tables. He collapsed into a chair, yawned, rubbed his face and eyes, and stretched. The walls of Vittorio's were covered with pictures: the

103

Italian royal family, Victor Emmanuel III and his queen, and beside that the former king, Humbert; popes, the present one, Pius X, and the last one, Leo XIII. All were covered in a yellow film of grease and dust. Below them hung signed photos from many of New York's Italian boxers. Doolan looked at them vacantly for a while, then took a deep breath and shook himself awake.

"Peader!"

Tom was sitting in a booth near the window. He had a newspaper spread out on the table in front of him, an empty plate pushed to one side. He wore a neat, dark grey jacket with a clean white shirt and tie. His dark wavy hair was brushed to one side, and he looked disgustingly healthy. As if reading his brother's mind, Tom lifted his mug of coffee in a mock toast.

"Come on over and join me."

Doolan got up and sauntered over to Tom, meeting Vittorio en route with a large coffeepot in his hand. Vittorio was in his late forties. He had lost most of his black curly hair, but some still remained, clinging tenaciously to his temples and the back of his head. It would have made him look like a worldy friar, but the thick, dark handlebar moustache added the touch of an opera villain.

"Sit down, Mister Lieutenant."

"I'll have some more of your great sausage," Tom said with a wink, "that is if you're still serving breakfast, Vittorio."

"An' you, Lieutenant?"

"Just coffee. There's something at the back of my head giving me signals in Morse code."

Vittorio poured some hot, black coffee into Tom's mug. He left the pot and walked back to the counter for another mug, slapping Doolan on the back as he shuffled away. Even the smell of the coffee was revitalizing, pushing back the night's phantoms.

"Good morning, young brother. If it isn't the proud

boy in blue, out to face a new day of crime."

"I haven't yet decided if I'm talking to you."

Tom grinned the winning, crooked smile of a ten-year-old.

Vittorio returned with a mug for Doolan and some more sausage for Tom. "Listen, Lieutenant, that reporter Harkins, he been looking for you already."

"Shit, no. I couldn't take that this morning."

"I told him you'd been and gone."

"Then at least I can eat my breakfast in peace. God, they hang around here like vultures. Vittorio, what about a plate of toast?"

Vittorio shuffled back through the other tables filled with truck drivers from the docks and warehouses, shop assistants, and cab drivers.

The brothers sat for a moment in silence. Tom picked up his paper again and Doolan took another satisfying gulp of hot coffee. From behind the paper, Tom watched his brother. He was sure that something had happened last night before Peter had met him in the bar. He had not seen that look of bleak despair in his brother's eyes since their father's death. But Peter would say nothing, and that was an end to it. Tom consoled himself with the thought that many things could bring that look of distraction. Maybe there was a woman. Tom thought of yesterday afternoon with the whore. Something had passed between them, something precious.

Vittorio placed a large plate of toast on the table.

"Toast; but a man needs more. You should have sausage, bacon, eggs, something."

"Tomorrow, Vittorio, tomorrow."

Vittorio turned away in mock disgust and shuffled back behind the counter to shout abuse at his sons. Tom folded his paper and stared over it at his brother.

"I see your murder got front page, a gruesome, bloody thing."

Doolan slowly looked up and stopped chewing. "I

105

start work *after* breakfast, Tom."

"Sure, ah, you're right, sure."

Tom drained his mug. "You were talking in your sleep."

"How would you know?"

Tom grinned. "I didn't collapse like you. All that rum they feed us on Dutch ships has inured me to alcohol."

" 'Inured'? Planning to take up literature?"

Tom shrugged, not willing to rise to the bait. "You were shouting about our father."

"Oh."

Doolan turned away, glancing around the room. His chin was set, and Tom could see that the conversation was ended. He picked up the paper again and pretended to be engrossed in the stock market, but he kept looking at his brother. He recalled his daydream, the one in which he had seen his brother as a priest, his head obscured by a writhing snake. Suddenly Tom felt afraid for his brother.

"Peter, is it this case that's bothering you?"

Doolan shook off his black feelings. "Hmm? What would bother me in that? It's just the usual butchery and horror." He stopped. The joke had turned sour on him. "I must get back to work."

They walked over to the counter and paid Vittorio.

"If I see Harkins, whaddo I tell him?"

"Tell him to write a better paper."

Outside, Tom grabbed his brother by the arm. "Shall I meet you here tonight?"

"I tell you what, Tom, make your own plans and leave me a message."

"Fair enough. And Peader . . ."

"What?"

"Get a bloody shave before your boss sees you. You look like a bloody Boer with that stubble."

Doolan quickly passed his hand over the roughness of his chin. Christ, he'd forgotten.

"You and the drink, Tom, you're a menace." Doolan grinned and slapped his brother on the back. Tom landed a friendly punch on his arm.

"Look after yourself, Peader."

Doolan quickly walked off, turning east onto Grand. He would go to Rudi Saalberg's, the barber at the corner of Elizabeth and Canal, just behind the Thalia Theater.

Tom stood for a while looking after him. He smiled approvingly as the man, tall and broad shouldered, made his way along the crowded sidewalks with his long loping walk. He wasn't the kind of man you'd want to lose.

CHAPTER 16

THE WATER WAS dark and dangerous. Jenny had been there for what seemed like an age, standing on the last stone step. Just below, the frothy waves lapped seductively against the green-and-brown-slimed walls. Jenny looked out into the river, knowing that something was there waiting to claim her. Then she heard the soft, accented voice whispering in her ear. It was warm, reassuring, almost sexual.

"There is no danger. There is nothing there, it is all in your mind, child."

She stepped down. Her foot slipped into the icy river. Something plopped into the river in the darkness. Jenny knew it was the snake.

The Snake of Knowledge was coming to her in the water. She would have to go with it, let it take her away. Then she heard the voice of the sailor, the dark-haired sailor with the gentle eyes.

"Jenny, come back. Come back, don't leave the land. Don't leave the faith. . . ."

His warm smile floated before her. The water was encompassing, seductive. She wanted to fall into it, slide toward that new truth, but his smile was a call to something else, a stirring she had thought long dead.

She felt something brush against her in the water. Something slithered between her legs and grabbed her ankles. It tugged, and she knew she was lost. It was horrible and exhilarating at the same time. Her feet slid out from under her. The grotesque face of a fanged snake came close to hers, and a harsh, raucous laugh echoed over the water.

"Come to me, Jenny, come to me. I will help you pass through the veil of the flesh, shake off the clay of flesh that traps your soul, bring you to the master, Simon."

The coils of the snake tightened like a steel clamp. There was no escape. She screamed.

"Aaaagh!"

She shot forward in the bed and found herself grasping the sheets, her body bathed in sweat. The room was shaded, the dark red curtains drawn. For a moment she couldn't tell where she was. Someone was standing at the foot of the bed, gently pulling on her leg.

Her scream faded into rasping breaths. Furiously she rubbed the tears and sleep from her eyes. The young cockney girl, Susie, grabbed her by the shoulders.

"Lor' Jesus, Jenny, what's the matter? You've gone 'n' 'ad a bad dream, that's all. Come on, wake up, luv, wake up."

Jenny stared up at her, glassy-eyed at first. She focused slowly, staring up at the girl. Poor Susie. The worry over the syphilis and her constant smoking of opium over the past few weeks had left her drawn and haggard. Her beautiful curly blond hair still flowed voluptuously over her shoulders and breasts, but her skin was sallow, her cheeks sunken, her eyes ringed and reddened with opium and weeping.

"What was it, luv, a nightmare? What was it?"

"Nothing, Susie, nothing. I can't remember."

It was not true, but Jenny did not want to talk. She wanted to push the dream out of her mind. She looked over at the clock; ten-thirty; she had slept late. The morning would be over before she pulled herself together.

Susie sat down on the bed. She looked at her

dark-haired friend, studying Jenny's pouting lips and liquid, dark-blue eyes. She started to cry, very quietly. She opened her loose robe and rubbed her hand over her stomach, as though to relieve some deep pain. Beneath the robe she wore a black-and-white-striped underskirt that flared out just below the knee. On top she wore a yellow taffeta silk blouse that lay open, the ribbons untied.

Susie rubbed away the tears with a shaky hand, then hugged herself tightly. She was trembling as she looked over toward Jenny.

"What am I goin' to do, Jenny? Oh, Jesus, Jesus."

For a moment Jenny thought she should tell Susie about Abyssos. But Susie was mumbling something.

"You were talking about the nightmare, Jenny, luv, well that's how it is with me, waking up every day. I wake up into this nightmare, 'n' the only relief I get is with the pipe, the opium, every blessed day. . . ." She swallowed hard and stared at Jenny. "Even with that, it's not enough."

She lunged forward and grabbed Jenny tightly by the arm. Her eyes were wild, desperate. Her naked breasts brushed lightly against Jenny's hand. Her voice was a hoarse, desperate whisper.

"Please, Jenny, I know you've got morphine."

Jenny pulled away from her. She looked beautiful in the soft, late morning light that filtered through the heavy red curtains, but it was obvious from her face that she was angry. She glared at Susie. She had tried to keep her morphine habit quiet and now this girl had blabbed it out.

"What the hell d'you mean, I've got morphine. Don't ever say that to me again. Are you trying to get me kicked out of here? You know what Mrs. Flanagan thinks of that!"

"Please, Jenny . . ." Susie began to cry again, falling face forward onto the bed.

Jenny stood up and sighed. She moved to her

110

dresser and slipped on a long, blue silk dressing gown. She walked around the prostrate girl and stood for a moment, listening to her sobs.

Jenny thought about the last phial of morphine in her drawer. She knew that it would give poor Susie some pleasure, some relief from her frightening daily reality. Old Mrs. Flanagan would probably throw her out on the streets by the end of the week—after all, it was not good for business to keep saying "No, sorry, you can't have Susie, she's got the clap." It would be funny if it wasn't so awful.

She glanced down at the sobbing girl again and decided that she would give Susie the phial and tell her about her supplier, Morasini. Maybe the Naples Pavilion was the place for her to go. After all, not many of the drunks down at the waterfront would care if she had the clap or not.

She leaned over and grabbed Susie by the shoulders, tugging her onto her back. Holding her firm, she shook her until the crying stopped.

"Susie, don't ever talk to Mrs. Flanagan about this. . . ."

She stood over the girl until the tears subsided into dry sobs. Then she leaned close and lowered her voice.

"Susie, I'll give you some morphine, but god damn you, girl, if Mrs. Flanagan ever finds out, I'll kill you."

Susie's face brightened. Her whole quaking body seemed to relax. "Thank you, Jenny, thank you. I wouldn't tell that old—I mean Mrs. Flanagan. I just want to get away in my 'ead for a bit, you know, luv. I mean, I ain't an addict, 'n' I ain't gonna become one 'cause I—"

"Shut up, Susie, I don't care. We all go to hell in our own way."

She walked to the dresser, recalling Bertha's words: "But the chosen can be taken beyond heaven and hell, if they allow themselves to be led to the Light." She

111

slid open the drawer and pulled aside her silken underskirts. At the back was a red leather jewelry box. She took it out and placed it on the dresser, then opened it to reveal a phial of morphine wrapped in a piece of white cotton. For a second or two she stared at it, and a distant thumping began in her stomach, an echo of desire.

Then she steeled herself. No, she wouldn't use it. She would give it to Susie. If she became desperate later, she could always go to the Naples Pavilion. She wanted a clear head today. She had that meeting to go to with Bertha, if Mrs. Flanagan would let her away for a couple of hours; Bertha would lead her through the gates and into Abyssos.

She placed the phial on the bed, closed the box, and put it back in the drawer. Squatting, she pulled a metal trunk from under her bed and opened the lid. A smell of lavender wafted into the room. Carefully she lifted out a small linen bundle. She untied it deftly and took out the syringe. She placed it on the bed, next to the phial, and then tossed the linen down beside them.

"There it is, Susie. Now, get it done before anyone finds us."

Jenny went to the door and locked it. Susie was watching her, doe-eyed. Jenny went to her wardrobe and slipped off her gown. She stood naked, smooth-skinned and lithe of limb.

Susie stared vacantly at Jenny's body; the white pureness of her skin, full breasts and firm thighs. She thought how beautiful Jenny was and how warm and caring she could be. Her eyes filled with tears again. Jenny turned and looked at her.

"Come on, Susie, come on, use it if you're gonna, and if you're not, for God's sake, stop crying."

The little cockney quickly rubbed away her tears and picked up the phial, then stared at the syringe as she placed it in her lap. She broke the seal on the phial and tried to place the needle in the morphine. Her hand was shaking and the steel of the needle clicked against the sides of the glass.

"Don't you know how to do it?" Jenny said impatiently. She took the phial and syringe away from the other whore. She pushed the plunger firmly and steadily.

"You can't leave any air at all in the syringe, or it'll kill you." Susie nodded and stared up at Jenny with big childish eyes. "Look, when the air's all squeezed out, you put it deep into the morphine. When it's full, turn the syringe needle up, then squeeze to make sure that no air is left. Here."

She handed the syringe to Susie and watched as she looked at it.

"You have to find a vein," Jenny said. "Try your right arm. Wrap the linen cloth around it, tight, then wait for a vein to swell."

Susie did what she was told and watched as the vein swelled along her thin arm. She took the gleaming needle and poised it over her flesh. Her hand started to shake. She glanced up at Jenny, her lower lip trembling like a child about to burst into tears.

"Oh, Gawd, Gawd. I want it, Jenny, I need it, I need it. But I can't put it in, I can't put the fucker in. 'Elp me."

Jenny leaned forward, kneeling on the soft bed. First she steadied the girl, putting her arm around her. Then she took the syringe and carefully laid the sharp tip of the needle against the vein. She pushed, then gently squeezed the syringe and pumped it firmly to the end.

She laid the syringe on the bed as Susie looked around at her. The panic slowly ebbed from Susie's eyes. Her face was beginning to relax. That unmistakable daze of pleasure started to cloud her gaze. With a sigh of comfort she slipped her hand around Jenny's neat waist and stared into Jenny's face, her eyes half

113

closed, pupils dilated. Susie could feel the full force of the drug now, pumping through her. It was a throbbing joy, like running fearless as a child, diving into a parent's welcoming arms.

They stayed like that for a few minutes, but if Mrs. Flanagan found them here, Jenny would obviously be to blame for Susie's drugged state. She would have to go back to her own room. Jenny stood up so abruptly that Susie almost fell over. She caught herself, a dazed distress creeping into her eyes.

"Come on, Susie . . . you'll have to get out. I gave you the stuff and I can tell you where to go if you don't have a friendly pharmacist, but you've got to go now!"

Susie staggered to her feet and tottered forward. She reached for Jenny, but Jenny swept her hand aside.

"No, Susie. Get out. You've got what you wanted."

The little cockney was still caught in the first rush, that numbing pleasurable thrill. She found it difficult to form words. She tried to speak, but it came out in a blunted garble. She staggered to one side and grasped at the bedpost. Then she gathered her gown about her, tottered to the door and out into the dark corridor.

Jenny felt like thin glass, about to explode. She saw the empty syringe on the bed and very tentatively reached out and grasped it. She upended it, so that the needle was vertical, erect and gleaming. She had to put this away before Mrs. Flanagan came. But she couldn't move. She sat staring at it, mesmerized.

It was like the Knowledge to her. The snake was the messenger who brought it, and when he brought it, it was sharp and quick, like the rush of the drug itself. When it came upon you there was no mistaking. Yes. She could believe Bertha; it was the key, the beginning.

But Susie had used it. The shiny steel had been deep into Susie's syphilitic veins. The corruption was on it, on the syringe itself.

Revolted and scared, she dropped it on the bed. She quickly leaned over and picked up the linen cloth. Using it like a glove, she snatched the syringe and wrapped it tight. She walked to the flowered wastebasket in the corner and flung it in, a tight grimace of distaste spreading on her lips.

There was a muffled sound of glass shattering. She cast a nervous glance toward the door, and then around the room. The reddish light filtering through the heavy curtains invested everything with a lurid, almost sinister quality, the ruffled bed, the clothes strewn about, the open trunk. She felt a wave of disgust at the narrowness of her life. Her dream seemed to imply a choice in her life, as though the sailor was in opposition to the clear message of the cult Abyssos. But the sailor was no one, just a john with a twinkle in his eye. Simon and Abyssos offered her a way out of this and out of this evil world of Ialdoboath/Jehovah. Wasn't that what her friend Bertha promised?

She gave a bitter smile as she fell back on the bed and looked up at the ceiling. By now the sailor was probably in some other cathouse.

Jenny was wrong. Tom could no more rid himself of the memory of that sexual encounter than she could. All day long as he trudged through the stores, shopping, he saw her. Every dimpled smile on a plump shopgirl stirred him; every flashing eye caused him to recall her languid yet gentle glance.

Tom was to go home to Johnstown after his week in New York with Doolan, and it was one of his theories that a bundle of presents made up for, in the words of his sister Ann, "an inexcusable dearth of letters."

He had spent a long morning going through Saks and Macy's on Herald Square. He was a great believer in one-stop shopping, but today he was not doing well. Everything he touched he saw as a gift for the dark-haired whore. When he ran his fingers through a silk scarf he could see her beside him, looking up with half-taunting, half-smiling eyes. When he saw a lace shawl, she was there, sliding it over the smooth fullness of her breasts. Many times that morning he found himself standing stock still, wanting only to stretch out and caress the soft curve of her thighs.

Finally he could take it no more; he needed to sit down and clear his mind. He gathered the gifts that he had managed to find, left Saks, and shouldered his way across Herald Square to the steps of the *Herald* building. Around him, the city whirred and snarled like some crazed machine, but the steps provided him a momentary island of sanity. He looked for a place to sit amongst the clerks and shop assistants with their lunch bags and sandwiches.

He loved this building. It reminded him of Venice. It was like a two-story version of a doge's palace with the steps around the pillared arches, the covered walkways, the striped, conical awnings. The only touch of the twentieth century was the sound of the *Herald*'s presses inside, and the sight of the gigantic, grey-white rolls of paper being unloaded from the trucks. He stared for a while at the line of proud stone eagles on the edge of the roof, and then sat near Horace Greeley's greening statue.

He tried to focus on the trucks, on the workers in their long leather aprons, as they skillfully juggled the rolls of paper, on the cabbies arguing at the cab stop just across the street. But he could not absorb himself in the lives of others. He could only think of Jenny, her tempting dark-blue eyes, the softness of her smile, the full rounded shape of her thighs under the black frilled underskirt.

"Jaysus."

He shuddered as his pulse leapt. He could not stand it any longer. He had to go and see her.

CHAPTER 17

ARAYA CATAPULTED FORWARD from his kneeling position. The carrier of the evil burden was about to fall within the sphere of Abyssos.

Araya unclutched his hands, which had been clasped tightly in prayer. His whole body was tense and aching, and his black knitted shawl had slipped from his shoulders. The cold needled into his flesh. A feeling of imminent danger had pulled him back from the iron rim of his concentration. He shook himself and drew the shawl around him, shivering. It was a warm afternoon, but his hotel room was frigid. He had experienced this before, at the end of a long period of fasting and prayer. It was as if he had drawn all the heat and strength from the air. He would need that strength for the struggles to come.

Slowly he rose and crossed to his bed. There he had laid out his most precious possessions. He had brought few things with him on his journey out of that high desert mountain, and now they lay before him, the essentials of his life: the prayer mat, woven with the sacred texts and symbols; the Holy Book; his beads; his small iron cross and the black amulet. And something else, something he felt even more uneasy about than the accursed amulet.

He knelt beside the bed and pulled the parcel toward him. Very carefully, he unwrapped the heavy cloth covering. The first part revealed was the ribbed, ivory handle, stained brown and dark yellow with age.

Tentatively he touched it with one finger, tracing up and down along its carved surface. Then he grasped the handle and pulled the knife free of the cloth. The blade was about six inches long, and it glittered in the afternoon light that leaked in through the shaded window. Three inches from the hilt, the blade split in two. The vicious twin points were about two inches apart at their tips. Gazing at it, Araya was forcibly reminded of his enemy. The knife was the forked tongue of the snake, evil and deadly.

Araya shivered and placed the dagger back on the heavy cotton cloth. He would wrap it up again until the final hour.

He laid a gentle hand on his prayer mat. Since early in the morning he had sat upon it, legs tucked under him, hands clasped in prayer, his face calm, his eyes closed. He had to reach the Holy One here, here in this city that never slept. It was a struggle to find that well of strength.

Here, men moved through the days, morning to night, without a thought for their souls. It was so different from the place where he had grown up, even though life there was also built around commerce. The city of Makale lay just north of the Danakil, the searing hot desert that stretched from the high Ethiopian plateau toward Eritrea and the coastal plain to the east.

Araya's father was a rich salt trader, and his whole early life focused on the weekly markets. The salt caravans wound their way slowly from the massive dried lake beds in the desert for these weekly meetings with the merchants. The plodding camels were goaded by skillful, proud, and reserved Danakil tribesmen. They had cut their precious bars of salt deep in those parched lands where the sun burns all life from the rocks and sand. Only the thorn scrub and the Danakil could live there.

The family had a large house facing the wide,

118

mud-baked square. Standing on the high roof, Araya could easily see the entire town. Somehow that little town was always stirring; the market, feverish with the salt traders and herdsmen every Monday; the Coptic churches, swarming with the devout every Saturday and with pilgrims on the numerous feast days. And then there was the army, the small garrison of the emperor Johannes the Fourth, its soldiers constantly moving to and from the frontiers and the war with the Egyptian khedive Ismā'īl Pasha.

The emperor Johannes had come from Araya's home province. He had been the regional governor there before being helped to the throne by a British expeditionary force in 1872. Johannes' family name was Kassai, and so Araya, along with almost seventy other young family members, was given the privilege of attending school in the capital, close to the imperial palace.

Except for summers at home, he lived there for ten years, learning English from the British advisors and Italian from the Catholic priests whom the emperor had invited to teach at the palace school.

As he grew older, he would journey alone from the city to the rock churches of the Highlands.

On the day that he first saw the monastery of Abba Salama, his heart had almost stilled. He stood at the edge of a cliff that fell away for two hundred feet below him. Across the parched land of shrub and rock rose one of the mesalike ambas, towering into the cloudless sky. He could see two white-clad figures slowly pulling their way up the amba.

He scarcely remembered the journey down the cliff, across the dry riverbed, and then up the steep slope. But he clearly recalled the three old monks who had waited for him at the top. As though welcoming him home, the eldest monk lowered the intricate wrought-iron cross toward him. Araya fell to his knees, trembling, and gazed up at the old man's smiling eyes.

"Welcome to the monastery of Frumentius, Abba Salama." The old man extended his hand and helped Araya to his feet. "Come join us at our church, and pray with us."

Araya's next trip home had been to tell his father of his determination to become a monk. His father had listened carefully and only once had his eyes betrayed the sense of loss that he felt. Afterward he sat for a while in silence, then pulled his son into a strong embrace. His throat was full with tears. He held Araya and spoke in a low voice.

"Araya, I have one thing to say to you. You can listen or not, as you wish. After all, I am a salt trader, not your abbot, your memhir. But you are my child, and the vessel that God will fill is of the proud Kassai clan." His voice was gentle and calm, but very firm. "Remember that God is to be found not only on rooftops and high among the cliffs and ambas of the Central Plateau. God is also of the earth. God is also of the marketplace. He is to be found amongst the sand and camel dung, amongst the mosquitoes and tsetse fly, and in the mud and filth and garbage of the cities. Seek him in silence, but remember the world beyond."

His father's words seemed to echo through the dingy Manhattan hotel room. Araya quickly stood up. He had to return to the place where Bellarma stayed.

The maid was startled when she opened the front door. The black man who confronted her had an authoritative look in his eyes, the look of someone who demanded unqualified attention. Gladys simply stared at him, wide-eyed.

"I have come to talk with Mr. Pendleton," he said.

"I'm sorry, but neither the master nor Mrs. Pendleton are in at this time."

He stared at her with his dark penetrating eyes as if assessing the truth of her statement. Then he smiled.

"In that case I have come to see the priest, Bellarma."

"Oh, I see. If it's about the manuscripts, a man has just returned them."

"I do not understand."

"A man came just now and delivered Father Bellarma's case—"

Suddenly, from high up in the house, came a muted, terrified scream. It was a chilling sound. The maid fell back against the open door and gasped.

"That was the father, upstairs."

Without a second's hesitation, Araya sprinted past her with the long, limber strides of a natural athlete. As he reached the bottom of the wide stairwell, he heard a more guttural, choking sound. Araya did not wait for an invitation, but bounded up the steps in broad leaps.

Gladys scrambled up behind him, gasping for breath. Her mind was caught somewhere between fear at the sound of the screams and anger at the presumption of this black man intruding into her household.

Araya stopped for a moment at the top of the stairs, then strode forward along the hall, all senses alert, a Danakil hunter close to his prey. He heard a rustling to the left.

"That's his room."

The maid's breathless whisper stopped Araya in his tracks. He raised his hand as she reached for the door handle.

"No. I will go in."

He twisted the ivory handle and pushed the door open. The room was deeply shadowed, but as his eyes adjusted, he took in the shapes of the furniture. Over by the window he saw a bedside table and on top of it, a battered leather suitcase, lying open. A small movement drew his eye to the bed. The sight of the priest jolted him.

Araya had almost missed him, propped among the

121

embroidered pillows. Bellarma's grey hair was wild, his features gaunt and complexion sallow. His eyes were wide open and glassy white. This was the man Araya had followed through deserts and across oceans. Bellarma was so still that he looked as if he was dead.

Then Araya saw it. He froze. It sat before the little priest, coiled on the counterpane with its head stiff and erect. It seemed like one long, taut muscle under the sinewy, multicolored, scaly skin. The slit eyes stared fixedly at Bellarma. Man and snake seemed bound in a battle of wills.

Araya had seen many poisonous snakes and he knew that this one was tensing before its death strike. Slowly and quietly, almost without breathing, Araya slipped off his jacket. He brought it in front of him, holding it wide at the collar. Silently he moved toward the snake. It was then that he heard the door open behind him.

Araya froze, knowing that he would endanger the priest by turning, knowing that any movement could cause the snake to strike. He held his breath as the maid spoke.

"Father . . . Father. . . ."

He heard her edging into the room. There was a pause—it seemed like an endless silence—and then she screamed. His heart jumped. He barely registered the thump as Gladys fainted against the door. Now he had to move. He threw the coat, making sure that it fell between Bellarma and the venom that shot out toward him.

Araya quickly grabbed the coat and held down the squirming reptile. It fought strongly. Araya twisted the material into a sack. The snake thrashed, but Araya held it tight. He staggered back to the suitcase and threw the whole thing inside, then snapped the lid shut and locked it. For a moment there were dull thuds against the sides and finally that too stopped.

Araya turned to the bed. The priest's eyes were closed and he seemed to be unconscious.

Araya carried the maid into the next bedroom. He laid her on the small single bed. On the table by the window was a decanter of water and a glass. He poured some and tried to get her to swallow it.

She choked on the first mouthful but then awoke and gulped down some more. Then her eyes flickered around the room. He reassured her.

"It's all right, it's all right, it's gone, the snake's gone."

"What? Where?" She was confused and scared. Then she remembered, and sat up. "Is the Father all right?"

"He seems to be. I think he fell asleep. I managed to get the snake into the suitcase." Someone had intended to murder the priest, but there was no point in frightening the young woman further with complex explanations. For a moment it looked as though she was about to cry and then she steadied herself.

"What're we going to do about . . . the snake?"

"Leave it to me. If you could just go down and get something to drink for the father."

"Yes, all right."

In a daze, she made her way to the door. Araya followed her and watched as she walked along the corridor and started down the stairs. Then he turned and walked back to the other guest room. The priest was staring at him.

"Thank you, you have saved my life. That is the second time that they have tried to kill me."

Araya had sought out this little priest, thinking that the struggle would be with him, but now he knew there were others. They had to be of the cult of Abyssos.

"They are here? Abyssos is here?"

Bellarma was staggered that this stranger knew of Abyssos. "Who are you? Are you one who has met the

123

snake?" The priest's eyes narrowed with fear.

Araya saw this and put his hand forward in a gesture of friendship. "We will talk later—but this you should know: I came to Gebel Kalat soon after you. You have carried this burden of evil far, and now you need my help."

Bellarma stared at him for a moment with a penetrating gaze. Araya felt as though a light was probing into the shadowy corners of his mind. Then Bellarma's face relaxed as though he had found his answer.

"I am not safe here, now that they know where I am. I must leave, and you must help me."

Araya helped the little priest out of bed.

"Come. I have a room, and you can share it."

CHAPTER 18

IT WAS LATE in the afternoon when Tom finally found himself pushing open the door that bore the legend "Mrs. Flanagan's Modeling School." He hastily glanced around, feeling awkward and furtive. But there was no one there. To his right a door lay open. As he looked toward it, a piano started up. For a moment there was a cacophony of sound, then the player seemed to find the note and launched into a version of the old English tune, "Greensleeves."

Tom edged over to the velvet-covered ottoman and sat down. Somewhere a young girl started singing. He listened, detecting an English accent, and his mind drifted, wondering at the disparity between the tune and its surroundings. The gentility and pageantry of court life, the half-timbered houses of Tudor England, the neat, ordered gardens, contrasted strongly with this place where you could almost smell the raw, animal sexuality.

"Oh, hello. I'm sorry, I didn't know you were here."

He looked up and saw a young woman coming in from the piano room. She was dressed very primly in a grey dress with a white apron, somewhere between a housemaid and a nurse. She had a very trim figure, long fair hair tucked firmly under a small lace cap, and a broad toothy grin. Tom thought he detected a Boston brogue.

"Can I help you, then?"

"Eh, yes, I was looking to talk to one of your girls."

She smiled at him sweetly.

"Talk, sir? You mean 'meet' with one for a while."

"Oh, yes, Agnes luvvie. The darlin' gent'll want more than talkie talkie, won't you, sweet'eart?"

Tom hadn't noticed the music stopping, but now the musician slumped against the edge of the door. She was a small, thin girl, with thick curly blond hair that fell over her shoulders. Wisps of hair straggled carelessly across her face, making her look even more vulnerable. She tried to take a step forward, then lurched back against the doorpost. She slammed her shoulder hard, but was apparently oblivious to the pain.

The yellow blouse she was wearing fell open and revealed her small pert breasts. Her eyes were glazed, unfocused, but the ghost of a smile flickered on her lips.

"Hit's all right, Agnes my dear, I'm great. I'm fine. I'm sure the gent 'ere thinks I'm fine."

She pressed her head back against the doorpost and spread her arms wide, causing the silk blouse to slip off her shoulders. She stood now naked to the waist. She had the body of a nubile fifteen-year-old, but a whore's sensual sneer curled across her lips.

"Wot about a bit o' time wiv Susie then?" Her cockney accent seemed to get thicker as she slipped into her role.

Agnes deftly pulled the blouse back onto her shoulders. She wrapped it over at the front, tucking it into the black underskirt. Susie watched as she did it, helpless but bemused.

"But 'ow's the gent gonna see the goods, luvvie?" A new voice then intruded on the scene.

"Agnes, keep Susie out of Mrs. Flanagan's way. I'll be back in—"

Tom spun around; it was Jenny. She looked beautiful, dressed demurely in a light grey suit. Her eyes flickered with recognition, and she flashed him a warm smile.

"Oh, hello."

"Hello." He felt awkward, like a child caught with his finger in the honey pot. He could feel the red flushing his face and neck. "I came to see you."

"I'm sorry, but I'm not working now. I have a few hours to myself."

"I meant—just see you."

A smile sprang to her face. The sailor was back!

Agnes watched them for a moment, then turned to the parlor door. "If it's all right with you, Jenny, I'll get back in to Susie."

"Yes, of course."

Agnes closed the door after her, leaving Tom and Jenny facing each other, girdled in a breathless silence. Their eyes flitted around the room, avoiding each other's gaze. Then Tom heaved a throaty sigh.

"I was thinking about you."

"Well now, Mr. Sailor, maybe the thinking wasn't all on one side." The statement held the first hint of her carefully concealed brogue, and Jenny laughed at her lapse, laughter that was not mocking but effervescent and joyful. This man made her relax, allowed her to drop her defenses.

"Did I hear the touch of an Irish accent?"

"Now, maybe you did, and maybe you didn't." She smiled again.

"I just thought I'd like to see you one more time," Tom said, then blushed. "I mean, just see you."

"Why don't you sit, then, take the weight off your feet. I don't have long, I have to be somewhere within the hour."

Her face flushed as she thought of Bertha and the others waiting for Simon to come. Waiting for the promised word.

Tom stepped back, bumping into the edge of the

divan. The armload of presents fell from his grasp, spilling across the floor.

"I've been shopping," he said, reaching to pick them up.

"I'd never have guessed it," Jenny said, helping him.

"I have no doubts now that you're Irish," Tom said, "with that sharp edge to your tongue."

"I'm pulling your leg."

"I know." He gazed up into her clear blue eyes. That something passed between them again; the haunting gossamer touch of their past intimacy. He caught his breath, remembering the taste of her, and that fire began to burn again in the pit of his stomach.

"They're for my family in Johnstown."

"Ah, now, sure, I could tell you were a good boy!"

She gave a light, mocking laugh. He saw the shape of her thigh against her skirt and once again caught his breath at the thought of her naked beauty. She passed him some of the parcels and he took them from her awkwardly.

"There's one for you, if you'll accept it."

Somewhere in this mess of gifts was a silk scarf that he had bought for her. At the time it had seemed a wonderful idea, but now he felt foolish. He stood very still, his eyes flickering over the carpet so that he would not have to look at her.

She stared at him in surprise and saw a blush creeping up his neck, reddening his cheeks and ears. Suddenly she saw an awkward country boy, and her heart went out to him. She wanted to step forward, smooth his forehead, and reassure him with a hug, like a child being gathered into its mother's lap. She took the parcel he was holding and smiled.

"Yes. Yes, of course I will."

He let the parcel slip from his grasp, not knowing what to say. It was not the scarf, but the present for young Joseph, his cousin in the seminary. He wanted to say something, but he was so tangled in his own embarrassment that he could not speak.

Jenny pulled off the paper and opened the box. Her eyes widened. There was a look of fear and confusion on her face. She lifted out the little silver Celtic cross and held it toward the light. It lay neatly in the palm of her hand, glistening.

Her eyes filled with tears. She thought of Simon and the cult Abyssos, and then of this simple cross of her childhood. Within her heart, one system of beliefs was warring with another.

Her early morning nightmare flashed into her mind. She saw Tom standing on the pier with his hand outstretched and she wondered if this was what he had been offering her. Was he a messenger of the old faith? Then she shook herself. He was a sailor and she liked him. It was that simple.

Tom saw the confusion in her eyes and touched her hand gently.

"I didn't mean to upset you. This is a mistake."

She turned from him and quickly wiped the tears from her cheeks. Damn! Why was she still so affected by this poisonous religion? She shuddered, clutching the tiny emblem in her clenched fist, then shoved it deep into the pocket of her skirt.

"No. It's all right. Thank you, but now I have to go. I'm expected somewhere."

Once again she thought of Bertha and the others waiting for Simon. She did not want to miss that. Then she stared deep into Tom's eyes, and for a moment she thought of inviting him. But she knew that she could not.

He cleared his throat. "Could I see you again?"

"I don't know."

"You see, I came here with a letter, because I didn't know if you'd be free or not. It gives my address. I'm staying with my brother, and if you thought we could meet, outside of this . . ."

"I'd know where to find you. I like that."

She took the note and, smiling, slipped it into her pocket beside the cross. She started to walk away from him, then stopped and turned back, giving him a quick, nervous kiss on the cheek. "I've got to run. Good-bye."

"Good-bye."

He watched the door slam behind her, and slowly sank onto the divan. He could still smell her perfume, still feel the feather-light touch of her lips on his cheek. God in heaven, what was happening to him? He had a schoolboy crush on a whore. A whore! He picked up the empty box that had held the cross, and crushed it slowly in his hands.

CHAPTER 19

BRIDIE LET THE young people in, one by one. They were a strange, eclectic bunch. Some of them had haunted eyes; others slumped under the cares of the world as though the burden was about to crush them. A few disturbed Bridie, for their eyes gleamed with the hope of expectant disciples.

Bridie rebelled against such subservience. It was wrong that these people needed the young father Schmidt so much. It was wrong that they needed any man this much, even a priest.

"Good evening, Bridie."

Bridie looked at the speaker and recognized one of the regulars. The girl was strange but interesting-looking, not more than twenty. Though not pretty, there was an almost handsome quality to her face that was reinforced by her determined jawline. She had, however, managed to undermine nature's gifts by pulling her brown hair back into a severe bun and wearing unflattering wire-rimmed glasses. The overall effect was that of a mousy, retiring girl, barely out of school. Bridie had forgotten the girl's name.

"Eh . . . good evening . . ."

"Bertha."

"Aaah, yes, Bertha, yes. You've been here before."

"Indeed I have, Bridie."

There was something smug and condescending in the girl's tone. It was obvious that she held the woman

131

and her simple ways in deep contempt.

"Listen, you don't have to wait at the door. I can let people in, if you like."

"Well, I . . ."

Usually Bridie guarded her duties jealously, whatever they were. But this evening she was happy to be relieved of the job of doorkeeper. She gave Bertha a wavering half smile.

"Thank you, dear, I'll take you up on that. I've a lot to do yet in the kitchen."

She walked quickly back along the hall, through the door, and across to a large pot full of clothes boiling on the stove. She lifted a wooden pole, edged the lid aside, and pushed at the steaming mess.

She had thought about the horror in the chapel for two days. Father Schmidt had been sympathetic but had told her to forget about it. He had also told her not to tell old Father Brautsch.

She jabbed at the clothes as though she were wagging her finger at young Schmidt. She would not keep it from Father Brautsch. She did not dismiss the sacrilege as airily as did the young father. Father Brautsch would just be finishing his after-dinner nap, and she would go up to him.

She pushed the lid back over the pot of washing and then rubbed her hands on her apron. She would go up the back stairs; that way she wouldn't have to pass all those lost souls going into the meeting. Nervously she smoothed her grey hair back behind her ears, and started up the stairs.

It was not easy talking to Father Brautsch these days. So many times he seemed distant, almost dazed, as though his mind was elsewhere. Oh, how things had changed. Shortly after Father Schmidt had first come, the old man seemed to get some relief from the crippling pain of his arthritis. Bridie did not know the cause—perhaps it was the faith of the younger man, or some skill that he had. Whatever it was, it worked, and she was glad. But over the years, something else happened. It was as though Father Brautsch was losing all his energy, as though his life was slipping away. Before her eyes, Brautsch the extrovert became the recluse.

San Salvadore had become a church of secrets and whisperings, of guarded mutterings. At times she was swamped by an oppressive feeling of loneliness.

Bridie knew that Father Brautsch would be in the library, seated in his rocking chair by the window. She stopped outside the door, a smile flickering across her face. How often had she chastised him for writing his sermons that way, the sheets of paper balanced on his knees, the inkpot beside him on the floor. Of course, it was a long time since he had written a sermon. Now he rarely delivered one, and when he did, it was written by Father Schmidt.

She knocked. There was a low sound, as though someone was clearing his throat after sleeping. Then she heard a weak voice.

"Come in. Come in. Please . . . Please . . ."

She pushed open the door and stopped dead.

Father Brautsch sat slumped in his chair, facing the door. He seemed more wretched and shrunken than ever. One sleeve of his shirt was rolled up and his bare arm was held out toward her, like a defeated beggar. His jaw fell slackly, his lips trembled, and his eyes, full of tears, flickered with a mixture of desperation and shame.

The crumpled body went into a momentary spasm. The outstretched hand clenched and unclenched as though clutching in desperation for something.

"Please, please, I need it now. Schmidt."

Father Schmidt strode past her to Father Brautsch's side, his eyes glaring with an authority she had never seen before.

"You must leave. He needs my help. I will minister to him."

133

Just before the door slammed in her face, Bridie caught a glimpse of a syringe and a small phial lying in a dish. The door was locked with a sharp click. Bridie fled back to her sanctuary.

In the kitchen, she once again pushed aside the lid of the boiling pot and stirred the wash, staring fixedly at nothing as the steam wafted up. Her stomach churned with the sense of having witnessed someone's silent secret shame. And that look in Father Schmidt's eyes, an ice-cold glance of authority. She shivered as she began to lift the clothes out of the pot.

It was then that she made her resolution. Tonight she would go to the meeting. She would slip in the back and hear what Father Schmidt had to say.

Bertha settled into a chair at the side of the room and stared at those seated around her. She knew many of them, though some were new and some of the old faces had dropped out. She thought of how long she had been coming to the "Open Group," as the inner cult called it. She had continued to come long after she had entered Abyssos, because they had requested it. She was good with new members, and Open Group was the best place to fish for disciples.

Bertha had been driven by a deep zeal almost from the beginning. She had wanted to draw everyone into that deeper meaning, to open up the staggering truths to them. But there was a barrier, a darkness over which they would have to leap. Jehovah had circled their lives with fear and it took a brave heart to journey beyond his strictures. Here, though, she would slowly interest newcomers, then persuade and cajole them, helping them to break Jehovah's rules. It was exciting.

Antonio glanced at her from across the room. Bertha saw the fire in his eyes. That look was for her and her alone, the look of recognition, of a shared voyage through darkness into light. Antonio had

134

drawn her into the family of Abyssos. At first she was attracted by his dark, handsome looks, but then she had seen the fire in his eyes. She knew that he was close to Father Schmidt, he whom they knew as Simon. Some said that Antonio had brought Simon here from Italy, but Antonio did not talk much of such matters.

Bertha watched as Antonio sat beside a young girl. She saw him smile; it was warm and inviting, but he always was the gentleman.

Bertha looked back at the door and saw that Jenny had just walked in. Bertha waved and Jenny smiled. Bertha felt a thrill go through her at the sight of her friend. Jenny had come to many meetings, but Bertha still feared that her friend would turn away from Abyssos. She sensed within Jenny that paralyzing fear of Jehovah, which was strange because Jenny's profession continually brought her into conflict with Jehovah's morality.

Bertha felt a tremor of excitement deep in her stomach when she imagined the sordid situations in which her friend found herself. Jenny rarely spoke of her encounters, but anything she did mention was stored away by Bertha, to be relished later. Jenny was so close to Abyssos—it was written that "all must fall through that putrid pit of degradation in preparation for the call."

Bertha's eyes glittered with an almost sexual energy. This week she would give herself in the ceremony of the snake. The Snake of Knowledge would undo the work of the Archon of Fornication, Saclas. Her hand slipped down to her lower stomach. Somewhere in there another trapped soul was stirring. She quickly pulled her hand away.

Jenny slid into the empty chair beside Bertha and gave her a nervous smile. Meeting with Tom had thrown her into turmoil. All of her confidence in Abyssos had been shaken by his appearance. On the way to the meeting she had clutched the small Celtic cross so tightly that her palm bore its mark. She knew that a man, no matter how gentle and warm, could not change her course of action, but something else was stirring in her. She knew it was the old, deep conflict between her old faith and this new revelation.

Bertha sensed her friend's dilemma, but before she could speak, a silence spread through the room. The priest had come in. The expectant audience sensed his deep inner strength. He had an engaging face, boyish good looks, a mass of tight dark curls, and olive skin. But it was his eyes that marked him. They were deeply blue. When he smiled they seemed to exude warmth, but when angered, they were as hard and cold as ice. This was a man not to be crossed.

As the session began, Bridie slipped into the back of the room to listen. She saw that the listeners focused totally on Father Schmidt. The session began like any other Bible reading class, but then came the questions from the anxious listeners.

"What God of Love would allow . . . ?"

All the questions seemed to start that way. As Bridie listened, the litany of doubt and misery grew. Something malignant was growing in the room, and all eyes and ears were trained on Father Schmidt in the hope that he could defeat it.

"What about the concentration camps of the Boer wars?"

"Have you read about the horrors of the Russo-Japanese war?"

"Father, millions are threatened by cholera in China. . . ."

The questions and accusations came relentlessly, one after another. And more and more their doubts ate like an acid even into Bridie's practiced certainties. A lulling, hypnotic desperation filled the room, and Bridie felt that she was being sucked under. Her simple faith was being prized open to reveal hidden, festering sores.

Bridie suddenly realized that Father Schmidt was saying nothing to meet this onslaught of doubt. They had all placed their faith in him and he was leaving them with questions, only questions.

A young woman with a thick East European accent was recounting the plight of the crowded East Side tenements. The hunger, the crime, the lack of medical care. She turned slowly so that she could take everyone in, her large, sad eyes surveying the whole room.

"Two months ago, my brudder die, vrom street accident under iron truck veels—" She stopped abruptly and looked down, then she glanced up again. Tears began to drip down her cheeks. She wiped them off as though they burned. "Two days ago my mother die vrom childbirth . . . too old. Vee are only in America vive years. . . ."

Her voice faded away, stifled in sobs. She clasped her hands to her face. The woman's breath came shorter and shorter, until finally she collapsed into her chair, heaving with sobs. Bertha walked over to her, placed a caring hand on her shoulders, and led her gently to a seat at the side of the room. Bridie watched Father Schmidt. He sat quietly, smiling sadly. It was as if he were saying "Tell me more about the evil of this world," as if he drew out all of this putrid despair, yet offered no help or respite.

Suddenly Antonio was on his feet.

"My uncle was buried this week."

Bridie was startled. Antonio Gallenini had always seemed so reserved, so cool and distant, like his uncle. Now he stood in this strange company, spewing out the darkness in his heart.

"Buried. And from his first stroke two years ago I saw him wither, a strong man, a generous man, a man of love. I saw him die. He was tortured in his death and dying—and if there is a God, how can he be a

137

God of Love? He can only be a vain and arrogant God, a God of Malice and Vengeance. He is evil."

That was it! Behind the probing and questioning, behind all the assaults, Bridie had felt something else, something unnamed. Oh, Sweet Jesus, God would accept any sin, except denial of Him. And Sweet Lamb of God, here it was.

She gazed at Antonio. He was no longer the quiet young man she had known. His eyes were ablaze.

She turned to Father Schmidt and saw that same fire in his eyes. He agreed with Antonio!

They were assaulting her God, just as surely as had the person who had defiled her chapel.

She moved as quietly as she could to the door. Outside in the hall she half staggered, half ran to the kitchen. The whole way she felt she was being watched. She shivered. The devil was clawing at her, the devil who could tear you apart and take your soul onto his loathsome breast. If doubt separated you from your God, you were doomed to eternal damnation.

She stood by the sink, pressing her hands hard on the ribbed side of the washboard as she looked out to the dark shape of the church.

Holy Mary, Mother of God. Eternal Damnation.

Oh God. Oh God. Denial. It was the ultimate evil, the ultimate sin.

Bertha caught up with Jenny halfway along the rectory path. Jenny was pale and trembling. Something was distressing her. Bertha had thought Jenny was farther along than this, but now she felt as if Jenny was turning her back on them, on Abyssos.

"Jenny—"

"Bertha, I must go. Mrs. Flanagan will think I've left for good." She walked quickly away, thinking of Tom and her doubts.

Bertha angrily watched her go. She could see that

138

Jenny was paralyzed with fear of Jehovah, but she hoped it would pass. It had to pass. She wanted to confide in her friend, tell her that soon she would take the ceremony of the snake and Saclas. She wanted to share so much with Jenny.

She felt a spasm in her lower stomach. She rested her hand there and smiled. Soon she would enter the next level of Abyssos.

CHAPTER 20

VIRGINIA HAD RETURNED home soon after Bellarma left the house. She found Gladys sitting at the bottom of the stairs, trembling, looking off into space.

Virginia led her into the front room and sat her down, then carefully prized the whole story out of her. She was shaken by what Gladys told her, shaken and angered. She dismissed the maid almost curtly, then paced the room.

This was her house, her home, a place of supposed safety for her and her family. Now Pendleton's dabblings and his damned secrecy had made it a place that was "dangerous to stay in." Dangerous for the priest—dangerous perhaps for herself and her children, her precious darlings who had just come in from the park with their nanny.

She ran over the events. Pendleton had brought home a wounded priest, a man who spoke to her of long journeys and evil manuscripts. Then someone sent a poisonous snake to kill the priest, but he was rescued by a strange black man who seemed to know him. It was a pantomime, a farce! It was something that would be funny if it were not so frightening.

Virginia stormed into the hallway and phoned Pendleton at his office. She didn't have to say much. As soon as Pendleton heard that Bellarma had gone, the phone went dead.

Virginia was sitting in the front room, waiting, when Pendleton rushed in. After a brusque greeting, she gave him a brief account of what had happened. She saw fear in his eyes when the delivery of the suitcase was mentioned, but when she told him the details of Bellarma's departure, his face reddened and his eyes narrowed. She had never seen him so angry. He ran his fingers through his beard and tugged at it distractedly.

"But he must have left an address."

"No."

"That's impossible; he couldn't just leave without—"

"No, Ernest, I said no."

Then something seemed to occur to him; he looked up and glared at her. "Stay here. Don't move!" He ran from the room. Virginia slowly sank into the chair by the window, feeling as if she had been kicked in the stomach.

The children jumped in fright when he slammed open the nursery door. Mary was trying to dismantle one of her dolls and Ernest Junior was drooling over a comic book in which Jack Presley, boy reporter, was foiling a bank robbery. Mary burst into tears when she looked up and saw her father's angry face. The nanny, Cecily, quickly scooped her up and out of his way.

"Cecily, please take the children somewhere else."

The woman quickly took Ernest by the hand and, hugging the tearful Mary, went out the back door.

Pendleton was a man obsessed. He went to the doors that led to the front and back hallways and locked them. His mouth was dry. Bellarma was gone. If the manuscripts were gone too, then he had nothing. Nothing to barter with them, nothing left for himself.

He scrambled over the toys and books and pulled aside the rocking horse. Once again he pulled down the top trunk and threw open the bottom one. He searched through it, scattering clothes in wild desperation.

141

When he found the manuscripts tucked in between the little pink dresses, he clutched them to him, letting out a muted laugh. Now, where could he conceal them? He took a moment to steady himself, thought, then resolved that he would leave the bundle in the trunk until he could make a deal with the cult. He smiled grimly, certain that they would respond to his advertisement again. He tidied the children's clothes away, replaced the trunks, then unlocked the room's doors.

Now if only he could find Bellarma.

Doolan ran his forefinger around the rim of the glass, occasionally dipping it into the whiskey. The resultant circles made a light humming sound. He wasn't daydreaming, in fact he registered everything that Pendleton had to say, but he was determined to keep his eyes averted. Virginia was sitting beside her husband on the couch.

On those rare moments when he did look up, Doolan caught glimpses of her blue-green eyes. She would quickly look away. Then, for a few seconds, he would allow his gaze to linger on the sculpted smoothness of her skin.

Pendleton talked on, unaware of anything but his own fixation, and when Doolan finally interrupted him to ask for the maid's version of the events he seemed surprised. Then his lawyer's sense of procedure asserted itself and Gladys was called up from the kitchen.

She stood in front of the fireplace like an awkward schoolgirl and nervously repeated the afternoon's events, glancing at Pendleton as though expecting him to interrupt her.

"And then, then Father Bellarma left with the man."

Pendleton jumped forward in his chair, his fingers frantically scratching at his beard.

142

"You see, Lieutenant, it was duress. This person—well, it was akin to kidnapping."

It was obvious to Doolan that the lawyer's heated emotions were affecting his judgment. Pendleton was consumed with only one thought; he wanted Bellarma returned. Doolan leaned forward and flashed the maid a friendly smile.

"Can you give me a description of this man who went with the priest?"

"Gladys told you he was black," Pendleton said.

Doolan chuckled. "There are, Mr. Pendleton, quite a few black people in this city."

Virginia sat forward. A nervous smile flickered across her face. "Ernest, perhaps Gladys should speak."

Doolan stared straight into Virginia's eyes, admiring her quiet strength. Gladys looked at her mistress and then spoke.

"Well, he was very tall, very, well, very regal looking, with a beard . . . and his eyes . . . I remember his eyes." Gladys stopped. Doolan had flinched as the memory of the black man at the rails of his brother's ship flashed into his mind.

"Please, go on."

"That's it," Gladys said, then added, "Oh, yes, I think I heard him saying that he was just off a ship. . . ."

Pendleton leaned forward, excited by the new thought.

"You see, Lieutenant, that narrows it down. I mean you could institute a search of ships, or hotels frequented by sailors, or bars."

Doolan took a deep breath. A black, bearded sailor. Maybe it was the same man. Still, this was not his case.

"I'm sorry, Mr. Pendleton, but in order for me to carry out such a search, you would need to take your complaint to the commissioner. I would venture to suggest that he might think it was a wild-goose chase. For a start, there is no evidence that a crime has been committed, and without proof of a crime, we cannot allocate men. . . ."

The policeman's semi-ironic tone and cool, assessing eyes returned Pendleton to momentary sanity.

"Lieutenant, you need say no more. I was getting carried away. You are, of course, completely right. I apologize for dragging you here."

"Not at all. I was happy to be of help, sir."

Once again Doolan's eyes flickered to Pendleton's left and caught a glimpse of Virginia just as she looked away. Then he quickly made his excuses and left.

That night Virginia and Pendleton slept in separate rooms.

CHAPTER 21

THE SALLOW-FACED little man was nervous. He fumbled as he quickly buttoned his fly and slipped on his old-fashioned jacket.

Jenny watched him dreamily as he turned from her. He walked over to the small bamboo table and picked up his glasses, an expensive, silver-rimmed pair. He adjusted them and walked quickly to the door.

"Bye."

"Eh . . . oh, yes . . . good-bye."

He sidled out, his eyes focused on the floor. Jenny smiled at his furtive exit. She lay back in the bed, pushing her head deep into the pillow. The sound of an English vaudeville tune floated down the hall. Susie must be playing the piano again. The song was bright and cheery, and occasionally she would tinkle off into her own version of ragtime. Fragments of the lyrics drifted through the smoke and perfume of the whorehouse.

Jenny sighed and wiped some sweat from her breasts. Her lace bodice lay open. It was late, and she felt tired and slack. She stared along her body, dreamily. The black satin underskirt lay crumpled under her firm buttocks. One of her stockings lay at the bottom of the bed; the other was still on. Idly Jenny ran her hand up the black silk and over the crushed velvet rose on the garter, then slid her fingers under the strap of the red-and-black suspender belt.

Poor Susie. Well, at least she had the piano. Jenny recalled the cockney's desperation that morning, but at least the morphine had taken the edge off her despair, and all day long she had kept "topped up" with opium. When Susie had first heard that her dose wasn't being shifted by the "miracle mercury" she had screamed for a good fifteen minutes.

"I got the pustules again, the pustules, the fuckers won't go. I'm done, I'm done. Oh, Lord Jesus!"

She wouldn't stop screaming. Everyone was to blame. It was the end for her. Jenny had listened and very coolly thought that Susie was right. There would be no more whoring, for Mrs. Flanagan or for anyone else; no brothel would take her.

Jenny stretched her legs over the side of the bed. She suddenly felt dirty. The same thing could happen to her. Any john coming through the door could carry the pox with him. She pressed the douche and felt the cold water squirting up inside her. She shivered, but it was more than the fear of pox. This evening's meeting had left her in a state of confusion. Earlier she had determined to walk with Bertha into Abyssos, but now something was tugging her away. She shivered again, and cradled her head in her hands. This evening of all evenings she could do with some good morphine. She cursed Susie for persuading her to give it to her that morning. She tried to steady her breathing in the hope that the pangs would pass, but they didn't.

She squirted more water inside her as though that would wash away the desire. She worried that she was addicted, that she couldn't live without the stuff, but Bertha assured her that morphine was a sacred instrument that could be used to get closer to the Light.

Jenny waited for the water to seep out between her legs and tried to keep her breathing steady. As she did, she remembered a few weeks before when she had met Father Schmidt walking through the rectory garden.

146

He had thrown off his priest's disguise and spoken to her as Simon, entangling her in the ice-cold fire of his eyes. He had told her how anything was of use as long as it brought her closer to Abyssos and the true Light of Godhead. He had told her that there was no such thing as addiction. Morphine gave fire to the flesh, he said, and, "Always remember that he who is near Me is near the fire and he who is far from Me is far from the Light of Abyssos."

She didn't fully understand, but when she ran the words over and over in her head she felt warm and comforted. That was the day that she decided to join the cult and make Simon her master, but that was before the sailor and before the nightmare. She shook her head as though that would banish her confusion. But still, two roads lay ahead of her, and she had to make a choice.

She got up and doused a flannel in a bowl of water, then gently rubbed it all over her body. If she could not make a decision she could at least complete her toilette. After washing, she picked up a white towel embroidered with bluebells, and dried herself. A tin of Excelsior Borated Perfumed Talcum Powder sat on her dresser. She picked it up to powder herself and stared for a moment at the baby on the label.

Why had she said that to the sailor? "I sowed no children for the ruler." It was one of Bertha's favorite sayings. Bertha had said it would be explained to Jenny when she joined fully with the cult.

Jenny started to tremble. The choice was there again. On one side they demanded barrenness; on the other, fertility. She herself promised fertility, but did everything to avoid it.

"Damn, damn, damn!"

She could face her inner turmoil no more. She would go down to the Morasinis' and get just enough to help her through the night.

She changed into her street clothes. As she did up

147

the last buttons on her high-necked print dress, a series of shudders coursed through her. Her mouth began to go dry. She needed the drug, how she needed it! The thought pounded in her head. Her fingers trembled as she forced the last button into its hole. Pinpoints of sweat appeared on her forehead. Shaking, she clung to the footboard of the brass bed.

After a minute the shudders subsided. She patted her face with the towel and some astringent. Then she looked into the mirror.

My God, she looked white and shaken. It would not do for old Mrs. F. to see her like that. Jenny would soon be on the street if the madam thought she was on anything harder than opium. She took some rouge and lightly rubbed it in. Now all she needed was one of her satin wraps. It was a warm evening.

When she was finally dressed for the street, Jenny reached under her bed and pulled out an old stocking. Inside she had a roll of notes. It was her private money, kept away from Mrs. Flanagan. She peeled some off and put them in her bag, then crossed the hall and knocked on Mrs. Flanagan's door.

"Yes?"

Her voice sounded warm and drowsy, as though she had been nipping the brandy again.

"It's me, Jenny, Mrs. Flanagan. . . . I was wondering if I could step out for an hour or so."

"Huh. That's the second time tonight. Oh, well, I suppose we've seen the last of the thundering herd anyway. Go ahead, but be careful . . . it's a bit on the late side to be sauntering along."

Jenny chuckled. Mrs. Flanagan sounded more like her grandmother than her madam.

"I will, Mrs. Flanagan. I'll be back soon."

She walked down to the parlor. Susie was sitting glassy-eyed at the piano, swaying to the music. She was playing "Greensleeves," and some of the notes clanged dissonantly. Her singing was slurred, but this only seemed to add to the sadness of the song. Two of the other whores, Tess and Ingrid, sat nearby, exhausted, brushing their hair. Marie Louise, the French girl from New Orleans, had spread herself on the rich, golden embroidery of the divan, her small breasts exposed, catching the greens and reds and blues from the Tiffany lamp above her head, like a filigree on her smooth skin. Her eyes were closed and her mouth lay slackly open, like a child's, red and sweetly dark.

Jenny turned and quietly left the room. She did not want Susie to see her leaving. She might guess Jenny was going to the Morasinis', and cause trouble.

Jenny walked to the end of the block and turned right, walking north along Eighth Avenue. She had been wrong about the weather. There was a cool dampness coming off the river and she could have done with a heavier wrap. Still, the mist did give the streetlamps a romantic golden halo and muted the grating sound of the iron wheels on the paved streets. She quickened her pace to keep warm. She didn't want that awful trembling to start again.

At Thirty-fifth she turned left, toward the Hudson River. It was not the best area of the city to be walking in at one o'clock in the morning, but she did not have far to go. She was headed for a run-down Italian restaurant and bar called the Naples Pavilion. It was owned by two brothers, the Morasinis; they controlled the whole drug trade on the Hudson docks down to Fourth Street.

A few hundred yards ahead, she saw the lights of the bar. Someone inside was playing an accordion, singing a ballad in a smooth, Italian tenor. She could have been in Italy, in any small town south of Rome. She gazed at the reddish light in the windows, and for a moment the street seemed to take on the romantic hue of another world, away from the crime and the grinding poverty. Then the shivers came again.

Jenny quickly pushed into the bar. Inside, the

smoke was thick, immediately making her eyes sting. Along one wall were tables covered with red-and-white-checkered cloths. They were crowded with people eating and drinking. The bar along the other wall was three to four deep with bodies elbowing for drink, arguing, laughing, shouting. These were dock laborers, rivermen, and deep-sea sailors, and with them were numerous street whores, red-faced, vulgar women with cracked, blackened teeth and shrunken cheeks.

She stared at them, wondering if she would end up like that, then pushed her way through the crowd to the bead curtain at the rear, ignoring the rude comments that followed her. Those men were not evil; just vulgar. The Morasinis, however, were different.

The back room was furnished with two long tables, one dull yellow gas lamp, and a line of wooden kitchen chairs in various states of disrepair. In one corner, wedged between a table and the wall, a thin, disheveled man in his late twenties sat slumped in a battered chair. A well-worn derby covered his head, and his eyes were glazed, half closed; his mouth hung slackly. A syringe and phial lay on the stained table-top before him.

Suddenly a man came into the room through a side door. He was small, heavyset, with black, curly, greased hair brushed back from his forehead. His small eyes found Jenny as she moved into the yellow glow, and a lecherous smile spread over his face.

"You come for a little fun, huh?"

"Yes, yes, and I need a syringe."

She swallowed hard as she remembered smashing the one that Susie had used. She could feel the trembles coming on again. God, she needed it quickly. She needed the rush.

Morasini looked at the money she held out. He took it, but before he could count it, he saw the addict lying crumpled in the corner. His face hardened, his eyes narrowed in anger. He turned and called back through the door.

"Frederico, what the hell's going on? Get this bum outa here. *Buttalo in strada.*"

A young man in an open laborer's shirt rushed in. Seeing Jenny, he instinctively slowed, smoothed back his hair, and strutted. Sucking on his teeth, he settled his shirt into his trousers and leered at her. The older man slapped him on the arm, glaring.

"Lasci stare la puttana, butta fuori quella schifezza."

He pointed to the skeleton-thin human wreck seated in the corner. The creature groaned, and smiled moronically at them.

Frederico pulled the addict from behind the table. He slipped off the chair, gashing his forehead on the table's metal edge. He yelled as blood trickled into his eye. He started to whine like a child.

"Please, no. Please lemme stay. No, no, lemme stay."

The words came thickly, but the young Italian was not listening. He dragged the pipe-thin addict to his feet and pulled him out of the room by his shredded jacket. The syringe slipped from his hand and smashed on the floor. He began to sob.

"No, no."

Frederico crushed what remained of the glass under his heel, then kicked the needle across the floor. Jenny turned away. She could no longer bear to watch the man's squirming helplessness. But she was aware of Frederico's every move as he lifted the man with one hand, like a sack. Then he punched him viciously in the stomach and dragged him out through the bead curtain.

The sleazy smile returned to the elder Morasini's face.

"Trash, just trash, a girl like you shouldn't see such things."

He flicked the dollars in his hand and slipped them into his trouser pocket. Turning, he shuffled into the other room. Jenny's mind was beginning to race again. Her breath was coming short and fast. Her eyes flitted around the filthy room. How had she sunk to this?

"Here, best stuff. From Turkey."

Jenny started. Morasini was standing beside her. He held out four phials and a syringe, its needle gleaming with the promise of relief. He leaned forward and stroked her hand as she took her hard-earned "goods."

"Sweet girl, lovely skin . . . bella, bella."

"Only four?"

He stared at her and gestured in mock apology. "The price, what can I say, she always go up." Then he grinned and winked at her, a vulgar, sexual smirk spreading across his face. "Hey, you justa pass it on to your customer, huh?"

She turned away from him, wanting to get away before the shudders came again.

Outside, the air felt cold and heavy as Jenny stumbled along the cracked sidewalk. She had to get to somewhere quiet, a place where she could quickly pump the morphine into her. She hated coming down here, but at least there were no questions asked, and any quantity was available. Of course, it was more expensive than buying it over the drugstore counter, but pharmacists were becoming leery of freely dispensing it because of the recent outcries about an epidemic of addiction.

She searched for a gap in the line of warehouses. There had to be a small wharf or an open shed somewhere. Muffled voices emerged from the street ahead.

"Stand up, ya stupid whore."

As Jenny came closer she heard a woman sobbing drunkenly.

"I'm all right. Please, don't take the money. I can stand. . . ."

Approaching, Jenny looked for the speakers. Under a flickering light, she saw a redheaded woman and a balding man, obviously a prostitute with her client. Her skirt was hitched high above her knees; her thin legs gleamed whitely in the flickering glare of the light. She pulled the man to her, fumbling at his trousers, forcing out a nervous laugh.

"Come on, now, come on, it'll be fine."

The man lunged forward. Jenny felt sick. She turned and ran. Bertha had told her that through degradation they would leave the flesh behind and come to the Light. But tonight, for the first time, Jenny saw that that path could bring her to this, could reduce her to soliciting on the streets, to swaying senseless against a stable door among the manure and axle grease.

Jenny ran across the cobbled street to the grey-painted warehouses by the Hudson. Her heart was pounding, sweat poured down her body. Fear and confusion mingled with her desire for the morphine. A throbbing pain twisted through her. She stumbled toward the river and found a place to conceal herself among some bales of hessian.

Jenny fumbled in her pockets for the syringe. With shaking hands, she assembled it and carefully took out one of the phials. She thrust the needle in deep and sucked up the precious liquid. She could almost feel the relief when she saw it surge up inside the glass.

She unbuttoned her long sleeve and pulled it back, ripping the cloth in her desperation. She tightened the material into a tourniquet. Slowly she injected the morphine and almost immediately felt its warmth.

"Aaah, sweet Lord."

Her fears started to ebb. That pit where the lowest prostitutes eked out their last days, that was for others. The old, the ugly, the haggard. That would never happen to her.

She stood up and felt the power flooding through her. A great oozing sleepiness lifted her, like the deep swell on a sea. She floated forward, to a rail that led down to the water's edge. The river glistened invitingly. The pier lights snaked and bobbed along the waves before being swallowed by the fog.

Perhaps Bertha was right, perhaps it was time for her to make the commitment and join the cult. Bertha had spoken to her about depravity leading to the highest Knowledge. Her morphine habit was one of the keys to that Knowledge. Jenny felt as though she was near the gates of some great Truth. She could almost hear Bertha whispering in her ear.

"If ye make not the below into the above and the above into the below, the right into the left, and the left into the right, the before into the behind, ye shall not enter the gates of Abyssos."

Jenny mumbled the prayer as she slowly glided down the steps. She would throw the empty phial into the river. She would never need the morphine again, for she could feel the truth now. She could cross the threshold. But still she held the other three phials tucked in the pocket of her skirt.

She held on to the rail, and with her other hand tossed the empty phial far out into the black water.

Jenny heard the phial plop into the water. It was the sound she had heard in her dream. She suddenly had a creeping, shivery sense of déjà vu: the pier; the steps; the black river. But then she clenched her teeth. No! That was a dream and this was reality. She squatted down on the steps and stared at the lights. For a few minutes the blues and greens and reds of the reflected dockland lamps danced and bobbed just for her on the dark waves. She became one with their swaying rhythms.

Then she saw something else dancing out there. She

154

stared, open-mouthed like a child, not able to make out the shape at first. It bobbed closer. Soon the light from the gas lamp on the dock behind her picked out two gleams of light. A thin mist drifted on the waves like smoke, here obscuring, here revealing. The thing came toward her. She began to see it more clearly in the yellowish light from the dock, and her whole body was filled with a rush of horror.

The eyes of the floating, severed head stared at her wildly, caught forever in a silent scream. Strands of dark hair, matted with blood and water, choked the open mouth. As it bobbed to the step below her, it flipped over, showing the raw red flesh of the lacerated neck, the grey of the spine and the purplish hollow of the windpipe.

A wave caused the head to turn again like a gruesome football. The wide, white eyes flashed and seemed to shriek out against the horror of death.

Jenny screamed. She knew the girl. Even with that waxy, bloodied skin, she recognized the face.

The wharf, the lights, the water and its grotesque burden, swirled around her. She staggered away from the river, sobbing. Her screams echoed past the darkened warehouses, across the deserted wharves.

CHAPTER 22

"IT'S A NICE breakfast gift, huh, Pete?" Frank Cassassa had a sick smile on his face.

"Yeah," Doolan said as they clattered up the echoing stairwell. Just what he needed to start the day.

"This is better than the crossword in the *Sun*. Each day you add a piece and finally you get a whole body. Wonder what the prize is?"

Doolan grimaced. "Cut it out, Frank. Where's the girl who found it?"

"The sergeant says he brought her up here to wait." The two men reached their office. O'Neal was sitting with a young woman, taking notes.

Doolan strode in, offered her his hand, and gave her a sympathetic smile.

"Miss McGreevy?"

"Jenny McGreevy, yes."

"My name is Doolan; I'm the lieutenant in charge of this case."

She took his hand and shook it limply. She was obviously exhausted. Probably she had not slept all night. Still, Doolan could see that under normal conditions she would be an attractive woman. Doolan took the notes that O'Neal had made, scanned them, and turned to the young woman.

"I can see you're tired. I won't keep you long. We seem to have almost everything here."

* * *

Tom was waiting for Doolan in Vittorio's. He was dipping his toast into the yolk of his fried egg when his brother walked in. He glanced up, gave a wry smile and then saw Jenny. He dropped his fork; it clattered onto the plate. Then he stood up awkwardly.

Jenny stopped dead, her face registering a mix of confusion and relief.

"Tom, this is Miss McGreevy—"Doolan stopped in midsentence. It was obvious that they knew one another. He would not ask how.

During the halting conversation, Vittorio bustled about the table, bringing coffee, eggs, bacon, toast, and more coffee. Tom and Jenny began to relax. Doolan had brought Jenny to the café here to help steady her nerves after the night's ordeal, but Tom was doing a better job than he could have.

He felt it was safe to leave them alone for a few minutes and strolled over to the counter to get a quick look at the morning's headlines. He was glad to see that his case had disappeared from the front page. But then he heaved a sigh; when the revelation about the head came out, it would be front and center of the evening editions. He walked back to the table.

"So if you're not working," Tom said, "you could come out to Coney Island with me."

"I don't know. I feel so tired."

"Have a sleep in a deck chair on the beach."

"Well . . ."

"I'll take that as a 'yes.'" Tom grinned and stood up. "Come on, then, we should go."

Jenny gave him one of her half-cynical smiles and then shrugged. "All right. Do you know where we catch the train?"

Tom winked. "Now, do I look like a traveler or do I look like a traveler?"

Jenny stood up and was about to go when Doolan laid a gentle hand on her arm.

"Did you go to anyone—about the . . . the head—before you came to us?"

"Yes, I went to my priest. I was afraid. I didn't know what to do. He told me to go to the police."

"He was right. Who is your priest?" Doolan would double-check Jenny's story with the cleric.

"Father Schmidt at San Salvadore," Jenny said. Then she and Tom were gone.

"San Salvadore," Doolan repeated.

It had a chilling echo.

CHAPTER 23

PENDLETON HAD STARTED walking to work that morning, as he always did. But he was tired. It had been a long night. His back was bothering him, and he had a slight crick in his neck. He would have to buy a new bed for that guest room. As Pendleton crossed Sixty-second Street, he saw one of the new, shiny red automobile meter cabs bearing down on him. He patted his girth, heaved a sigh, and laughed.

"It's a sign, a sign."

He stepped out from the sidewalk and hailed the cab.

"Ninety-six East Fifty-second Street," he said, settling into the back seat.

"Right, sir."

The driver sounded sharp and efficient. It was a quality that Pendleton had found in many automobile drivers. They seemed to share a pride in being the aristocracy of a new technology.

Pendleton's back gave a twinge. He rubbed it with one hand. Last night he had slept badly. He and Virginia had had another violent row after the policeman, Doolan, had left. She had told him that she no longer wanted her home to be a staging post for his strange friends.

Pendleton would not be ordered about by his wife, and certainly did not want to hear her opinions of his philosophical searchings. Finally he lost his temper and threatened to hit her if she did not keep quiet. It was at this point that she locked him out of the bedroom.

He slept in the guest room next to his study but woke up after only a few hours thanks to dreams filled with Bellarma and the more mundane effects of a bad mattress. While the streets outside were still dark and damp, he went next door to his study, locked the door, and scribbled down all he could remember of Bellarma's words. He flinched at the task, but he had no other option unless he found Bellarma again. The manuscripts in the nursery were indecipherable to him.

He gazed at the scrawled pages now, then he crumpled them in his fist. He was sick of grasping for straws. Perhaps today they would approach him. He felt like a man standing outside a banquet. Someone had opened the door for a few seconds and let him see the feasting inside, then slammed it again in his face.

The cab drew up outside his office, and he pressed the balled fist into the throbbing pain in his lower back. He cursed Virginia and then squeezed out of the cab, paying the driver and tipping him generously.

Pendleton had two junior partners, Arthur Kretch and Douglas Watts, as well as six secretaries. His head secretary, Elizabeth Barnes, was an attractive woman in her late twenties. She had decided early in her life that she was to have a career, and she had pursued it as successfully as any woman of the period. She had her own typewriter, her own telephone, her own swivel chair, and a small electric fan, but she still felt like an underpaid slave. Elizabeth was standing beside her large oak desk outside Pendleton's office when he arrived.

"Everything in order, Miss Barnes?"

Without listening for an answer, Pendleton disappeared into his office. That was the usual routine. Elizabeth straightened her starched, white office apron and followed him. The office was darkly pan-

160

eled. Neat rows of law books lined the walls. The desk was of mahogany; the chair was upholstered in deep green leather. The desk was clean, looking as though no work was ever done there. But Elizabeth knew differently. Pendleton was, at times, unpleasant to his staff, but the man was close to being a genius in his interpretation of business law. He had had a good teacher in John D. Archbold, Standard Oil's chief counsel. Pendleton had worked for Archbold for five years, through the great battles between the corporations and Teddy Roosevelt. The corporation lawyers found themselves in the front line, pitted against the newly created Department of Commerce and Labor.

"Some people have their money in oil. My money is in legislation; the more there is, the richer I am," Pendleton had once quipped to Elizabeth.

"Well, Miss Barnes, what have you lined up for today?"

"Firstly, sir, Mr. Van de Veer has already called twice this morning about a quick resolution of his interests in Venezuela."

Pendleton let out a long sigh. "I want Arthur to take care of that."

The phone on his desk rang. Pendleton picked up the earpiece and pulled it toward him. "Yes."

"Mr. Pendleton?" The voice was unfamiliar.

"Yes, yes. This is Ernest Pendleton."

"I would like to talk to you about the manuscripts."

For a moment it was as if his heart had stopped beating. The office seemed very far away and he felt as if something immortal was within his grasp.

"A moment, please." He covered the mouthpiece and turned to his secretary. His face was flushed, his manner brusque. "Miss Barnes, I'd like to take this call in private."

"Yes, sir." She left. As the door closed, Pendleton uncovered the mouthpiece. His stomach was jumping and he had to make an effort to keep his voice steady. His mind raced as he thought of the bloodstained manuscripts wedged between his daughter's pink baby dresses.

"Who am I talking to?"

"There is no need for you to know. But if you do indeed have the manuscripts, we would like to meet with you and talk. It must be somewhere discreet, somewhere quiet. There is an old warehouse at the end of Fourth Street, by the river, Bendlers. There, at four o'clock. Bring the manuscripts."

"And what would I gain from this?" Pendleton asked.

"What do you want?"

"Entrance to Abyssos." He managed to say it calmly.

There was a sharp intake of breath at the other end of the line. "How do you know? Ah, yes, of course, the priest." The words were spat out like poison.

"Well?"

"Bring the manuscripts and we will talk. Four o'clock."

The phone clicked off instantly, but Pendleton held the earpiece for a moment before replacing it. He would arrange a deal. They would get the manuscripts and he would get into Abyssos. It was a logical exchange. But until he was sure of the cult, he would leave the manuscripts hidden in the nursery at home.

He shivered as though touched by a passing shadow of evil.

CHAPTER 24

On his way to the church, a newspaper tucked under his arm, Doolan thought about the black sailor. Tom had spoken about him one evening while they were out drinking and said he had told Araya to contact him through Peter at Police Headquarters.

Doolan smiled cynically. If this black man was involved in some kind of shady activity with the missing priest, he was not going to walk into Centre Market for a chat. As he mulled over the puzzle of the black man and Bellarma, the whole strange interview at Pendleton's house flooded back. He blocked it out immediately. All night his dreams had been filled with Virginia Pendleton.

At the corner of Broome and Elizabeth he stopped. The rectory lay at the back of the church, and as he peered down the street, he could see the house behind the trees.

He had pushed his terrible experience in the crypt to the back of his mind. But now the church had come up again. He was beginning to feel that his life was full of fragments. Sometime they might come together, but just now those connections were shrouded in fog. It was a far cry from the logic preached by Inspector Ferrais.

Doolan abruptly jumped away from the edge of the sidewalk. A cab horse, standing by a hitching post, had emptied its bowels into the gutter beside him.

Doolan looked at the steaming pile of ordure, and then at his shiny patent leather oxfords. His quick side step had saved them.

"Bastard!" Doolan swore at the absent cabbie, then turned into the street and then down the short path to the rectory; the gravel crunched under his feet. The front door was a heavy, paneled affair that had newly been painted black. The brass handle of the bell gleamed with daily polishing. He leaned over and pulled it.

As he waited, he wondered why he had come. There was enough police work to be done, lists to check out, businesses to be visited without him testing some kind of feeling.

A plump, grey-haired woman in her midfifties opened the door. She wore a starched, full apron over her faded check dress; obviously a woman who took pride in herself. She gave him a shy but pleasant smile.

"Yes?"

"Morning, ma'am, my name is Doolan, Lieutenant Doolan of the N.Y.P.D. I've come to talk to the priest—Father Schmidt—about the incident in the church a few days ago."

He got no further. Bridie's face drained of color and a look of incomprehension clouded her eyes.

"I don't understand. The father told me not to say anything, that we were to keep the shameful thing to ourselves."

Doolan knew immediately that he had stumbled on something other than his own nocturnal adventure. He led her, using the old security blanket of the law.

"Don't you think it's better for you to talk to us?"

She stood for a moment, struggling with her orders. Then a look of relief passed over her face.

"Yes, of course. I . . . I . . . Please come down to the kitchen."

"I will if there's a cup of coffee in it."

She blushed and gave him a warm smile. "I thought you had to be Irish, but now I'm sure of it. Come on in; of course there's a cup of coffee for you."

In the kitchen Doolan slowly, almost painfully, drew her story from her. Amongst the aging copper pans, gleaming tiles, and lines of drying dishcloths, Bridie revealed what she had seen that morning. She was visibly shaking by the time she had finished. Perspiration stood out on her face, and she stopped to pull down a dishcloth from the overhead line, and wiped her face dry.

Doolan sipped his coffee and watched her.

"Father Schmidt was first to return, and when he saw, he was angry. I've never seen him so angry. He told me to tell no one, not even Father Brautsch. Except, I'm afraid." She tugged at the cloth and wiped her face again. "It's the work of the devil!"

Doolan smiled. Hardly, he thought. The devil was always accused of such petty little swipes against God. "Mightn't it be some poor demented soul, someone with a grudge?"

"Mr. Doolan, there was real evil in that chapel. I could feel it. The father took the poor animal away and buried it. I think he killed the snake too. After a while I went back and cleaned up the blood. He said we should tell no one, that such things bring the church only infamy, and that . . . well, that more evil could come from this, if it were known. I think he's wrong."

She stopped, shaking. For a moment she sat still, tracing the blue pattern at the edge of the cloth. Doolan watched her closely.

"What does Father Brautsch say? Who does he think is responsible?"

"Father Schmidt told me it would be better not to tell him. He . . . he's not that well—this weather . . ."

The woman started to fidget, her plump, work-worn fingers tapping against one another. She was obviously embarrassed that she had conspired to keep this from the priest.

Doolan stood. "If anything else happens, you'll let me know, won't you? There's no use in bearing the burden yourself."

"I will. Thank you. And if you do come back, I hope I'll have some soda bread baked. My bread's famous, even if I do say so myself."

"I might just try and get back for that." He gave her a wink and walked to the door. "Take care of yourself, Bridie."

She gave him a sad smile. Biting his lip, he turned from her. She could have been his mother, crying as he told her of his decision to leave the Church; his mother, unable to speak to him the day he refused to accompany her to Mass. He looked through the kitchen window at the church and nervously drew his hand through his reddish fair hair. It looked so quiet and unobtrusive, and yet it was the deep chord that stayed with men through birth and death, peace and war. Bridie stirred behind him; he turned to see her closing a drawer by the sink. She held out a sealed envelope.

"There was something written on the back of the door. I wiped it off, but I never told the father that I wrote it down." She pressed the small sealed envelope into his hand.

"Thank you. Would it be all right if I took a look at the chapel?"

"Surely. I'll let you in the side door. Ah, poor Saint Dismas."

Bridie scurried ahead of him, taking a large bunch of keys from her apron. She stopped at the heavy iron-and-wood door and searched through them. Doolan yawned as he came up beside her.

"Did you not sleep last night?"

"Not much, Bridie." She was like all his aunts rolled into one.

"I was up at three myself. Some well-dressed young

woman came to the house, sobbing, looking for Father Schmidt"—she glanced around at Doolan and gave a tired smile—"but I'm sure you've more to do with your day than listen to my life story. . . ."

Doolan leaned forward and placed his hand against the wall. He flashed her a boyish smile. "Go on, Bridie."

"Well, I've seen the poor girl at meetings here before, and in much better shape than she was last night, poor article. Her mind was wandering. She kept talking about a head floating down the river. . . ."

"Bridie, she was right, I'm afraid. She had found part of a body."

Bridie looked stunned. "Oh, my God, my God! I know the father told her to go to the police directly, but I didn't really think she was . . ." She turned away, blushing. Then she turned the key in the lock and swung the door open. She led him through the presbytery. The calm and quiet of the place, the sense of perpetual waiting, wafted over him. Bridie opened another door and entered the nave.

Doolan followed, and his mood suddenly darkened. He began to feel swamped with the same feelings he had had on that other night. It was as if he could smell evil, like the first whiff of smoke before a fire. He gazed through the shadowed arches to the side aisle. In the dull light he could just make out the iron door to the crypt. It sent a nauseous shiver through him.

Bridie stopped and looked at him.

"What is it?"

"Nothing." Doolan pulled himself together and strode forward.

"It's a lovely chapel, this, and I've always felt great comfort in here—at least until yesterday," Bridie continued.

"Yes. And whose chapel did you say it was?"

"Saint Dismas, the patron saint of the chronically ill and deformed."

167

Her words resonated along the empty, polished surfaces of marble, brass, and varnished wood before being swallowed in the heavy velvet curtains.

All around him Doolan could feel that heavy gloom, as if, just beyond his grasp, some horror was readying to strike. He shivered again and glanced once more toward the iron door of the crypt. Bridie may have found comfort in this place, but to him it was a place of evil.

"Yes, it's cool in here. It always is, even on the hottest day."

She lifted the heavy brass latch. Doolan saw her set her chin and pull the door slowly open. Inside, she took a box of matches from her pocket and lit a candle. Placing it in one of the holders on a side table, she knelt by a pew and bowed her head toward the cross at the front.

Doolan felt as though he were spying on a very personal act. He turned aside. The small chapel seemed to swallow the glow of the candle. The only other light came through the chinks in the thick velvet curtains. His eye was caught by a painting on one wall. Beside a Roman ruin, a man held a child in his arms. At least it seemed to be a child; the face was completely covered by the cloak in which it was wrapped. At the side and in the background, other people stood, anger in their faces, as though expelling the man.

"It's a painting of Saint Dismas," Bridie said. "There he is, taking some deformed child away from people who would only hurt her. He was a man of great love and compassion. It was a gift from the man who built the chapel."

"Who was that?" Doolan asked.

"There's a stone plaque in the corner." She took the candle and led him to the right of the small altar. Pulling back one of the long velvet curtains draping the walls, she pointed down to a granite plaque set into the brick. Doolan knelt down beside it and brought the candle close. The reflection of the flame danced in the black polished surface.

"GIUSEPPE V. GALLENINI. MDCCCLXXXVI"

"Gallenini!"
He barked the name out before he could think. Everything was weaving together into a bizarre pattern; a pattern that was no pattern. There was more to the inscription than the man's name.

> *"Exemplum Dismas Sancti faciat*
> *propositum Dei tolerabilius*
> *pro infanti innocenti."*

"Do you understand Latin, Bridie?"
"'Tis the great shame on me, but I don't."
Doolan smiled. It was the great shame on him, for he had forgotten almost all he had learned. He took out a pencil and wrote the sentence on the back of her envelope.
"Do you know much about this Gallenini, Bridie?"
"Not much. He kept to himself, and this chapel was built before my time here. In later years it was Father Schmidt who was close to him."
"I see," Doolan said. But really he did not see. Pieces of information floated in his mind like lilies on a darkened pond. Somewhere there must be a connection. He turned over Bridie's envelope.
"Where was the writing, Bridie?"
She cleared her throat and coughed nervously. The sound made a ringing echo that spoke of total silence, like breath suspended. She shuffled nervously beside him. "On the back of the door."
He walked over, taking the candle with him. The swaying flame reflected dully in the dark varnish.
"I cleaned it off."

169

"Chalk?"

"Blood . . . I think I should go. . . ." She pushed past him into the main body of the church. He could hear her footsteps echoing along the cold marble. With the click of a latch, she disappeared into the presbytery.

Now there was only the sound of his own breathing. A lonely, brooding quiet stretched into every dark corner of the building. Doolan leaned forward and pulled the door toward him. It was clean. Bridie had done a thorough job.

The darkness was closing in again. Icy fingers worked their way up his spine to the back of his neck. He shuddered and spun around. Nothing but the grey darkness, the crucifix, and the figure of the saint carrying the child.

He flipped over the envelope she had given him and ripped open the top with his finger. Inside there was a sheet of cheap, green-lined paper. He held it close to the candle.

"BEWARE. TRULY, IALDOBOATH IS THE ARCHON OF VENGEANCE."

Suddenly there was a gasping hiss, as though the whole church had been filled with a legion of the dying, sucking in their last breaths. He felt as though someone were squeezing the air from him. He had to get out. He had to leave.

The candle fell from his hand. Crumpling the paper, he stuffed it in his pocket and ran out of the place.

The church was silent again.

CHAPTER 25

ARAYA'S HOTEL ROOM smelled of burnt candles and incense, and of something more: fear. He had dared to perform the ceremony of purification, the ceremony he had first learned from his memhir at Gebel Asoteriba, and he was left exhausted.

At the rite's beginning, Bellarma sat before him, cross-legged, his hands resting palms upward in his lap. Araya placed the black amulet into the mouth of the dead snake that had been sent to take Bellarma's life. He laid the snake on the priest's palms, then set his cross upon the serpent's coils. Finally, he covered the priest's hands and the body of the snake with his prayer cloth, leaving the reptile's eyes staring up at Bellarma. Araya's chanting quickly drew the little man into a deep trance.

While Bellarma was in the trance Araya prayed as he had never before: the prayers of James, the brother of Christ; of the saint Taklu Haymanot, and of Johannes and Mark, Elijah and Enoch; all chanted to the tinkling sound of his finger bells.

Araya watched every flicker of Bellarma's eyelids, every twitch of his lips. He had sent him into the trance under the eye of the snake, because that was the influence under which Bellarma had lived for so long. But then Bellarma was caught in the struggle between the snake and the Christ of the cross. Araya drew on his every drop of spiritual strength in his battle to bring the priest back into the fold.

At first he feared he would fail. He was alone in a godless city. The hotel room, with its faded, cracked wallpaper and its fly-stained blinds, could not compare with the stark splendor of the rock-hewn church of his first monastery, Abba Salama. There the monks swung the thuribles, and the scent of incense mingled with the sand-dry smell of the church before drifting into the valley beyond. Nor could this hotel room give comfort like Memhir Mark's small chapel at Gebel Asoteriba, where the monks' prayers would linger for a moment amongst the dark vaults before gyring off into the high arch of the desert sky. No, this dingy hotel room in lower Manhattan was no sanctuary—but then Araya recalled the words of his father. God could be found in the mud and filth of the city, in the dirt of the market. And the presence of Christ was summoned to the small, dirty room.

When Araya felt that Bellarma was tiring, he allowed the little priest to slip from the trance into a deep sleep. Araya stayed vigilant, refreshed in his faith, and in the morning, when Bellarma awoke, they began again. It was a relentless, enervating purge, but Bellarma's soul *was* slowly being purified. By early afternoon, both men were exhausted but elated, feeling as if they had rowed through a storm and finally arrived safe at port.

Araya left Bellarma to wash. He then went out and bought some bread and cheese and milk. When he returned, Bellarma was sitting by the window, looking out over the dockland. As the priest turned toward him, Araya saw that his gaze was clear. Here was a man who had reclaimed his purpose for living.

He smiled. It was the smile of rebirth.

"I have no way of thanking you, Araya," he said. Then his manner firmed. "How did you come to search for Abyssos—and for me?"

"I don't know if this is the time to explain," Araya

172

began, but Bellarma interrupted him.

"Araya, we have no time to waste."

Bellarma gave him a sad, chilling smile. After a moment, Araya nodded and brought the food over to the small table by the window. Over their shared meal he spoke.

After the death of his father, Araya had left the monastery of Abba Salama and become a mendicant, journeying through the high tablelands and the scrub deserts. Finally he had come to the monastery of Biet Giorgis at Gebel Asoteriba, in the scalding-hot deserts of the Upper Sudan.

It was in his third year, during the fifteen-day fast of the Assumption, that he made his decision. One morning, while the desert air was still sweet and crystal clear, he sought out his memhir, the aging father Mark. He was a venerable old Egyptian from Alexandria. His thin face was creased with wrinkles, but his eyes were alert and ever joyful.

The old man was tending the vegetable garden outside the southern wall of the courtyard. Araya quietly approached him and asked that he be allowed to retreat into the desert for seven days.

Araya never forgot the image of him standing there, so at home with the earth. The memhir held some onion plants in his left hand, and leaned comfortably on his hoe. He stared into Araya's eyes, then smiled and laid the hoe aside. Still clutching the young onions, he shuffled off toward the monastery wall.

"Araya, come with me to the church."

The tall young man followed his memhir through the arched gate into the courtyard, past the citrus trees, and along the church's outer wall to the last of the three small chapels on the eastern side.

The old man knelt, with difficulty, before the brick altar. For a moment he glanced at the ceiling, searching for inspiration. The dome was covered with a richly colored fresco, showing eight of the disciples and James, the brother of Christ. Araya knelt beside him.

"It is the rare monk who is made for the rigors of the lone spiritual life. Since you came here three years ago, Araya, you have always seemed to be such a person. The desert is truly a place where one can find God, but it also is the place where one will find evil in its purest of forms. Human intensity can be mistaken for Divine Grace. And the anchorite must always beware. Remember that Christ himself was tempted in the desert. The pleasures of the flesh are nothing to what man can face when he is alone with his God."

His voice coarsened, as though some deep and painful memory was stirring. He stared at the floor, then at the door which led to the courtyard and daylight.

"In this desert, nearly two millennia ago, there lived a sect of people who are accursed in the eyes of the believers. They twisted the world and the word of God and made it seem that good was evil and evil was good."

A shiver of fear crept into Araya's stomach. The old man studied him carefully and then continued, "The early Church despised them for their doctrine, for they had as central to their belief that the Lord God was evil, malignant, proud, and vengeful. They were led through this to the most inhuman and sinful of practices. They called themselves the cult of Abyssos, but the early fathers called them the church of the damned, and they reveled in the name, saying that only through Christian 'damnation' could the Truth of the world be found. They said they sought the knowledge that Jehovah would deny them. Their last apostles were thought to have died in the caves where they worshipped and practiced their abominations. But the desert peoples believed that they had made a promise to keep the texts until another age would

174

come, an age that would be more open to their evil teachings."

The old man seemed very tired. He slowly turned to Araya and reached out, taking his hands and holding them firmly between his own.

"My son, I am not blind to the world. I spent much of my life in the city of Alexandria; for five years I studied in Paris. I have read the so-called learned philosophers of the new Western thought and I know that a new age is upon us. Men have begun to question the existence of God, and behind that thought is something black and frightening beyond measure. It is the thought that because of the world we are building, God himself must be evil. Araya, I think we have come into that time when the accursed teachings of the cult will take root. Somehow it will be brought into the light of the world again. Somewhere in that scorching desert, their teachings lie hidden, perhaps guarded.

"If you are to journey alone into the wilderness, you must be ever alert, for I have felt since the first day we met that you are the one who will be called to fight them when they come to challenge our faith again."

Araya sat very still. There was a great heat in the old man's hands. He felt the memhir's strength flowing into him, along with a heavy burden. He did not feel adequate for the challenge. The old man sensed his apprehension.

"You are right to doubt your strength, for it is only in the continual renewal of your faith, in the welding of yourself to the will of God, that you will be prepared. I give you my blessing, Araya. Go into the desert. You will be regenerated by it, and you will wish to go again. North and west of here there are anchorites who have lived beyond the world for years, alone, strong in their silence. You will be as they, but you will return to us and again leave and again return. Yours is a long and hard road of preparation, and for a battle that may never occur. But perhaps you will meet that hideous challenge and then your life will change forever. When that day comes, I want you to be strong and prepared. Remember that the seduction of the mind is more potent than the seduction of the flesh."

Bellarma had long since pushed the bread and cheese aside, engrossed in Araya's story. Now he leaned in close and gently touched the black man's hand.

"Your memhir was a wise man." His voice died away under a canopy of self-accusation, and for a while he looked out the window at the river, but saw nothing.

"And while you were being prepared, I was already making my way to Gebel Kalat."

"Yes. One day, in the desert to the north, I met some Sunni pilgrims. You had passed through their village. From that moment I had a marker, a trail to follow, and I made my own way to the cave at Gebel Kalat."

"And so in this way you learned of Abyssos, but not of their teachings."

Araya slowly ran his forefinger along the edge of his cup. His eyes were troubled.

"No," he said, "I do know part of their teaching."

Bellarma's question was an awed whisper. "How?"

Araya then completed his story. When he told Father Mark what he had seen in the empty cave at Gebel Kalat, the old memhir was deeply troubled. He had led Araya into his room and crossed to a cupboard built into the whitewashed wall. Inside were clothes, books and other tiny mementos, the debris of a cloistered life. He had pulled out a leather-bound manuscript.

"I have kept this for you. Now you have the burden, now you are the guardian." His sharp eyes peered deep into Araya's. "When you read this, it will make

176

many things clear to you. But above all, remember that evil can easily mask itself in the cloak of reason.

"These writings came to me in the same way that I pass them to you. When I had returned from my studies in the West, the last memhir gave it to me to keep safely. Like me he prayed that the main body of the cult's books had been destroyed. Now we know that they have not, and that struggle will be yours."

Araya looked up to confront Bellarma's intense gaze.

"And so, Father, like you seeking in the library of the Vatican, I know something of Abyssos. I read in the manuscripts of their challenge to our God, Jehovah, and how that challenge had caused the early Church Fathers to reject them. I read of the cult's journey into the desert. I read of their frightening philosophy and their abhorrent practices."

Bellarma suddenly stood up and started pacing from the door to the table by the window.

"And I, I took all that from the cave and brought them again into the light. The old monk was right. It takes a brave man to start on that search, but it takes more than bravery to complete it."

Bellarma gave a deep sigh and shuffled back to the table.

"It takes a man filled to the brim with God's grace and love. Araya, your memhir at Biet Giorgis was the last in a long line of guardians, but those guardians had only half the truth. There is mention in the New Testament, in the Acts of the Apostles, Chapter Eight, of a man from Samaria, a man called Simon."

Bellarma paused, letting the name die in the dusty dark corners of the hotel room. The silence inched forward as he picked up his cup of milk and sipped.

"Simon. The Acts say he was a magician, and a charlatan, who converted to Christianity, hence his name Simon Magus. But the manuscripts from Gebel Kalat tell a different story. They say that before the cult's dispersal and persecution, he was their master. He had many magical powers, and legend had it that he could raise himself from the dead.

"But when they went into the desert, he would not go with them. He told them that his was another path, and that he wanted them to keep the manuscripts safe in the depths of the desert. When the time was right, he and the sacred writings would join again in a world more open to the path of knowledge. This is all written in a book called the *Hypostasis of Simon*." Bellarma tilted his head and quoted from memory.

> *"Simon, the master, has revealed to us that he is the Snake of Knowledge, that he was there to help us in that first garden, and that he shall return through the ages to help man along his path past the evil archon Jehovah, whom we know as Ialdoboath, to the unnameable Godhead of Light. He shall return."*

Bellarma sank back into his chair.

"There is one in this city who believes he is Simon, and I have brought the manuscripts here to him, as it is written in the *Hypostasis*. But he does not have them, at least not yet. I must go back to the Pendleton house and destroy the books before Abyssos destroys me."

178

CHAPTER 26

CONEY ISLAND WAS not busy; after all, it was midweek and the end of September. But the giant Steeplechase Park was open, and from the boardwalk the sound of the attractions was enough to convince Tom that this was the place to bring Jenny.

Mrs. Flanagan had told her to take off as much time as she wanted; she had even given her a small wad of money.

"This is one time that you shouldn't be waiting on a man," she had whispered as she pressed the money into Jenny's hand. "You've had enough happen to you with that . . . that horror. . . ."

Jenny's first thought had been to go and buy morphine; to send herself into a dream for days. But her last dream had quickly turned into the worst of nightmares, and the thought of a day with the sailor, doing ordinary things, seemed like a life raft.

But when Tom took her through the red-roofed, Italianate entrance, he insisted on paying, and she could tell from his smile that she would have to listen to him. He was like a little boy on a big outing!

They strolled through the entrance and over the medieval bridge that crossed the Venetian Canal, heading for the fake sailing ship. Tom led her in and walked her up to the stern. There he regaled her with such funny stories about his travels that the tears started to roll down her cheeks. Behind them the roller coaster rattled away, and in front the small gondolas swished their way along the Venetian Canal.

Then they walked around the edge of the roller coaster, keeping the canal to their left, past the stadium and back around to the Arab Mosque. This was a square building, decorated with geometric tiles and topped with three gaudily painted onion domes. Inside, they tested their skill at the shooting galleries, tossed rings, and tried in vain to hit the coconut. The sideshow, featuring the man with India rubber skin, did not attract them. This was not a day to be reminded of the distortions of the human body.

They wandered on through the park, past elephant rides and wooden Frontier Cabins, over rope bridges and up watchtowers, like two children on a school outing. Laughing, joking, teasing one another and occasionally touching. Slowly their deep mutual attraction eroded her lingering sense of horror at the night's events.

In the afternoon, they hired two deck chairs and sat on the beach. Lulled by the warm sun and the sound of the waves, Jenny drifted into a light, relaxing sleep while Tom watched over her proprietorially.

The rhythmic sound of the tide brought back images of home to Jenny. The sound of the waters of the North Channel was a mother's lullaby. She recalled how, night and day, it washed over the dark grey rocks around the headlands of the Ards peninsula. When she closed her eyes, she could almost see the froth-tipped waves dancing out into the Irish Sea to the Isle of Man beyond.

"A penny for them."

She opened her eyes and saw Tom staring at her. She smiled. "Just listening to the sea."

"Remind you of home?" he asked, his eyes gleaming with sympathy.

Why not tell him? She described the cottage in the northern county of Down and the coarse, savage beauty of the headland on which it was built. All around their small farm the light and dark greens of the many grasses were woven like a crazed patchwork amongst the spiky gorse bushes. Jenny especially loved it in spring, when the gorse would burst with yellow teardrop-shaped flowers and sprinkle the countryside with Easter Gold. But the land was poor; what was not rock was too saline to farm. Her father could only keep the family together by fishing and herding cattle for the rich Protestant farmers farther up the peninsula.

"A Catholic has no way to be rich in Ulster, girl," her father had often said while she was growing up, but somehow she believed it was possible. She was the eldest, and she saw herself working to send the other seven to school. She determined that she would travel to Newtownards at the head of Strangford Lough and get a job in one of the new textile factories. She had heard of many girls from Portavoe going there and sending money home every week. Her father's opinion was scathing.

"They're Protestant girls, lass, it's farther than the Ards peninsula you'll have to wander to find a good-paying job."

Jenny told Tom about the day that she found out that her father's warnings were true. She had gone to Barnell's factory on Movilla hill at the edge of Newtownards, a day's journey with Johnny Mullen on the horse and cart. For an hour she had waited outside the manager's office, under the line of stern portraits of the Presbyterian owners. Finally a dour-faced clerk came out and told her to enter.

The manager sat behind his desk, stiff and superior. His name was MacDonald and he sat on the town council. She trembled at being in the presence of such an eminent person. He asked her name, her age, and where she had gone to school.

"Saint Bridget's convent school, Portaferry, sir," Jenny said.

That was all she had to say. Mr. MacDonald's bald head wrinkled in surprise. He pushed his gold-rimmed glasses back up his nose and coughed. A dry, polite hack.

"Well, thank you very much, Miss McGreevy, but we have no openings at the moment."

So that was how they told your religion, especially if you had a name that could also be Protestant. Simply find out what school you attended. Saint Bridget's was obviously Catholic.

She had gone home the next day; and that night, after she wept the truth out in front of her father, she walked along the rocky path, to the Giant's Head. It was her own special retreat, a large boulder of granite that projected into the cold waters of the North Channel. There she sat, watching the lights of the steamships coming out of Belfast Harbor and edging south along the coast. She cried for a long time and then finally set her chin and clenched her teeth. That was the last time they would deny her work. She would show them her tail, as her grandmother said. She would take one of those ships and find a new life.

Oh, but that was so long ago, before she became pregnant by one of the Colvin boys over in Ballywalter. He was a Protestant, so neither side would countenance a marriage.

Then there was that day her father had stood with her down by the grey, wind-chopped waters of the North Channel, and made her swear on the Bible to give the child away.

"Fernenst the shame to us all!"

Jenny fell silent, and for a long time stared out over the smooth rolling surf. Tom wanted to touch her, stroke her troubled brow, but he waited.

"I couldn't give up the baby," Jenny said. Her fervor surprised Tom. "I went off to Glasgow the next day and worked in a linen mill. I had the baby on my own with a midwife to help me. She was a little girl,

Kathleen. Soon afterward there was a typhus outbreak and . . . and she died. . . . The midwife said she wouldn't have lived anyway, that she wasn't strong. So I buried her, just a month after she was born. I had to borrow money for the coffin." Tears rolled down her cheeks. "I couldn't go home and I had no one where I was living. Mrs. Flanagan had a friend in Glasgow. A girl I knew at the mill had left to work for her. She asked me would I work for her, but I told her no, for if my father ever found out it would kill him. Then she told me about Mrs. Flanagan in New York. I didn't really know what I was coming to, but I had nothing else, nothing, not even Kathleen."

Tom stretched out his hand and gently stroked hers. She looked at him, afraid of his reaction, but saw only warmth in his eyes.

CHAPTER 27

PENDLETON WATCHED THE cab do a U-turn and head north. He had decided to walk the last few blocks, thinking that it might settle his nervous stomach.

As he straightened his jacket he glanced across the street, catching glimpses of the river sparkling in the afternoon sun. He turned left, and sauntered past the rows of horse-drawn trucks waiting outside the sheds and warehouses.

The smell of horse manure was overpowering and the flies seemed to be everywhere, buzzing swarms of black malignancies. Each horse had its tail in constant motion, but the poor animals could do nothing about the ones that crawled around their mouths and noses. No amount of head shaking could banish their persistent little torturers.

Beelzebub. The name floated into his mind, and he curled his lip in distaste. No wonder the devil was called the Lord of the Flies. The pest-erer. He spat into the manure-laden gutter, then strode forward.

Two blocks farther on, the street was less busy. Some of the warehouses had been closed and the area was beginning to have that air of diseased abandonment that settles on old commercial neighborhoods. He stopped at the corner of Fourth and saw, some thirty yards down on the left, a sign half dangling from the wall. It said "Bendlers." He started toward it, feeling the throb of excitement in his stomach. He did not see the black carriage parked before the side entrance.

Just past the sign there was a large gate, its brown paint peeling, the wood at the bottom rotten and crumbling. A small boy sat there, jabbing a knife into the wood and gouging out large chunks. Hearing Pendleton's footsteps, he looked up warily, his eyes furtive, alive to any approaching danger.

Pendleton sniffed. The child was barely clothed, and every part that was uncovered was crusted with grime. Pendleton's hand instinctively tightened on his cane, but almost immediately relaxed in shame. God, the kid couldn't be more than eight years old.

"Hey, mista, you de geezer de udder nob's waitin' for?"

"Yes, how did you know?"

"Folla me den." The boy jumped up and pushed open a small door in the gate. By the time Pendleton squeezed through, the boy was halfway across the cobbled yard, inside. It was a clutter of debris, boxes, broken trucks, and large piles of garbage. The boy stopped by a large open shed and pointed.

"He's dere, mista."

As Pendleton walked toward him, the boy hopefully jerked out a filthy paw, then drew back, expecting a blow for his impudence. Pendleton stopped, and for a second stared down at the emaciated little face, white beneath the dirt.

"You were paid, weren't you?"

"Yes." The child looked crestfallen. Another dinner gone. He bit his lip and turned away. As he did, Pendleton touched him on the shoulder and took a dollar bill from his inside pocket. What the hell, no one deserved to starve.

"Here, take it." The boy's eyes lit up, and Pendleton grinned as he watched the child skip toward the gate.

185

The boy got to the little door and then yelled over his shoulder, "Sucker!" He slammed the door after him. Pendleton laughed.

The struggle against the ether-soaked rag was the last thing he remembered before the darkness swirled in.

He woke up slowly, feeling adrift in a timeless dark. At first his mind was numb; then he recalled the last moments before he had lost consciousness. The smell and taste of the ether lingered in his nasal passages, but there was something else. He sniffed hard, trying to clear his nose. Beyond the musty smell of neglect there was something sweet and fresh. He sniffed again. Fresh-cut flowers.

Slowly his eyes became accustomed to the dark, and he saw a doorway. He staggered to his feet and shuffled over to the door. Cautiously he looked out. In the greyness all he could make out was a long, dark corridor. There was a noise in the distance. Pendleton held his breath and listened. A tinkling noise, very muffled, very muted. Well, damn it, nothing would be gained by standing still. He stepped into the corridor. The sound of his footsteps rang off the stone floor and echoed into the blackness. The corridor was stone, and he could tell from the sound that it was low-roofed. He reached up and touched the cold, damp, arched ceiling. This all reminded him of something, something he couldn't quite recall.

Catacombs! That was it. The labyrinthine burial places of the early Christian dead.

He could feel his hair begin to crawl. Was he trying to scare himself to death? He moved on quickly, stumbling twice on the uneven stones. Abruptly the corridor opened on either side of him, into a T-shaped junction. To his right he glimpsed what seemed like a series of doors. He heard that tinkling sound again, like a tune being played on a music box. But it was only fragments of a song. It had to be from somewhere along there. He moved cautiously in that direction. The tinkling music seemed to be getting louder, seemed to come from behind the second door. Gently he turned the knob and pushed.

The tinkling sound of the music box filled the room. For a moment he was blinded by the light, then he stared in amazement. It was a nursery, crammed with dolls and kitchen sets, two large dolls' houses, and baskets full of soft toys.

A gaslight hissed on the wall beside him, casting wavering shadows over the dusty clutter. The floor was scattered with lilies, which accounted for the smell.

He searched for the source of the music. On top of a pink-painted, wooden, girl's dressing table sat a black-lacquered music box. It was open; its painted ballerina was turning on her toes. The tune was just beginning again, a nursery song, one of those sentimental family ballads. Pendleton recalled the words:

"*This is the father and mother, this is the baby dear;*
This is the sister and brother, all our good family here."

It was haunting, and deeply disturbing. God in heaven, what was this place? How had he got here? Drawn as if by some spell, he walked over and stared down at the tiny, twirling ballerina, then glanced up at the dressing table's mirror. But there was no glass in the frame; instead Pendleton found himself staring at the print of a painting. A man in Renaissance attire carried a child in his arms through a Roman ruin. The child's face and body were completely covered by a cloak. But someone had gouged at the head with a sharp instrument, then spotted it with red paint—

187

No. No. He looked closer, clicking down the lid of the music box as he did. Silence fell, a deathly hush.

No. It was not red paint. It was blood.

"My God. My God."

The light went out.

A voice cut through the black stillness. It half whispered, half growled in the darkness behind him, a terrifying voice.

"Do not turn, Lawyer. Where are the manuscripts brought by the priest Bellarma?"

Pendleton stood frozen. Fear jumbled his thoughts. The person lurking behind him growled. It was a savage, guttural sound.

"Where are the manuscripts?"

Pendleton gathered his wits and replied with his prepared lies. "You have them. You took them from the train. I wanted to get copies from you."

Like a whiplash, the voice sliced the air. "You know those are the notes, the ramblings of the priest. Where are the manuscripts, the Truths, the words of Abyssos?"

The voice was now raised in shrill anger. Pendleton thought it might be a woman standing there. He had to calm her.

"Very well. I have them, and you can obtain them —but I want to be one of you, one of Abyssos."

He spun to face her. Her shriek rent the air. "Do not look!"

He lost his balance, startled, and fell, knocking the music box to the floor. The door of the room slammed as the tune started again.

The acid tug of fear pulsed through Pendleton, but he steadied his breath and wrenched the door open. The gloomy corridor was empty. Behind him, the music box ground down to its last note. All was silent, except for his breathing.

Slowly he edged out of the doorway and stared to either side. Shadows. Then to the right, some light shone from a crack under a door. He moved into the corridor, and quietly edged his way along the wall.

When he came to the door, his hand fluttered out, feeling for the knob. He touched it lightly, then more firmly. It was warm and sticky. Instantly his mind was flooded with a premonition: his body hauled high by the feet, like a slaughtered steer, his stomach sliced open and the guts slipping a bloody mess to the floor. Terror and rage surged through him. He wrenched at the door's handle and ran into the room.

He stopped, staring around in disbelief. It looked like a chapel. There was a stone altar in the middle, with a red light above it. Around the altar stood cubicles with carved chairs. Suddenly the lights dimmed.

Another voice rang out. Clear and precise, warm and engaging. He stopped, immersed in the beauty of it.

"He who is near Me is near the Fire; and he who is far from Me is far from the Kingdom. For it is written, and passed down to us, 'Man, if thou knowest what thou doest, thou art blessed: but if thou knowest not, thou art accursed, and a transgressor.' The ignorant, not the sinners, are the victims of the world and its God, and Jehovah, who we call Ialdoboath, is our enemy, the enemy of our Godhead. Lawyer, you are accursed."

"What have I done?" Pendleton's voice was shrill, his throat parched. White, frothed spittle had dried along the edges of his mouth.

"You sought the books for yourself, but they are ours. Lost for two millennia, but ours, ours alone."

The voice was smooth, insistent, almost comforting. Pendleton wanted to be approved by it, to embrace the person who spoke to him so coldly.

"But I want to join you."

"If that were true, you would have brought us the manuscripts, brought them to me. We know that the priest Bellarma brought my words and the words of the other masters to you. We cannot let you see them or use them. Interloper! Persecutor!" The voice suddenly became sharp, excited. The words were repeated almost like a chant. "Traitor . . . interloper . . . persecutor . . ."

A searing-hot spasm ripped across Pendleton's lower abdomen. He dropped to his knees and clutched at himself, his face contorting in agony. Slowly the pain dissolved and a bull-like anger swept over him. Illogical as it was, he knew this pain was coming from the cult. He roared out,

"I am not a victim, I will not be ruled by you!"

Again the voice came, cool and soothing but like a long, thin stiletto, beautiful and deadly.

"We are all victims, Lawyer. Ialdoboath, or Jehovah if you wish, has made the rules, but we hold the keys, the keys of knowledge that will take us beyond his world of pride, wrath, and vengeance to the First Paradise. Where are the manuscripts, Lawyer? We must have them, for only *we* can hold the truth. . . ."

"I have them. But you must let me join you as an equal."

Pendleton's voice was cool and steady, but it masked a deep pulsing fear. All pretense collapsed when the voice seared across his mind again with cold fury.

"We are not merchants to bargain with! Where are they?"

Pendleton staggered to his feet and slowly stepped backward, toward the door.

"But you *will* bargain. I have your precious Truth, and you have nothing but your criminal act. You attacked the father. I could go to the police."

He kept his eyes focused on the closed curtain before him. He would bull his way out of here! No one had ever stopped him doing what he wanted.

One more step back. Suddenly a screech rent the

air. It bored in through his skull, spreading like a thousand writhing snakes through his brain. He heard the silken voice shouting, "No. No!"

But the scream increased, like a siren wailing. He felt a rush of air, and quickly turned. Something cold and hard ripped across his throat. Bright red blood exploded over his coat and shirt. It bubbled into his windpipe, choking him. He fell backward, coughing out gobs of blood over his beard and white shirt.

Dying, he saw over him a white porcelain mask with black, eyeless sockets and a dark slit of a mouth.

Somewhere in the room above him someone spoke.

"Only we hold the truth."

A glittering knife swooped into his sight and plunged downward. He felt it pierce the top of his stomach and rip through the layers of fat, down to his navel.

Pendleton passed into darkness.

CHAPTER 28

VIRGINIA WAS SITTING on one of the benches near the Central Park Reservoir. A sharp, throbbing headache crept into her skull and came to rest just behind her eyes. Cecily, the nanny, was supervising the children; their laughter trilled over the water. Occasionally Virginia looked up from her book to glance at them.

Ernest had a model sailboat; a small skull-and-crossbones flag flew from its mast. But there was no wind, and for a long time he watched it loll listlessly in the water. Finally Cecily tied a string to each end and Ernest and Mary pulled it back and forth between them. Twice, a tug of war developed and Cecily had to adjudicate.

Perhaps the children's laughter was causing the headache; perhaps it was the glare from the water. She looked down at her book, Stephen Crane's *Maggie: A Girl of the Streets*. She had covered it with a brown paper wrapper, so that neither the children nor Cecily could see the title.

Cecily got up and walked over to the children. They were arguing once more. Ernest had pulled the boat onto the walkway and was keeping his sister at bay. Virginia closed the book and slipped it into her bag.

Tonight she would confront Pendleton again. Last night had been awful and she had had every right to lock him out. The thought of it made her angry all over again. She was no longer going to be a doll for

Pendleton, a possession to be paraded around for his society friends.

Suddenly an intense pain whipped across her skull. It stabbed at the back of her eyes with a blinding flash of light. She doubled over, hands clapped to the sides of her head, pressing in hard on her temples. For a moment she was paralyzed; then, slowly, the pain receded. She looked at the nanny and the children to see if they had noticed. But they were still embroiled in their squabble. Poor Cecily—she had to contend with them all day.

Virginia straightened, and nervously adjusted the top of her lace blouse. She fished her little watch out of her bag and glanced at it: four thirty-seven. She wondered where her husband was. Pendleton had left the house that morning without a word to her. Where was he? She saw his face before her. It was blanched white; his eyes bulged in terror. Virginia fought for breath and sank back against the bench. The vision faded slowly. She gasped and relaxed.

She looked at the children, at the other wives and nannies. Everything was in order here. She was living in the middle of a civilized city. Still, Pendleton's selfish insanities were nibbling away at the foundations of her life. She had no choice; she would face Pendleton again. If she had to, she would take the children and go up to Maine.

She stood up and smoothed her skirt, then walked over to her family.

"Cecily, children, we must stop playing now. It is time to go in."

"All right, ma'am, but don't we have to take the children to your Aunt Eleanor's for dinner?" The nanny spoke quietly, not meeting her employer's eyes.

"Damn, you're right, Cecily—the chauffeur's to pick us up at the park gate. I had forgotten. Thank you for reminding me." She glanced at her little watch

193

again. "Come, children, we must go."

Pendleton's arrangements once again assured that Virginia would be kept out of her own house until darkness had fallen.

While Virginia was fretting in the park, Bertha was impatiently waiting for the end of her shift at the Spring Exchange. When six o'clock finally came, she rushed out of the building. She needed fresh air, but West Houston Street was full of traffic. The grating of iron wheels and the clip-clop of horses did not help her headache.

She liked being a telephonist, liked doing a job that was so special and modern, but some days the buzzing in her earphones caused a throbbing pain to fasten around her temples and across her forehead.

As Bertha leaned against the wall, Julia and Emma, fellow telephonists from her shift, walked by.

"Will you join us for a cup of coffee?" Julia asked.

Bertha pulled herself up and forced a smile. "No, I've got to get home to my uncle's for dinner. Thank you, though."

The two women waved as they went off arm in arm. It was a lie, of course. No one must suspect where she was going.

She pulled a newspaper out of her bag and read once more about the head being found in the river. Her stomach knotted. It must have been horrible for Jenny. Bertha jammed the newspaper back into her bag and headed for West Twenty-third.

Mrs. Flanagan was pleasant but distant. She looked at the mousy girl with her eyeglasses and her hair pulled back in a bun and thought that she and Jenny were a strange pair.

"No dear, I'm afraid she's gone out for the day. It'll help her get over what happened to her. Terrible thing, wasn't it?"

194

"Yes."

Bertha felt uncomfortable. She adjusted her blouse collar and nervously patted the bun at the back of her head. What if Jenny did not come back right away? Perhaps Bertha would not see Jenny before her own entry into the next level of Abyssos. She would have to somehow let Jenny know she had been thinking of her. She reached into her bag and pulled out a small leather-covered diary. For a long time she had wanted to give it to Jenny. It would be a symbolic act, a giving up of her past life. It would show Jenny how she too could journey toward the Light.

"This is for Jenny. Could you see that she gets it?"

"Of course, dear." Mrs. Flanagan showed her to the front door and smiled. "Watch the stairs."

Bertha walked down and heard the door close behind her. Halfway down she stopped and looked back. There was such depravity here, such a stripping away of Jehovah's laws. She could almost smell the Archon of Fornication, Saclas. Yet tonight she would sit down at her uncle's table, with her aunt and her cousins, and eat dinner. It would all be proper and ordered and they would know nothing of her other life.

She smiled, half-mischievous, half-lewd. Soon Jenny would know. Jenny would have her diary and at last understand her journey.

Bertha pulled open the heavy front door and walked into the night.

Bellarma had spent the early evening in the small church of St. Joseph's, half a block north of Canal Street. He sat in a shadowed corner behind one of the pillars, his head bowed, his hands clasped before him. He prayed as he had not done for years.

Araya had brought him across the dark river. He was on the sure ground of faith once again. He would reclaim the manuscripts and destroy them.

195

Araya had wanted to come with him, but this fight Bellarma claimed as his own. He had brought the evil from the caves in the desert into the light and he would send it once more into the darkness. For twenty years he had been obsessed, blinded by a kind of lust. Now this black monk had given him the chance to right himself.

He said a last prayer to his special saint. Saint Stephen the martyr, Stephen who had died so brutally at the hands of his persecutors, battered by stones. Then Bellarma crossed himself and left the church to make his way uptown.

Mary was asleep on Virginia's lap by the time the automobile turned onto Sixty-fourth Street. A cool dampness seemed to swamp them, surging up from the East River. Cecily shivered and Virginia pulled the lap robe up over the sleeping child.

It had been a teeth-grinding evening. Virginia had only finally managed to escape when Mary collapsed fast asleep on the rug.

Aunt Eleanor was a bore. How could she go over that tedious play again, scene by scene? They had seen it together, and it was such a bloodless comedy, not worth discussing. The woman had no taste; Virginia had gone to the play with her under duress.

As the automobile drew up outside the house, she glared up at Pendleton's study. The light was off. Well, she wouldn't wait up for him, but tomorrow there would have to be a showdown.

She smiled at her western metaphor as she passed her sleeping daughter to the nanny, who stood on the sidewalk. Gladys opened the front door and light poured out of the house. It was a welcoming sight.

No one noticed the black carriage as it edged up Fifth Avenue and stopped at the corner of the street.

Ernest Junior skipped out of the auto and clattered his way up the steps.

"Ernest! Do not wake your sister!"

With exaggerated caution, the boy continued into the house. Virginia got out of the vehicle and turned to the chauffeur. "Mervyn, we won't need the automobile again tonight. You can put it away."

"Right, ma'am." He released the brake and pulled smoothly away.

It had been a long day. Virginia desperately wished she had someone to talk to; not Pendleton, who would lecture her as if she were a child, but a person to share with her. Her thoughts turned to Lieutenant Doolan, to his pleasant face and sympathetic eyes. His visit had disturbed her deeply. She remembered his eyes, watching her and then turning elsewhere when she looked at him.

She sighed. God! Was her life to be forever made up of such improbable dreams? She walked up the steps and stopped at the door. It had swung shut after Ernest. She looked down at the brass plate. "Pendleton." Virginia traced her finger along the deep engraving and wondered where Miss Virginia Coles had disappeared to. Had she been forever swallowed up by that heavy brass, or was there still a way to freedom?

Behind her, the throbbing sound of the automobile faded. It was replaced by another sound. Light at first, then growing louder and nearer: the clip-clop of the horse, the grinding of the carriage wheels.

Virginia's finger froze on the O in the name plate.

The carriage came closer. A clammy cold suddenly enshrouded her. She felt brushed by the fingertips of death. She shuddered.

The grinding wheels mixed with a throaty, rasping breath, a low growling that tailed off into chilling, malicious laughter. Virginia fell back against the door, transfixed by the sight of the black carriage before her. Its curtained silence was terrifying. The horse was still; the driver was muffled in layers of clothing, unidentifiable.

Suddenly Virginia smelled the dampness of death,

197

musky and pungent. It filled her nostrils and choked her. A figure moved in the dark of the carriage, framing itself in the window. As the face became visible in the yellow glare of the street light, a terrified scream burned along Virginia's throat and died in her mouth.

Virginia felt trapped in the fluid slowness of nightmare. What looked like a nun's black veil was draped over the head. The face was like death. It gleamed dully in the gaslight and she abruptly realized from its rigid stillness that it was a white porcelain mask. The hairs on her neck rose in fear and her hand fumbled along the door, seeking the handle.

A cold breath rattled from the creature. Virginia gazed, frozen, at the black, eyeless sockets and the pouting, dark slit of a mouth. It was a death mask— but whose? All will seemed to leak from her. Her legs began to move, as if the eyeless creature and the black carriage summoned her. Suddenly she fell backward, into her own front hallway. Her body jerked in horror, as if she had fallen to her death. Gladys seized her arm, supporting her. Virginia clung to the young woman, gasping.

"Dear God—are you all right, ma'am?"

For a moment Virginia could say nothing. Her mind raced. Then she slammed the front door and locked it. She turned to Gladys, forcing a smile. She would not put anyone else in danger.

"It's nothing, just the evening chill. . . . I slipped." She knew that the eyeless monster was still out there. It was waiting to walk into her dreams, waiting, eyeless and mouthless, hissing out its cold breaths. "I think I'll sit down for a moment, Gladys." The maid led her mistress into the drawing room. "Get me a brandy, please."

Gladys went quickly. She had never seen her mistress so distressed. Virginia stood in the middle of the room, trembling with fear. She felt drawn to look out the window at the coach. She moved over to the curtain and touched it, then pulled back her hand as though she had been stung.

Outside, the creature shouted *"Andiamo pronto."*

Virginia shuddered at the seething voice. The horse's hoofbeats faded away. As her trembling subsided she felt a great relief. It was gone. But what had it to do with her or her house?

Bellarma knew the answer.

He turned into East Sixty-fourth Street just as Virginia fell through the doorway. He was unaware of what had happened. His mind was filled with his mission. If the lawyer was in, he thought he could persuade Pendleton to hand over the manuscripts. If he was not in, then Bellarma would surely be able to find the manuscripts in the study, or wherever Pendleton had put them.

Bellarma gazed along the row of townhouses with their elegant stoops and intricate iron railings, at the trees under the lights of Central Park. All was quiet and still. The priest did not see the black carriage, but as he started across the street toward the Pendleton house, the creature inside saw him.

"Andiamo pronto," the voice whispered through the mouth slit.

Bellarma turned at the sound of the carriage. It halted before him, and time ground to a halt. The carriage was silhouetted in the light that spilled from the lamps along the street. It sat in the middle of the street, threatening and perfectly still. Bellarma had never seen it before, but he knew it from his dreams. They were here, here to take what they believed was rightly theirs. His mind filled with terror. All he could think was that there was no escape. He took a step backward. The horse snorted and tossed its mane. Bellarma turned and ran. The carriage followed.

The avenues were busy, but the priest paid no

199

attention to the traffic. He was driven forward by a wild panic. His mind seemed to have gone blank. He was narrowly missed by an automobile that swerved around him with a screech of brakes. The young driver stood up behind his wheel and screamed out a torrent of abuse.

Bellarma heard none of it. He glanced back to see the black carriage give the open Packard a wide berth, and grind relentlessly after him.

He increased his pace, but they were unshakable. He would do anything to escape them, anything. His unwitting service was over. Something loomed over him. He looked up and saw the latticed, dark shadows of the Third Avenue El. To the right, he could see the lights at a set of stairs that led up to a station.

Somehow his quickened heartbeat pumped ideas and voices into his head until they spun in a dizzying conflict. Bellarma could hear the carriage coming closer, the horse starting to canter. Bellarma dodged between the support girders under the rails. Within seconds the carriage swerved in behind him, and it was as if there were only the two of them in the world, the hunter and the hunted. The noise of the grinding wheels filled his ears. He could almost feel the hot breath of the horse on the back of his neck.

He swerved to the left, between two support girders. The steps were only twenty or so feet ahead. The carriage attempted to head him off. He glanced at it as it passed, and saw the dark interior and the smooth porcelain face at the window.

Panic stirred him to a last effort and he sprinted to the bottom of the iron steps. He leapt up them, two and three at a time, loudly clanging his way to the wooden platform at the top. He clambered over the turnstile, ignoring the shouts of the ticket booth attendant.

"Hey, you! Come back here and pay your damned fare!"

Suddenly he was thrust aside and slammed into a billboard. As he slid down to his knees, he heard the swish of robes, and a vengeful hiss. "Traitor!" it called over the rumble of the approaching train. The robed figure forced Bellarma to the edge of the platform. A knife glittered in the gaslight. Bellarma lurched. The pain in his throat was terrible. A jet of dark fluid arched out across the platform. His assailant growled. The knife flashed again, jabbing. Bellarma fell backward onto the tracks. The creature fled, robes flying.

Somehow Bellarma staggered to his feet as the express train bore down on him. One hand tried in vain to seal the bubbling slash that was his throat. The other stretched above him, reaching for the heavens.

The priest's last feeling was of exquisite relief. He had been driven by fear to the edge of his soul, but now the struggle was no longer his. Araya would carry on the fight.

The high-pitched shriek of brakes filled the air, but the driver had had no time to stop.

CHAPTER 29

VIRGINIA'S SLEEP WAS troubled. The black cab pursued her through her dreams. It rumbled after her through the streets of Brunswick, Maine, straight to her father's newspaper office. It floated after her across the small boating lake at Mount Holyoke, where she had gone to school. In the final dream, the carriage followed her to the door of her house on East Sixty-fourth Street. Walking along the street, Virginia could hear the slow, persistent hoofbeats drawing closer. She was trapped, wanting to run but afraid to show panic. She reached the top of the steps and froze. A bitter breath had touched her neck. She wanted to turn and face the eyes that she felt boring into her. But she couldn't move. A rasping hiss filled her ears.

Virginia jerked the door open and rushed into the house. She ran directly to the nursery, her footsteps echoing on the checkered marble floor. She heard the creak of wheels behind her. She flung open the door, looking to protect her children.

The carriage stood in the middle of the room, evil and brooding. Behind it she could see the frightened white faces of Ernest Junior and little Mary as they cowered in a corner.

Terror struck at her heart. She had to reach them. As she took a step, the horse snorted and stamped. The harness jingled. Virginia stood very still.

The mask appeared at the window, even more chilling than before. Something glittered in the black eye sockets. A lascivious tongue snaked around the dark pouting slit of a mouth. The whole mask radiated malevolence.

Virginia screamed, awakening herself. She struggled for breath, beating at the air with her hands. She was bathed in a cold, clammy sweat. It was morning. Pendleton was not beside her. Had he even come home last night?

She got up quickly and took her watch from the bedside table. It was an inexpensive little Edgemere that her father had given her when she first went to Mount Holyoke, but she valued it more than any of the costly jewelry that Pendleton had given her.

Eight-thirty; she had overslept.

She dressed, went downstairs, and looked into the study. Pendleton was not there; the room seemed undisturbed. Virginia turned; Gladys was crossing the hall, a dustcloth in one hand.

"Gladys, when did Mr. Pendleton leave this morning?"

"Well ma'am," Gladys said, "I don't think Mr. Pendleton came in last night."

"Oh yes, of course, I forgot, he told me he might be staying with that Mr. Van de Veer on Long Island."

Virginia stopped. She was overexplaining. She gave Gladys a cool smile. After all, a lady must not show her suffering.

"Will he be back tonight, ma'am?"

Virginia looked closely to see if there was even a hint of malice in Gladys's face. But if there was anything there, it was sympathy, and that was almost worse.

"He may, but it's more likely that he will stay away."

Virginia walked toward the nursery, back straight, head erect. Her mother would never have suffered such an indignity. Her husband was absent again and he had not had the decency to tell her where he was or why. There would be a time of reckoning. One day Pendleton would realize what a good marriage he had destroyed. She had endured such a spate of absences before, before the Brownlea scandal had exploded. One afternoon, at a tea party, she had overheard that Pendleton had been seen at Hammerstein's Roof Garden on top of the Olympia with some "vulgar person." The emphasis on "person" left no doubt that Pendleton's companion had been female.

Virginia opened the nursery door. For a moment she expected to see the stamping horse and the black carriage. But she was greeted by nothing more than the usual preschool bustle. Ernest Junior was up and ready to go. He had already finished his breakfast, and was waiting for Mary to finish hers. Billy, the ginger cat, was sitting on his chair, hoping Mary would leave some milk in her bowl.

"Good morning, ma'am," said the nanny.

"Good morning, Cecily."

"Mama!" Ernest ran over and gave Virginia a hug. Though only seven, he was already a big boy, with light brown eyes and fair hair. "Mama, are you going shopping?"

"Yes." Mervyn was to collect her at ten o'clock.

"Would you buy me some comics?" the boy asked.

"Ernest, you know what your father says about comics."

He looked up at her for a moment, obviously thinking. "Yes, but you don't say that."

She had to smile; already he seemed to have a lawyer's mind.

"No, I don't. I shall bring you one—but only one, and you must not tell your father."

"Thank you, Mama, thank you."

Cecily grinned. "He hoards them like they were gold, Mrs. Pendleton. Come now, Miss Mary, eat up your wheat berries. We have to walk your brother to school."

"What price are these comics?" Virginia asked her son, smiling.

"Five cents each, Mama."

Poker-faced, she held out her hand. Disheartened, Ernest reached into his trouser pocket and fished out five pennies. Slowly he handed them over. She counted them with exaggerated care.

"Five cents. So you want just one."

"I suppose so," he said, hanging his head.

"We shall see." Ernest looked up at her, saw her smile, and grinned.

Mary ran over and hugged her at the knees, her blond curls tumbling out from under her tiny white bonnet.

"Mama, can I go with you?" she begged.

"Mama has to go shopping, but after Cecily leaves Ernest at school, she's going to take you to the swings."

Cecily took the little girl by the hand as Ernest picked up his tan satchel.

"Are we all ready?" she asked.

There was a chorus of yeses as the children bounced out.

Virginia laughed, watching them skip down the hallway. There was a chinking sound in the nursery behind her. She turned and saw the cat, sitting on the small table, lapping up the rest of Mary's milk. She clapped her hands, startling the animal, which stared at her.

"Come on, you ginger beast, move!"

Billy moved off with magisterial dignity. Virginia surveyed the empty nursery, the dolls and the enameled battleships, the kite and the two "Weedon" steam engines, the tin soldiers peering over the walls of the toy fort, Ernest's metal farm wagon, in which Mary had arranged three of her dolls for a tea party. All so gentle and innocent. All serene. And yet something was wrong. A slimy coldness shivered across her. She backed out of the room, jerking the door shut behind her.

CHAPTER 30

BY NINE-THIRTY DOOLAN'S office stank of cigarette smoke and cheap cigars. Doolan had the window open, but it didn't help much. He glanced across his desk and stretched as he watched O'Neal and McKenna scribbling notes.

O'Neal looked up and yawned. He was a plump-faced man in his early thirties with a thinning head of mousy brown hair. Morning was not his best time. He gave a lazy grin and stretched.

"God, Lieutenant—I haven't seen so many cloth stores since I went shopping with the little lady."

McKenna laughed and pulled his jacket from the back of the chair. In his midforties, he had a gnomish look about him, with a slightly bulbous drinker's nose and a seemingly fixed half smile. Slipping into the jacket, he searched the pockets and pulled out a bag of boiled sweets.

"Hey, McKenna, you addicted to those things?" Frank Cassassa said as he entered the room, a sheaf of papers in his hand. He walked past McKenna, dropped the papers on Doolan's desk, and snatched a candy from the bag.

"Okay, you knights of the street," Doolan said with a sigh, "I've divided today's shopping list into four. Help yourselves."

Each selected a paper. Cassassa spat out the candy, dropping it with a clatter into a metal wastebasket.

"Holy shit, McKenna, how long've these been in your pocket?"

"Nobody asked you to steal them," McKenna retorted.

The three detectives trooped out the door, leaving Doolan alone. He walked to the window, sucking in the raw city air. The whirring and grinding of the city's morning traffic wafted up from the street below. At least he'd had a good night's sleep last night. Tom hadn't made it home. Doolan wouldn't inquire where he'd been when he finally surfaced; presumably he was old enough to look after himself. Presumably.

Doolan heard the door open and turned. Albrecht walked in.

"Pete."

"Abe. How goes the day for you?"

Albrecht shrugged. He was a tall, thin man with a somber face, deep-set grey eyes, and heavy, protruding eyebrows. This grim appearance concealed a wicked sense of humor, but Doolan could tell that he had not come to offer his usual new joke.

"I believe you have the word out for a priest, name of Bellarma," Albrecht said.

"Yeah," Doolan replied. "Have you got something?"

"Why'd you need him?"

"A friend of mine was looking for him."

Albrecht stared at Doolan, searching his eyes.

"Come on, Abe, cut the meaningful looks. What've you got on him?"

"I've got him—on the slab in the morgue."

Doolan stepped back and sank down on the windowsill. "What? How?"

"An El sliced his head off." Albrecht rarely minced words.

"Jesus . . . Was it an accident?"

Albrecht shrugged and gave a bitter, thin-lipped

207

smile. "I don't think so—the ticket-booth attendant saw something, but it sounds like a tale outta Edgar Allan Poe. The fellow says he saw someone in robes and a mask—a porcelain mask! Can you beat that?"

Bellarma had not returned. Araya waited and waited, then finally allowed himself to sleep. His dreams told him what his conscious mind would not allow: Bellarma would never return; Bellarma was dead.

Gebel Kalat, the mountain that held the caves of Abyssos, towered above him. Its ocher, saffron, and sulfur-yellow cliffs rose sheer into the depthless blues of the Nubian sky. Araya set his feet on the path and slowly made his way up, around the massive outcrop of rock. The wind rose and whistled between the peaks with a sad, enervating sound, like a cathedral organ. The eerie music was clearly a warning, but Araya could not heed it. He had his mission.

Suddenly the path opened on a high cliff that was pockmarked with caves. Araya's stomach churned as the odor of death and decay filled his nostrils. But there was something else, something beneath the smell of rot: pure evil. The stink catapulted him into the cave, past the pile of mud bricks and through the gaping black hole.

The altar sat still and brooding, just as Bellarma had found it. But the desiccated lovers were gone. Instead, the priest lay there, his face covered with blood. His hands were wide open, empty, showing that he had failed to obtain the manuscripts. Araya fell to his knees, and the dream returned to its beginning and once again unreeled before him.

When Araya finally woke from his fitful cycle of nightmare, it was a warm, clear morning. He looked out his window and saw the river glittering. He could stay in his room no longer—he needed to walk, to breathe some air other than the stale smells of the

208

hotel. Then he would return and wait for Bellarma. He dismissed his dreams. They had to be wrong! Bellarma could not fail. He would bring back the manuscripts and they would destroy them together, using the centuries-old Coptic rite of purgation. They would cleanse the words of Abyssos from the world.

Araya turned left from his hotel and walked along South Street. The dockland buzzed with activity. He stood for a good hour, watching the dockworkers unloading a shipload of hardwood into Krevit's furniture trucks, then walked inland, along Clinton Street.

He was as much of an oddity to the people he passed as they were to him, for he cut an exotic figure, tall, lean, and muscular. His ebony skin, high cheekbones, and tight, curly beard gave him a majestic, otherworldly quality. His mind was troubled, but his face was placid and serene.

He walked on, across Division to Hester, where the buildings seemed to squeeze out the sky. Araya wondered how the citizens could live, piled on top of one another. His attention was captured by a large billboard at the bottom of a stairway leading to an El station. It was covered with advertisements for theaters and nickelodeons. He peered at it in wonder. Posters were layered one on the other; years of entertainment history bound into a solid mass of paper and paste. Where weather and vandals had torn sheets away, old announcements mingled with new. To Araya they were all meaningless—*Aida* at the Metropolitan with Caruso; the Vanderbuilt Cup, "showing automobiles on stage"; *The Jesters,* at the Empire, this poster adorned with a photo of Maude Adams.

"*Heral'* . . . *Heral'* . . . read all about it!"

A husky-voiced boy sauntered past, chewing on a stick of licorice. He jabbed his papers at the passengers clattering up and down the steps, then flicked his unruly mop of black hair out of his eyes as he glared over at Araya.

"*Heral'* . . . *Heral'* . . . Priest dies on El track. . . . Priest dies. . . ."

Araya lunged toward the boy and snatched a paper.

"What the hell!" the boy shouted in surprise, then jumped away from the giant black man with the glaring eyes. Araya scanned the front page, grimacing as he read the headline, "Italian priest dies on El tracks: Foul play suspected."

Araya staggered. He felt as if someone had struck him a mortal blow. For a moment he could not think. Finally his mind conjured up the image of his friend Tom, and the man Araya had seen from the ship, Peter Doolan. It was time to enlist their help. So far he had failed, and Abyssos was winning.

Bellarma was dead. But what had happened to the manuscripts?

The newsboy watched until Araya was at a safe distance, then picked up the discarded paper, smoothed it, and placed it in his bundle.

Overhead a train rumbled into the morning heat.

CHAPTER 31

THE LIGHT, APPLE-SCENTED breeze ruffled the curtains
and made the room into a theater of dancing shadows. Bertha felt warm and protected. Her words
drifted lazily over the blue-and-white-checkered
counterpane, over the perfumes and powders on the
dressing table, and mingled with the flickering shadows that died in the dusty corners. Hers was a drowsy,
girlish voice, and her strange prayers blended easily
with the sounds of the children at play, drifting up
from the garden below.

Bertha was only twenty years of age and in the last
year or so she felt that she had gained more knowledge
of the world and the universe than her uncle had
acquired in a lifetime. She knew that Father Schmidt
was Simon reborn, Simon Magus: Simon the enemy
of the apostles of Christ, Simon the master of true
knowledge, master of the cult of Abyssos. His words,
and the depth of his knowledge, had led her past the
despair of the world created by the Christian Jehovah,
to the truth in Abyssos. Each time she joined in sexual
union with one of her brothers in Abyssos she felt the
divine electricity as it rushed to pull another spark of
light from the First Fire. Simon had taught her that
she could touch that current, feel it, wallow in it—but
if a new life was created, it had to be destroyed. The
ultimate sin in the eyes of Abyssos was to trap another
spark of the divine—the soul—in the foulness that
was the body.

In the temple of Saclas, the Archon of Fornication, she had touched that current of sex often, snatching hungrily at that godlike knowledge. She had created a new life, and now she would release the divine spark that had been trapped in the new flesh that had formed within her body.

Bertha lay back on the bed and began to undo her corset, gently rubbing each velvet-covered button in turn. She started at the bottom and worked her way up, her stomach relaxing a little more with each unfastening. It was only four months and already she could feel the swelling and thickening of her waist. Tonight she would be with them. She had only one regret, that she could not share the secrets of the inner temple with Jenny. But that time would come.

She worked her way up to the three crimson silk bows that tied the front of her frilly, blue satin underblouse. She undid them one by one, enjoying the gentle touch of the warm air on her small, firm breasts. Now she lay naked from the waist up. Slowly, almost tentatively, she covered her nipples with her fingers and began to massage herself. Her eyelids drooped in sensual delight; the smile of a wicked child crept onto her lips.

"Bertha Langman, you have a lovely figure," she murmured.

Indeed she had. Usually it was hidden, lost under layers of corset and bloomers, slips and ankle-length skirts; but now, as she gently writhed on the bed, her curves and secret sensuality were exposed for anyone to see. But no one would—this was secret to all but Abyssos.

To the world, she was the youngest assistant supervisor at her telephone exchange, only twenty years of age. She was intelligent and looked it, not an advantage in this first decade of the century. Her eyes held alertness, not compliance. Most young men were intimidated by her firm gaze, sparkling behind her

212

eyeglasses. Her mousy brown hair was the bane of her life and seemed to defy all attempts to coif, curl, or set it into a shapely style.

Still she had her beautiful body and her secret lust. Away from home and work, she had another life.

She got up from the bed and stood in front of the large mahogany wardrobe. A full-length mirror covered one door. Studying her image, Bertha pulled the pins from her hair and allowed it to fall over her smooth white breasts. It parted around the mounds, revealing small, erect nipples. She let the ruffled, black sateen slip fall to the floor, and stepped out of it, closer to the mirror, closer to that other self.

Watching her hand on her stomach, she moved it slowly and sensuously, farther and farther down with each stroke. Beneath her skin, life was stirring, but not a life she wanted. It was a trap set by the evil one; it was to be a fleshly tomb for another soul. She would not perpetuate that evil.

Tonight they would gather and challenge this arrogant, ignorant Jahweh, this Jehovah who had imprisoned them all in flesh. Only knowledge would release them to beyond him, to their rightful place in the plenitude. Abyssos.

The rhythms of her body vanquished thought. A throbbing warmth coursed through her loins. She spread her legs to firm her stance, and then leaned forward, rolling her forehead along the hard, cold surface of the mirror. She shrugged out of her corset. One hand slid beneath the elastic on her white drawers and inched down to the soft hair between her legs. The white muslin of her drawers rubbed sensuously against the fine hair on the back of her hand, and her fingers coiled into the warm dampness between her legs.

She saw each of them coming to her, each of them slipping off their trousers, revealing themselves, one after another. And one after another, they came into

213

her. Slowly at first and then pumping at her, harder and harder. She drew breath in short gulps. Her jaw dropped open and she ran the tip of her tongue lightly along her lower lip. Oh, yes. Oh, yes.

She tasted the tang of salt on her skin. She moved, imagining that Antonio was in her, that they all entered her. She wanted to scream with the ecstasy of it. But she stifled her groans; the household must not hear.

She stared into the mirror. If her mother could see her now, her legs spread like a five-cent whore, clad only in a pair of extravagantly ruffled and ribboned bloomers . . . Her mother with her brittle, starched righteousness, who saw all pleasure tainted with the devil. And who was the devil? Some bogey, set up to keep us from the gates of true knowledge. So said her master, the dark-eyed Simon. Was not Helen a prostitute and yet the Goddess of Wisdom?

Wave after wave of throbbing pleasure raced through her. Tonight she would penetrate to yet one more mystery. Through her quickened breath she intoned, "I sowed no children for the ruler, but I tore up my roots, and gathered together my limbs that were scattered abroad."

Tonight, she would destroy the unwanted life stirring within her. And she would free another soul from Jehovah's rule.

"I sowed no children for the ruler," Bertha gasped, sinking to her knees. She arched back until her head touched the blue and green of the flowered Brussels rug. The Serpent of Knowledge writhed toward her, into her. Her pale breasts heaved with the final shudders of her ecstasy.

"And the two shall be one . . . shall be one . . . the male with the female, when ye tread upon the vesture of shame."

She thrust upward against the motion of her fingers, groaning deeply. It was as though she could feel the

214

hot, forbidden liquid of the master mingling with her own. A last tremor, a moment of total abandonment, and then it was over. Outside, the laughs of the children spiraled off into the air.

Bertha took a deep breath and smelled the apple tree mingled with the sweat of her passion.

Now she would rest and wait for the night to come.

CHAPTER 32

TOM AND JENNY had just arrived in Peter's apartment when there was a loud knocking at the door. They were seated at the table drinking coffee. Neither of them moved as they smothered their laughter. They did not want to answer it. Last night at the hotel in Coney Island, they had created a cocoon of love, a time set apart from the world, and they did not want to break that shell, to allow the nuisances of daily life back in. But the knocking continued.

"They won't go away," Tom whispered.

"Maybe it's your brother," Jenny replied, her voice soft.

"No, he's chained to his desk by now."

Jenny smiled as Tom got up from the table and crossed to the door. There was another knock as he reached up to pull back the bolt. "All right, all right, hold yer horses!" He swung the door wide open. "Araya—my God!"

"Tom." Araya offered no further greeting, and after a moment Tom stepped aside.

"Well, come in."

The tall man entered and quickly looked around him. He saw Jenny but did not acknowledge her. "Is your brother here?" he asked.

"No, he's at work. How are you, you bugger?"

"I must speak to him—and I must speak to you."

Tom would have been angry if he had not seen the intensity in his friend's eyes. Tom indicated that he should take a seat, and closed the door. "Well, no problem, you can talk to me now."

"And your brother?"

"I'll take you to him at Police Headquarters, if that's what you want! Araya . . . what the hell's all this about?"

Araya turned and looked at Jenny. Tom went to stand beside her, smiling. "I'd like you to meet a friend of mine."

Jenny said hello, but Araya merely nodded in distant response. She saw the dark, disturbed look in his eyes and knew that he needed to be alone with Tom.

"Tom, I should go to Mrs. Flanagan's."

"No, you don't need . . ." She wasn't going back to that place if he had anything to say about it!

"Yes, I do. All my things are there. I'll come back, I promise."

She gave him a twinkling smile and lightly touched his hand, hoping that the previous night was not a dream. He took a key from his pocket and gave it to her.

"All right, I'll see you back here later."

"Later," Jenny said, and gave him a smile as she left.

When she had gone, Tom turned to Araya and saw something akin to terror in his friend's eyes.

"Well?" he said, curious to know what could unnerve such a man.

"I have much to tell you, but I can only tell you part of it now, and then you must take me to your brother. We have little time. We are in danger from the Snake of Knowledge, the Snake of Abyssos."

Tom tensed as he heard the word "snake." He had a flash of his dreams, and as he listened further he had the terrifying sensation that those dreams were becoming real.

* * *

217

Virginia sat alone in the dark, paneled dining room. The house was quiet. Half a cup of coffee rested before her. Every so often she would pick up the spoon and stir the cold liquid, then set the spoon back on the saucer. She stared across the polished table, not knowing how to think or react. Some twenty minutes before, Elizabeth Barnes, Pendleton's secretary, had phoned from the office, looking for him. The woman's efficient, businesslike voice had disturbed her.

"Well I'm sure there's no cause for alarm, Mrs. Pendleton. Mr. Pendleton has often . . . well . . . he can be impulsive. . . ."

Impulsive. Virginia mulled over the word long after she put the phone back in its cradle. Miss Barnes was certainly diplomatic; diplomatic and condescending all in the same breath.

Miss Barnes had promised to contact Mr. Pendleton's business associates and make inquiries. She promised to phone Virginia later. The secretary's call was enough to plant a seed of worry in Virginia's mind. She had presumed that this was just another of Pendleton's "male jaunts," and judging by Miss Barnes's tone of voice, she thought the same. But it was possible that something else had happened.

The phone rang. Virginia reached it on the fourth ring.

"Hello?"

"Mrs. Pendleton?" She recognized Doolan's voice immediately. It had a firm, warm, reassuring quality. She soaked it in like a sponge.

"Yes, this is Virginia Pendleton. Is that Lieutenant Doolan?"

"Yes, it is," he said.

"I'm so glad you called—it's so good to hear your voice—"

She stopped in midsentence. She was rushing ahead of herself. There was such a thing as decorum, even if she was in need of advice and someone to turn to. A

218

lady did not throw open her emotions to the world. She kept them private and controlled.

"Mrs. Pendleton, are you all right?"

"Yes, yes, of course." She covered her embarrassment with a light laugh. "Can I help you?"

For a second they both knew that Doolan was about to say something beyond his immediate inquiry. Then he retreated. "I'm looking for your husband."

"He's not here."

"Yes, but I don't have his office number."

"Well, he's not there either, and he didn't come home last night."

There was a silence as both of them reviewed the implications of Virginia's statement.

"I see. Do you have any idea where he might be?" Doolan's tone was soothing.

"No, I'm afraid I don't."

Again there was just the crackling of the telephone line. Virginia believed he was thinking of the Brownlea affair, the whorehouse murder and the much-whispered high jinks of Pendleton's business associates, but in fact he was not.

"Mrs. Pendleton, there's probably nothing to this, but the reason I called your husband was that we found Father Bellarma."

"The priest?" She was surprised. The conversation had lurched in the wrong direction.

"Yes. He was killed last night— I mean, he was in an accident on the El."

"Oh, my God! My God!"

"I'm sorry to tell you this way. When your husband returns, perhaps you could get him to call me." Doolan paused, obviously considering his next words. "Unless you wish to put him on the missing list?"

"No, no. I think he would be quite angry if he was just . . . just . . ."

"I understand. You may get a call or a visit from a Lieutenant Albrecht; he's on the case. He will want to

219

know how you and your husband know—knew—Bellarma."

"I see. Thank you." The seconds ticked by, with just the distant hum of the line, broken only by the occasional burst of crackling. Then Doolan spoke. His voice was gentle and concerned.

"If you need someone to talk to, I would be happy to listen."

"I know . . . and I thank you." But she was not ready, and he knew it.

"Yes, well, good-bye."

"Good-bye." Virginia replaced the earpiece and stood looking along the hallway toward the marble Athenae. She felt numb. The little priest was dead. Dead! What had he said to her? "Sometimes when you find what you search for, it is like the taste of poison on your tongue." She shivered, feeling the first pang of fear for Pendleton. Had he found the taste of poison on *his* tongue?

No, that could not be. Pendleton was absent on one of his jaunts. That was all. Damn him.

Doolan put down the phone and stared across the room at the empty desks. Every turn he made seemed in some way to lead him across Virginia's path. He slammed his fist on the desk and jumped up. He walked to the window and leaned his forehead on the cool glass. He could make no sense of it. Pieces of information floated disconnected in his mind. Here he was, investigating the possible murder of a prostitute, and meanwhile his own life was cracking at the seams. And the case grew ever more complicated—the nun figure at the church—Pendleton and Father Bellarma—the black sailor, Tom's shipmate—his "kidnapping" of the priest—and now Bellarma was dead, the "nun" had resurfaced, and Pendleton was missing!

He slammed the window frame with his open hand

and rattled the glass. "Jesus, Mary, and Joseph!" After a few seconds, he started to laugh. To think this had all started with a severed torso!

"I hope this is in memory of my many fine jokes, Peter."

Doolan swung around. Abe Albrecht was standing in the doorway, watching him. Doolan arched an eyebrow and ran his fingers through his tousled hair. "Just one of those mornings, the kind you offer up to the God of Absurdity."

"Tell me about it." Albrecht sauntered over and stood by the desk.

Doolan turned again and looked out over the city, into a blue sky dotted with ball-like clouds. In the glass he saw Albrecht nosing around the papers on his desk.

He turned around. "What's this, a raid?"

Albrecht took out a cigarette and continued poking around. "I need some matches."

"Forget it, you're not smoking in here. I've got enough with the other three."

"What's this?" Albrecht picked up Bridie's envelope and was looking at the Latin on the back. "I didn't realize you went in for Latin epigrams, Pete!"

"Can you read it?"

"Exemplum Dismas Sancti faciat . . . hmmm . . . may the example of Saint Dismas make God's will more . . . more bearable for the innocent child. Pretty good, huh? That comes from having a fourteen-year-old in high school!"

Doolan took the envelope and wrote the translation directly on it. Then he stared at what he had written. It meant nothing to him.

"Hey, Pete, I got better ones than that, genuine licentious Latin graffiti collected from the seminaries of the world."

"Uh-huh."

"Where's this from?"

"Just a chapel I went into recently," Doolan said.

Albrecht nodded and gave a sly smile. "A chapel. Good, Pete, glad to see you're drifting back to your roots."

"Yeah, thanks for your concern, Abe. You ever hear of a man called Gallenini?"

Albrecht lifted his eyebrows. "Sure, Giuseppe the Weird."

"My wife's brother used to do a lot of business with his import firm. It's a big place down on Vestry; they work out of docks Twenty-five through Thirty."

"Why'd you call him weird?" Doolan asked.

"Unfortunate would be a better word. Some years ago he had a bad time with his daughter. She wanted to marry someone he didn't approve of, so he bought off the suitor and shipped her to a convent upstate."

"Is she still there?"

"No. She killed herself."

Doolan let loose a whistle. "Jesus. How?"

"I don't know, knife, I think. Anyway, the poor bastard never got over it, just went slowly downhill. He became a recluse and rarely left his mansion, up on Riverside Drive. My brother-in-law had to go there once; he said it was like a morgue."

"I came across his funeral early this week."

"You must've been up early," Albrecht said.

"You knew about it?" Doolan was surprised.

"Sure, from Vittorio and my brother-in-law."

Doolan took a deep breath and let out a long, voiceless sigh. "What a world! Did he have any other family?"

"I don't think so. His wife died in childbirth, about twenty-odd years ago, just when I joined the force."

Doolan looked at the date on the envelope. "1886?"

Albrecht gave a puzzled smile. "Yeah, 1886."

"So the chapel must've been built in memory of his wife . . . ," Doolan said.

"What does that get us?" Albrecht asked.

"Nowhere. I still have a murder to solve, you still have a murder to solve."

"Okay, I get the message. Sure you have no matches?"

Doolan just grunted, and Albrecht started for the door.

"Anything on Bellarma, you know where I am, right?"

"Yeah."

Doolan looked out the window again, over the rooftops toward the church of San Salvadore. How did Saint Dismas figure into all of this? Perhaps he should pay another visit to Bridie.

Someone knocked on the door. Doolan turned to see Tom, looking in the prime of health, giving him a mock salute and smiling. Doolan gave him a sour look.

"Where the hell've you been?"

"I spent the night in Coney Island, minding me own business." Tom's smile spread to a grin and Doolan found himself smiling back. God, but he sometimes envied his brother's simple life!

"Come on, give up the worried brother look," said Tom. "I have a friend who wants to meet you."

Tom moved aside, and Araya stepped into the doorway. His clear, bright eyes focused on the policeman.

"This is my friend from Abyssinia, Araya Kebbede Kassai."

Doolan could tell it was going to be a long day.

CHAPTER 33

JENNY FELT STRANGE, sitting in Mrs. Flanagan's room. She had only been away for a night, yet she now felt like a visitor. The whole place seemed different to her; she looked at it with the feeling that her whole life had been turned around.

Mrs. Flanagan sensed this change and watched Jenny carefully as she ushered the younger woman into her room and offered her a glass of sherry. Jenny refused the drink and sat nervously at the edge of the overpadded ottoman. For a moment Jenny imagined that she was about to hear a speech on commitments. Mrs. Flanagan smiled, poured herself a drink, and seated herself in the winged armchair near her rolltop desk.

"You're thinking about leaving us, aren't you?"

Jenny swallowed hard, and looked away from Mrs. Flanagan. Leaving? In truth, she didn't know what she was thinking. Yesterday and last night at the hotel in Coney Island, Tom had opened up the prospect of a new life for her. There, in his arms, it had all seemed clear.

Now, without him, that "new life" seemed like a dream. She had slid down so far since she'd left the small farm at the end of the Ards peninsula. A week ago there had seemed to be only one salvation for her, through Bertha and Antonio and the words of Simon.

Jenny shook herself. Somewhere she heard Mrs. Flanagan repeat the question.

"Jenny, I said, are you thinking of leaving?"

"Maybe . . . I don't know. . . ." She looked at Mrs. Flanagan again. "Are you angry?"

The older woman smiled and twirled the sherry in her glass.

"No. And I will give you time to make up your mind. You can keep your room while you think about it."

"Thank you . . . thank you. I was going to collect some of my things."

"Whatever you want, Jenny."

Jenny smiled awkwardly. She was relieved. She stood up and walked to the door.

"Oh, one moment, dear."

Jenny turned back to see Mrs. Flanagan taking a book out of her desk. The madam handed it to her. "A young friend of yours left this for you yesterday."

"Thank you." Jenny took the book and gave it a quick glance as she left. It looked like one of those five-year diaries. It had a black-and-gold-leather spine, a flowery cloth cover, and a leather flap that led into a small lock.

She went into her room, closed the door, and sat on the bed. Who had left their diary for her? She took a deep breath, clicked open the lock, and opened the book. There was an inscription in a childish hand.

"THIS BOOK BELONGS TO BERTHA LANGMAN.
A PRESENT FROM HER MAMA AND PAPA.
CHRISTMAS, 1901."

Bertha! Jenny shivered. She remembered how she had walked off and left Bertha after the last meeting. And now Bertha had placed her life into Jenny's hands. She stared at it, not knowing if she dared read the diary. It might drag her back into the orbit of Abyssos.

For a long time Jenny sat, propped amongst the pillows, running her finger along the book's ridged spine. The smell of perfume leaked in under her door, and somewhere Susie was drowsily singing an English lullaby.

Jenny felt that she should leave the diary in her bedroom, unread, walk out, and meet Tom back at his brother's apartment. But something drew her to the book. Perhaps she had not fully closed the door on Abyssos. The thought made her shudder.

She took a deep breath and turned the pages. The diary seemed to divide into two parts. It started on January 1, 1902, but it also fell open somewhere late in the year 1904 where two pages were stuck together. Carefully she prized them apart with her forefinger. A dried flower fell into her lap. Very gently she picked it up. It was a small red rose, scarcely beyond the bud stage. The blossom was a dark, wine red, so rich in color that it seemed painted. She carefully laid it on the table beside her bed.

Flicking back to the beginning, she started to skim the entries, stopping occasionally to read in more detail. Bertha's life jumped off the page, in an elegant handwriting. It was the portrait of a young woman isolated from her neighbors and too old to play with her young brothers.

Jenny began to feel a little dirty. She should not have been reading this. She was rummaging around in a delicate and very private world, spying into a life that was meant to be closed. But that was absurd—Bertha had left the diary and must have intended her to read it. As she turned the pages, she began to feel a great tenderness toward her friend.

Before Jenny's eyes, Bertha grew older. At the beginning, she was filled with that special spiritual blossoming of the teenager, that first and very special thrust toward God.

"I will pray harder, so that His divine plan may be revealed to me."

It was a trusting, naive statement that pulled Jenny back to her own first declarations of faith. Jenny skipped through the months of early pieties. Then Bertha's attitudes began to change. It was time for her to enter the world.

Bertha started working as a claims clerk with the Long Island branch of the Industrial Audit and Policy Division of the Metropolitan Life Insurance Company. The women she worked with opened up a new world to her. They talked to her of things unmentioned in her strict home, of working women's rights and the love life of men and women.

One of them, Maisie Dixon, was older than the others. She had moved to New York from a small town in Kansas. Jenny determined from Bertha's comments that Maisie was sassy and outspoken.

"Oh, Maisie is so independent. To think, she left home and traveled so far, on her own. Now she can live her own life. I wish. I wish."

More and more, Maisie took over the pages. The mentions became obsessive, more passionate, the youthful adoration of an older person of the same sex. Those warm, exciting flushes of teenage love that bordered on the sexual. There was nothing clearly stated, but it took little skill to read between the lines of Bertha's sometimes breathless prose.

"Maisie looked so lovely today. She is so tall and yet so elegant. I wonder, are all Western pioneer women like her?"

And later,

"She is such a warm person. She is always sharing, yet always the leader. We love to hear her talk."

There were many entries about the "talk" and the "sharing." The obvious physical attraction was mingled with an intellectual stimulation. Pages were devoted to the books that Maisie loaned to Bertha. There were summaries of newspaper articles on the National American Woman Suffrage Association, notes on meetings she had gone to in Brooklyn. For weeks she was obsessed by her reading of *The Woman's Bible* by Elizabeth Cady Stanton. Bertha wrote:

"A commentary on the scriptures, written by women and from their point of view. It is very interesting, but scares me a little. I hide it from my father. My goodness, what would he think? He is so strict and Old Testament. I call him the patriarch, and Maisie laughs at me. Nonetheless, I shall return the book to her when I have finished it. I do not believe I could stand up to my father's wrath on its chance discovery in my room."

On the next page, Jenny read something that chilled her—the first intimations of Bertha's drift away from orthodoxy to the waiting chasm of Abyssos.

"Mrs. Stanton writes, 'In general, the Old Testament makes woman a mere afterthought in creation; the author of all evil; cursed in her maternity; a subject in marriage; and all female life, animal and human, unclean.'

"I read this late last night, and it stayed with me. I have risen early this morning to write it down, before I return the book to Maisie. I don't know what to think about it. It is somehow frightening. I know it will stay with me for a long time."

Jenny looked up. She could hear the piano in the parlor. A dreamy ballad of summer nights and moonlit rides rolled along the corridor. She looked down at the book again. Mrs. Stanton's reading of the Bible had indeed stayed with Bertha. It was one of the first books she had asked Jenny to read.

The Woman's Bible was returned and Maisie continued to open Bertha's mind to new women thinkers: Anna Howard Shaw, Carrie Chapman Catt, Elizabeth Blackwell, Susan B. Anthony. These names appeared over and over again, along with mention of the National American Woman Suffrage Association.

The young women at work had formed a kind of club of their own. Through the many earnest references, Jenny found herself creating a mental picture of their meetings, at a café called the Mayflower. She saw its spartan decor, the plain wooden furniture, the red-checkered tablecloths. On some evenings, but mostly on weekends, they would meet there for an hour's talk. Iced tea in the summer, hot chocolate in the fall. And opinions—round-faced, smooth-skinned, pretty girls, full of opinions. Rose, Margaret, Gertrude, Sadie, and of course Maisie, always Maisie. Maisie the leader, the eldest, the one whose ideas were always carefully recorded and nearly, but not always, agreed with. Bertha the girl was becoming a young woman, confident in her own opinions. In late November of 1906 she wrote:

"A glorious day. The sky was blue, oh so blue, and the brisk chill wind blew clouds across the heavens like fitful spring lambs. We met after church and went to the hall on Winderly Avenue. The tall elms are stark and bare, but strong and beautiful. Maisie talked to us on the way. She told us about the meeting, and all I could think was how she was like those elms, so strong and so sure.

"The speaker, a Mrs. Baldwin from New York City, was so wonderful and lucid. I think that soon

229

I shall decide to join the National American Woman Suffrage Association, no matter what Father thinks."

Jenny turned the page. There was a single stark entry scrawled in a jerky, hurried hand. It was violent in its brevity.

"Maisie told us that last night she became engaged to Mr. Lane, one of the agents of the Metropolitan. She was so happy! How could I have been so blind not to have known?

"I wish her only happiness!"

Jenny let out a little sigh. Poor Bertha! She was being allowed a glimpse into a hurt soul.

More blank pages; then, a week later;

"Late. Very late, Saturday night.

"I don't know what to write. Why? Why? Why did she do that to me! I thought she—"

Those last three words had a line through them. Jenny smiled sadly as the tears welled up. For a moment she set the diary aside, trapped in her own sorrow.

She remembered walking over to Ballywalter to see the father of her child. He was one of the Colvins, a rich, landowning family. William was a tall young man with a slight stoop and lank brown hair. She looked into his soft eyes and for the first time knew that what she had taken for warmth was, in fact, weakness.

He would not go away with her; didn't she understand how difficult that would be? He would be cut off from his family and friends if he married a Catholic. His father had arranged a job for him in India.

Jenny never saw him again. Her uncle had cynically

commented on how the long tentacles of the Protestant hierarchy stretched to the farthest ends of the Empire. She cared nothing for the politics; she knew only that her child's father was gone forever.

But that was years ago, and another past life. Jenny picked up the diary again. There were two weeks of blank pages and then a moderate-sized entry.

"I did it. I had an argument with her. I told her my objections to the Suffrage Association. It's funny, but when you stand back from her, Maisie is really a shallow person."

A number of similar entries followed, in which Bertha obviously exorcised her anger over her slighted love.

Then the entries became briefer.

Life was not as wonderful as it had been, and the sourness spilled into the contracted prose. There were complaints about her father's strictness, the boredom of her clerk's job, and the discomfort of having to see Maisie on a daily basis. Then came a strange episode. Bertha had gone down to the cellar late one night, with all her remaining pamphlets and newspaper clippings on the National American Woman Suffrage Association. She had opened the furnace and tossed them in, one after another, until they were all burned. Jenny could almost picture the glow lighting Bertha's face, her eyes glittering coldly with the passion of a youthful zealot.

That seemed to break the emotional logjam, and soon she came alive with a new idea. She got a letter from a cousin in Baltimore. The girl had become a telephonist. She could do that, too! She could be independent. New York City beckoned; that was the place for real advancement for a woman—Manhattan. The diary noted the arguments between her and her family.

"I have decided that I no longer wish to live here. My father, however, forbids me to leave. I want a new and modern job. There is something exciting in the new telephonist profession. I shall go to Manhattan, whatever he says. I must start a new life, and he shall not get in my way."

Jenny pushed the diary aside and quickly got up. Start a new life. That was what she herself was trying to do. She knew that Bertha's new life would lead to the brotherhood of Abyssos. But she didn't want to go that way. She put the diary in her bag. She would go back to Doolan's apartment and wait for Tom.

Doolan sat in Araya's hotel room and listened. Hour by hour Doolan sat, caught by the black man's clear, penetrating eyes. He heard the story of a man obsessed with seeking. He heard about Bellarma and the cult of Abyssos, of the manuscripts taken from the urn, and of how Araya had followed Bellarma halfway across the globe.

Doolan listened, and was deeply disturbed. He had the strange feeling that this man's tale could mend the cracks in his own shifting universe.

Tom was also entranced by the Abyssinian's story. He had known from the very first time they had met that this was a man who was different, set aside from others. But now, after he heard Araya's tale, he was in awe of the black man's mystic journey.

He recalled the day he had first seen Araya, at the port of Suez in East Africa. The man was striding along the newly constructed dock, walking around the creaking gantries and under the swaying bales of cotton, toward the gangplank of Tom's ship, the *Pretoria*. There was something almost regal in his straight-backed stride.

As he set foot on the gangplank, a small fat man in

an officer's cap appeared beside him and grasped his arm.

"Vat you vant, Kaffir?"

"Excuse me, what did you say?" Araya's English was stilted, but clear and precise in contrast to the coarse, corrupted accent of the Boer. The white man was taken aback by Araya's speech, bearing, and firm, unyielding look. For a moment he loosened his grip and stared. Then he let go.

"I say, vat de hell you goin' on de ship for, Kaffir?"

Araya lowered his head after a moment.

"I am sorry, sir. I wanted to see if there was work. Shipping across the Atlantic."

The Boer seemed satisfied. A tight, malicious little grin curled over his weak chin, and he stepped back from the giant Abyssinian, slapping the chain on the gangplank as he did.

"No, black boy, not vor you. Get de shit off dis plank."

Tom had seen all this. As the tall man turned to leave, he ran down the gangplank.

"Hey, sailor, wait a minute!" The man stopped and looked back. "I think we can use you, fella." Araya nodded, and Tom turned to confront the fuming Boer.

"Vat you doing, stoker?"

"I don't have to be reminding you, that due to the fine temper of our illustrious captain, we lost two of our blacks at Port Sudan. Now, if we don't get another man before clearing the canal, you'll be down in the boiler room yerself shoveling the black stuff. I'm telling you, two men along the coast I can do without, but midseas and a full watch, and we're done for."

The Boer looked from the stoker to the tall Abyssinian and back again. Clearing his throat, he spat over the edge of the dock. Then he shoved past Araya, and up the gangplank.

"Vell, de Kaffir's big, you may try him."

233

The stoker waited for the Boer to get out of sight, and then addressed his new crewmate. "You're hired. Have you ever shoveled coal before?"

"No, I have not, but I am sure I can do it."

Tom burst out laughing. "Bejaysus, I'm sure ye can; aren't you the honest beggar, though. Here, I think we're gonna get on well together."

He extended his hand. The man was apparently surprised by the spontaneous warmth of the gesture; for a moment he just stared. Then he leaned forward and pressed Tom's hand firmly.

"Thank you," he said.

"Ah, I need another hand. That wasn't a bowl o' mulligatawny I was handing him. Wait'll we get out in the Med. My name's Tom, Tom Doolan."

"And mine is Araya. Araya Kebbede Kassai."

Now Araya stood in a dingy Manhattan hotel room, revealing the true purpose of his journey.

For a long time quiet reigned. There were many questions to ask, but there was also much to absorb. Tom looked past Araya to the late-afternoon sky over the river and his mind drifted; to the sky over Suez; to the sky over Coney Island.

The previous day had been an oasis of love—and more, it was a dream of future and family. Jenny, Jenny. He had arranged to meet her at his brother's apartment. They were to go out to a show. He wanted to show her that there was a life beyond the sordid survival of the brothel.

He became aware that Araya was staring at him.

"You have something to do, Tom, please do not stay."

Doolan knew about Tom's arrangement and gave him a crooked smile.

"Go, for heaven's sake, you can't leave the lady waiting."

Tom frowned, wondering if they had some reason

234

to be rid of him. But that was impossible—they had just met.

"Tom, I have already told you of Abyssos and of Simon and the Snake of Knowledge," Araya said. "Now I must tell your brother."

"But don't you need me?"

"We need you, Tom, but not yet."

The words rang in Tom's mind as he turned to Doolan. "I may stay at a hotel tonight. Don't wait up."

Doolan nodded. His mind was filled with all the untied strands of the last week. Now everything was placed against the background of this monk and his obsessive search.

Tom left, and the door closed with a click behind him, a strangely final sound. Afterward there was silence, except for the noise of activity along the river. Araya closed the window and shut out the world.

He took a bag from under the bed and pulled out a book with a scarred leather binding. He held it for a second, then walked back to the table and sat down.

"The priest Bellarma took the manuscripts of Abyssos from their caves at Gebel Kalat, but there were other writings, writings about them. They were kept by the memhirs of my monastery, Biet Giorgis. We were meant to be the guardians. I think that you should hear what we know of the teachings of Abyssos. . . ."

Araya took a small cross from his pocket and kissed it. Then he placed it beside the book and opened to the first page.

CHAPTER 34

BERTHA WAS READY. As she walked along she repeated that to herself. Ready . . . ready . . . it was a chant of reassurance.

Oh, yes, of course she had doubts, lingering fears from those days when she had lived by the Christian ethic, but she would crush them. Now she had that acid gnawing of fear in the pit of her stomach, but when she joined the others they would help bring her through. They would make her proud, they would make her feel that this was the final act of denial against Jehovah/Ialdoboath. Through this she would release herself from her bonds, she would experience the releasing of the Light within her. Tonight she would free a soul trapped in her own flesh, free that spark of the divine so that it could join again with the true Godhead beyond the evil Jehovah.

She stood near the majestic Brooklyn Bridge, gazing north along the East River. The water shimmered, catching the last rays of the evening sun as they filtered between the clouds. To the west, reds and pinks glowed ominously over the New Jersey skyline. Her spirit soared: this city, this fiery cauldron of knowledge, reflected the heart of Abyssos. Knowledge wrought in the crucible of the fire. Yes, she was ready!

By the time she reached San Salvadore, the streets were buzzing with evening rush hour traffic. She walked up the alley behind the rectory garden and went in through the old gate in the wall. As she did she left the noise and the rush and the smells behind. The closing door shut her into silence, and for a moment she breathed it in, leaning back against the wood, gazing at the softening silhouettes of the trees in the growing dusk. All was quiet. The smell of the apples and pears mingled in a rich, sharp aroma. She breathed it deeply, then moved out of the shadow of the wall.

She had strolled through this walled garden approximately once every two weeks, during that whole, long summer, and somehow it always reflected her own inner changes. As the trees blossomed and bore fruit, so she had become a woman, and become a woman in a way that her friends would never know.

In the darkening night the church seemed a dark, brooding place. A cool dampness crept into her bones, causing her to shiver. She turned away for a moment, pulling a grape from a vine and rolling it between her fingers, breaking the skin. The red juice coated her flesh; she lifted her hand to her mouth, and slowly licked her fingers, saliva flowing freely at the tangy taste.

She plucked more grapes, filling her mouth with red sweetness. The rush of sensation opened the floodgates of anticipation. Tonight she would lie with three of them—a magic number. With the drug, her pleasure would whirl off into timelessness. Her heart began to beat faster. It was as though every nerve in her body had come alive again.

Across the garden came the sound of a door slamming. Bertha quickly stepped back into the shadow of the wall. She saw Bridie standing on the gravel path. The housekeeper dropped some keys into her bag. So, she was going out. It really didn't matter what she did anyway. Simon, whom she still knew as Father Schmidt, did not allow her access to the vaults. Those catacombs under the church were the gift of Gallenini and only Simon had the key, Simon and the veiled one, his handmaiden. She felt a breath of cold on the hairs along her neck. The shadowy one. They whispered that she . . . no, she would not think of that tonight. They were waiting for her in the catacombs and corridors beyond Gallenini's tomb.

Jenny had thought that the walk back through the crowded streets to Doolan's apartment on West Fifty-third would rid her mind of thoughts of Bertha and her diary, but it was not so.

Inside Doolan's apartment she paced from room to room. Then she felt that familiar stirring deep in her stomach, and a cold sweat rushed to her brow and neck. The dark, beckoning memory of the morphine was beginning to surface. She began to gasp, then steeled herself. Damn it, no! She would not go back to that. She must do something, anything, to divert herself until Tom arrived. Bertha's life would take Jenny's mind off her own.

She cleared a space at Doolan's cluttered desk and opened the book.

"I must start a new life and Father shall not get in my way."

Jenny almost laid the diary aside again. A new life . . . Wasn't that what she wanted too?

Then she started reading. After a few pages, the tone changed. The news was better. Bertha's father had relented. She was allowed to flee the nest.

"Father told me that my uncle Henry has invited me to live with him and his family. They have a fine house on East 29th Street. I like my three little cousins, though I am sure they can be monsters, like Bill and George.

"I think it will be fun. Pray God I pass the telephonist's test. I go for it on Tuesday, at number 52 West Houston Street, the new Spring Exchange.

"Tuesday night, late. I got it! I got it! I can't believe it. They want me to start next week, if I

238

can. What am I saying? Of course I can. Mother and Father grudgingly say it is all right. And I owe no long notice to Metropolitan Life. Oh, I feel so excited! I will change my life. I must discipline myself, to get ahead. The world is mine oyster!"

The account became more of a work log. Bertha gave the times of her shifts, the hours she worked, the names of her co-workers and superintendents, the number of calls she logged. It was all dry and businesslike. The new Bertha was a lady of the world.

Jenny flipped through weeks of an occasional personal note sprinkled in a barrage of work. Then she stopped: here was something different, in a different pen.

"This was the first time that I spoke to Antonio."

Antonio. Jenny put the diary aside for a moment. She had known that Bertha and Antonio were close, but now she could see more clearly. He must have been her first introduction to the cult.

Jenny picked up the diary again. It was pitiable and frightening at the same time. Bertha was full of the flutterings of new love, but Jenny suspected that on Antonio's part this was just a cynical attempt to bring Bertha into the brotherhood.

Jenny wanted to see if they had used the same ploys on her. For days there was a simple repetition of the same entry,

"Antonio phoned."

Then the entries grew longer. Jenny could see Bertha becoming more and more intrigued by her telephonic suitor. Of course, the business woman did not completely disappear; there were still notes on work, but the hot breath of romance was there. Flicking forward, Jenny stopped at the page with the reddish stain. The imprinted outline of the rose stood out against the white paper. The entry read:

> *"I met Antonio today for the first time. Oh, he is handsome! I did not wear my eyeglasses."*

In the pages after the imprint of the rose, the prose began to blossom. Bertha wrote of a moment in the park, of walking by the river, of hours spent dallying in restaurants.

Jenny felt a great closeness to her. She remembered her day with Tom, sauntering through the amusement park, drifting on a gondola along the Venetian canal, and the hours of talking and lovemaking at the hotel last night. But Bertha's love took a different path.

> *"Antonio has talked to me of his group. They are enlightened young men and women like him, interested in another way."*

Another way. Jenny felt a twinge. These were the same words that Bertha had used to her. Now she could watch the angler dangling his bait.

> *"A. is so intelligent and lucid. Everything he says makes sense. He tells me that he does not want to say more, but I press him to do so. Above all else in this world, I want that knowledge, and tonight I told him this. It seemed to please him, more than anything I had said before. He told me that if I was sincere, then he would help me, for knowledge would indeed bring me to the true God-Beyond-God.*
>
> *"I feel so excited, so alive that I can scarcely write."*

Jenny could feel the nerves in her stomach tightening. One part of her wanted to put the book away, but she was drawn on, fascinated. There was a gap of about a week, devoid even of the hieroglyphics of work schedules. Then another late-night entry:

"I have met some of them, some of the group. They are wonderful people. Tonight, I heard for the first time of Simon and the cult of Abyssos. They say it is an understanding, like light breaking over one, but I have felt it already. If there is more, then truly, as they say, knowledge will be ecstasy for me."

Then,

"I met Jenny."

So now she came into the story.

"Met Jenny again at one of our 'front' meetings, where we fish for converts. Oh, but she is an innocent for all her profession!"

Jenny felt like an insect under a microscope. She read on, feeling angered and slightly violated.

"Jenny and I talked again. How her life intrigues me! It is difficult to get her to talk about it, but I love to inveigle bits and pieces from her. In that way I can piece together her encounters and imagine them, treasure them, in the quiet of my own room. I lie there, feeling only the touch of sheets against my skin, and I think of the men she has had, and then I wish—oh, how I wish!"

Jenny clamped her hands to her forehead. She pressed hard, then ran her hands through her hair as though that would somehow brush away the memories. She felt a great rush of distaste for herself and her life. She wanted to see Tom again, someone who would make her feel clean.

She took a couple of deep breaths and steadied herself. It was both scary and in a strange way a gift to be able to see yourself through the eyes of others.

She brushed beads of sweat from her temples and glanced at the diary again. Surely she still had some courage left.

"*A. has asked me to join the inner circle of the cult. I am deeply moved. Soon I shall have to leave this diary aside. All my thoughts and all my energy shall be given to the brothers and sisters, the seekers of the Light.*

"*I would love to bring Jenny with me, but she is so very much on the outside, not daring to take the step to join the brothers and sisters of Abyssos. I cannot understand. I wallow in the thrill of degradation. She does not understand that her life has brought her halfway to the Truth. She does not know the secret scriptures, but if she did, then she would see how close to Light she is.*

"*It is written, 'For the Light of Knowledge will come when you have eaten of every pasture, and when you have trod upon the vesture of shame, and when two shall be one, neither male nor female.'*

"*Oh, Jenny, how I wish you would join with us.*"

Jenny shook her head in disbelief. Had her life brought her halfway toward their Light, their Truth? She thought of Bertha and the laughter they had shared. Now she saw her friend walking down this road into the shadows. She would have to talk to her, to make Bertha see.

There was a noise of a key in the door. Jenny jumped up, and when Tom came in, all thoughts of Bertha left her head. She could talk to her friend tomorrow.

It was a decision that was to open the dark doors of guilt.

242

CHAPTER 35

BERTHA SAT IN the stillness of the chapel, deeply inhaling the incense-laden air. Here was a power that would bring her beyond this world and the horror that was Jehovah's creation. She had touched the Light and would touch it again, would consume herself in the fire of the Truth. When she had smashed through the deceptions and the tricks, the laws of the Torah and the Christian Bible, then that Light would be hers. She was one of the elect.

She had asked Antonio to leave her. He would be with the others, down in the sanctuary of Saclas, the Archon of Fornication.

She looked up at the flame behind the red glass, which threw its light over the smooth surface of the altar. She would be lying there soon.

She shivered. The chill of fear was rising again within her. It was something she would have to conquer. Surely it was embedded in the guilt that Jehovah had molded into her. It was a sickening feeling in the pit of her stomach. She embraced herself tightly and slowly rocked to and fro on the floor. They must not see her like this. This was her night. She would join them in the sanctuary of Saclas, and then come back here for . . . for . . . She dug her nails into her forearms. The pain drove her fears away.

It was time. Beside her on the dark polished wood floor was a syringe. She stared at it for a moment. The others had used theirs, she was the last. She picked it up and examined the purity of the sharp point. Like a lover, it would enter her, like all lovers combined into one, and shoot pleasure through her. It would bring her comfort, the rich warm feeling of belonging. Then she would know again the Truth within her. She murmured, "For there is Light within man and it illuminates the whole world."

She pulled up the sleeve of her blouse and yanked a leather strap tight around the flesh. She watched the soft, pink flesh in the crook of her arm as the bluish vein first showed itself and then slowly bulged. Holding up the syringe, she saw the lamp glow through the pure liquid. Yes, this would bring her closer to the Light that was within her.

She placed the needle against the vein, and clenched her teeth as she drove it in. Soon all Knowledge would be hers, Knowledge that would allow her to burst beyond the evil Jehovah/Ialdoboath to the True Godhead. The drug pumped its way through her veins. At first the rush was almost unbearably pleasurable. The red light danced bizarrely over the altar, her breath sounded like wind in her ears. But soon everything steadied and she felt a strong flow of confidence.

She waited for a few minutes and slowly got to her feet. She felt almost as though she were floating. They were waiting for her in the sanctuary of Saclas.

"I sowed no children for the ruler." She mumbled the words in a gentle slur, and rubbed her hand over her stomach. Something was stirring in there, another trapped soul, pulled from Abyssos, imprisoned in the fleshly creations of Jehovah.

She smoothed her dress and moved to the door, then along the dimly lit corridor and down the circular stone stairwell. As she neared the lower level, she could hear laughter spiraling over the wild beat of a drum. She walked down another set of steps. The sounds grew louder and wilder. At the bottom, Bertha entered a large cellar. There were stone pillars stretching along its length, each supporting dim oil lights, and scattered throughout were couches, piled high with cushions. In one corner a young man sat, playing a pair of tall African drums. His look was vacant; his head swayed to the rhythm of his hands.

On some of the couches, couples were in various stages of fornication. It stimulated Bertha to stand and watch. Bodies naked and half-naked, all immersed in a tide of debauchery. And debauchery was the only way, for only by despising and degrading this physical prison of flesh could the soul go through to the true paradise, Abyssos. That perverted thrill at committing what Jehovah/Ialdoboath named Sin was really the rejoicing of the soul as it reached out to Abyssos. These were the teachings of Simon, and Bertha felt a deep electricity, a knife-edge thrill of ecstasy as she watched the couplings.

She felt someone touching her arm and slowly focused on Antonio's face. He was staring down at her.

"Are you ready, Bertha?" he asked.

"I have prepared myself," she replied.

There was no more to be said. Tonight, three of her lover-brothers would come inside her, one after another. And thus they would repay to the flesh the things of the flesh, and to the soul the things of the soul, for the soul resided in the semen.

Bertha moved as if in a dream to a large couch near the center of the temple, and stretched back on it. The drug swirled her off into pulsing fantasy. Pleasure broke in waves upon her as first one, then another, and another came into her and left.

Afterward she lay as though floating on water in a netherworld. She felt satisfied. Every man who had pushed himself into her had struck another blow against the laws of the upstart God Jehovah/Ialdoboath. A hand passed gently over her body. She

245

looked up and saw Antonio. She groaned a little and extended her arms.

"Come . . . please, Antonio. . . ."

"We must go, Bertha. Simon is waiting."

"Please, Antonio—just you alone. . . ."

She sat up and stretched out to touch him. He flinched and stepped backward.

"No. They are waiting for you."

They. She could not remember who "they" were. She was unable to keep control of her thoughts. The throbbing, sensual feeling once more engulfed her.

"Please, Antonio . . . plea—"

She found herself standing. Antonio had her under the arms.

"Do you want to disappoint Simon?"

"No, no. I'm sorry. . . ."

"Come on, I'll help you."

He half carried her to the base of the stairs. She staggered upward, supported on his arm. At the top, he steered her toward the chapel door. This was the final act after the indulgence with Saclas, the Archon of Fornication.

Antonio opened the door and led Bertha into the room. Everything seemed fluid. There was a dreamy inevitability to her actions. She walked forward and laid her hands on the cold stone of the altar. A firm, cold shudder of reality went through her as she stared up at the flickering red light, the flame struggling to ascend to the unknowable Godhead, beyond the evil, prideful One who proclaimed that there was no other God but Him.

She could feel Antonio's hand on her elbow, helping her to climb onto the stone. The surface was sensuously cold after the hot sexual thrusts of her lovers. Once more the drug surged through her, a sweetness beyond measure. She spread her legs.

The voice pierced her dream, clear and alluring.

"You are welcome."

Then that other voice, the whispered half growl, a chilling echo of the other.

"Welcome."

Bertha slowly opened her eyes and gazed at them where they stood on either side of her. Suddenly she recoiled in fear. The one with the porcelain face and the veil of a nun! The porcelain had been painted, like a drunken whore; a slash of red across the mouth; red-spotted cheeks and blue-lidded eyes. Somehow this was more terrifying than the blank white mask Bertha had seen before. But beside her stood *him,* smiling. He, whom the church knew as Father Schmidt, the snake master, Simon. Slowly he lifted above his head and donned the mask of the snake.

Antonio came into view between them. He carried a tray, which he set down on a shelf near the altar.

Simon spoke in a soothing and sensual tone. He asked, and Bertha answered. This was the catechism of Abyssos.

"What were we?"

"Light."

"What have we become?"

"Slaves."

"Who enslaved us?"

"Ialdoboath, who calls himself Jehovah, the jealous god."

"Where were we?"

"Residing within the Light of Abyssos, in the pleroma."

"Where have we been cast?"

"Into the mud, the creation of the Archon Jehovah."

"Whither do we hasten?"

"Back to the unknowable, Abyssos."

"From what are we freed?"

"From the foul corruption that is flesh."

"What is birth?"

"The smothering of the flame."

"Are you prepared, sister?"

The answer was in her head. She had thought of nothing for the last week. The words were there, damn it. The words were there. Why couldn't she grasp them? She was awash in the dulling tide of the drug.

Bertha felt a needle prick the skin in her groin, and a numbness spread from it. She stared dreamily at Antonio as he withdrew the syringe, and then turned to Simon, his eyes glittering in the coils of the snake mask.

He spoke firmly but seductively. "For it is written in the texts, 'Death shall hold sway as long as women bring forth.'"

She started to respond, but the breath caught in her throat. At last she found her voice and spoke out loud and clear.

"I gather myself from all sides. I sow no children for the evil Archon Jehovah. I tear up His roots. I know Jehovah for what He is, because I am from the realms beyond. I am Light, and Light resides in me."

So it was finished. The two stepped aside, making room for Antonio. He bent over the tray and turned back to the altar, holding a long, thin needlelike instrument. For a moment it was poised, glittering in the wavering red light. Then he moved toward her. Suddenly they grasped her legs and held them firm. She looked up to see the quivering stilettolike needle, and sucked in a sharp breath.

Doolan stood by the window of Araya's room and gazed out over the East River. Here and there, lights were reflected along its dark surface. Tugboats chugged along, pushing barges, churning up a white phosphorescence behind. On the opposite bank, Brooklyn glowed against the September night sky. All seemed right with the world, in order, as it had always been. But Doolan's mind was reeling. Araya had conjured up an alien world, opened a window into a chilling darkness full of heresy and perversion.

Araya began to read again from the book of the memhirs.

> "'They have milestones in the growth of their "knowledge," on the journey to their Godhead. Epiphanius, a father of the Roman rite, has written in a book called the Panarion: "And though they would have sexual union, one with another, man with man, and woman with man, the bearing of children is anathema to them. It is their teaching that the act of sex glorifies Abyssos through the intercession of Saclas, the Archon of Fornication. Thus are their degraded orgies exalted, and their fornications transfigured into religious acts. It is also their teaching that the imprisonment of another soul in flesh is an evil that cannot be tolerated."
>
> "'It follows then that if a female of their number is found to be with child, it behooves them to destroy it. And thus they distort the meaning of the Scriptures, which say "For behold, the days are coming when they will say Blessed are the Barren, and the wombs that never bore, and the breasts that never gave suck." Luke chapter twenty-three: verse twenty-nine.
>
> "'The state of barrenness is thusly perverted into a holy state and within their circle all new life is terminated.
>
> "'Those who are of the inner group of initiates perform an inhuman act of abortion in denial of Jehovah and in celebration of Abyssos. The embryo is extracted and smashed with a pestle in a mortar, and when they have mixed in honey and pepper and other condiments and spices to prevent vomiting, they each take a piece of the discarded life in their fingers and eat it.'"

Doolan turned away toward the dark river again, disgusted. God, but the Church Fathers loved their lurid details—and yet, wasn't that his own job, the reconstruction of personal descents into hell? He recalled his discussion with the coroner, Feinberg, earlier in the week. "She would have become a mother, had she lived." Was there a connection?

Araya spoke again, in a more conversational tone. "There is one in this city who believes he is Simon of the cult Abyssos, Simon reborn. Bellarma told me this, and I believe him. He told me that this Simon did not want the knowledge in the manuscripts to be seen by any who were not of Abyssos, wanting the word only for himself and his followers. I believe that Bellarma was killed by one of those followers. Bellarma either had the manuscripts on him, or they are still in the Pendleton house."

Doolan closed his eyes, trying to make sense of it all. He wanted this week to disappear from his memory. He turned to Araya. "All right then, tomorrow morning I'll go to the morgue and search Bellarma's effects for these manuscripts—and if they're not there, then they must be with Pendleton or in his house."

Doolan thought of Virginia. He would go back to Centre Market and phone her. He would find out if she had heard from Pendleton or knew anything about the manuscripts.

CHAPTER 36

Bertha woke slowly. A red light flickered rhythmically above her, and in her half-dream state she thought she was watching her own heart pulsing and pumping. She hugged herself, shivering as she slowly emerged from her drowsiness. She realized that she was lying on the altar, and the memories flooded back: the cold instrument slipping deep into her, its sharp point gouging out the new life that had begun.

She sat up on the altar and gazed around the empty room. A large silver chalice glistened on a side table. She stared at it for a long time. The drug was still pulsing through her body, distancing everything. She started to tremble, violent shudders that spread outward from her loins. She had done it, she had rid herself of the life inside her. The silver chalice came into focus. She saw the drops of blood, congealed on one side, crusting orangy red. At the base rested three silver spoons.

She swung her legs off the altar and, grasping its side, stood. She tottered forward. The room started to spin around her.

She stopped and stared at the chalice and spoons again. Yes, they had gone through with it. She had given them their offering. She felt sick; a weakness swept over her. She sagged down onto her knees and rested her forehead against the cool stone. It had really happened!

She tried to piece together all the teachings of the

cult so that she could justify her actions, but found her eyes fixed on the chalice. Dried, crusted blood stained the vessel's lip and side. Bertha growled despairingly through her teeth. She wanted to cry, but the tears wouldn't come. She staggered toward where she had piled her clothes. She needed to get dressed.

Then she remembered Antonio had told her to lie still, that it would not be good for her to move around. She couldn't recall why—all she wanted to do was to get away from this horror.

She put her hand down between her legs and touched a bandage of some kind. The numbness was ebbing and she could feel a growing soreness. She began dressing. She had to get out, to get away. She glanced once more at the blood drying on the chalice, then with trembling hands buttoned her jacket.

She didn't want to see any of them now, not even Simon. She just wanted to get back to her room and go to bed. She wanted to slip into the lavender smell of her sheets and nuzzle her face deep into her pillow.

Bertha tottered unsteadily toward the door and carefully opened it. The corridor was quiet and empty. She staggered into the dark stone passageway. She was trembling, covered in a cold sweat.

She had to get out. Then she heard footsteps in the stairwell. In panic, she started looking for a way to escape, anywhere. She staggered across the corridor and fell against a heavy wooden door, wrenching at the handle. She twisted it one way and then another, and when it finally opened, she pushed in and slammed it behind her.

The footsteps stopped at the top of the stairwell as though the person had heard something out of place.

Bertha held her breath. Please, God. Please, someone—Abyssos, Saclas, even Jehovah. Don't let them come in here. She clenched her fists tightly by her side. A gas lamp burned with a low flame on the left wall. Bertha quickly moved over to turn it down, and heard the footsteps start again. They were coming toward the door. Terror was paralyzing her mind. Her eyes darted around the room, searching for another way out. On the back wall was a door. As quietly as possible, Bertha scurried across the room, opened the door, and slipped into the closet. Drawing the door shut behind her, she heard a click as the door to the room opened. Someone walked in.

Bertha could scarcely breathe. It was dark and stifling in the closet. Panic was choking her, but she held it in. She knelt and put her eye to the keyhole. At first she could see nothing; then the figure of the nun came into view. The chilling porcelain face peered around the room, and for a moment that white mask pointed at the closet door. Bertha felt a hand reaching in and stilling her heart, a cold, icy gauntlet clutching at it. The black gouges that were the eyes glared with a dark malevolence. The woman, if that's what it was, always scared her in the ceremonies, and here they were alone, just the two of them.

For what seemed like an hour Bertha stared at the door. She felt weak in the legs; her whole body was drenched in sweat. As she began to faint, she saw the nun slowly turn and leave the room. Bertha collapsed in relief.

It was still in the closet, very still. There was only the sound of her own breathing. She closed her eyes. Oh, God, she wanted to sleep, to get back to the safe comfort of her bed. It was then that she became aware of the plopping sound.

It sounded so close, as if it was inside the closet.

She jumped up, hands reaching for the cold stone behind her. Her gaze swept the dark recesses of the closet as her hand groped for the door handle. The light filtering through the keyhole allowed her to see something bulky in the greyness.

She located the handle of the closet door, twisted it open, and fell backward into the room. Regaining her balance, Bertha peered into the closet. An agonized scream choked in the dryness of her throat. Eyes wide in horror, she staggered back, shuddering.

Pendleton's body hung, head down, over a pan half-filled with blood. The plopping sound was the blood dripping from his wounds. The liquid in the pan shimmered with each falling drop. The body slowly pivoted. The bloodied face came into view, and the whites of the eyes caught the light and glittered. It was as though he had blinked into life. Bertha choked, and fled the room, racing along the corridor.

A wild, terrified screech was ringing in her brain, but only a stifled sob escaped her. Death was everywhere! The death of the fetus within her, the death of this man. Within her the pain started again, and with it, the fear. Was this the beginning of her own death?

She reached the top of the circular stairwell and lunged downward. At the bottom she tripped, falling hard onto the stone floor of the corridor, gouging her left knee. But she felt nothing; she was possessed only by the frantic need to escape. She picked herself up and staggered forward.

There was the way out—through the door into Gallenini's crypt. But she was afraid to go that way. She turned and headed for another stairway that would bring her up to an entrance by the side of the church.

She ran up the last steps and fell against the outer door, felt for the latch and lifted it. The door swung open. Bertha ran to the nearest part of the orchard wall and followed it to the gate.

A jagged pain cut across her abdomen. She reeled back against the stone. A searing bolt of pain twisted into her. She doubled over, clutching herself. Antonio had warned her to be still afterward. God only knew what she had done to herself. She threw open the gate, lurched into the street, and staggered away from the church. She would get home, whatever else. Home, away from the faceless terror of the eyeless mask.

Jenny had finally become engrossed in the show. She turned to Tom, and for the first time that night he could see a smile in her dark eyes. She had been distracted since he picked her up. He knew that something was bothering her, but he did not press her. He just wanted them to be together.

Jenny laughed loudly at the quick patter of the comedian, and was held rapt by the tricks of Menzinni's juggling act. But most of all she was mesmerized by the color and flair of the chorus girls. Her mouth fell open every time the Ziegfeld Girls danced across the stage, in yet another set of costumes. There were girls in furs and silks, girls decked with feathers and flowers, and every one of them glittering. It was as though someone had thrown a thousand diamonds into the air, and captured it all in light.

During the intermission they stayed in their seats and held hands. Tom told her a story from his childhood, something about bees and a glass jar and his brother Peter. She didn't hear the details; she just watched his eyes sparkle when he talked to her and realized that she wanted his child: a child that would be like the child that lived in his eyes.

Then suddenly a startling thought came to mind. Was that the cause of Bertha's actions? Was that what the ominous tone of the diary foretold?

The drums began a long roll, and Tom and Jenny glanced quickly back at the stage. At first it was dark, then the spotlight snapped on to reveal a man dressed as an Indian maharaja. He wore a bejeweled turban and a long flowing gown.

The music from the orchestra pit took a vaguely Eastern turn, and one of the chorus girls, dressed like an Arabian houri, came out and slipped off the man's robes. Underneath, he had on nothing but an elaborate loincloth, and his slender build and deep brown color suggested that he was indeed Indian.

The houri gave a deep bow and spoke: "Ladies and gentlemen, presenting Maharani, the grand fakir of Delhi, India."

The audience applauded politely as Maharani walked to the backcloth and gestured it to rise. As it did, the lights came up on what looked like the contents of a medieval torture room. The women in the audience gasped at the sight. Knives and swords dangled from a beam, glittering. A long wooden board covered with spikes lay atop a table. The points glistened viciously. Maharani took a short piece of metal and tapped each. A series of clangs reverberated through the auditorium, and then the act started in earnest.

The man lay down on the bed of nails. He balanced swords on his face. He took long, thin rapiers and thrust them through the pinched skin of his side. By now the audience was squirming. A number of ladies were stifling screams behind perfumed handkerchiefs. Jenny gripped Tom's hand so hard that he felt his fingers going numb. Her eyes were wide in disbelief. He watched her more than the fakir—he had seen these tricks before, on voyages to Bombay, Calcutta, and other ports around the Indian Ocean.

The music changed, and Tom's attention snapped back to the stage. There was only a lone Indian flute being played now. The fakir was sitting beside a large reed basket. Notes tumbled from the pipe in a lulling drone. After about half a minute, the houri entered and untied two cords that held down the basket lid. She left quickly. The fakir waited for a moment, leaned over, and lifted the woven top. He placed it beside him, and gripping the pipe in both hands, launched into a hypnotic drone.

Within seconds a dark yellow, diamond-shaped head appeared over the rim of the basket. For a moment the audience did not notice it, then the snake's forked tongue darted out, and a long, dangerous hiss jolted the watchers. This time Tom grabbed Jenny's hand, squeezing it hard.

Suddenly his dreams of the last few days made sense. He had not put it all together when he was listening to Araya. The snake that he had seen obscuring their faces in his dreams was the Snake of Knowledge! They were all in danger from this thing they called Abyssos!

The fakir swayed from side to side and the snake seemed to mimic his movement. It uncoiled slowly, its weaving muscularity looking more and more dangerous as it cleared the basket's rim.

Tom was not a squeamish man, but he felt a strange panic rising in him. The snake had finally come for his brother—for all of them. He stared at the sheen on its skin, gasping. He stared at the dangerous, tempting eloquence of its swaying motion, and he knew it was a sign.

There was a moan from an aisle seat only five rows ahead of him. A large matronly woman could take it no more, and, standing up in an attempt to leave, she fainted, tumbling onto the floor.

There was a general stir in the audience. All eyes turned to her as an usher came forward and helped her to the back of the stalls. Tom did not look. He kept his eyes focused on the supple body of the snake. Midway through its swaying motion, it jerked, and Tom knew what had happened.

The commotion in the stalls had broken the primitive, mesmeric bond between flute and viper. Tom watched helplessly as the cobra's hood flared out like a scaly disk. The white spots caught the glare of the lights, like eyes.

Suddenly the snake's tongue darted out with a long threatening hiss. The fakir yelled and fell back, grasping at his eyes. Tom was transfixed. He could think only of his dreams of Araya and Peter. He stared as the fakir lunged forward blindly and grasped the cobra by the neck. As he wrestled it to the stage floor, the assistant rushed on and together they put it back in the basket. Rubbing his eyes furiously, the little fakir stood to receive the applause of the audience.

Tom could not tell if it was all a trick, but it was a potent symbol. When the curtain fell and the orchestra started a medley of sprightly tunes, Tom turned to Jenny. He felt drained and sweat soaked, but he was surprised to see that she was white and trembling, her eyes fixed on some point beyond the curtain.

"Jenny?"

"Tom . . . let's go, please, right now."

"Of course."

Jenny and Tom started up the aisle. The lights dimmed and the audience turned to listen to the hit song of the year. The curtain lifted, revealing a hay wagon with Nora Bayes and Jack Norworth perched on top. A full moon appeared on a deep blue sky and they started to sing "Shine on, shine on harvest moon . . ."

The young lovers did not hear the singers. Their minds were filled with knowledge and fear. The Snake had invaded their lives.

CHAPTER 37

GLADYS OPENED THE cellar door and looked into the mirror on the back of it. "I look a sight!" She took her comb from the shelf under the glass and stroked the hair back from her forehead, sighing. She was through for the night. She had served her mistress's dinner and now she could leave.

The tension in the house was unbearable. Mr. Pendleton still had not returned, and that awful thing had happened to the little priest. She gave a shudder. Well, she would go out and relax. She took the comb and leaned into the mirror.

She was so engrossed in fixing her hair that she did not hear the footsteps. There was only a light padding on the stone steps that led down to the basement door. It was that blind time of twilight, when shapes meld with deepening shadows. At the bottom of the steps, the figure stopped, and for an instant, an eye peered through the small, dusty window, seeing the maid combing her hair, the jacket and hat nearby. She was going out. Already another servant had left. Soon the house would be almost empty. Almost.

Gladys spun around and squinted at the window. She was sure that someone had been watching her. But there was nothing there. She dismissed her feelings. The events of the last few days were making her jittery.

She set down her comb and grabbed her jacket and

hat. Gladys ran across the kitchen, up the back stairs and into the dining room.

Virginia was seated at the table. She turned as Gladys entered.

"I'm off then, ma'am," the younger woman said.

"Have a nice evening, Gladys. When will you be in?"

"Oh, I . . . I might be staying with a friend. I'd be back by seven in the morning, if that's all right?"

Gladys was blushing and Virginia quickly looked aside so as not to embarrass her further. "Of course, I didn't mean to pry. I just didn't want to wake up in the middle of the night, and think someone was prowling." Virginia laughed dryly at her own attempted levity. Gladys said good-bye and left the room.

Gladys's departure from the kitchen spurred the watcher to action. It slipped inside silently, and flitted across the large room, past the stoves and under the lines of copper pots and pans gleaming dully in the flickering yellow gaslight.

Then it heard Gladys returning. It pulled back, seeking a hiding place, its breath rasping.

The wine-cellar door was still ajar. The intruder swished over the polished floorboards and halted under the lintel. On the back of the door was the mirror. Turning to look for the maid, the prowler caught sight of its own reflection. It gave a savage growl and swept the glass to the floor. The creature pulled back into darkness.

Gladys sprinted down the last few steps to see the mirror lying splintered on the floor. How could that have fallen? She leaned over to see the damage. It wasn't too bad. It had broken into three main parts. There might be small fragments, but she could collect them later. She picked up the large pieces and laid them on the long wooden bench by the sink. There went seven years' bad luck. And it would start with

Mervyn, if she didn't leave soon.

Outside, she carefully locked the kitchen door. But she had locked in some of the dark.

Sitting at the dinner table, Virginia heard the distant smash of something on the kitchen floor. She dismissed it as a plate, and then set her dinner aside. She could not eat; her mind was in turmoil. Her earlier conversation with Detective Albrecht had all but convinced her that Pendleton was dead. She jumped up from her chair and paced the room. It was a terrible thing to contemplate. She had prepared herself to be angry with him, even to sue for divorce, but not to hear that he was dead.

She needed to talk to someone. She needed to have some perspective on the last few days. Doolan came to mind once again. She had left a message for him that afternoon, but he had not called her back. She glanced toward the hall door. Perhaps she should swallow her pride and call him again.

No. She shook her head and took a deep breath. She would occupy herself. She walked purposefully into the living room and crossed to the cherrywood desk. She would finish the household accounts.

Suddenly the telephone rang and she spun around with only one thought.

Doolan.

When Doolan had walked into his office, he was suddenly swamped with the responsibilities of the real world. He found it comforting. His journey with Araya had left him drained.

There was an ashtray on his desk, jammed full of cigarettes and cigar stubs. The air felt heavy and stuffy. Doolan crossed to the window and slammed it open, gulping in the cool night air.

"Goddamn smell!"

The desk was cluttered with lists and notes. He gazed down at the mess and slumped into his chair.

He pinched the top of his nose with his fingers and rubbed the corners of his eyes. He yawned and started in on the pile.

There was a note from Cassassa:

"No breakthrough on the cloth—see our work sheets—if you had similar luck, maybe we should take up fishing the Hudson for more parts!"

Doolan sniffed. Sometimes Frank crossed the line of good taste. He read on.

"O'Neal is off for two days—remember weekends? Ferrais might be moving McKenna to Albrecht's priest case; seems like they're taking the ticket collector's story seriously.

"Tomorrow's a bad day in the garment district—Saturday closedown—I want to try something else, the morphine angle. I have good contacts along the riverfront."

Saturday already. Lord above, where had the week gone? Doolan grunted. So Frank would ask among the illegal morphine dealers. It was a good idea. He should have thought of it himself. He was losing his touch. He read on.

"Where the hell were you?

"Mrs. Virginia Pendleton called—an enticing voice."

Doolan tossed the note onto the desk. Enticing. Cassassa was a sharp one. He never used words carelessly. There was also a note from Albrecht:

"I spoke to Mrs. Pendleton—thanks for the lead—a strange tale my friend, manuscripts and snakes—I think I prefer dollar bills and guns—

Don't tell your society ladyfriend, but I have a hunch we may be looking for another body soon."

"Christ!" There was a bluntness about policemen that sometimes took his breath away. Doolan looked through his other notes and stopped as he came to a brief one in police stenographer's copperplate.

"Mrs. Virginia Pendleton called. She asks you to return her call when you come in."

Doolan glanced up from the note and out into the night. Then he picked up the phone and asked the police operator for the Pendletons' number. While he listened to it ringing, he scanned Albrecht's note again.

Another body. He had thought that himself but he had not voiced it. For almost half a year he had allowed himself the occasional daydream that Virginia would one day need him. And now, since the death of Bellarma and his talk with Araya, Doolan was certain that she did need him.

Finally someone answered the phone. He was just about to slam down the earpiece and take a cab up to the East Side when he heard the click and a female voice.

"Hello."

"Oh, hello. Mrs. Pendleton?"

"Yes?" she said.

"It's Lieutenant Doolan of the N. Y. P. D."

"Oh, Lieutenant, I was hoping it was you."

Doolan didn't know what to say, but he knew that he had to keep his guard up. This woman was too much in his mind and heart as it was.

"Is there any news? I mean, has your husband returned?"

"No, no he hasn't. Is there any news from Lieutenant Albrecht?"

"No, but that doesn't mean anything." Doolan gazed at Albrecht's note. "Another body." He would not tell her.

Virginia broke the strained silence. "I would like to talk to you—in person."

"I'll come over as soon as I can." Doolan didn't think before replying.

After speaking to Doolan, Virginia felt elated. She stood for a while in the shadowed hallway, wondering exactly what she had done. But then she reassured herself. She was alone with the children. She could hardly talk to them of the possible . . . she could not even think the word . . . anyway, she could not talk to them about their father.

She walked back to the dining room and put her dinner things back on the tray. She would take it down to the kitchen and then go upstairs, read the children a story, and tuck them into bed.

Very carefully she descended the back stairs. They were badly lit by a single gas bracket. She had often asked Pendleton to put electric light there as well as in the rest of the house, but he was of the opinion that servants could do without modern equipment.

The last two steps creaked as she came down. Before the events of yesterday, she had never felt afraid in this house, but now everything seemed to unnerve her. She stopped and listened. Nothing. Her father had always said that if you take the first step to run from something, you'll keep on running. She took a deep breath.

She was mistress here. It was her house. Safe. Locked.

She strode into the kitchen, and placed the tray on the table. The open wine-cellar door caught her eye. Why not? She would bring up another bottle of cognac, and after she had put the children to bed, she would pour herself a glass and listen to some of

Pendleton's phonograph recordings.

She didn't bother to light the gas. She knew the wine cellar like the back of her hand. She moved inside. In the dim light from the kitchen she could see the vague, shadowy outlines of the wine racks that ran the length of the room. The spirits were on the left. She moved along the lines of bottles, stopped, and ran her hand down the rack. She located the squat shape of the cognac bottle, and gently pulled it from its nest.

Suddenly she froze. She could have sworn she heard a breath somewhere close. She listened, clasping the bottle like a club, and whirled around. But there was nothing, nothing but the deep silence of a closed dark space. Her eyes peered into that darkness, scanning row after row of bottles.

She quickly moved to the door and stopped, then looked back. Nothing. Virginia went back upstairs. She had not seen the eyes that were watching her every movement, staring past the gleaming curves of the bottles.

She left the bottle on the table in the dining room, and walked along the rear hallway to the nursery. The children were surprised to see their mother come in the servants' door. Ernest skipped over to her, toy soldiers in hand.

"A story, Mama, tell us a story!"

Mary looked up from the book she was drawing in.

"Yes, a story, read us a story!"

"All right, I will. But you must get into bed first."

Ernest lunged at his bed, then carefully placed the soldiers on the bedside table. Meanwhile Mary wriggled under her sheets and popped her head out to watch her mother at the bookshelf.

"Hansel and Gretel, Mama, Hansel and Gretel!"

Ernest glared at his sister. "No, Mama! She's only saying that because she knows I hate it!"

"Ernest, that's silly, we have to read it sometime. She likes it, and anyway it's only a story. You're not really afraid of it, are you?"

Virginia settled herself on the bed, pushing the pillow behind her back. Then she opened the book and began.

The two children and the kindly father woodcutter. The new stepmother and the dark forest. She was sailing through it when suddenly it all seemed to sweep over her. A sense of the horror of the story, the horror of betrayal. She slowly ground to a halt as the witch started to test the children for their plumpness.

Ernest had long since buried his head in her lap and fallen asleep. Mary's eyes were struggling to stay open. Virginia settled her son in the bed, rising to her feet. Earlier, she had thought she heard a creaking on the back stairs, but she had dismissed it as her imagination. Now she thought she heard a faint padding of footsteps on the floor above, in Pendleton's study. Mary too was asleep.

Virginia kissed her and left the nursery. The house was silent again. She marched into the living room and across to the phonograph. She opened the top drawer, and while she wound the machine, scanned the neat rows of cylinders. There was a piece by Lucien Muratore and Lina Cavalieri that she particularly loved. Virginia took it out and slipped it onto the machine, then fetched her bottle of cognac and a glass from the dining room. She switched on a small side lamp, then leaned over and clicked on the phonograph. After the initial crackling, the voices soared out, filling the room. It was a joy that she was still not accustomed to: the great performers in her own house, at her beck and call.

She sank back into the cushioned armchair, and placed the glass under the potted plant on the table beside her. She started to sing along with the aria as she opened the bottle. The mellow, distinctive smell of cognac drifted into her nostrils. She was beginning to feel relaxed. She poured a glassful of the golden liquid.

Heavens, but Italian was a beautiful language; perhaps she should take it up one day. Putting the glass to her lips, she took a sip. It was delicious. Virginia leaned back, closing her eyes and letting the music waft over her. Images of Italy floated into her mind: the canals of Venice, the splendors of Rome, the serenity of hillside vineyards. She took another sip. Her imagination lifted her into a land of blue skies, wayside inns, terraces overlooking wide, fertile valleys. And everywhere the fragrance of spring flowers. Perhaps one day she would go there. Perhaps Pendleton could be persuaded to . . .

With a jolt she was brought back to her present situation. Pendleton was not here, had not been here for days. She feared both the turmoil of his return and the turmoil if he did not return. And then there was Doolan.

She stared across the room. She felt so alone, even with the children in the nursery. As she looked along the polished marble tiles to the first steps of the sweeping staircase, the music came to an end. The phonograph horn bellowed out the grinding and scratching of the needle on the cylinder.

Virginia leaned across the fern, its fine leaves tickling her face, and clicked off the machine. Then she froze. Somewhere there was a persistent scratching, like an animal at a door. Her eyes flickered to the phonograph, to see that it had indeed stopped. She jerked backward, knocking the potted plant with her elbow, sending it crashing to the floor. The earthenware pot smashed inside its embossed silver container, and spilled its soil across the carpet. The cognac bottle also fell, cognac gurgling into the mess.

Virginia ran to the bottom of the hall stairs, then stopped and listened. Silence. But her pulse was racing and she was determined to find out what, if anything, was there. She scurried along the hall, through the dining room, to the servants' hallway. She looked around cautiously, at the nursery door and the head of the kitchen stairs. Nothing. She looked up. There was no light on these stairs. The gas fixture had not been lit. Damn Pendleton and his penuriousness! Well, she had no time to search for matches. Carefully she placed her foot on the first bare wooden step. She lifted her dress and climbed. Halfway up, three of the stairs creaked. The noise seemed to fill the whole house. She cursed herself. Anyone would know she was coming.

The thought of anyone, of a person actually being there, rooted her for a moment in midstep. Beads of sweat broke on her forehead. Once more she looked up, into the darkness and beyond, to a dim light, the frayed edge of some stronger illumination at the corridor's far end. She took a deep breath and completed her ascent.

"Hello?" she called. The word died in the heavy silence.

She edged forward a few steps, and peered along the corridor. The main bedroom was there. She placed her hand on the wall to steady herself. The bedroom door was slightly ajar. Didn't Gladys usually shut the doors when she had cleaned? The black strip of shadow between door and jamb beckoned to her. She heard a slithering whisper, like paper being rustled. But she could see nothing.

Again there was silence.

She turned back to the door and threw it open. The light from the stairwell flooded across the empty room. Everything was in order, the beds neatly made, the sheets tucked in, counterpanes pulled back at an angle, just as she liked it.

Perhaps the rustling sound had come from Ernest's study. Silently, Virginia crossed the hall and opened the door. Sliding her hand along the wall, she felt for the light switch and clicked it on. A greenish light illuminated the rows of books facing her. Virginia quickly entered the room. Here as well, everything seemed to be in order.

Pendleton's desk was strewn with papers, as usual. Virginia walked forward and gasped. The desk had been ransacked! Had Ernest left it like this? It was possible that he had been looking for something in haste. Probably nothing was wrong at all, and she was overreacting to the clutter.

Even as she stood framed in the doorway, Virginia was being watched. Eyes flickered maliciously in the darkness, taking in her every move. It watched intently, as though through her it would find the answers. But there was nothing to be learned from the woman's stillness, and the shadowed intruder let out a long, hissing breath.

It was barely audible, but Virginia heard it. She turned, seeking the source of the threatening noise. Her eyes darted to the desk, just as the ginger housecat, Billy, slithered across the pile of papers on the chair, clawing noisily as he went. He leaped from the desk and shot past her, into the hall.

She steadied herself. She was being silly! Unseen above her, the figure glided into the maid's room, gently closing the door.

Once again Virginia glanced at the mess of papers. Pendleton could tidy it himself, if and when he returned; after all, he placed such value on it being his private room.

She switched off the light, stepped back into the hall, and closed the door behind her. She would check on the children. Her shoes sounded noisily on the bare steps as she quickly descended the staircase. She went quietly to the nursery door and carefully opened it. The blue-shaded side lamp cast a soft light across their beds. Ernest lay on his side, his arm tucked under the pillow. Even in his sleep, he was a neat child. Mary, however, was already half off her bed, one leg dangling, the other caught up in the sheets.

Virginia walked in. She crossed to Ernest and gave him a peck on the cheek. It was funny how big he looked during the day, and yet lying here asleep, he was a tiny boy again.

She stroked back a lock of hair from his forehead, and smiled. Turning to Mary, she pulled the child into the center of her bed, settling the sheet around her. Soon they would have to think of putting Ernest into his own room. Already Aunt Eleanor had made some disparaging remarks about a boy and girl sleeping together, but it was so easy this way, with the nanny so close by.

Cecily had gone out to see her sister's new baby. Perhaps she could give them some of the children's baby things. She certainly had no intention of having more children.

The baby was a girl. Where had they put Mary's baby clothes?

She had put most of the toys and clothes into the trunks, hadn't she?

She slid the top trunk off. It was quite heavy, but finally she had one end on the floor, the other end still resting on the bottom trunk. She stepped over to that end, and edged it out, holding onto the leather strap. It fell to the floor with a dull thud.

She glanced back. The children were still fast asleep, though Mary had once more kicked herself free of the sheets.

Turning back, Virginia pulled at the clamps. The trunks were strongly made of basswood, edged in steel and bound with leather. She liked the look and feel of them.

She opened the trunk. The smell of stored clothes greeted her as she stared down at Ernest Junior's clothes. The little sailor suit, with the rip in the trousers. He had snagged it on a barbed wire fence, on a trip to Connecticut, and had cried about it for hours.

Virginia smiled. If it had been Mary, she would probably have gone around showing it to everyone. Well, Ernest was nothing if not a tidy child. She searched through the hats and coats, beautiful knits her mother had made for him, and then caps, all the little caps that her father had sent. Below all that were the baby clothes. But they were mainly blue, only an occasional piece in white. She took out two long white flannel shirts, and a hand-embroidered shawl. The other trunk must hold Mary's clothes.

She closed the first trunk and opened the second. Again there was that smell of long-stored clothes. But beyond that, there was something else, something strange. She gripped hard at the steel-rimmed sides and, lifting her head back, took a deep breath.

That steadied her. Rushing her meal, gulping the brandy and then padding around the house like a Pinkerton sleuth after a phantom, it was no wonder she felt a little light-headed.

She gazed into the trunk and slowly her face relaxed into a warm smile. This was where she had stored the crib blankets and shawls. She lifted up one of her favorites, a delicate white crocheted piece. It had been made by her aunt Judith, her mother's sister. Only a way to pass the winter evenings, she had said, but Virginia could tell the love and care that had been put into it. She lifted it up and smoothed it against her face. No, she couldn't give this away. This had too many sweet memories. But there were other little dresses and baby shirts and bonnets. She pulled aside the blankets and delved deeper into the trunk.

The intruder had looked through every room upstairs and found nothing. Now the figure turned and carefully edged its way down the sweeping staircase.

Virginia had removed a whole layer of soft toys from the trunk. Little Mary was past that now and very much the mother of a "herd of dolls," as Pendleton jokingly called them. Perhaps she could slip some of these out of the house for Cecily's sister's baby. She would have to be careful; Mary was quite possessive.

Virginia stared down at the neat layers of little dresses. Why did little girls have to wear pink and little boys wear blue? It made life with young children so visually boring.

Sighing, she smiled. So many grand thoughts and no one to share them with. Sharing, wasn't that what a marriage should be?

She leaned into the body of the linen-covered trunk. Carefully her fingers traced over the delicate embroidery on the front and shoulders of the little rose-pink dress in the corner. Mary had last worn it at her first birthday, and even then it was small. She would not miss it.

Using both hands, Virginia lifted it by the shoulders. It was strangely heavy, and as she lifted it, she saw that a manuscript of some kind was stuck to the fabric. It suddenly tore free with a loud ripping noise, all but the last page, and fell back into the trunk. Gasping, stifling a scream behind her hand, Virginia jerked away from the trunk.

Calming herself, Virginia studied the redly stained paper, which had gotten snagged on the metal clasps along the back of the dress. She pulled it away from the fabric and stared at it. Bloodstained, it looked as though it had been gouged at by a knife. What was it doing in her baby's clothes? She peered into the trunk again. The manuscript lay splayed open, over the clothes. Two other similar manuscripts were there, loosely wrapped in a bloody cotton cloth. Placing the dress and the loose page on the inside of the trunk lid, she lifted up the ripped cloth package and the manuscript that had fallen out.

Suddenly a chill filled the room, and a seething hiss of breath seemed to rush from behind her. She spun around, focusing on the darkness beyond the partly opened door. But she saw nothing, not the eye that peered malevolently at her from the dark, not the gleaming white mask spitting out the short rasping breaths.

The doorbell echoed along the marble hall. She could not work out what was going on. This looked like the parcel that Bellarma had had by his bedside. She remembered him laying his hand on it. "I searched for years," he had said, "and I found when I got it that I had grasped evil, pure evil." Virginia shuddered.

The doorbell rang again, more insistently.

Virginia quickly crossed the nursery, clutching the parcel to her bosom. As she opened the door to the hall the bell clanged once more. She ran along the polished hall, past the bottom of the stairway, and pulled open the front door.

Doolan smiled at her.

"Good evening, Mrs. Pendleton. I got here as soon . . ." His voice trailed off as he registered the distraught look in the woman's eyes and the stained parcel clutched tightly to her breast. A scream ripped through the hallway. Doolan sprinted past her. His hard leather boots echoed hollowly in the hall.

He burst into the nursery, Virginia close behind him. There was another scream: the piercing, high-pitched yell of a petrified child. Mary was sitting up in bed, thrashing with her hands, wide-eyed in terror. Ernest was valiantly trying to stagger to his feet, still half asleep.

Doolan's eyes darted to every corner of the room, seeking anything out of place. Some toys were scattered, books thrown down, but apart from that it was

273

just a child's room. Then he saw the opened trunk, the clothes spewed over the side, and quickly moved toward it.

Virginia threw the manuscripts down at the bottom of the bed and gathered the sobbing child into her arms.

"There, there, Mary. It's all right, Mama's here, Mama's here. There there, it was just a dream, just a dream."

She pulled the damp hair back from the child's face and kissed her gently on the cheeks. Mary continued to sob, clinging tightly to her mother. As Doolan walked toward them, holding a small pink dress in his hand, she pushed herself from her mother's grasp. Screeching, she scrambled to the top of the bed.

"She rip it! She rip it!"

The little girl grabbed at the pillow as though trying to hide under it. Doolan looked at the dress in his hand and stepped back. Virginia moved up and pulled the girl to her once more.

"Don't, Mary, don't. There's nothing to be scared of, it's just your silly old dress. And you had a dream, that's all."

The child hugged her mother again, sobbing. "No, Mama, she was here! A lady like a nun with a doll's face!"

Both Doolan and Virginia froze. Each had their own separate and distinct memories. Then Doolan asked, "Are you sure, Mary?"

Virginia stroked Mary's head and the child looked up with large blue eyes at the tall, pleasant-faced man. "Yes, yes. She hissed and then, she tore my dress."

Doolan examined the dress he held. It was indeed ripped. Virginia's eyes widened as she saw it. There was a crashing sound from the servants' corridor. Doolan catapulted toward the back door, flung it open and peered into the darkness.

There was another hollow crashing noise, the sound of heavy pots rolling over a stove and tumbling onto the floor. Virginia shot up from the bed, and then ran to Doolan, calling "The kitchen, the kitchen—down the stairs."

He clattered down the bare wooden stairs.

Virginia snatched up the dress he had dropped. The part where the paper had been attached to the cloth was completely ripped away, and the rest shredded as if by an enraged beast. The nun *had* been here.

Doolan ran to the bottom of the stairs and stopped. The kitchen doorway was just ahead of him. There was a loud banging noise like a door being flung open. But Doolan was cautious; he had seen that trick before. He stepped over to the other wall, pressed himself against it, and looked into the dimly lighted room. There was silence.

He gazed past the stove and wooden kitchen bench. Two large copper pots were lying on the floor, and the outside door was slowly swinging shut. Doolan ran through the room and up to the street outside. His eyes searched into the night. There was no one there, no pedestrians, just the traffic, rattling along Madison. Nothing out of the ordinary.

For a moment he leaned against the iron rails, slowly pounding them with his large, clenched fist. Then he remembered the woman inside the house. He started down the stairs toward the open door.

Tom woke up many times that night. Each time, Jenny stroked his brow and hugged him like a child. Each time, he slipped back into sleep, mumbling her name.

His nightmares were great black pits into which he tumbled helplessly. He would scream into wakefulness, bathed in sweat. Jenny was always there to hold him.

Once he woke with a start to find Jenny nuzzled

beside him like a purring cat. A streetlamp cast a shaft of light through a gap in the curtain and across her face. He looked at her for a long time. Was there a future for them?

He sighed. Perhaps the answer was that they were here now and that was all that life would promise. It was in this mood that he slipped into his final nightmare.

Peter and Araya were walking across a grey desert. Above them a moon slowly turned to blood. They looked up and made for the shelter of a cave. A sandstorm was coming.

At first everything seemed right. They knelt on the floor, dust all around them, and clasped their hands in prayer. They were thankful to have escaped the storm that raged outside.

As Tom stared, he saw the floor under them begin to writhe. One snake after another rose from the dust and wound its way toward them. Unhindered, the snakes began to slither up the men's bodies.

Behind them a figure appeared, half snake, half man. Araya and Peter knew this creature was there, and despair began to crush the light in their eyes.

Tom could feel the pulse of evil within the cave quicken, and suddenly knew that he had within him the strength to banish it. He knew now why he was there. They needed him. He clasped his hands and started to pray. As he did, pain ricocheted through his skull, as though his mind were being ripped in two. Something was stopping his intercession for them. He looked across the cave and saw malevolence in the eyes of the man-snake. This was his adversary. Tom prayed on, ignoring the pain. He raised his arms as though he could wrench strength from the heavens. For a while a godlike strength seemed to flow through him and he saw the light of hope in his brother's and friend's eyes. But it did not last. The man-snake reared high above the writhing mass and shot out a tongue of pure red flame. In that moment, Tom doubted his strength, doubted his God. The one tongue became many tongues, then a consuming fire, and Tom knew that they were all lost. He saw the slit eyes of the man-snake glitter, and watched as Peter and Araya slipped helplessly into the writhing mass. He had lost. A scream gurgled from his throat. He broke from sleep, thrashing on the pillow. This time Jenny had not wakened.

Doolan insisted that he stay the night at the Pendletons'. Virginia did not argue with him. He first locked all the doors and searched every room in the house. It took him a good hour, but when he was finally convinced that the place was safe, he went down to the nursery. Virginia was lying in bed with Mary. She had fallen asleep with her arm crooked around the girl.

Doolan watched Virginia for a long time; this woman had become an obsession in his life. He saw the strand of dark blond hair that fell across her cheek, quivering with each breath, and the gentle rise and fall of her breast against her little girl's face. Her beauty was partly as a mother, a life-giver, a protector, not just in the sculpted smoothness of her face or the athletic elegance of her figure. Doolan saw the crow's feet and the one deep crease between her eyebrows and felt that his heart was stretching out to her as a complete woman, not a "bird in a gilded cage."

Quietly he took the manuscripts, shot a last look at Virginia, and went into the living room to read. He settled into a chair, placing the manuscripts on his knee. Were these what Araya had searched the globe for? Had these caused the death of Bellarma and perhaps Ernest Pendleton?

Doolan scanned the writing on the first few pages, but it was indecipherable to him. His friend in the rag trade, Herbie Gutman, had once shown him a family

Torah, and that was close to this script. Araya had said it was Sahidic, one of the ancient languages of the Upper Nile.

He settled into the chair. It had been a long day. He laid his head against the lace antimacassar and closed his eyes. His hands tightened around the manuscript.

It was good to touch something tangible, something that might bind together all the loose strands of the week. Araya's tale no longer seemed so bizarre. There was a cult here in the city and they wanted this! His fingers played along the uneven edges of the leather binding. But how did they link to the church of San Salvadore? Perhaps he should pay another visit.

The thoughts trailed off and he slowly fell into a deep sleep. His dreams were troubled. He kept replaying the case that had first brought him into contact with Pendleton.

In his dreams, the scene of Brownlea's murder was transplanted from the extravagantly decorated whorehouse on lower Fifth Avenue to the Pendletons' living room. The Jamaican whore sprawled broken-necked across the piano, blood trickling from her mouth. Then Doolan saw her in the nursery, stuffed into the trunk. She lunged out at him like a jack-in-the-box, holding the manuscript in her hands.

The porcelain-faced nun lunged past Doolan and snatched the book. Doolan gave chase, first up the stairs and then out of the house. Finally he cornered the creature in a large warehouse of copper pots. He reached forward and ripped off the porcelain mask, then staggered back, stunned. A creature half-snake and half-man leapt at him, hissing. The slits of eyes widened and the tongue darted out toward Doolan's face.

Doolan shot forward in the chair and gave a muffled yell. At first he thought Virginia was part of his dream.

"I'm sorry," she said. "I didn't mean to wake you."

He shook the sleep from his eyes and saw that she had changed for bed. It was a gesture of trust. He watched her, bathed in the light from the hallway. He did not dare think of them together, as man and woman. He watched her move, watched the white lightweight silk wrap as it hugged her body.

"I must've fallen asleep myself," she said. She sat down on a chair beside him. "You've got the manuscripts."

"Yes," he sighed. He had them—what would he do with them?

"I don't want them near me," Virginia said. "Take them away."

He would give them to Araya, Doolan thought. He would know what to do with them.

"I want to thank you for being here," Virginia said.

Doolan smiled awkwardly. "It's my pleasure."

Was that the wrong thing to say? But she didn't seem to mind. She smiled again and looked at the carpet. He saw the lines form around her eyes and he wanted to lean forward and kiss them.

"You're a beautiful woman—" The words were out before he knew it. "I know I shouldn't be talking like this." He fell silent.

Virginia flashed him a nervous smile. This was new territory for both of them.

"I've felt like this for a long time," he said. "I . . ." He was about to slowly but surely twist himself into a know when her cool and quiet voice filled the room. "So have I, Lieutenant."

He looked up and saw a smile playing around her blue-green eyes. Her lips trembled slightly.

He wanted to walk over and take her in his arms, to feel the smooth sheen of her wrap, to take it from her and touch her skin. He wanted to stroke her, to make her feel secure and loved. But he didn't move. He squeezed the arms of the chair, trying to stanch the flood of emotions. Adultery was a word that tasted foul in his mouth.

Virginia sat still and poised. She gazed past Doolan. Her eyes grew large, and tears spilled over the lids and down her cheeks. It was the hour, and the day, and the years of bad marriage. It was the fear that Pendleton was dead and the fear that he would come home again to disrupt their lives. She could not stop sobbing.

Doolan knelt beside her. He took her by the shoulders, grasping her firmly but gently. He brushed back her wayward hair and planted a firm kiss on her forehead. Very slowly, she looked up. She brought her hand up to his and they twined their fingers, tight.

When the morning sun finally found its way through the net curtains, it found them asleep on the couch, arm in arm like the brother and sister in the Hansel and Gretel story.

They looked as if they were comforting each other against the impending evil of the new day.

CHAPTER 38

DAVEY WAS THE youngest of Bertha Langman's three cousins, but for a little boy of six, he showed a marked degree of determination. He had set his mind on waking up early so that he could get a chance with the new kite. After all, his father had bought it for him as well as for his brother and sister. It was just that he was the smallest and they never gave him a chance to get near it. Well, if he got up before them, they wouldn't be able to stop him.

At first he lay very still in his bed. He stretched his toes, and turned them up, making two mountains in the sheets.

A slight breeze blew through the window. If the wind could billow the curtains, it could raise up the box kite to a splendid height.

Pulling back the sheet, Davey quietly placed his feet on the floor. His toes nosed over the threadbare rug seeking his slippers. He stood up and glanced over at Eddie. His older brother was, as usual, lying with his head half under the pillow.

Eddie had gone to bed after him. Where had he left the kite? Davey's eyes flickered about the room. Maybe on top of the wardrobe? No. Maybe with that pile of toys by the desk? No.

His eye stopped at the bottom of the bed; there was the string snaking out to the ball left on the window-sill. He tiptoed over and leaned down, pulling out the precious flying machine as carefully as possible. It felt good in his hands. He had scarcely been allowed to hold it yesterday. Sometimes he really hated his brother and sister.

Davey would steal out as quietly as he could. He clasped the kite by one corner and sneaked over to the door. His clothes were lying on the chair beside it. The floorboards creaked, just as they always did. Davey could feel the hair standing up along the back of his neck. For a moment, he stood stock still, just like an Indian. He glanced back.

Eddie was still asleep. Davey scooped up his clothes and gently opened the door. Every moment he expected it to creak loudly and wake his brother to his daring theft. But it didn't.

Outside on the dark landing he leaned the kite against the rails of the banister. Then he slipped off his long cotton nightgown and threw it back into the bedroom. It landed on his bed, and Davey shut the door. Eddie had not moved. Naked, Davey realized that he had to piddle. Well, he would get dressed first.

He bent down and picked up his shirt, slipping it over his head and shooting his arms along the sleeves. Even his dad said he was quick at putting on his clothes. He pulled on his trousers, and glanced at his cousin Bertha's door. She didn't like either him or Eddie going in there; in fact when she was out, she kept the room locked. His mother said that that was right. She was a young lady and had a right to her privacy.

What did she do in there? What did she keep hidden from them? The pressure on Davey's bladder was forgotten as his curiosity rekindled. Maybe she had a treasure in there!

Davey walked a few steps across the landing. This would be the perfect time to look in and discover the truth. But what if she caught him peeking in? What if she was sitting in the armchair, waiting for him to open the door? Then there would be trouble. His mother would shout and his father . . . well, his father would use the strap.

He stepped backward, toward the top of the stairs. No. No, he wasn't afraid. He would just wait for another time, when Eddie was with him. Anyway, he had the kite. That was the reason he had gotten up early.

Davey sat down on the top step and put on his socks. He buttoned the bottom of his britches and put his slippers back on.

When he stood up, he got a whiff of a sweet smell. It was strange, rather sickening. He had smelled something like it before, but couldn't remember what.

The landing was getting a little lighter; it was time for him to get outside. He moved down the steps as quietly as he could, wincing at every creak. At the bottom, he stopped to look along the second-floor corridor. The bathroom was at the top of the main flight of stairs, just beside his sister's room.

He left the box kite by the top step, and padded across to the door. It was slightly ajar, so he edged it open a little more and slipped inside. He was in a small dressing room, lined with cupboards full of bed linen and towels. The smell lingered, but he had gotten used to it. He was excited about getting out, and getting the kite up into the wind. The stimulation was making him burst for a piddle.

It was dark in the small room, but he easily found the handle to the bathroom door.

It was dark in there too. Someone had left the curtains pulled over. But that didn't matter, he knew where everything was. He marched straight over to the toilet, and pushed the seat up with a clunk. He opened his fly and aimed as well as he could, hearing his pee splatter against the bowl, and then the more satisfying sound of it splashing in the water. Slowly he turned his head.

It was a big bathroom, and the long, white enameled bath lay against the other wall. If Davey stretched, he could just touch the edge of it. It was a game. Could he still aim into the toilet and grasp the lip of the tub? As his hand closed on the rim, he could tell that someone had left it full of water.

He finished his piddle and then shook his willie with exaggerated care.

"No matter how much you shake your peg, there's always a drop'll go down your leg."

Eddie said that every time. He had learned it from the big boys.

Davey shuffled over to the bath, his eyes becoming more used to the lack of light. The white outline of the bath stood out now, like chalk on a blackboard. But the water was very dark.

He stared along the length of it, half dreaming, thinking of the kite soaring up to the clouds. There was a cloth floating . . . no, it was like that seaweed you got at the shore. Seaweed in the bath?

He reached out and grabbed the black mess. It was like seaweed, the fine, hairlike seaweed you find in those deep rock pools. He tugged at it and let go—it was heavy!

A strange thing happened. His tugging had a peculiar aftereffect: that displaced motion that occurs when an object is moved through liquid. There was first of all a ripple through the water. Then, slowly, the whiteness began to rise. It was chalk white, bone white, emerging from the darkness of the liquid. It was fully up and floating on the surface before Davey was able to recognize it. Then his heart seemed to skip a beat, and the air choked in his throat.

It was his cousin Bertha! But how could she be under the water?

"Bertha?" he whispered in a tentative voice. But there was no answer. Her head lolled to one side; the eyes flashed whitely in his direction. Davey looked at the sleeve of his white shirt; it was dark with the water. It was not water.

The little boy screamed. It echoed through the halls of the house. And as he was screaming, he remembered where he had smelled that strange, sweet smell before. It was on a visit to a slaughterhouse with his grandfather. Then, as now, he had been surrounded by the smell of blood.

CHAPTER 39

DOOLAN FELT LIKE a man set apart from the world. Even though the Third Avenue El was noisy and crowded, he felt a great internal calm, as if he were adrift on some benign sea.

He thought of Virginia, and smiled. When they had woken that morning, she had shown him to the bathroom off the main bedroom and given him Pendleton's shaving gear. She had watched him shave, leaning on the door and smiling gently.

"I haven't had this much attention in years," he said, but she did not reply, just smiled.

He held that smile of hers in his mind as he stepped out of the El, clutching the small carpetbag containing the manuscripts. They were dangerous. Abyssos was probably still after them, and still thought they were at the Pendletons'. When he got to the office, Doolan would ask a uniform cop to keep an eye on the house until all this passed over.

The wind was blowing with some force from the southeast. The papers said there was a storm moving up the coast, and these gusts were its precursors. The trees around San Salvadore swayed, and the leaves shimmered, alternately showing their dark tops and their light undersides.

Doolan looked up at the front of the church and

stopped. The doors were closed and a notice was tacked to one of them.

"Closed for repairs."

Doolan raised an eyebrow. Since when was a church closed for repairs? Had the congregation grown so small that they could just be off-loaded on another parish?

As he stood there a familiar voice cut across his musings.

"Is that you, Lieutenant? You must've smelled my baking clear across town!" Doolan looked at the corner of Elizabeth Street and saw Bridie standing there holding a basket of freshly cut chrysanthemums. The blossoms were brightly colored, butter yellows, deep reds, pure whites. "I was in the garden and saw you walking by," she explained.

He walked over to her, smiling. "Hello, Bridie, how are you?"

"I'm fine. Did you come back for some soda bread?"

"No, I was just walking by. I saw the sign on the door."

Bridie frowned and bit her lip. "I'm fed up trying to work out what's going on. Young Father Schmidt gets queerer by the day and Father Brautsch . . . well . . . I just don't know. . . ."

She glanced around nervously, as though someone was listening. Then she gave a resigned smile.

"Come on in and have a slice of that bread."

Doolan could not refuse. As Bridie opened the back door of the kitchen, the smell of baking wafted around him. It was a warm, nostalgic smell. Bridie shuffled over to the large sink unit and placed the basket on the drainboard. She turned on the tap and quickly washed her hands.

"I'll have coffee ready in a minute," she said.

"Bridie, I'm taking you away from your garden," Doolan protested.

"It's a happy stroke of luck; I think every bug in New York State has had a taste of me by now."

Doolan laughed and watched her as she crossed to the marble-topped bench by the oven. On the bench was a line of cooling racks, filled with little mounds of soda bread and two apple pies.

"You've got enough to feed an army there," Doolan commented.

"I do this every Saturday," Bridie said, slicing one of the loaves of bread. "It's for the parishioners, the regulars, those that are left. Now there won't be services tomorrow, but I was already at work." She gave a grunt of disgust.

"Who decided that, Bridie?"

"Young Father Schmidt," she said, removing a dish of butter from the small ash-panelled icebox. "He seems to decide everything these days."

"Is he in at the moment?" Doolan asked.

Bridie stabbed at the cold butter and Doolan got a clear impression of her feelings for Schmidt. "I don't know where he is now. He's in and out, always with one of that crew he picked off the streets."

"What are they doing to the church?"

Bridie took down two plates and loaded them up with freshly buttered slices. Her jaw was set and he could see that his questions were upsetting her.

"Look, Lieutenant, as things are, I'd be the last to know. Father Schmidt told me they were going to start work on the Gallenini tomb again, though as far as I can tell, it doesn't need to be any bigger."

At the mention of Gallenini, Doolan recalled his conversation with Albrecht about the Latin inscription. Doolan chewed one of the crusts and wondered if she knew any more about the family.

"Do you know if Gallenini had any children baptized in the church or anything about his wife?"

Bridie shook her head. "That was all before my time. Father Brautsch would know, if he can remember. These days he can scarcely recall his own name." She paused, staring at the plates before her. "I must take some of this up to him."

Bridie put one dish onto a tray, then crossed to the icebox and pulled out a jug of milk. As she was pouring a glass, she turned to Doolan and gave him a cheeky smile. "But if you want to do some detecting on your own, you could go through the parish records." She offered Doolan her keys. "One's for the presbytery, the other's for the cellar. While I'm getting this up to the father, why don't you just slip across and find out whatever it is you're after?"

Doolan looked at the two keys. This was insanity. He had a pile of work to do and a thousand unresolved questions. He took the keys.

She edged past him to a large cupboard under the sink, opened it, and pulled out an oil lamp and a box of matches.

"They never bothered to put a permanent light down there," she said, handing him the lamp.

Doolan thanked her and left the kitchen as she went back to the tray. He crossed the garden to the presbytery. The wind was blowing in gusts that caused the leaves to whisper like a fast-ebbing tide. It lifted his reddish-fair hair and tousled it. He carefully unlocked the heavy iron and oak door of the presbytery and slipped inside. There was that familiar church odor again, the faint whiff of incense and the smell of starched linens.

He stopped and listened. Silence, except for the sound of his quickened breathing. Fear flooded into him. The crypt was there, the tomb where he had his terrible experience. If they were indeed going to work on it, then maybe it was open. The thought of the dark stairwell caused a wave of dampness to break out on his neck and forehead.

He would not go into the church. He would go down, look at the records, and then leave. He would find out about Gallenini and get out.

The cellar door proved difficult to open, but finally yielded, creaking a little on thick iron hinges. The musty smell of disuse drifted up the steps from the dark cellar below.

He lit the lamp and went down. Soon he found himself in a room about the same size as the presbytery and obviously directly beneath it. The place was full of boxes and trunks. Along one wall bookcases stretched from floor to ceiling. Doolan held the lamp high. Each volume was dated.

He would start with 1886. Perhaps there was some clue there to why Gallenini had built the chapel.

He pulled over one of the packing boxes that littered the room and placed the lamp on it. Then he stretched up and pulled down three volumes: 1884, 1885, and 1886. He set them on the top of the box and dragged over a small three-legged stool. Adjusting the lamp so that it threw its yellow light over the books, he opened the 1886 volume.

Marriages, births, deaths. Here it was, the whole social life of the community, concentrated into a series of facts and figures. He became so absorbed that he did not feel the change of air, did not hear the soft footsteps padding across the tiled floor above him.

His mind was totally focused on the job before him. He skimmed the pages. Suddenly a white hand swept across and slammed the book shut.

Doolan recoiled and staggered to his feet. He fell against the row of bookshelves. The lamp on the makeshift table shook for a moment and then steadied itself, and in the wavering light, Doolan saw a white-haired old man standing before him.

The man laid a shaky hand on top of the closed volume and stared deep into Doolan's eyes. Doolan had seen that look before, amongst drug addicts. The man's eyes, once dark, were blurring white at the edges. They held Doolan in a fixed stare, that fierce glazed look that comes with the misuse of drugs. "I'm sorry," the man said in a wavering voice, "I didn't mean to startle you. My name is Father Brautsch."

Doolan collected his thoughts and stepped forward, offering the old man his hand. It was a strange meeting, here in this crypt, bound by this small circle of light. Once more he felt as though he had been tugged out of the mainstream of his life. He shook the feeling off.

"I'm Lieutenant Doolan."

"Yes, I know. Bridie told me." Brautsch sank onto Doolan's vacated stool. The lamp highlighted the strange brightness in his eyes.

"You have been asking about Gallenini."

"Yes, but . . ."

Brautsch kept talking. "I want to speak to someone. Perhaps it is too late. What do you need to know?"

"I was interested in the chapel that Gallenini had built, the one to Saint Dismas. Was it dedicated to a particular child?"

The old priest nodded, and then glanced down at the volumes stacked in front of him. He picked up one, flicked through it, and showed Doolan an entry. It was a baptismal entry for 1884. Elaine Maria Gallenini.

"Gallenini's daughter?"

"Yes."

"That's the one who died in the convent?"

The old priest sighed. "Yes, she is dead."

"Was there another child, one who died at birth?"

The old man seemed confused for a moment, then turned back to the books. "His wife . . . she died."

In the book for 1886 he found the death entry for

Doolan to see. "Mrs. Christiana Helena Gallenini, died in childbirth."

"And the child?" Doolan asked.

The old priest flicked back a page, and pointed. Another birth entry: "Helena Maria Gallenini."

"So he did have another child."

"Yes."

"Was this child the reason for the chapel?"

There was a silence. Far away, outside, the wind was blowing in a long, low howl, under the eaves of the church.

"Yes," Brautsch sighed.

"God, the poor man. His wife dies in childbirth, and the child is born, deformed?"

"Horribly deformed."

Doolan began to turn the pages of the book, scanning the entries. "When did the child die?"

The priest leaned forward and grabbed his wrist in an iron grip. Doolan's eyes fastened on the old man's haggard, drawn face.

"She did not die," he said in a stronger voice. "Everyone believes that she is dead, but it is not so."

"Then where is she? Some home, some hospital?"

The priest slowly shook his head. "Once she lived in Gallenini's mansion, but now . . ." His voice trailed off. He released Doolan's arm and leaned back. Doolan waited, but the silence stretched, seeming endless. When the old man finally spoke, it was quietly and with hesitation. "You saw the painting in the chapel, the figure holding the child covered with a cloak. No one saw the child, but I saw the horror on Gallenini's face. It ripped him from God's bosom. He had established the chapel, as though with his wealth he could buy God's pity. But when that did not work, he turned from the church."

Doolan was puzzled. "Didn't Bridie tell me that the other priest here and Gallenini were close?"

The lines around the old priest's mouth deepened

292

as though he was recalling something extremely distasteful.

"Ah, yes. Father Schmidt."

For a moment the old man sat still, for all the world like a photographic portrait. Then he shivered, automatically pulling his jacket tight around him. His eyes flickered toward the door. He peered into the darkness as though expecting someone to appear. Suddenly he turned back to Doolan, fixing him with sad eyes.

"Gallenini was a man of great power and wealth in the Italian community. He was also my friend, before his tragedies. Not long after the death of his daughter in the convent, he had a stroke. I know what pain is—it can make you want anything, anything, to relieve the suffering. . . ." For a moment it looked as though tears were going to overwhelm him, then he regained control.

"He brought Father Schmidt from Rome. The bishop explained he was a close family friend to the Galleninis and I was to be accommodating about any special duties he had to perform for them. Lieutenant Doolan, inertia is the worst sin of all. I let him take over, let him 'help' me, and now I am surrounded by secrets. . . ."

The old man's voice trailed off. He coughed, then spat into a worn handkerchief. He carefully wiped his lips and placed the cloth back in his pocket.

He turned and once more peered into the darkness of the doorway. The man's obvious fear was beginning to affect Doolan. He wondered what Brautsch was expecting.

"Schmidt seems warm and loving. He collects the despairing and wretched, and that's good, but somehow God seems to take a back seat to the priest. The servant of God becomes all-important. I have seen him work. He allows faith in God to falter, and dependence on him to grow. Slowly doubts creep in and corrode the strongest of faiths. I don't know how

293

to explain it, but I have felt weakened myself. It's like a slow poison. . . ." He sat forward, eyes blazing. "I have seen Father Schmidt rarely in the last few days, and I feel more alive than I have in months. I fear seeing him again, fear looking into his eyes!" He spat again into his handkerchief.

Doolan spoke. "Have you ever met a Father Bellarma?"

"No, no."

"Have you ever heard of Abyssos?"

The old man looked blank and then slowly shook his head. "No . . . What is it—what is wrong?"

Doolan did not answer. He picked up the carpetbag containing the manuscripts and held it under his arm. There was no proof of any connection between Schmidt and all of this. Such leaps of logic were very dangerous, and yet . . .

"I must go. I have a lot to do, a lot of things to piece together." He waited for the priest to rise. The old man sat for a few seconds, unmoving, then with a rumbling croak cleared his throat. Turning, he got up and lifted the oil lamp.

"I shall walk up with you."

There was no conversation between them as they mounted the stairs, each burdened with a private silence.

At the door of the presbytery, Brautsch gently took hold of Doolan's arm. Doolan turned; the eyes that met his were tired.

"I shall stay here in the church for a while."

"Thank you for the talk," Doolan said, smiling. He patted the manuscripts in the carpetbag and set off toward Centre Market, forgetting Bridie, her soda bread, and her keys.

Father Brautsch watched him for a moment and then stepped back into the presbytery, closing the door. For a few minutes he leaned back, feeling the

heavy iron hinge across his shoulders. He was very tired and yet, in a strange way, he was also relieved, as if a great burden had been lifted and he was suddenly aware of how it had been sapping his strength.

He sank into one of the heavy choir chairs. In moments he was asleep.

CHAPTER 40

JENNY FELT GOOD. Last night she had given to some-one, given to Tom when he needed her. She had held him and mothered him, brought him through his nightmares. She had not felt so wanted since the death of her baby.

She turned into East Twenty-ninth Street and caught a gust of clean air off the river. The wind was rising, but she found it invigorating. She slipped her hand into her bag and felt the cover of Bertha's diary. Yes, she would talk to her. The snake incident of last night was an omen. Even the diary itself was Bertha calling out to her. She turned and walked up the stoop to Bertha's front door; she would dissuade her friend from becoming further involved with Abyssos.

She knocked. The door was soon opened by an obviously distraught woman. Her reddened eyes be-trayed that she had been crying.

"Yes, may I help you?"

"I'm a friend of Bertha's," Jenny said, "and I was wondering if I could talk to her."

All color drained from the woman's face. "A friend of Bertha's," she whispered. "What is your name?"

"Jenny."

"Jenny! Oh, yes, I've heard her talk about you." The woman wrung her hands. "Oh, Jenny, she . . . Bertha's dead!"

Jenny stepped backward, as though she had been struck. She had arrived too late!

"Oh Jenny, I'm sorry, you couldn't have known. Please, come in." She led Jenny into the house and ushered her into the front parlor. A large bronze and marble clock with a mounted horseman on top dominated the mantelpiece and ticked away with relentless precision. Jenny perched at the edge of a large, overstuffed velvet ottoman. The woman, who had to be Bertha's aunt, sat down nearby. Jenny found her voice.

"How did she . . ." She began to weep, and drew out her handkerchief.

The other woman swallowed hard. "My husband went with her, to the morgue. She had drowned in the bath, but . . ."

Jenny suddenly knew what Bertha's aunt was about to say.

"My husband came back about an hour ago. He said that the coroner said she lost consciousness due to blood loss. She had an internal hemorrhage from an illegal operation. . . ."

"Oh, Jesus!" Jenny shot out of her seat and embraced the other woman. "When did it happen?"

"Last night. We didn't hear her come in. I wish we had." Bertha's aunt started crying once again and turned from Jenny. "Oh, Lord, who could have gotten her into this? If my husband had known his name this morning, he would have killed him."

She stared at Jenny, eyes demanding. "Do you know who it could have been?"

Jenny thought of the diary, the mentions of the "sharings," and she shivered. "No, I don't. We went to a Bible-reading class together, but we were drifting apart."

"She was the same with us, Jenny. Lately she'd become distant, secretive. Oh, God, oh, God, what will her father think?"

Jenny felt unclean. She was hiding something from this good woman, but she could not bear to tell her

297

about the diary. This family had suffered enough. She suddenly felt nauseous. She paled, and sweat broke out on her forehead.

"Are you all right, dear?" asked Bertha's aunt.

"I feel a little sick. Could you show me the bathroom?" Her hand flew to cover her mouth in embarrassment. But the other woman smiled gently.

"It's all right." She led Jenny into the hall and pointed up the stairs. "It's up there, on the right."

The doorbell rang as Jenny started up the staircase. Bertha's aunt turned to answer it. "I hope it isn't another of those undertakers!"

The bathroom door was firmly closed. Jenny opened it and stepped into semidarkness. Downstairs, she heard Bertha's aunt taking the visitor into the sitting room. Not an undertaker, then.

Jenny found herself in a small dressing room. The inner door was half open and Jenny could see the toilet bowl. She moved into the bathroom.

The curtains had been pulled back and the room was bathed in late morning sunshine. Everything gleamed whitely, from the toilet bowl to the long, enameled bath. It was scarcely believable that her friend had died here; that Bertha had stepped into a bath and sat there until her life slipped away.

Jenny thought of the blood leaking from her friend's body and draining down the pipes. Her stomach heaved, and she staggered over to the toilet and threw up.

After a moment she steadied herself and wiped the sweat from her face. She splashed her face with cold water and rinsed her mouth.

"Did you know my cousin Bertha?" Jenny gave a muted scream and spun around to see a small boy watching her with large eyes.

"Uh, yes."

"I'm Davey. She's dead."

"Yes, I know. Your mama told me."

"You wanna see her room?" the boy asked. "She's not there anymore. If she was, she wouldn't let us in. But she's gone. She leaked away in the bath." He turned and marched away, up the stairs.

Jenny stood for a moment and then thought that she would like to see her friend's room. She hurried to follow Davey.

At the top of the stairs, the boy stopped and pointed. "There."

Jenny tried Bertha's door. It was not locked. The curtains were drawn but the window was open. It was a simple room, not large, but everything was so neatly arranged that it gave the impression of more than adequate space. A tall, elegant chest of drawers stood along one wall, and the simple cane chair beside it had a pile of neatly folded white blouses on the seat. A bedside table held an assortment of knickknacks—two dolls, a jewelry box, a powder box, a porcelain clown, and some silk flowers. Jenny stepped closer and saw a sealed envelope behind the clown. The envelope bore her name, "Jenny McGreevy." She slid it into her pocket and turned to the door.

"She always locked her closet door. She locked all her doors," Davey said. "Is it open now?"

It was. The closet seemed very ordinary. Toward the back there was a clothes rack, half filled with dresses and skirts. Shoes were placed in a neat row on the floor, and above, on the shelves, two hatboxes competed for space with cardigans and blouses. One shelf held books and notebooks, and the wall above was covered with drawings and photographs.

Jenny was so shocked that she found herself suppressing a nervous giggle. Of course she had seen pornography; some of the girls at Mrs. Flanagan's had used it, but it seemed so misplaced here. Her eyes skipped from one drawing to another. She could scarcely believe what she was seeing. Every position, every variation.

299

"Can I see?" Davey was poking his head around the door. Jenny stepped forward, blocking his view, and he looked up with big, innocent eyes.

"I don't think so," she replied.

The boy shrugged and skipped over to the window. He pulled back the curtain and stared down at his brother and sister playing in the garden.

Jenny stared once again at the drawings. They were obscene. There were no redeeming features to them, nothing artistic, nothing romantic, just pure, vulgar sex. There was something blatant and rebellious about it. Then it clicked in her head. This was the next step into Abyssos after the meetings. This was the pit into which her friend had fallen.

Suddenly she stepped forward and snatched them from the wall, thinking of the poor woman downstairs. The pictures had not yet been discovered, and now would not be. She stuffed them into her handbag. Davey yelled, "Eddie!" and ran from the room. Jenny closed the closet and followed.

As Jenny reached the first floor Bertha's aunt walked out of the sitting room. She closed the door behind her, but Jenny caught a glimpse of a man in clerical collar sitting on the ottoman.

"I hope you feel a little better, dear," she said. "Our minister has come and . . ."

"I understand. I should be going. Do you know yet when the funeral service will be?"

"I don't know. We haven't completed the arrangements. If you'll call again on Monday, I'm sure we'll know then." She showed Jenny out.

Standing on the sidewalk, Jenny made a resolution. She would go to the church and talk to Father Schmidt, whom Abyssos called Simon.

CHAPTER 41

FATHER BRAUTSCH AWAKENED slowly. He stamped his feet to restore circulation, then shuffled into the church. The vast darkness overwhelmed him. He tottered to a halt just past the altar, and automatically genuflected in the direction of the red sanctuary lamp. The oil lamp he was carrying cast a yellow pall over the carved altar. For a moment Brautsch considered slipping to his knees and praying, but something drew him on, beckoning him into the blackness of the nave.

So many faces had looked to him from those pews, so many souls had stretched toward him for sustenance. He moved forward, feeling the thin red carpet under his feet. It was his church; he knew every inch of it, every molding that needed to be replaced, every piece of guttering that was blocked, every floor tile that was cracked. But more and more he felt like an alien. The old congregation had almost gone, and the new ones? They were lost sheep, but sheep whom he could not help, sheep who looked to a different shepherd. The thought chilled him.

Father Brautsch looked across the church to the door of the Gallenini crypt. He could barely see it in the shadows. It was wrong, he thought, wrong that there should be such secrets. Perhaps this time he should go down? No. Not now. Now he needed solace. He did not want a confrontation with Schmidt.

He turned along a cross aisle toward the small chapel of Saint Dismas. He approached the door, and paused before lifting the gleaming brass latch. Beyond the wind, beyond the sound of his own breathing, he thought he had heard something, a slithering, as though something or someone was trying to approach him as soundlessly as possible. He peered beyond the circle of lamplight, but could see nothing, only the looming shapes of pews and pillars. Perhaps Bridie had followed him in. How long had he been asleep? Perhaps she had been worried and come over to see what was detaining him.

"Bridie?" His voice echoed through the nave, only to die away, swallowed in the silence. "Bridie, are you there? Is that you?"

Again the echo died away, fading into the gloom. Nothing. He was imagining things. He stepped into the chapel.

Inside, the heavy velvet curtains smothered all sound. He shuffled along one of the short pews, and all at once a great sense of weariness flooded over him. He sagged onto the seat, placing the lamp beside him, and passed into unconsciousness.

When he awoke, some kind of invisible, numbing cushion seemed to surround him. It was like one of those dreams where he wanted to run, but his legs would not obey him. Slowly he turned his head toward the painting on the wall. There were the steps, the pillars that looked as though they were part of a Roman ruin, the crowd with ugly, angry faces, the man with the child in his arms.

Brautsch recalled Gallenini's anger and bitterness. The canker of cynicism had finally ruptured and devoured his spirit. Brautsch wept for his friend, for the unseen child. How could God allow such suffering, such horror?

Father Brautsch shivered with terror at his thoughts. God was not to be put on trial by man. God was a God of Love, but he was also a jealous God, and a God of vengeance. The priest struggled to sit up, to move, but could not. He sucked desperately for air, gasping.

Then he heard it. Another hissing sound, close to the back of his head. He could not move. There was another hiss and then a slithering sound. He felt something firm and muscular press against the back of his neck and squeeze between his shoulder and the pew.

On and on it came, winding its way slowly but surely around him. Finally it came into view. At first there was the blur of the tongue darting in and out, then the head, hard and diamond-shaped. The slits of eyes gleamed evilly in the yellow glow of the oil lamp. He watched as it slithered down his leg, then turned and stared into his face.

A vicious, rasping voice exploded into the silence. "You have betrayed us!"

Mesmerized by the snake's gaze, Brautsch lay still. The creature in the porcelain mask eased up behind him. "Betrayer," it hissed.

The priest saw the blade out of the corner of his eye and watched as it fell with a shining whisper.

CHAPTER 42

ARAYA WAS WAITING for Doolan when he arrived at Police Headquarters. He could tell from the policeman's step that he was carrying a heavy burden. They walked up the stairs in silence. Inspector Ferrais's stenographer handed Doolan a note as they headed for Doolan's office.

"Lieutenant, please come to my office as soon as you can. Feinberg."

Doolan sighed. He swung the carpetbag onto his desk, looked at Araya, and opened the bag.

"Last night, Mrs. Pendleton phoned me," he said. "When I went to her house, she had found these." Doolan lifted out the manuscripts. Araya stared at them, visibly trembling. Doolan lay them on the desk.

"Stay here and read if you want, I'll be back in a few hours."

Those hours were an eternity for Araya. The gate was slowly opening.

Jenny could scarcely remember any of her journey through the crush of Saturday-afternoon shoppers. She felt only a deep pain for the loss of her friend, a pain that was deepened by the feeling that somehow she could have prevented Bertha's death.

Fifth Avenue was crowded by a group of banner-waving Socialists proclaiming Eugene Debs the next

President. On the corner of Twenty-sixth, a fight erupted between a drunken Taft supporter and an ardent Socialist. Jenny shrank away, clinging to the wall as the banner proclaiming "Ten million Socialist Americans" was pulled into the gutter. She quickly sidestepped the fight and rushed on.

Marie Louise, the dark-haired French girl from New Orleans, was the only one in Mrs. Flanagan's boudoir when Jenny arrived. It was just as well; she did not want to face all of them. Marie Louise was lying back on one of the ottomans, reading. She was dressed like a Sunday school teacher, with a white blouse and a high ruffle at the neck.

"Jenny! I thought you had left us."

"Almost. I've come back to pick up some of my things."

"You aren't really going to go, are you?"

"Yes." Jenny nodded. She went quickly to her old room. She felt as though she were walking into her past. A cold shadow passed over her. It was less than a week since she had worked here, since she had taken men to her bed. She walked inside and slammed the door behind her. God! If only she could close the door to her past in the same final manner.

She sat on the bed, opened her handbag, and pulled out the pornographic pictures and Bertha's letter.

Jenny stared for a long time at the pictures, then picked up Bertha's envelope. Taking a deep breath, she ripped it open.

Doolan was pleased that he didn't have to go down to the slabs again. Morgue workers were callous about other people's reactions to corpses, and no matter how many Doolan saw, he always grew slightly nauseous.

The attendant in the yard had told him that Feinberg was up in his office. Doolan plodded up the stone steps. It was always cold in the building, even in the middle of summer. At the top he turned left along a bleak, green-painted corridor, marveling that institutions always seemed to favor the same sickly shade. He came to an open door and knocked on the doorpost.

"Come in, Lieutenant, I saw you walking across the yard."

Doolan walked in. Feinberg was sharpening a pencil with a pocketknife. The coroner looked up and pointed the pencil at Doolan. "Well, sir, we might have another one!"

Doolan's heart sank. He would have to go down to the slabs. "Who?"

"Another young lady, but of good family—and not murdered."

"What?" Doolan dropped into a chair. Feinberg pulled over a folder, opened it, and referred to the papers inside as he talked.

"Let me give you the circumstances as I can piece them together. Sometime last night this young woman had an abortion. It was, in layman's language, botched. She started bleeding. When she arrived home later that night, she drew a bath. From what I can tell, the uterine muscles went into spasms, inducing a massive hemorrhage."

"She bled to death?"

"Well, yes and no. She was bleeding heavily; that produced light-headedness. She blacked out. At that point she slipped under the water and drowned."

"In a bathtub?"

"My young friend, most drownings occur in less than one foot of water, and the young lady was in no condition to fight off choking. In addition to the blood loss, she was suffering the effects of a large dose of morphine." Feinberg smiled.

Doolan straightened in his chair. "Like the girl we fished out of the Hudson!"

"Yes," Feinberg said. "The veins in this girl's arm

had a number of puncture wounds, indicating that she was a frequent user, if not an addict."

"Holy Christ!"

Doolan thought of Frank Cassassa making his run along the Hudson docks amongst the morphine suppliers. Perhaps he would indeed turn up something.

"Do you have her name? Her address?"

Feinberg nodded and handed over a sheet of paper.

Virginia went into the sitting room after lunch and sat in the armchair by the window. The policeman that Doolan had sent over was downstairs in the kitchen, drinking coffee with Gladys.

Virginia sighed as she thought about him being in her house. She felt strange about the whole business. Outside, the sun was bright and the air was filled with children's laughter. Her own children were playing in the park with their nanny. And yet here was a policeman sent to protect her from . . . from what?

She glanced out and up at the clouds drifting across the blue sky. Somewhere life was simpler than this, surely. She thought of Doolan and suddenly felt a wave of guilt. They had broken the rules. She laid her head back against the antimacassar and closed her eyes. Why did she have this urge to be with Doolan, to hear him, to see him, to touch him, and at the same time feel this whiplash of guilt?

She sank into a light sleep; Doolan was waiting for her in her dreams. They were standing by the sea, somewhere with blue skies and warm breezes. He slipped his arm around her and she felt his warmth and strength. They turned from the sea toward the church where they would get married. But as they walked, people began to appear along the path: parents, school friends, society friends, business associates. They hissed and booed, but Virginia and Doolan went on to the church. Doolan turned to her and she drew strength from the sureness in his eyes. Bellarma appeared at the door and stretched out his hand toward them. Malice seemed to drip from his smile like green saliva.

She wanted to turn back. She did not want to enter the black door of the church. A hand was laid on her shoulder; she spun around and found herself face to face with the eyeless white mask. She screamed and woke. Gladys was standing beside her, smiling gently.

"The phone's been ringing for ages, ma'am. I just answered it. A gentleman wants to talk to you. Shall I tell him to call back?"

"No, I'll take it."

Gladys walked ahead of her along the hall, heading for the back stairs. Virginia took up the phone.

"Hello."

It was a stranger's voice, and from his first word she was chilled. "Mrs. Pendleton?"

"Yes," she replied.

"You must listen to me carefully, for I will not repeat this. Your husband has in his possession manuscripts that are ours. You must get them and bring them to us, if you wish to see him again."

Virginia dropped the mouthpiece and nearly fell. Pendleton! God, was it possible that he was alive? She fought for breath and then pulled the mouthpiece back again.

"Where is my husband?"

"Do not ask questions. You will bring the manuscripts to the church of San Salvadore at Elizabeth and Broome. You will do this now, and you will tell no one."

The line went dead. Virginia stood for a long time listening to the buzzing on the line. She could not abandon Pendleton. She would phone Doolan and try to get the manuscripts back. Then she would go to the church and meet with them. She would beg for Pendleton's life. And if she could not find Doolan, she would go anyway.

CHAPTER 43

ONCE HE HAD been Erik Klaus Schmidt.

But that was before he knew the truth. That was before Rome and the Vatican and the long-neglected vaults. Then had come that moment of revelation, that powerful surge of knowledge and faith, and from that time forward he had known that he was Simon, Simon Magus, Simon of Abyssos reborn.

He had hidden the truth behind that other persona. To casual observers he was the parish priest, the simple Father Schmidt. But beyond that outward appearance he gathered initiates to his side and created a circle of power and knowledge.

Now all he needed was the book, the book that the cult had sealed away in secrecy at the time of their last persecution. He waited with patience, for it was written that Simon and the Word would once more be reunited. Now the woman would bring the sacred writings to him.

He walked into the altar room and took his place in one of the carved cubicles. Around him sat the elect. He smiled at them, and his blue eyes flashed in the dim red light from above the altar. His face radiated total faith, total knowledge.

"We have returned. . . ." His voice was gentle and reassuring. He looked around at his inner circle of believers. They were completely his. He could read their thoughts, enter into their minds, play with their moods. This power had come to him at the moment of his revelation. He used it to save his followers from doubt. He had used it the night that the policeman had entered the crypt. And each time he pushed himself one more step beyond the rim of Jehovah/Ialdoboath's moral laws, his strength of mind increased. He knew that he was entering into the power of the snake, into the power and knowledge that was Abyssos.

He had drawn his elect from the fringes of society, from those who already doubted Jehovah. They were the outcasts, the disenchanted.

Erik, a young, sallow-faced man with long greasy hair and deep-set eyes: he had slashed his way through the underworld, stealing, living only in the moment, preying on the weaknesses of others. He was driven by a deep anger which he laid at Simon's feet.

There was Sean Thomas, the barrel-chested dockworker. The burn scar that disfigured the right side of his face was a daily reminder of the night he had burned down his home in a drunken stupor. Only Simon had given him the will to live after the death of his wife and children.

Irene, the young Polish immigrant: eyes darkened with suffering, body racked by consumption. Only Simon's words enabled her to make sense of her shrinking world.

And then there was Antonio. Antonio, the nephew of Gallenini, who had seen Simon in the eyes of the priest almost before he had known it himself. Antonio, the first acolyte, who shared Simon's visions and drew the dispossessed from the streets.

These gathered were just a few of his disciples and their number was growing.

Simon lifted the shimmering snake mask and showed it to the assembled. The one with the porcelain face came out of the shadows and knelt before him. She, more than any, knew of the twisted malice that was Jehovah/Ialdoboath's world. He placed his hands on her veiled head. Deep in the dark eye slits, there was a glitter of joy. Simon's voice rolled out rhythmically in a paean to his God.

"I will take the chaff from the grain, I will take the castoffs from this world, I will take the human garbage from the gutters, I will take the failures. Just as I took you from your prison, took you and made you my handmaiden, took you and made you the instrument of the Snake of Knowledge. The first sister of Abyssos was Helen of the desert brotherhood. She lay down her mortal clay beside the sacred manuscripts, as I did. As I was reborn, so were you! You are reborn!"

He looked around at his inner circle.

"I promised you Light. I swept you out of the black hole of despair. I took you out of the gutters of the harsh world of Jehovah/Ialdoboath. I snatched you from His hatred and His vengeance and I showed you the love that can flow from the great Unnameable One that is beyond Him."

He walked forward to the altar and raised his hands, then set them on the top and looked up. His eyes burned with an inner fire.

"The Snake of Knowledge has come to us as he came to us before, for we are of those called the cult Abyssos. Once our enemies called us the cult of the damned. We were persecuted by the Church of Rome, by its bishop Hippolytus, and driven from the cities of Constantinople and Alexandria. The desert was our last refuge then, our last church. But now we are reborn!"

Before him, he saw the ochre cliffs of Gebel Kalat, the cave of the last altar.

"The Snake of Truth is the vessel of the Knowledge and it shall bring salvation to the elect."

He slowly slid the top of the altar aside. From the hollow interior rose a horrible hissing.

"Ialdoboath is cunning and vengeful, but the Snake will conquer. The Snake will lead the soul from its

311

prison, past Ialdoboath's abode of vengeance and pride to the Eternity that is the soul's rightful heritage, beyond the dust that is the flesh and the corruption that is the body. We must never fear to pay the last quadrant."

By the light in their eyes he knew that the elect understood that the "last quadrant" was that which Jehovah called death. Their eyes said they would follow him through that last gate. They rose and approached. As each stepped forward, Simon leaned over and removed a snake from the writhing pit. Each grasped the snake in firm hands.

"And now the Snake will choose who will join the Godhead, and who will remain here for the work that is still to be done. Soon those chosen to remain will travel to other cities. There we will do what we have done in New York. We must work for the destruction of Jehovah's stranglehold on the souls that truly belong in Abyssos. Our goal is the destruction of all flesh and all matter. We are the messengers of Abyssos!"

And the elect responded: "We are the messengers of Abyssos. . . ."

Their chant echoed through the dark corridors.

CHAPTER 44

TOM FELT JUBILANT. The wind blowing from the southeast carried the smell of the sea, the smell of hope and travel and new horizons. Along Eighth Avenue the canvas shop awnings flapped in the wind, and Tom thought of the high-masted schooners that he and his brother stokers had virtually put out of business. Well, now he would put himself out of business, if Jenny would listen to his plans.

Drawn by the smell of fresh bread, he turned into Villachi's bakery at the corner of Fifty-second. He would bring home a fresh loaf for lunch. The plump, grey-haired Italian lady behind the counter wiped her hands on her apron and gave him a motherly smile. Tom paid for the bread and dropped it into the bag with his other purchases—salami, tomatoes, oranges, and milk. Then he started for his brother's apartment on Fifty-third Street.

That morning, after Jenny left, he had remembered the bosun off the *Christiana,* a tall gangling Swede by the name of Olaf Jacobsen. He was one of Tom's best friends. Ollie had gone "dry land" as he called it, and bought a tugboat in San Francisco harbor. He had written to Tom only a year ago, offering him a job, telling him that the whole area was thriving since the earthquake. But Tom had never considered it until he met Jenny. Now that foggy bay beckoned like a promise of paradise.

Tom opened the door to the apartment, walked over and dumped his packages on the kitchen cabinet beside the stove. Jenny would be back within the hour and he had to have his arguments worked out before he spoke to her.

The apartment had an unused smell about it; his brother had obviously not slept there last night. Tom pulled back the living room curtains. He would move the table over there and they could look out the window as they ate. Turning, he saw the envelope on the floor by the door.

He stared at it and felt a strange sense of foreboding. He picked up the envelope, ripped it open, and read.

"Dearest Tom,

"I went to visit a friend of mine this morning and learned that she had just died. I'm very upset.

"I used to belong to a group with her. I need to go and talk to the others about her death.

"Tom, I don't know how to say this, but I held something back from your brother about the girl who was fished out of the river. I knew her. She went to the group too. Her name was Anna Kresge and she was part of the inner circle. I need to find out what happened to Bertha. I am going to talk to Father Schmidt at the church of San Salvadore. I shall be home in a few hours.

"I love you.

"Jenny."

Tom looked up. He did not understand any of this. Why had she lied to his brother? And why would she go to this priest?

Araya's presence in Doolan's office caused quite a stir. They were used to seeing black men in the holding cells, not sitting in one of the offices, behaving as if he had every right to be there. After three stenographers and four of the policemen had walked in, stared, and then excused themselves, Araya decided to shut the door.

His journey through the manuscripts had to be a solitary experience, as solitary as his journeys through the high tablelands of the Ethiopian plateau, and the deserts and gebels of the Upper Sudan. This was in many ways the final part of the pilgrimage that had begun in that hot, dusty town of Makale at the edge of the Danakil desert.

Even though the book of the guardians had prepared him for this, it staggered him when he finally started reading. The words in the manuscripts of Abyssos ripped across his mind like a jagged-edged saw.

In the hours that he was left alone in the office, he set the pages aside many times. He would take the small cross from his pocket and pray. On one occasion he took the amulet out of its leather pouch and laid it on the manuscripts.

Each time he returned to the words, he was struck by the insidiousness of the message. In the book left by the guardians, the teachings seemed stark and odious, but in the manuscripts, the masters of Abyssos spoke for themselves and they wooed with gentle, seductive voices. Everything was made so reasonable, so believable. More than once Araya found himself being swayed, and more than once he lay the manuscripts aside so that he could bring the clear vision of his own faith into focus.

When the phone on the desk rang he was startled. The battle of good and evil slowly receded in his mind as he looked at the instrument. He lifted the earpiece. The ringing stopped and he heard someone talking. He placed the black piece to his ear as he had seen Doolan do that morning, then leaned forward, putting

315

his mouth near the other part.

"Hello?" said a voice in Araya's ear.

"Hello."

"Can I speak to Lieutenant Doolan?" the woman asked.

"He is not here, but he will return soon." There was a long pause, and for a while Araya thought the machine had stopped, but then the woman's voice began again.

"Could you please tell him that Virginia Pendleton phoned? And tell him that they have phoned me, offering Mr. Pendleton's life for the manuscripts. I have gone to the church of San Salvadore to talk to them. Will you tell him all that?"

"Yes," Araya replied through a dry throat.

The phone went dead. He listened to the strange tone and then fitted the earpiece back into the cradle. So Bellarma had been right. The church of San Salvadore. He must go there.

Jenny kept replaying the words in Bertha's letter over and over in her head as she walked to the church. They sent chills through her.

"And I asked Simon how long death would hold sway and he said so long as women bring forth, for I come to end the works of the female."

That was how Bertha had died, denying the works of the female.

Jenny walked on, feeling a knot of fear and anger growing in her stomach. The warm, sticky wind whipped along the streets of the island, swirling the dust from the gutters and blowing it into her eyes. Dark clouds had started to scud across the first spectacular beginnings of sunset.

The front door of the church was closed, but Jenny knew from Bertha's letter that there was a side entrance to what Bertha called the sanctuaries. Jenny hoped to confront Father Schmidt there.

316

She went in through the gate in the wall. The house was dark, and she wondered where the housekeeper was.

The door was near the bushes according to the letter. Yes, there it was. Jenny tugged it open and walked down the steps. At the bottom she found herself in a labyrinth of corridors. Here and there a gaslight gave off a dull yellow glow, and as she walked past, shadows danced along the walls.

The hissing led her to the altar room. The door was open. Inside she saw a red light flickering over the altar. It beckoned her like the heartbeat of her lost child. She shivered at the thought. What was happening to her?

"Hello? Is anyone there?"

She walked in. The top of the altar was pulled aside. A number of agitated snakes coiled and wreathed themselves around each other, hissing and slithering. The door slammed behind her and she swung around. Father Schmidt was standing there. His intense blue eyes held her in their clear gaze and she felt his love and warmth flowing around her. Jenny began to relax as he walked toward her and placed his hand on her brow.

"So you have come to me at last."

She had come here to confront him. She had come here to accuse him in the deaths of Bertha and Anna, and yet she now saw him as a friend, a confessor. It was as if he knew her questions before she could ask them.

"You have come to ask about Bertha and about Anna."

"Yes," she murmured.

Again the soothing hand gently stroked her brow. "You must forget your questions, Jenny, for I can assure you that Bertha and Anna are in a paradise that is beyond your imaginings."

Jenny tried to shake off the lulling influence of his

voice, but she found herself listening, almost believing.

"You must forget those questions, Jenny, and you must ask the real questions, the ones that pierce to the root, for only then will you find the real answers." He took her by the hand and led her to one of the chairs along the walls. Then he moved back to the altar and slid the cover shut with a final, resonating clang.

"The question you must ask," he said, "is the one that I ask of all of us. What would the world be like if the devil and not God had won the great struggle at Creation?"

Jenny stared at him, intrigued in spite of herself.

"What do you mean?"

"I mean, what would this world be like if Evil ruled . . . if Jehovah was in fact Evil."

"No . . . no. . . ."

"Abyssos asks you to look at the world as it is, not as you wish it to be, to look at the horror, at the death by disease and starvation and war. Look at the hatred and envy, the shortness of life and the fear of death, the scarcely controlled desperation of most men. Look at all that agony and then tell me if the God who created such a world is a good God. What kind of being is it that has buried us in such mud?"

He paused, watching her intently.

"We answer that such a God is evil, a proud and malignant being. In his own words, he is a jealous God and a God of Vengeance. We poor beings are less his creations than his victims."

A chill crept up Jenny's spine. In the yellowish light from the flame, the priest's eyes took on a serpentlike glint, growing cold and impassive. For a moment she felt as the fakir in the follies show must have, certain that the snake was about to strike.

The warmth in his voice attempted to belie the piercing, analytical stare. He was again soothing, cajoling.

"Jenny, we were not always enslaved in this mud. The True Light, The Unknown Father, is beyond this horror, in the realm of Abyssos. Once, eons ago, the essence that we are dwelt with the Forefathers, dwelt in his Light and was a spark of that Light.

"We have that spark within us still, and that spark can lead us back to the fullness of joy in Abyssos.

"At the time of the Creation there was a dividing of the great Original, and from that dividing came seven Archons.

"One of them called himself Jehovah, the Lord of Hosts and God of Gods. We of Abyssos call him Ialdoboath. This Archon was prideful and arrogant, and all that is written in his Testament is an expression of this pride. In Isaiah Chapter forty-five: verse five it says, 'I am God and beside me there is no other.' This God of arrogance has imprisoned our souls within the flesh of mortality. But we can travel beyond him to something greater, and that journey can be made through knowledge. The snake in Eden was a messenger from Abyssos, saying 'Knowledge is the path.'"

Jenny stared straight ahead of her, drinking in the darkness of the words. She could not look at Simon, whose voice was so smooth and seductive. It all sounded so reasonable. It would explain the horrors that daily took place around her, the loss of her child and her family, the early death that surely waited for her. But what he was saying had to be wrong. It had to be!

Simon smiled, and she felt a wave of reassurance sweep over her.

"This evil God, Ialdoboath, has enslaved our souls in our bodies, and set rules to keep us in thrall to him. These 'laws' must be broken to allow the soul to escape back to Abyssos. Every sin, especially those that smash the chain of procreation, is a glorification that will take the worshipper one step further along the road to Abyssos. Jenny, you are especially blessed. You have already broken the sexual commandments. Now you must go on to reject the evil archon Ialdoboath."

Jenny felt as if she were burning up. His words swept across her mind like the fire of a new truth devouring the old. Yet somewhere in her heart, one corner held steadfast. She pressed her hands against the sides of her thighs and felt something sharp dig into her right palm. From her pocket she tugged the small Celtic cross, the one Tom had given to her. Her confusion cleared like smoke before a refreshing wind.

"No more. You are wrong. It is you who are evil," she said. The words were a cry from her soul.

Simon strode across the room and picked up the cross. He held it high, so that it glittered in the flickering red light. "Jenny, this is the cross of sin. You know that it promises only suffering and torment. By its laws you are doomed to suffer again and again." His eyes narrowed and a moment later Jenny felt a blinding pain ripping through her skull. Consciousness ebbed away.

Centre Market seemed empty. The building echoed like a mausoleum as Doolan ran up the empty stairwell. He rushed along the dimly lit corridor and into his office, expecting to find Araya there. Instead it was his brother who greeted him.

"Tom! What the hell are you doin' here?"

"I was to meet Jenny, but she didn't turn up. I waited and waited. I'm worried, Peter." Tom pulled the note from his pocket and handed it to Doolan. "She left me this."

Doolan read the note and paled. Lord God, it had come full circle. He closed his eyes and rubbed his brow. He didn't want to think anymore. All his doubts and fears had gelled in that one moment, and he knew he could not stand against them. Then he shook himself, reached down, and pulled a .38 revolver from the middle drawer of his desk.

"I suppose you'll want to come with me?" It was a question he did not need to ask.

CHAPTER 45

VIRGINIA RUSHED DOWNTOWN in the cab, her mind whirling in anguished confusion. She kept replaying the events of the last week. She felt like someone falling, with excruciating slowness, unable in any way to stop herself. She was so absorbed that she did not notice that they had stopped until the cabbie spoke, and then she looked out the cab window at the church. The building was stark and uninviting against the stormy-looking sky.

She quickly stepped out and paid, then watched as the cab turned east. The horse first snorted and stamped as it faced the wind, then galloped off. Crossing the crowded sidewalk, she made her way up the church steps to its front door. How could all these people be going about their ordinary lives when she was immersed in an otherworldly struggle? Peddlers and shop assistants, paper boys and seamstresses from the garment factories pushed past in a seemingly endless throng, all consumed with their end-of-the-day tasks. And here she was, about to negotiate for the life of her husband. A small, neat notice was tacked to the dark wood of the front door. 'Closed for repairs.'

But Virginia knew that was not for her. She gripped the handle and pushed. The door opened and the smell of candle smoke and incense tumbled into the warm windy evening. She stepped inside, through a second door, and into the church itself. There was little light. It filtered dimly through the high windows, casting deep shadows across the empty pews. To Virginia's left a few votive candles burned in front of a glistening Virgin. Virginia stared at the lily-white sheen of the face, fascinated at how the wavering flames gave the features life.

Somewhere a door creaked. The candles in front of the Virgin flickered. Virginia looked away from the Virgin's marble niche and saw a large iron door standing open a few inches. As she stepped toward it she thought she saw it move.

"Hello?" Her voice died somewhere out in the dark nave.

She walked up to the ring of candles below the Virgin and took one. A thought struck her—if the church was closed, who had lit the candles? There had to be someone here, even just a caretaker.

A faint whispering sound filled the church, then faded. The door creaked again.

"Who's there?" Virginia called.

She held the candle out and watched the dark shadow made by the door's edge dance as if in slow invitation to enter.

The candle reflected dully in the shiny black enamel surface of the door. She reached forward and pulled the door open. A sibilant, inviting voice in her mind urged her on. It had to be her imagination. She stepped forward.

The candle opened up the dark before her, and she saw a stairway winding down below. She shielded the flame from the wafting air and took the first step. There was a smell of cold dampness mixed with a mustiness.

She kept her hand against the wall as she glided down. Near the bottom, the brickwork gave way to the cold hardness of the rocky foundations. Darkness spread out before her. She moved into it. To one side, she saw a black casket and gasped in fear. It was a chilling, ominous symbol.

323

The whispering came again, the swish of cloth on cloth—right behind her! Virginia tried to turn, but she stumbled and fell, dropping the candle. The smooth, white porcelain mask gleamed above her in the wavering light. She took in the molded lips, the dainty nose and tiny nostrils, the elegant high cheekbones that curved into the black eye sockets. And this time she saw the eyes, deep inside—eyes full of hate, eyes full of vengeance.

The creature pressed a rag over Virginia's face. The woman struggled against the bitter fumes of the ether-soaked cloth, but quickly lost consciousness.

Araya felt refreshed by the wind. It was a breath of God from the sky and the sea, from beyond the creations of man, the buildings, the streets, the cars and trucks. The streets were busy with the end-of-week traffic from the docks and warehouses and factories. As Araya strode along he began to feel the city bearing in on him. All around were desperate people, full of sadness and agony, begging for relief. All human suffering seemed to call out to him tonight.

He wanted to push it away and clear a space full of silence. He yearned for the silences of the desert hills and ambas. The desire grew within him, but he knew it was wrong. Almost like a soothing hand, the words of his father drifted into his head.

"Araya, remember that God is to be found not only on rooftops and high among the cliffs and ambas of the Central Plateau. God is also of the earth, God is also of the marketplace."

It was true. God was among this crush of peoples of all nations. A gentle smile formed on Araya's face, for if he was not big enough in himself to encompass the crush of human misery, surely God was. He was only one of God's conduits.

And now he would fight God's battle. San Salvadore was just across the street. The dark wooden doors of the church were closed. Araya's body tensed, preparing for the assault he knew would come.

A pounding nausea suddenly swept through his skull. He had not felt like this since he walked the rocky path up to the caves at Gebel Kalat. Waves of doubt attacked him, feelings of fear and unworthiness. He swayed slightly and clutched the manuscripts tightly. He would not fall! The mist started to clear.

He crossed the street, walked calmly up the steps and, ignoring the Closed notice, entered the church.

In the darkness of her half sleep, memories tumbled from the deepest corners of Jenny's mind. She saw the bleak despair in her father's eyes. She felt the cold panic when the Colvin boy told her that they could not marry. She stood sobbing at the grave while the tiny coffin of her child was lowered into the damp earth.

Slowly she began to waken, and as her eyes adjusted to the light, another world faced her. As the delicate numbing web lifted from her mind, she staggered to her feet. She was no longer in the room with the altar. All around her, naked bodies were stretched out, entwined, caught in the act of intercourse. She stared, wide-eyed. They were writhing, but absolutely silent. The shapes began to take on more positive outlines. The people were still, still and white in the eerie glow. Something else was moving, squeezing and writhing through the bodies.

Her eyes focused on the closest couple. A blond young man was locked between the legs of an older woman. Her plump thighs were spread wide. As Jenny watched, something stirred around the man's neck and started to slither over his white back and buttocks, and down between his legs. For an instant the snake's sleek head turned toward Jenny. There was a jarring hiss as the tongue slithered out and in.

Jenny stumbled backward. She fell against one of

325

the couches and grabbed, feeling the clammy touch of a naked thigh. She recoiled in terror, but as she tried to turn away, she tripped and fell onto two bodies. Panic swamped her. She pushed hard into the soft flesh of a woman's stomach. The body jerked up, eyes popping, as the air rushed to escape. There was a rattling groan as it was expelled from the corpse's throat.

Jenny was close to fainting. In this half consciousness, she saw Simon moving amongst the bodies. Some rose at his touch, nearly as pale as the dead. They embraced and vanished into the stairwell.

Simon came to her. Jenny felt the touch of his hand in hers and looked up to see those eyes, bright and penetrating, boring in on her. Once again her mind flooded with images. She saw the Naples Pavilion, the Morasinis leering at her across the table. Her arm was outstretched like a beggar's, and all along it the skin was broken with a welter of ulcers and purulent sores. She saw the stableyards and the dark dockland alleyways; the prostitutes offering what remained of their diseased bodies. That was her future, that was her, being banged senseless against a stable door!

Simon laid a hand on her brow. His voice was filled with a gentle assurance that quickly changed to vicious arrogance.

"This is the temple of the Archon Saclas. The Snake has chosen. Some have gone to Abyssos at last. Others I have sent to take the Word to the world beyond. But you have betrayed Abyssos, you have chosen Jehovah/Ialdoboath, and you will suffer for your choice."

The beauty of his voice resonated through her mind, and yet she shivered at the threat. Her throat dried with fear and she could not swallow. She sank back, paralyzed. His eyes seemed to burrow into her. A throbbing pain filled her groin. The pain ripped through her like a knife sawing at her nerve endings. Jenny looked down at her stomach and legs. The skin was breaking out in large, ugly sores that oozed pus.

Jenny collapsed; her whole nervous system had been suddenly eaten away. Her skull thumped against the hard floor. She tried to scream, but only a strangled gurgle spilled out. At last she fainted. As the darkness closed in, she heard Simon laughing.

Doolan opened the back door of the rectory and let himself into the kitchen. Bridie was nowhere to be seen.

"Bridie? It's Doolan. Bridie?" There was no answer. Tom entered the kitchen behind his brother.

"No one's here," he said.

"I hope Bridie isn't mixed up in this," Doolan responded.

He crossed to the stove, touched the handle of the blue-speckled coffeepot, and then jerked his hand away.

On the Japanese lacquer tray beside it he saw two cups and the unfinished plate of soda bread.

"Let's get into that church now," Tom insisted. "We'll look for your lady friend later."

"All right." Doolan tossed them in his hand, then crossed to the large cupboard below the sink, opened it, and pulled out an oil lamp and a box of matches.

"Is there another lamp there?" Tom asked. "I want to find that side entrance that Jenny mentioned."

Doolan looked at his brother for a moment and was about to argue. Then he saw the look in Tom's eyes and gave a grunt.

"All right, but be careful."

Araya walked through the dark passageways under San Salvadore, possessed of an inner vision. He saw in his mind the small church in the town of Quorquor; and that moment when his journey of years had begun. Once again he saw the old Debtera, a man from that class of ecclesiastical laity who ran the smaller churches, standing before him in a small chapel. A painted wooden crucifix hung over a brick altar. The Debtera walked to a fresco, held the candle high, and invited Araya to join him. The old man's eyes were heavy, tired. His beard was white and straggly and his face deeply wrinkled. He looked like a man who had carried a burden too long and was happy now to shift it.

Araya walked over and studied the faded but still rich colors of a wall painting. Eve in the Garden, being tempted by the serpent. The brown-skinned Eve stood open-eyed as the serpent whispered smoothly into her ear. Araya stared at it. It was truly beautiful. And yet something was wrong. Suddenly it hit him. It *was* beautiful. The snake was not malevolent, not evil and dangerous, he was warm and seductive. He was the messenger of knowledge and he had the ear of the woman.

The old man spoke slowly, obviously choosing his words with care. "I have waited for you. You are the one who will one day face this tempter and the knowledge he will offer. The painter was of the cult of Abyssos. Though they were destroyed, it has been foretold that they will return."

The old man walked to the foot of the wooden cross and opened a secret compartment. He pulled out an object wrapped in ancient cloth. The Debtera stared at Araya and slowly pulled the cloth aside. The metal glittered in the light. It was a strangely formed double-bladed knife. It swept out from one shaft to two vicious points.

As Araya walked along the corridors under San Salvadore he felt the sharp edges of the twin points under his coat and trembled at the thought of what he had to face.

"So, you have come!"

Araya stopped. He had walked into the pillared room, the sanctuary of Saclas. The smell of death lay heavy around him, and the sight of the bodies lying in the room wrenched at his stomach. In their midst he saw Simon. Around the room a number of bowls flamed yellow and blue. Mixed with the smell of death was the heavy smell of oil. He immediately knew that this was to be a human pyre.

Simon held him with his eyes and suddenly laughed. It was a wild, vicious laugh that lashed out across the temple like a snake's tongue seeking a victim.

As Doolan descended into the blackness of the crypt, memories of his earlier terror below flooded over him. Each step downward seemed to increase the chill threat. The yellow light from the lamp illuminated only a tight circle, and beyond that the light died.

At the bottom of the stone steps Doolan stopped. It was there that the black robes had billowed past him; it was there that he had caught his first haunting glimpse of the porcelain mask. He took a deep breath, narrowed his eyes, and peered into the darkness of the crypt. The flash of the lamp was reflected in the polished marble of the Gallenini tomb. It looked as ominous as the first time he had seen it.

He walked forward, trying to piece together all the elements that had led to this place. The dissevered body of the girl, taken piece by piece from the river; the death of another young woman, Bertha; Tom's lady, Jenny; the lawyer, Pendleton; the priest, Bellarma; Father Brautsch; Bridie; the African monk, Araya. Everything led to this church, to the enigmatic Father Schmidt.

Doolan ran his hand along the smooth, cold surface of the marble. A cold draft of air swirled around him. It smelled of the dampness from rock and earth, a breath from deep, secret places. Doolan thought he heard a distant, rasping hiss. He spun around and pulled his .38 revolver from his pocket, listening intently. There was a deep, taunting silence. The memory of his father's death burst on him again, but he fought against it, struggling to fill his lungs with air. He would not travel down that road again. He squeezed the handle of the revolver and stepped forward into the crypt.

At each step he expected to see a figure lunge forward. He felt alone and vulnerable. Wave after wave of doubt and loneliness and fear swept over him. He felt like a child, alone in a nightmare of desolation.

He shivered as the breeze came again. He had moved to the center of what looked like another small crypt. The walls were lined with man-sized niches full of shadows. There was no exit—where was the wind coming from?

Doolan walked toward one of the arched niches. The back wall was solid, but the right-side wall had a narrow opening. Doolan squeezed through, and beyond it discovered a corridor.

Within twenty yards the corridor divided, and the right-hand branch formed a stairway down. The place smelled of dampness and disuse, and something else. Doolan sniffed, but quickly went down the stairs. His shadow danced and flickered beside him on the wall. Then in a flash it came to him: it was the smell of oil!

No sooner had he identified the odor than he glimpsed another light and the shadow of a person. He gave a garbled yell.

"Stop! Police!" But it was gone. Doolan clattered down the remainder of the stairs. The corridor stretched ahead of him, carved rough and jagged from the mother rock. On the left he saw a doorway. With his back to the wall, he edged toward it. The door creaked. Doolan froze for a moment and cocked his gun. He could see that there was no light inside and realized that coming in with the lamp would make him a perfect target. Carefully he laid it down on the floor, then stepped in front of the door. He sucked in a deep breath and lunged forward. The door crashed inward and swung back with a soft thud. Doolan fell into the room and dropped into a crouch.

It was an empty storeroom. The only light came from the lamp in the corridor as it cut a yellow swath across the floor. The door creaked. Someone else was in the room. Doolan lifted his revolver.

"Come out!"

The figure leaped at him from the shadows. Doolan's gun fired without any conscious action on his part. There were two figures; they swung back and forth. Doolan saw them turn in the slow ballet of a dream: Father Brautsch and Bridie. Their eyes bulged white and their mouths gaped. As he watched, they continued to turn in a strange liquid movement.

Then he saw the tattered and ripped flesh around their necks, the dark stains of blood soaking into their clothes. Ropes had been neatly tied under their chins and passed through hooks in a beam above.

Doolan staggered back against the wall, stricken with a sickening terror.

"Oh, God! Oh, God!" He was too late!

Virginia woke up to the sound of some kind of instrument playing an old song. She remembered the words:

> "This is the father and mother, this is the baby
>   dear;
> This is the sister and brother, all our good family
>   here."

The tinkling sound of the music became clearer as she struggled to consciousness. Then there was a whirring and a click, and the tune repeated. The mist began to slowly clear from her eyes. She looked around. Shadows played across a low ceiling. She was lying on her back. A dull yellow lamp cast a glow over the room.

Virginia gazed around the windowless, shadowed space, feeling that she had fallen into a Lewis Carroll fantasy. It was a little girl's room, filled with all kinds of toys. There were two large dolls' houses. The front of one, a miniature brownstone, was open, and she could see that it was filled from basement to attic with beautifully crafted model furniture. There were shelves of dolls, kitchen sets, painting sets, a blackboard on its easel, baskets of soft toys, and jigsaws and games. Virginia stared, wide-eyed. It was like a toyshop.

Against one wall stood a small, pink-painted dressing table. The music box was sitting on it. A small ballerina danced, twirling to the music.

Virginia crossed to the box. It was so delicate, so pretty. Close up, she could see the intricate hand-painted scenes on the black-lacquered wood, and the delicate painting on the carved ballerina. The little model twirled again, and Virginia jumped back, gasping. There was no face!

Someone had sheared off the features. She watched as the little clockwork machine ground to a halt. Behind her, the door opened. Virginia knew at once what stood there—the thing with the porcelain face! Slowly, Virginia turned. She would not give in to her fears.

"Where is my husband?"

A hoarse whisper came from the creature in the shadows. "Pendleton is dead. The traitor is dead. You have no manuscripts. You too must die!"

But before the thing could move, Doolan stepped into the room. He felt like he was walking through a nightmare. Virginia was supposed to be safe at home, but here she was, menaced by an evil being in this perverted replica of a child's bedroom. Then like a line of dominoes everything clattered into place.

"You're the child of Gallenini," he whispered.

The creature turned like a trapped animal, letting out a half groan, half screech. "I am Gallenini's daughter, yes."

Relief flooded over Virginia. She moved toward Doolan, but he lifted his hand to hold her back. The creature continued to speak.

"I am daughter. For years I was kept in the mansion by a loving father. Then he built this place for Simon, and me. Simon told me to come to Abyssos, to Paradise. Simon ask me to be his angel of death. Soon we will all be joined in Abyssos beyond Jehovah, who made me a monster."

Doolan slowly moved forward. He felt a wave of sympathy for this lonely person. "But surely you can be helped."

"Helped!" The creature's voice was raised to a shriek as she tore away the mask. Virginia staggered back and buried her face in her hands. Doolan gasped in shock.

The woman was grotesque. Her features were a combination of those of a pig and a human. Her nostrils were two large holes. Her cheekbones were so high that the eyes were only slits. She had no upper lip so her yellow teeth were constantly exposed. And her skin was ridged with deep scars and bulbous tumors.

"I am a monster! But you are traitors to the true God, Simon, who shows me the true Light and life!"

Doolan saw what was coming. He placed himself between Virginia and the glittering knife. His revolver was pointed at the creature.

"Stop. Stop or I'll kill you!"

Then he realized that he could not do that. She was one of God's most needy creatures and he could not hurt her. The revolver dropped to his side.

She screamed as she lurched forward. Doolan pushed himself between the blade and Virginia. The knife rose and fell, slashing his shoulders and upper chest. Blood soaked into his shirt and trickled down his chest and arms. Virginia pulled the gun from his bloody hand. She fired. Again and again the explosions echoed through the child's bedroom and along the corridor.

The creature fell back, and the mask fell from her hand and smashed on the floor. She staggered against the door and reeled into the corridor.

Virginia collapsed on top of Doolan, sobbing.

Simon's laugh reverberated through the dark, pillared room. He fixed Araya with a penetrating look. His eyes glittered in the yellow-and-blue flame.

"I am Simon and I live within this fire of knowledge."

He took one of the crucibles of flame and held it over his head. His voice rang out loud and clear. "You conspired with Bellarma the traitor, conspired to keep the Word from us."

Araya dropped to his knees. He opened his arms wide and began to pray.

Simon stretched out his hand and slowly walked toward the kneeling monk.

"Come," he said.

Araya heard his warm, caring voice. He was seduced—no, more than that—compelled. A darkness blurred his eyes, as though a misted glass had been placed between him and the world. The voice was a firm, insisting drone, lulling and inviting. Araya wanted to go to him, to feel the security of his embrace.

"I have come to show the world as it really is," Simon whispered. "Not as we have been blinded to believe it is. Knowledge is Jehovah's enemy, because knowledge will show us a way out of the mortal prison in which he has placed us."

Around Araya there grew a place of light and heat.

"Jehovah is a jealous God, a God of Vengeance, swift to anger and revenge. Such a God can only create a world that is filled with terror and horror. We lull our minds to forget that horror, to bury it. But when we face it, we are on the road to knowledge, and our original homeland."

The words tumbled around Araya like so many spinning tops. They were the crazed words of a carnival charlatan, a mountebank, a dealer in black magic. But even as he thought this he could feel the slithering tendrils of the manipulator writhing into his thoughts. Reality was being wrenched from him.

A dry, dusty heat settled around his body. His arms remained outstretched in desperate prayer. The wind whipped up, swirling the fine, hot sand into his nostrils. Araya staggered to his feet, instinctively placing his hand in front of his mouth and closing his eyes. This was like the rolling heat off the Danakil desert, the beginnings of a dust storm.

Suddenly he knew where he was, and when. He was being brought back to his father again, to that day of death between Aduwa and Adigrat. He shook his head violently, trying to lose the growing vision. He clenched his fists. He would draw on the strength within him. He would defeat this false magic with faith.

He felt the crush of the people beside him, the coarse language, the rancid smell of poverty. He was being pushed forward, staggering from shadow into bright, blasting heat. A roar went up not far from him, and a wave of excitement swept through the crowd. He was in a narrow, rocky street. On either side stretched low, flat-roofed houses with shuttered windows, and courtyards with scrawny palm trees.

He was back home.

Suddenly the crowd behind him shouted as one. A

low chanting began, followed by a ringing clang of metal. The chanting stopped.

Araya staggered forward. A man turned to him and smiled. The open face, the sympathetic smile, the cool blue eyes. The face was bearded, the clothes were different, but Araya knew who it was—the one they called Simon.

Araya pushed through the throng, and the priest vanished. This had to be an execution. There was a snarling savagery here that belonged nowhere else. But where was Simon?

Araya spotted him a few yards away, his blue eyes glistening in the sun. Suddenly there was the clash of steel on steel again. The crowd along the center of the road parted before the soldiers at the head of the death procession. Araya was stunned to see that they were Roman soldiers.

He scanned the procession. Above the bobbing heads and helmets, Araya saw the heavy wooden cross. This was not his father's death, but something far worse!

A wail of despair spilled from his throat, drowned by the crowd around him. He wanted to flee, but a tight wall of bodies held him in place. He felt as if he were bound in metal, as if a searing-hot needle were being rammed through his mind. He wanted to be anywhere but here, anywhere. Scalding tears brimmed in his eyes and coursed down into his beard.

Now the man was only yards from him; Araya could see him bent under the weight of the thick, rough beams. The man's hair fell tangled and greasy on either side of his head, and his beard was streaked with spittle and phlegm. The tattered purple cloth over his shoulders barely hid the deep lacerations that scarred his back.

He raised his head and Araya saw his face, deeply creased with pain and despair. Blood from puncture wounds across the forehead had poured down into one of his eyes, half closing it. He could see the man fighting back the pain, searching the crowd, seeking some relief. The eyes were magnetic. Araya could see past the crusted blood to the pellucid coolness of pure love.

The man's eyes locked on his, and the world stopped. The tumult faded away. Araya experienced truth and joy as he had never known them.

Araya was paralyzed. He watched as the man fell, helplessly, the flesh on his hands ripping against the rough edges of the wood. The heavy cross teetered for a moment, then fell on top of him. He gave a hollow groan as it pummeled the last of his breath from his lungs.

The crowd reacted with a mixture of whoops and groans. Pity and vengeance, a true carnival of emotions.

Araya broke through the cordon of troops. He rushed to the center of the road, and others followed. The soldiers restored order swiftly, and a centurion stood beside Araya. He motioned his men to stand back as Araya leaned over and gently touched the bloodied face. While he wiped the blood and sweat aside, he felt, pulsing through his hands, the energy that the man exuded.

Someone else pushed through the crowd and knelt beside them. Araya glanced up. It was Simon. His eyes were full of pity and tenderness. He looked at Araya, and then down at the man. The fallen one whispered, brokenly.

"I am forsaken."

Somewhere beyond the tight ring around the fallen man, the crowd began to chant again. Their circus was being interrupted. They had not ventured out under this boiling sun to see this. After all, the main event was to take place up the hill, at the Place of Skulls.

The man wept, slapping his bloody hand on the stones.

"Why . . . why?"

Simon spoke in a low voice.

"Yes, why? Why does Jehovah make us face such horror if he is a good God?"

He turned back to the man, and lifted him to his feet, supporting him firmly.

The centurion had had enough delay. He stepped forward and grabbed Araya roughly by the shoulders.

"You! You wanna help him? Well, pick up the cross and carry it."

Araya staggered to his feet. He propped up the heavy beam, and carefully shouldered it. As he did a searing-hot pain shot through him. This was the worst of all nightmares. This was the first and last of all horrors.

He staggered forward under the weight of the cross. The procession moved on. The heat became more intense. Araya choked back tears. His mind was numb. Simon stepped ahead of him, supporting the broken man. A strange trio of human misery, trudging on the weary road to execution. Araya knew that he was helping this man to his death, but there was no other way. It was written. It was the ultimate offering of human blood demanded by his God.

This was the God that he worshipped, the God of pain, the God of sacrifice, the God of blood and vengeance and jealousy.

The street seemed to be dissolving into flame. Simon beckoned through the fire. Araya could still feel the weight of the cross but instead he was carrying the manuscripts. Simon stepped from the heat and took the papers, smiling in triumph.

A scream rang through the crackling fire. The two worlds, real and unreal, jarred and shuddered.

The fire was real. The air was choked with the smell of burning flesh. The human pyre was alight.

The woman's screams ripped through the pillared

room again. Someone had extricated herself from the dead and was scrambling away from the fire.

"Jenny! Jenny, over here!" Araya spun around to see Tom standing at the bottom of the stairs.

As Tom was walking along the side of the church he had heard a door opening and the sound of muffled voices. He stepped back into the shadow of the wall and watched. About thirty feet farther along, a group of people walked up some steps and out of the bushes. He counted six: four women and two men. At first glance they looked like drab, ordinary people, like poor parishioners coming from an evening Mass. But even in the twilight and from that distance, Tom was shaken by their eyes. There was something too alive about them, something frightening about their gaze. It took Tom's breath away, that eye-bright glare of the zealot. He pulled farther back into the shadows, hoping they would not see him.

As he leaned back, catching his breath, Jenny's words about the cult came into his mind and he suddenly feared for her life.

He looked out again and saw them embrace, then one by one walk down the path. When the last one had disappeared into the dusk, Tom shook himself and rushed forward toward the steps, half-hidden in the bushes. He ran down and through the door where a dark corridor opened in front of him. At the end, a crude gas fitting gave off a dull yellowish light.

He left his lamp unlit and started along the passageway, like a man possessed. He had to find Jenny.

He heard the first shot echo along the corridor like the crack of a whip, but he instantly knew what it was. He yelled out, fearing for his brother.

He rushed along, not knowing where he was going, along passageways, down rock-carved stairwells, into empty cell-like rooms. Then he smelled it, a strange mixture of oil and something else. He gulped for air and was about to push forward when he heard the cracking sound of the pistol again. With the echo he could not tell for sure, but it sounded like two or three shots.

It seemed to come from the right. He had started toward the noise when he suddenly froze. A woman's screams echoed from the other direction.

It was Jenny. Lord Jesus, it was Jenny. He turned and sprinted along the passageway.

Another scream. And that smell coming stronger and stronger. Tom could scarcely think with the fear that tore at his mind. He came to the top of another stairwell and charged down.

At the bottom he was confronted by a scene of such horror that he could scarcely take it in. The place was strewn with naked bodies, and fire crackled and spat as it leapt along the floor, following the trail of oil, consuming all in its path. Jenny was trying to escape the flames. He called to her, then rushed into the smoke and heat and grabbed her under the arms. She looked up at him, gave a wail of despair and relief, and fainted. As he carried her from that terrible place he saw Araya standing in the path of the fire, hands outstretched, looking into its very heart.

"Araya!" Tom lay Jenny on the stairs and ran back, the heat on his skin like a blast from the furnaces. Araya's eyes were glazed. Gritting his teeth, Tom rammed his shoulder into his friend's stomach. The blow doubled him over, and Tom dragged him to the bottom of the stairwell.

He heard a clattering of boots and looked up to see his brother stumbling down the stairs followed by a handsome blond-haired woman. Tom could not stop to make sense of the growing chaos.

"Peter, help me!"

But when Doolan came into the light of the fire,

Tom could see that his brother was in no shape to help anyone. His chest was slashed and blood oozed into his clothes.

"Peter, for Chrissake!"

Doolan swayed forward. He looked up, eyes blazing, and aimed the gun at the center of the fire.

"Destroy him!"

Tom saw another figure in the fire. Though the flames erupted around him, this person stood unmoved and calm. His cold, crystal-clear, blue gaze seemed to plunge into Tom's mind and he was shaken by its force and intensity. He had seen the same look in the eyes of the people outside, but here it was magnified a hundredfold. It was like coming across the fire after seeing its sparks.

Tom wrenched himself away. His brother stood like a man bewitched, unable to shoot. Tom could see how badly wounded Peter was, and knew that he needed medical attention. The woman with him seemed in better shape. Tom gestured at Jenny, who was beginning to recover.

"Please help her up the stairs." Virginia stepped forward and put an arm around Jenny. Tom grabbed his brother under the arms and started to pull him away.

"Peter!"

But Doolan shook himself as though coming out of a trance, wrenched away from his brother, and aimed his revolver at Simon.

As Araya lay on the floor at Tom's feet, he heard the cool, logical voice of Simon echoing in his mind.

"There is no escape, Monk. The only way out is through the gate of true freedom. Death will release the soul to Abyssos."

Araya could feel darkness closing in over his mind. A crude, despairing prayer cracked from his throat.

"God. Strength, please, God."

And somehow it came, a pencil-thin beam. A voice of hope.

"Araya, I'm a simple man and I know and feel only one thing is certain: the love of the Lord God. I'm not worthy of that love, but I am given it anyway. So are you, Araya; so are you blessed by his love. Evil is all around you, but you are in the palm of God's hand, and you must let him use you."

It was the voice of his father, of the old Debtera at Quorqor, of his first memhir at Asoteriba, of the saintly old monk, Brother Johannes. God would come to you if you let him, God would give you strength if you opened your heart and let him past the arrogance of the throbbing intellect.

Araya stood gracefully. He easily removed the gun from Doolan's hand. Wide-eyed, Tom pulled his brother away as Araya walked into the inferno.

Simon stood in the midst of the pyre, waiting for his transformation. His eyes sparkled with a dark crimson, the color of malevolence.

"You will walk with me, Monk, away from Jehovah. My brothers have gone to prepare the way."

Araya took the double-bladed knife from his pocket and for an instant he saw Simon as the Snake of Knowledge. He threw himself onto the false priest, tumbling him to the ground. Araya swung his hand high, praying for God's strength. He looked up and let loose a deep vibrating yell, the shout of a tribal warrior.

"Oh, Lord of Hosts, help me! Elijah and Enoch, guide me! Guide me, Jesus of the deserts and the silence!"

With a wail, Araya plunged the blade deep into Simon's chest. The man roared in agony and disbelief. Araya stabbed again, slashed at the evil prophet. The twin points cut easily through flesh and shattered bone.

Simon struggled violently, but it was no use. There was no escape.

Araya suddenly heard a wailing cry from behind him. He turned, terror-stricken, to see the nun's disfigured face and flying robes. The creature's blade flashed in front of his eyes, tore across his throat. He had had no chance. Somehow he must complete his mission. He drove the snake knife into Simon's heart. The man shook, then fell still. With numb hands Araya tugged the coal-black talisman and the simple iron cross from his pockets. The world began to spin and he fell forward. Beside him, the creature clutched Simon's hand in a last grasp for comfort, but Virginia's shots had taken their toll.

Araya saw them, at the last, as lost souls, strayed from the true path. With a final effort he pulled himself up and placed the talisman in Simon's mouth. He laid the simple cross on his forehead. Then Araya's strength deserted him. He fell over the other two in a last, loving embrace. Around them, the fire raged, unchecked.

Outside, the survivors gathered in the rectory garden. An explosion rocked the church, blasting out a stained-glass window, showering fragments everywhere. The air was full of glass, sparks, and ash. Tom watched, frozen, looking desperately for his friend.

"Araya!"

"He's gone, Tom," Doolan said. "I saw him go into the fire." His pain seemed less, now.

Tom, Jenny, and Virginia pulled back as the heat grew, but Doolan walked closer, until the roaring sound swamped his hearing. Fire was cascading from the windows and spiraling high into the black sky.

He stood mesmerized, staring into the flames that were consuming the church, and for a moment he thought he saw Simon at the window of the church, hands outstretched. His smile was seductive yet leering, his eyes compelling.

Doolan heard a voice ringing clear in his mind.

"I will return!"

Doolan staggered backward. This was the threat that Araya had warned him of. How could he cleanse his mind of all this? He sank to his knees, weeping. A gentle hand touched his shoulder. He looked up at Virginia. Her eyes were warm with caring and love. She brushed his red-blond hair out of his eyes and traced her finger along the scar on his forehead. Her hand was trembling, but he felt the surety and strength flowing through him.

He looked at her and she attempted a smile.

"It's all right. It'll be all right."

He reached for her hand and squeezed it. There was a way back. Love and faith.

Together, Doolan and Virginia watched San Salvadore burn. The wind fanned the flames, spinning a thousand tiny embers into the air. They whirled and danced like blood-red snowflakes. By morning it would all be over.